MEDICAL MAFIA

R. GORDON HEPWORTH

Also by the author:

The Making of a Chief

MEDICAL MAFIA

A Novel

R. GORDON HEPWORTH

To Marion with sincere good wishes [signature]

PROTEA

www.proteapublishing.com/medicalmafia.htm

Published by:
Protea Publishing Company
Atlanta, Georgia, USA

www.proteapublishing.com
email: kaolink@msn.com

First Edition

Published simultaneously in soft cover and hardcover worldwide.

ISBN 1-931768-44-7 soft cover

ISBN 1-931768-45-5 hardcover

The author wishes to thank Dave Abbott, Suzanne Black, William Millin, and Mike Salvatore who gave invaluable advice during the writing of this story.

For Rilla

Those clamorous harbingers of blood and death.
– Shakespeare

CHAPTER 1

OUT OF ENGLAND

Sir William Williamson, the internationally known British surgeon, was pacing the operating room floor conjuring up the controlled yet caustic comments for which he was famous in addressing the staff working under him. He did not want to commence surgery without his house surgeon there and ready to assist.

"Laxton," he said, "I don't appreciate your tardiness. I was here at eight o'clock, and you didn't appear until five after."

"I'm sorry, sir, I was called to the emergency room," Laxton said.

"You should have told them to wait," Williamson said, without inquiring why Laxton had been called.

"It was a serious case. By the time I got there, the patient had died."

"All the more reason for telling them to wait. Obviously, if he was dead they didn't need you."

Williamson, although only five feet ten, was an imposing figure. His ruddy face and thin graying hair surmounted a morning coat. A white carnation, double breasted waistcoat, and the black striped pants turned him into a character who would have looked entirely appropriate a century earlier. It made him a unique personality in the hospital marking him as someone with special talents.

In the operating room he was always a gentlemen, never swearing or shouting at the house officers or nurses. He limited his frustrations to rapping the back of Laxton's hand with an artery forceps. He was a rapid surgeon who could successfully operate on several patients in one morning. He would remove a thyroid, stomach, gall bladder and colon on different patients between eight and twelve, and the patients rarely suffered complications. He knew his limitations and never attempted to operate in an area in which he was not qualified.

Much more volatile, less skilled, and evil tempered, was Sir William's junior, a consultant who shared bed allocation in the hospital with Sir William. Mr. Shillsmith, believing he was somewhere above God Himself, had the ability to reduce the house staff as a whole to silent, trembling hysteria. He was a short man, slightly on the heavy side, with dark hair and a pug nose, who pulled his shoulders back, clasping his hands behind him as he stomped down the corridors.

In the operating room he used the knife with great flourish, driving it lustily into an abdomen as though he was in conflict with the anaesthetized patient. This earned him the name "Slasher Shillsmith," which did nothing for his reputation among the house staff or the medical students.

Laxton struggled to please him and was always frustrated because nothing seemed to go right. One day he was assisting Shillsmith who was shouting: "Retract so I can see, retract, retract!"

Suddenly he shouted again: "Take your bloody dirty hands off the table before I chop the little buggers off."

When Shillsmith eventually removed the gall bladder there was a nasty, bloody ooze from the gall bladder bed which he stopped with a cauterizing instrument.

"Laxton," he said, "watch and learn."

Using the cautery he burned his initials on the surface of the liver giggling until he finally said to Laxton: "Close her up and don't take too long."

Sunday mornings were a trial for Laxton because he had to accompany Shillsmith on his ward rounds. Shillsmith insisted on taking his five-year-old son with him and he would occasionally pull out X-ray films and show them to the child as the rest of the staff waited.

"There, what do you think of that Shillsmith," he would say to the boy.

"Balls," would be the reply.

Shillsmith thought that very funny, and it was funny the first time, but as young Shillsmith's vocabulary of profanity increased it became tiresome. Laxton could not intervene if only because he sensed Shillsmith didn't like him. Perhaps this was because Laxton was tall, slender, and fair-haired, with blue gray eyes. He had a full mouth, square jaw and a smooth skin sloping upwards over high cheekbones. Shillsmith was small, squat, and looked older than his actual age. He did allow Laxton the opportunity to do a considerable amount of surgery on his own so he became very proficient for one of his age.

The more senior house officer had just returned from America where he had taken special training. When he resumed his post with Shillsmith, Shillsmith asked:

"Have those bastards learned anything over there yet?"

"Things are different over there and you have to see it to understand."

Shillsmith's expression was not one of approval. Laxton's curiosity led him to try to find out more about the American training program.

10

"There are tighter regulations in the cities anyway," he was told, "but some strange things seem to go on out in the country."

Although he was not very communicative Laxton's senior was supportive of Laxton. On one occasion when Shillsmith was particularly abrasive his Senior said to him, "Just because Shillsmith woke up this morning and put his foot in the piss pot when he got out of bed isn't your fault. Forget about it."

The occasion had been when Shillsmith performed a total gastrectomy and ran into difficulties because he wasn't good at the operation. It had only recently been introduced.

"I'm as good as anybody at any new surgery," Shillsmith said.

"It's not true," Laxton remarked subsequently when the fourth patient had died. He resented the fact Shillsmith turned the patients over to the house officers the minute the surgery was over and only became involved during the post operative period if some circumstance forced it on him.

There wasn't one query about the deaths. The British are a stoic race and Shillsmith eventually stopped doing the operation so criticism was limited to whispers among the house staff.

The long hours of tension suffered by all the house officers led to noisy drunken parties where dirty songs were sung and property was abused and nurses didn't get back to the nurses' home until the early hours. The worst night was when the house staff threw a piano out of an upstairs window onto the street below. No one was hurt, but the hospital authorities wanted to suspend the house staff, which gave Williamson a chance to show his empathy for them. He not only talked the authorities out of the suspensions, but bought a new piano as well.

Despite this, overall care was superb and the hard work didn't seem to be a burden to either the house officers or nurses. Emergencies were dealt with at once, whatever the hour, and Laxton learned to go without sleep. This probably contributed to a pneumonia he developed which started at a weekend. Laxton asked another house officer to take over for him for the whole day, and told the Hall Porter he didn't expect Williamson to visit the hospital that day, but if he did to call his colleague.

"You go to bed, sir," the Hall Porter said.

Williamson came in, of course, and insisted Laxton be called, and Laxton dragged himself along the corridor.

"Come along Laxton, it's ten o'clock, you should have been up and around these wards hours ago," he said. Williamson stopped. "My dear fellow, I can see you're ill. Sister, get him into one of my beds. Call

11

the medical specialists. Get the blood work done."

Laxton was impressed. It wasn't until two weeks later he found out that the Hall Porter had described his condition to Williamson and Williamson had known about it all along. Shillsmith was unsympathetic. He made one courtesy visit to Laxton by popping his head around the door.

"I don't know how he got sick," he said. "He does very little work around here."

Shortly after his illness Laxton sought out his senior who had just become one of the consultant specialists on staff.

"I am seriously thinking of going to Canada, Peter," Laxton said.

"What's the purpose of that?" his friend asked.

"I just can't see a future around here. Bluntly, there are two ways to become a consultant over here. You have to be brilliant and make all the right political moves or you have to take the vaginal route."

"Now just what do you mean by that?"

"Well you know Williamson married his Lordship's daughter and he was appointed a consultant about a month later. I know Lord Moynihan was considered the most brilliant surgeon in the country, and from all the statues and photographs around here was the most famous person in the city."

"I'm not sure those days aren't over, but if you think you need a helping hand of that sort, what about Williamson's daughter?" Peter said. "She's close to your age."

"I was at a party there once," Laxton said, "and I spent time with her. She was at Cheltenham College and is a total snob. She actually said to me, 'I know daddy thinks you're rather bright but you only went to a very ordinary grammar school, and even when you're a specialist it's going to be tough for you to move in the right kind of society.' Her attitude pissed me off."

"How on earth did you get into a conversation like that?" Peter asked.

"I took her out in the garden and we went into the summer house. It was when I got my hand on her thigh she started that conversation."

"What did you say to get out of it?"

"I told her it might be more appropriate if we visited the cow sheds."

Peter laughed.

"So I think if I go to Canada I can earn a lot of money over

12

there, do what I want to do, and then return."

"I'm sure you can find what you want over there but they are twenty years behind the times in medicine, and if you go, you'll never come back to stay."

"Why do you say that ?" Laxton said.

"Because you'll get too used to your Cadillac, color television, air conditioning and many material comforts."

Laxton said nothing. A year later he left for Edmonton, Alberta.

CHAPTER 2

LAXTON'S FIRST HURDLE

Laxton's passage on a Cunard liner was not a great experience. He had always been outgoing, and got along well with people, until he hit the deck so to speak. He was alone, unmarried, and there seemed to be no one to whom he could relate, and he would stand on the deck alone in the cold North Atlantic wind, a gaunt figure, tall and pale from all the time spent in the operating rooms, and excessively thin from an inborn nervousness. His face was still narrow and his lips thin, and he would moisten them with the tip of his tongue frequently, probably more from habit than necessity.

He was dragged from his bunk by the ship's surgeon one night to help with an acute appendix.

"Doctor Laxton," he said, "nothing could be worse than surgery at sea, but we have to do it. Come down and see the patient."

Laxton had to agree. The surgery was necessary. "The appendix is probably perforated," he said.

"We have what we need in equipment and I want you to give the anesthetic and I will scrub and get the appendix out," the officer said.

"Tell the bridge to hold the ship steady," he said to the orderly, as they were about to start.

Laxton gave the anesthetic. Open ether was all that was available. Pouring the foul stuff onto a mask while the patient coughed and sputtered was not Laxton's idea of modern medicine, but they were at sea. Nor did the ship's surgeon who stitched the wrong layers together impress him. Other than that the voyage was uneventful.

The journey across Canada took close to a week by train, and the immensity of the land was both surprising and depressing to Laxton. He arrived in Edmonton without work and had to start trying to find somewhere to practice. This entailed meeting several GPs who wanted help. He traveled all over Alberta. In one small town he was encouraged to enter practice there by the local GP but Laxton deplored his mercenary attitude.

"Hell," said the practitioner, "if someone has pain in their right belly, I call you and you consult and say 'Take his appendix out.' So you give the anesthetic and I take out the appendix and you get paid for the consult and anesthetic and I get paid for the surgery. It's a good deal for both of us."

"Don't you get a lot of normal reports though?" Laxton said.

"No, the pathologist always finds a bit of fibrosis or something."

"Do you do any gall bladder surgery ?"

"Never. It takes over an hour and a half to get a gall bladder out and I can take two or three appendices out in that time. It's easier. More money, less headaches."

Such contacts made Laxton hypercritical. It wasn't that some of the Canadian surgeons were self trained that bothered him. They were happy, patients were happy, and people got well. It was true he saw one self-trained surgeon in Southern Alberta go in to take out a gall bladder and end up taking out the uterus, but you could rationalize he couldn't find anything wrong with the gall bladder and the uterus did look a bit larger than it should have looked. There wasn't much wrong with it, except the pregnancy, but everyone was happy when it was all over.

Several stints at general practice led Laxton to conclude he should complete his surgical residency requirements. In the latter part of his residency in Vancouver Laxton saw one of the problems was that GPs were allowed to operate as well as trained surgeons, which was a big headache for the surgery department, but no one could do much about it because GPs were where the surgeons got their big cases. As a senior resident, one day he was grabbed by the Chief of Surgery who said: "Do you see who is starting a case in Room Four?"

It was De Louviers. He was a French GP who fancied his general surgical talents and had found one of his patients needed a hemorrhoidectomy, an operation done for piles. He probably booked one of these every two years.

"Get scrubbed and get into that room and grab that knife and those scissors and make sure you help him by doing the operation," the Chief said. "If you don't that poor bastard he's operating on will either never shit again or he'll shit all the time."

Laxton was glad to become one of the elite specialists in the city. Well, if not elite he was on the way anyway. Those hours of study spent in England, Toronto, in Vancouver and several places in between, had left him a trained and respected surgeon. He soon found out it was best to belong to the "club," and that didn't mean social. It was clear that the old adage "you scratch my back and I'll scratch yours," was operational. A lot of the guys were interested in what they were doing, and they weren't afraid. Everyone worked hard and there was the courtesy of not stealing each other's patients. Everyone worked together, operated

15

together, and played together. Those with skill supported each other.

Vancouver University had its tentacles throughout the city, and the city was a provincial enough community that there was academic inbreeding. There were few from out of town who could break into the tightly knit society which controlled the medical environment.

Being a tolerated son of the system, it worked out that a spot could be found for Laxton in one of the outlying hospitals where there was a Chief of Surgery who was not the easiest person to please, who had dogmatic and definitive views.

Laxton found Dr. Rugger was in many ways as English as his name implied. Born in Canada he had played a major part in surgery in the armed services during the Second World War, particularly in Great Britain. Rugger knew all the famous English surgeons personally, had worked with them, and probably should have been Professor of Surgery at the University in Vancouver. No one knows why that post was never offered to him, unless it was because his knowledge of politics, though profound, precluded him from ever practicing politics, an essential in the University environment. In any case Laxton divined immediately that Rugger was the epitome of the English surgeon, so he treated him that way, and despite the age difference they became good friends. That ensured that Laxton met many people he would never have had the opportunity to meet otherwise. Rugger knew many of the Judges, prominent attorneys, even prominent businessmen in the province, although Rugger was not a good businessman himself.

"I am very impressed by the meticulous way people are cared for," Laxton confided to Rugger, "and I know it's really done for money but everyone is doing some charity work."

This was limited by the fact that the hospital was Catholic, and Catholic hospitals in metropolitan areas were not in the business of providing charity. They were in the business of making money.

Laxton came to St. James Hospital and rapidly became their prominent surgeon, well liked because Rugger had already blessed him and given him hints on dealing with the nuns who ran the place. Laxton found that you either fit in with the nuns, the Chief of Surgery, and the conservative side of the community, or you were a rabble-rouser who was removed. This was never done overtly, but because there was a bed shortage, if you didn't fit in your patients waited an inordinate length of time for admission. There would be no beds for emergencies and your practice would slowly dissolve and you would choose to go away. A sort of unilateral divorce by common consent. Laxton saw many enterprising young men go that way.

16

Within such a structure there is always some misfit. Usually some old goat who has been at it too long, gained a reputation, receives work, but all his cases were difficult and complicated. Complicated because they always developed horrendous infections, obstructions, and underwent multiple surgeries for the same thing, while the surgeon's reputation apparently grew with the complications and deaths.

In Laxton's early days there was such a man on the staff. He wasn't that old. Residents began to notice and complain, and the word got around to the other surgeons, who first protected the miscreant, but subsequently turned on him when it was clear there was trouble on the horizon. Laxton had to admit that good medicine was practiced, and income wasn't bad. Everyone tried to do a good job. Except for Dr. Jamestown. Laxton concluded Jamestown was simply on a roll for money. Most of the others were not. The majority of his colleagues wanted an income, but didn't want to wallow in it. They wanted a good comfortable living without excessive luxuries. Jamestown was different. He was pretentious. He stretched the indications for surgery quite a bit. Occasionally Jamestown asked Laxton to assist him. One poor woman subjected to abdominal surgery by Jamestown clearly had extensive malignant disease, but Jamestown had to get a bit of tissue to prove it, an unnecessary procedure.

"I'm going to chop this ovary and tube out," he said, "then they'll have plenty to look at." With that he chopped out an indefinable piece of tissue between two large clamps, tied off the base of the clamps with catgut, and closed the patient up.

Laxton was uncomfortable. "I think you'd better look at that specimen,"

Jamestown cut the specimen open and found it was colon.

"Just a minute," he said as they prepared to wheel the patient out. "Can't leave her like that, not with the bowel tied off. Now she's obstructed."

The surgery had to be restarted, opening the woman up again and doing a colostomy. Laxton was relieved when she died in a few days, a relief from her suffering.

Rugger would not tolerate that kind of thing. Once he realized what was going on, Laxton was ordered to evaluate the surgeon's charts over the last two years and write a report. That was all precipitated by Jamestown's surgery on Mrs. Blanchette, the doctor's wife, who had a bowel obstruction. That much was determined by the autopsy. Jamestown had a couple of cracks at her abdomen before this. Neither surgical excursion relieved her obstruction, and in fact he converted a simple obstruction into a closed loop obstruction. That's where the music goes round and around but it doesn't come out anywhere. This led to a threat of a malpractice suit.

Laxton spent long evenings pouring over charts, which showed, for example, operations on the thyroid where no thyroid tissue was removed. In one case the same lady had three thyroid operations where no thyroid tissue was removed in any of the operations. When the material was presented to the Chief of Staff a meeting was held, and with the added blessing of Sister Superior, the culprit was thrown out. Jamestown went quietly down the street and got on the staff at the Vancouver General Hospital, where he had some friends who knew nothing of his practice, and he started that surgical mutilation and extermination all over again.

"I feel good about this," Rugger told Laxton, "how do you feel about it now it's all over?"

"He was the wrong man in the wrong place at the wrong time."

CHAPTER 3

THE INEPT

Laxton had the naive idea that the departure of Jamestown would mean the end of all contact with him, which was probably a reasonable conclusion at the time. The intermixing of staff members between each hospital was very infrequent. One stupid practitioner resigned from St. James hospital staff because Jamestown was gone, but only one. Most realized what a menace he posed to the patient population.

Laxton became lost in the hurly-burly of practice, and forgot about the whole unpleasant episode. As he watched those around him, the whole hospital and staff looked so innocuous and efficient he felt it was a high-class operation.

Rugger's new resident was a character. He had not been allowed to do much surgery, and eventually Rugger felt he owed it to this character to indulge him and supervise him taking out an appendix. This was part of the normal training process. Rugger should have known better, because there had been a number of incidents which pointed to instability, like the night the resident asked Rugger in front of a nice but obese woman if it wasn't a good time to slit her belly and look inside.

Laxton was sure Rugger must have had a drink or two prior to that episode and didn't notice the lack of protocol which Laxton would have called inappropriate rudeness, and so overlooked one of the more obvious indications of the resident's attitude. Attitudes in a physician, and more especially a surgeon, lead to modifications in performance, a matter overlooked by most.

The appendectomy Rugger gave the resident to perform was on a very slim woman, so there should not have been too much difficulty in the performance. The resident, whose name was Deakin, grabbed the knife and made a bold incision which penetrated not only the abdominal wall but two layers of bowel as well.

"Why the hell didn't you press harder and drive the knife out through her back?" Rugger yelled. "Give me the bloody knife and get your filthy hands out of there, stupid bugger."

By that time nuns were running in all directions in horror and panic, not at the act so much as the bad language. Rugger threw the knife across the operating room, pushed the resident in the chest, which sent him staggering, and resumed the surgery himself, first correcting

19

the mess created by the bold stroke. Of course the patient never knew what had happened, did very well, and only stayed a day longer than expected.

"We are not pleased because you upset Dr. Rugger so much he took to bad language," Sister St. Marie said to Deakin as he was leaving the operating room.

The whole episode did not deter Deakin one bit. In fact, he related the whole thing to Laxton just as it happened. Rugger never let him do another surgical case during the next seven months. Later he left the hospital and went elsewhere, and despite Rugger's terrible written report he became certified as a specialist in surgery.

If Deakin wasn't enough with his poor attitude and rather dangerous incompetence, there were others who made up for it. Laxton's friend Crawfish was a family practitioner who was friendly with an orthopedic surgeon called Wisham. Wisham had done many innovative procedures and was well liked by colleagues until he published a paper on spine curvature in which he had devised a method of correction superior to any other procedure of the time.

Probably few people knew that if anyone produced a paper without the blessing of the university and was lucky enough to have it published despite the influence and control of the university, they could count on abuse as well as being ostracized by the powers that be who were able to make out a case of incompetence even though incompetence did not exist.

Wisham incurred the wrath of the Professor of Orthopedics, who was himself marginally competent, and certainly not the thinker Wisham had proved himself to be. Wisham let the whole thing get to him, and began to drink. It probably wouldn't have mattered if Wisham hadn't turned up in the operating room drunk, for although this apparently didn't affect his skill or work capabilities, it offended the delicate sensibility of the nuns. That brought the whole matter to Rugger's attention. Wisham had done one of his new procedures with great expertise, and probably nothing would have been said if Wisham had not discussed his infidelities, his wife's sexual habits and preferences, and the fact that he would "throw the bitch out because I can't get a decent blow job at home." Sister St. Marie stayed until the whole conversation was over, no doubt so she wouldn't miss anything and could give a blow-by-blow description, so to speak, to Sister Superior who was also the Hospital Administrator. Sister St. Marie left the order about three months after this to get married. Sister Superior brought the matter of Wisham's behavior to Rugger's attention.

Rugger took Laxton and Wisham out to Rugger's Club to discuss the matter. Rugger and Wisham got totally polluted and Laxton took rather more than was good for him, but had to drive the others home. Strange as it seemed, Rugger's approach and method of discussing the whole business caused a marked moderation in the behavior of Wisham, who satisfied himself by divorcing his wife, and kept his drinking habits to his bachelor abode.

Wisham's new operative procedure became a standard method of approach to spine curvature, but only after a member of the university team had plagiarized the material in a more prominent surgical journal and given his own name to the method.

Shortly after this episode Wisham asked Laxton if he would see Wally Crawfish about a rather unfortunate event. Crawfish came to Laxton and told him that one of his patients had landed up in Jamestown's hands in Vancouver General Hospital.

"Wisham told me to come to you," Crawfish said, "because the whole thing is upsetting me. Jamestown took out part of the woman's thyroid, took out several segments of bowel, and operated on her varicose veins all at the same time. Trouble is she has feces flowing out of the incision in the belly, a big blood clot causing the neck to stick out, and a cold foot, which suggests there's something seriously wrong with the leg surgery. What the hell am I to do? I've looked after this woman for ten years and she trusts me."

"When you knew Jamestown was involved, why did you go there?" Laxton asked. "I told you about some of our problems at the hospital here."

"I guess I didn't believe it," Crawfish said, "I thought a lot of it was politics."

"The best advice I can give you is to tell her she's under Jamestown's care. You don't ordinarily go to that hospital, and when he releases her tell her she should come back to see you. She had to have gone there without a referral, didn't she?"

"Hell," Wally said sheepishly, "she phoned the office for a referral and I guess we let her go there to Jamestown since she asked for him."

"You've got yourself a great liability," Laxton said, "why don't you tell Jamestown and the patient you want to get a consultation by someone else?"

Crawfish grunted but gave no indication what he might do. A year later Laxton found out he hadn't done anything when he saw a judgement against both Crawfish and Jamestown for malpractice. Laxton avoided any comment on the subject, and Crawfish never brought it up, but he was very upset about it. Laxton found this out because Crawfish had separated from his wife, was drinking heavily, and was sharing space with Wisham.

Crawfish moved back in with his wife, but a week later, while she was away for a couple of days, Crawfish didn't appear at the hospital or his office. Wisham found him dead at home. The cause of death was never clearly established, but Crawfish was smart and Laxton concluded he had organized the whole thing. Laxton suppressed any personal guilt by rationalizing he may not have been able to prevent any of it.

"What do you think about all this?" Wisham said to him.

"He was the wrong man in the wrong place at the wrong time."

CHAPTER 4

SURGEONS' SHENANIGANS

That politics should have anything to do with opening a doctor's office Laxton regarded as ridiculous, but he found himself in a silly situation when he wanted to open his own office. The building where his office was to be located was under construction, but the structure was not far enough along to be divided into rooms, and Laxton knew the new telephone book was about to come out before he could put a phone in the building.

In dealing with the moronic sales representative for the phone company, Laxton knew he had been told many lies, but the upshot was he could not get his name in the phone book in the time frame he wanted. He wouldn't be in for at least a year. At that time he was involved in the care of the President of a major Canadian Airline, and got along well with him, so they had many personal conversations covering many topics. During one of these conversations Laxton told him about the problem with the phone company. The Airline executive looked at him.

"Just a minute," he said, as he reached for the telephone and placed a call, "I'll teach you something."

In five minutes or less the President of the telephone company called him back.

"You know I'm here in the hospital, Dean, and a young friend of mine here who's looking after me has a problem with your company and thinks it ought to be nationalized."

After a moment or two he handed Laxton the phone and Laxton was invited to describe the problem. He was assured everything possible would be done. The next day the sales rep was burning up the phone lines. Instead of answering the calls Laxton went to his patient friend and told him it really looked like there'd be some action, but he had not yet responded.

"Let me tell you a story," said the Airline President, "one time my airline and Trans Canada Airlines, had differential transcontinental fares and ours was cheaper. The President of Trans Canada Airlines asked me to lunch. Now, when a businessman asks you to lunch, he wants something. Always remember that. He didn't bring up what he was after until the end of the meal when he said: 'We're going to put our fares up.'"

"'Oh,' I said, 'we're happy with ours the way they are.' At that he got up and began to tremble. He was so angry I was terrified he might have a stroke."

"'You haven't heard the end of this,' he said, 'I promise you, there'll be more.' Well Trans Canada Airlines being government owned, I knew they could have pressure put on me, and I knew there was a week to the cut off date for the decision and announcement, so I told my board of directors I had to be away for a week and no decisions were to be made until I got back. So I packed my bag and took our flight to Rome. After a couple of days I decided I could be reached too easily there, so I went to Egypt. The telecommunications between Egypt and Canada were best about two A.M. in Canada anyway."

"Sure enough, two days before the deadline I got a cable from the Deputy Minister of Transport, and the cheap son of a bitch didn't even put down what he was cabling about. The cable simply said 'What are you going to do?' So I cabled back the next day 'I'm going to visit the Aswan Dam and the pyramids' and took the next flight to Rome. By the time I got back we had a cheaper fare than Trans Canada Airlines."

"So here's the lesson. Sometimes it pays not to be available."

Laxton never called the sales rep back and two days later the company's District Traffic Manager came to see him at the hospital. He told Laxton he didn't think he could do anything for him, except let him pick out his own number. It's funny, but when the phone book came out the new office number he'd picked was listed.

That wasn't the only thing this newfound friend taught him, but much of what he learned wasn't useful until much later. One day when Laxton was chatting with him in his room, the phone rang and an airline stewardess the executive had known for years was calling. He got all the details of the flight she'd been on from Hawaii and why it had stopped in Alaska.

When his Vice President, a cocky young man, came to report at the end of the day, Laxton was invited to stay.

"Oh," his friend said to the VP, "why did our flight 774 stop in Alaska?"

Laxton thought the VP would shit his drawers, especially since he didn't know the answer to the question. Laxton found his President friend knew everyone in his organization from the bottom up, and they could all reach him at almost anytime by telephone, so he was always well informed.

At that time Laxton was concerned with much more mundane pursuits, like curing people. He was right hand man to Rugger, although

24

he did a different type of surgery. Rugger was tough, personable yet compassionate. It seemed he was above politics. He was able to manipulate situations so that they became apolitical. One of the loud mouths on the surgical staff, although a good surgeon, couldn't stop gossiping and repeating every rumor he heard. His name was Farab.

Farab was ten years Laxton's senior. He was a tall thin man with the hint of sunburn on his face. He smiled a lot. He had verbal diarrhea, even in surgery he couldn't stop talking and it was usually unrelated to whatever he was doing. He was a good surgeon but he just couldn't shut up. He was his own worst enemy. On many occasions Rugger would say to Laxton:

"You don't tell Farab about this; I'm telling you, but keep it to yourself."

Yet Rugger often told Farab things himself which seemed inconsistent to Laxton.

"How come you tell Farab things but you don't want me to tell him anything?" Laxton said to him.

"Ah," Rugger said, pointing in one direction, "when I want to go in that direction, I tell him something that will point him in the other direction."

He pointed the other way.

"When I want false information disseminated, I feed it to him. It's cheap, and you get much better coverage than a radio station."

Farab never seemed to know he was being used. He enjoyed information, whether it was true or false, but he never stopped to analyze it. His unbounded enthusiasm for gossip nearly led to his downfall, an unfortunate occurrence, because he wasn't really bad.

It all occurred because Jamestown had stolen one of Farab's patients. That's not really true, as the family practitioner, Conman Patrick, had sent the patient to Farab for a hernia repair and Farab had done a good job. About two months later he developed a hernia on the opposite side, which was no one's fault. Conman Patrick liked to share the wealth so he sent the patient to Jamestown, who was at the Vancouver General Hospital. The patient was told Farab was on vacation. Since Farab didn't work that often, I suppose it could be argued that the information wasn't entirely false. Farab heard of it and just couldn't keep his trap shut.

"Jamestown has my patient, and he's going to do his left inguinal hernia," he told everyone. "Patrick blew his lid."

"I'd shut up if I was you," Rugger said.

"But his ball will fall off, maybe both balls, if Jamestown gets at him."

The conversation was reported widely throughout the city, amongst the medical community alone, of course. Everyone thought it was a joke, except Jamestown, who filed suit against Farab for slander. That got the case reported in the newspapers, probably a calculated gimmick on the part of Jamestown. He was always looking for publicity because it always seemed to bring more business. Little snippets would appear in the newspaper from time to time to propagate the story, and poor Farab was suffering loss of what little work he had, and loss of income.

The case was dropped before it even reached court, and there was no out of court settlement either, because Farab's prediction proved right. When the patient's testicle dropped off, Jamestown dropped the suit.

There was no malpractice suit against Jamestown, and his business increased because of the publicity, while Farab's went down for a very long time. In addition, Farab had to suffer the indignity of appearing before the Board of Licensure to be warned about criticism of another physician.

The worst feature of the whole case was that the truth never was publicized and the fact the suit was dropped did not appear in the newspapers. Jamestown's practice thus bloomed while Farab's struggled to survive.

At that time Jamestown embarked on a very unethical scheme which he concealed from other professionals, so few realized what was going on. He made a deal with the Lattrini brothers to look after some of the more questionable characters in town. It was good money, because most of the transactions were cash, especially if they were trauma. The real problem was that, although Jamestown was a traumatic surgeon, he was not a trauma surgeon in any sense of the word. The kindest thing which can be said about him was that he operated first and thought about it afterwards.

One would have thought that, that branch of criminal society would have protected its own, and taken the definitive action for which they are so famous, but it seemed Jamestown must have developed some inside track. As far as was known he never had conflicts with the group. This was despite the time he sutured a severed carotid artery in such a way it became connected to the jugular vein, and the patient ended up with an undesirable shunt where arterial blood was running into the venous system.

The local leader in that instance was a distant relative of the

Lattrini brothers, and his ultimate recovery makes a remarkable story, particularly since he was later arrested for two hideous crimes against children, and became a local notoriety.

The Lattrini brothers kept a club called The Pantyhose, which was supposed to be a good place to pick up a whore, but Laxton was sure many other activities went on in the club. Laxton was dating one of the nurses he had met at a dance. Diane was a curly haired blond girl who was attractive, slightly plump, but was called "wild" by other nurses who knew her. It was Diane who told Laxton she wanted to do something more exciting and suggested to Laxton they dine at The Pantyhose.

Although it was Saturday, there were few other diners. During the meal Lattrini Senior entered with his retinue of six or eight men, who looked like hoods. He was easily recognized because he wore a bright scarlet suit.

The food was barely tolerable and the place superficially dull. That proved to be an illusion of Laxton's, because the subsequent bust several years later revealed some pretty gruesome details about the club. Laxton's major discomfort was when the bill came and he gave a credit card to the waiter. The bill and card were taken to Lattrini who rose from the end of the table of hoods and approached Laxton and his date.

"I'd say this card was good," Lattrini said, "there's an MD after the name. I'm not interested in doing business with doctors right now, but I might be in the future. I'm going to keep your name on file. Maybe we can do something for you later. It isn't necessary to leave a tip. I'll just initial this and you sign it doctor."

He walked away and left the slip on the table. Laxton cursed himself for not paying cash, but it was too late now. He signed the slip after adding a generous tip. Laxton never went back but was never contacted. He had heard a rumor of Jamestown's connection and his only regret was he didn't see him there, as Laxton thought naively he might be in high visibility. Jamestown didn't need to be there because his contract was cut and dried. Several months later Jamestown escaped from the premises when there was a police raid connected with gambling. It should not have been a surprise to anyone he was almost caught there, because he gambled almost on a daily basis in the operating room where the stakes were higher.

CHAPTER 5

KILLING PRIVATE PRACTICE

The noose was tightening around the Canadian medical community as the government realized that there was a group of people out there who were not getting the medical care which the community required. Actually it wasn't the government who instituted complaints related to this as much as the news media, which began to insidiously insert bits and pieces of stories about the inappropriate way in which those who could not pay for their medical care were being handled. The first rumbles came in 1965, but reached a crescendo later when government sponsored insurance was introduced.

The favorite target of the news media was the medical profession, but the public, and the federal government also targeted them. The profession reacted in a typical fashion.

"What the hell," Rugger said, after a few drinks at his club, "there's a movement on foot to socialize the health services in this country, and you won't see me on the hustings disputing its necessity. Let all those idiots out there who think they know it all conduct this battle. They won't win."

Rugger had picked up the word "hustings" in England and used it every election so by now he had explained to everyone it meant the route followed by advocates in an election or some other kind of campaign.

"I refuse to be involved with the medical society," Laxton said, "but someone needs to warn the profession that the President of the Medical Association and his people will sell them down the river."

"Let me give you my view," Rugger said. "If I was in your shoes, I'd let them stew in their own juice. No one will thank you for interfering, warning, or advising them, and it might influence your practice. Don't forget you rely on other physicians to send you cases. You run a referred practice. What needs to be done is to make sure there's a clean up of all these morons who shouldn't be doing surgery, or obstetrics, or internal medicine, because they don't know what they're doing. There's something we can do something about."

"How in Hades can I do anything about Jamestown and those other people at other places who are just knocking people off?"

Rugger looked at Laxton and said nothing for a moment. He took a swig of his rye.

"If you think you can do a damn thing about what's going on in other institutions, you're crazy. All we can do is keep our own house in order. I want St. James' Hospital to meet any inspection the goddamn government or any one else might lay on us. I don't need the place called St. Judas. What I want you to do in house is just that. That's what I'll be doing. What you choose to do otherwise is your business."

Rugger's club was a good place to talk to him. It was one of those clubs catering to men only. When there was an event that included women, there were only certain parts of the club where women were allowed to visit. In fact it was an excellent escape place for any male who wanted to get away from home or just hide. If a wife called the club to reach her husband, the club called the husband on a separate line and asked if he wanted to take the call, or would ask him if he was in the club. If he didn't want to take the call the caller was told he wasn't there. It was in no way a family club. It was an ultra-conservative environment so exclusive that it was very expensive and membership was extended to the privileged few.

Perhaps Laxton's worst experience was when Rugger took the surgery resident Howard to the club. Howard was someone everyone wanted to get to join the medical staff. Howard was six feet three, had red hair, and was tremendously well built. Howard had excellent surgical skills and good judgement. Laxton's only reservation was that he had been to Laxton's home, got drunk and behaved like an asshole. Rugger decided to talk to Howard at the club.

He bought scotch for John Howard, in fact a whole bottle of it, and sat down with his own bottle of Canadian rye and began to talk in generalities, not really getting to the point right away, which was unusual for Rugger. Laxton was drinking rye and ginger ale while the two of them consumed the bottles. The conversation never really got around to John Howard's future as each became drunker.

There was no supper. About ten p.m. Rugger sort of choked and went a bit blue, and Howard told the waiter to call an ambulance. Fortunately, the waiter must have recognized Laxton was not as drunk as the other two and asked Laxton what to do. Laxton decided Rugger had not had a heart attack, that he would not welcome arriving at St. James totally polluted, and the best course of action was to get him home. Laxton called Rugger's wife at home and asked her to come and get him and said he would help get him home. Laxton took the risk of asking John Howard to drive Laxton's car to Rugger's house.

Rugger's wife arrived, and Laxton helped load Rugger in the car and accompanied her and the now passed out Rugger to his home, where they put him to bed. Shortly after that Howard arrived with the front end of Laxton's new car bashed in. It wasn't so bad it couldn't be driven.

Rugger's wife made bacon and eggs for Laxton and Howard, something both badly needed at that point in time. Howard was pretty well behaved considering his drunken state, so Laxton did not delay getting him back to the hospital resident's quarters. Laxton nervously looked for police and hoped they wouldn't encounter any, for he knew they would be in deep trouble if they did. The trip was uneventful and it was with a sigh of relief Laxton drove the short distance home to King Edward Avenue shortly after one a.m., unaware of what had been loosened in the hospital.

Howard walked in quite calmly, or so it appeared. There were always two residents, senior and junior, and the junior resident was in bed. Unfortunately, the resident quarters were off the two main wards of the hospital, close to the supervisor's office.

Howard marched past the supervisor's office and straight into the junior resident's room. He picked up the junior resident's bed, with the junior resident in it, and turned it upside down. Being a simple hospital type bed, it came apart. The din was enormous, and woke a lot of patients as well as the night supervisor, who should have been awake anyway. She arrived on the scene almost immediately.

"What's going on here?" she said, in an imperious tone.

"Ah, I've always wanted to get a crack at you," Howard said. "Come over here."

This was certainly untrue because Howard had told several people what an ugly bag the night supervisor was.

She ran from the room and called the hospital orderly to come at once. When the orderly arrived, it turned out he was not a very substantially built man. Howard fixed his eye on him.

"So, you want to get into this act, do you?" Howard asked.

"Oh no doctor, do whatever you want," the orderly said, and left the room.

Somehow the junior resident got Howard calmed down and off to bed.

Laxton told Rugger about the episode later and he didn't spare any details.

"We'd better wait awhile before we get into anything with him, because I don't remember too much of what was said. We didn't promise him anything, did we?" Rugger asked.

"No," Laxton said. "So far we aren't committed."

Two weeks later Howard started to screw one of the practical nurses who worked on the second floor, and the word got out around the hospital.

"You'd better know this," Laxton told Rugger, "Howard is screwing one of the practical nurses who works on the second floor here."

"Why the hell couldn't he go to the Vancouver General, or one of the other hospitals, if he wants to fool around. It's a cardinal rule as far as I'm concerned - Never shit on your own doorstep."

The problem was Howard had a wife back in Ontario, and everyone knew it. But even that wasn't the final straw. It was the B.C. Surgical Society meeting which put the final touch to any plans anyone might have had for Howard.

John Howard was taken to the meeting as a guest of Farab. Neither Laxton nor Rugger attended the meeting, so the description of the activities came entirely from Farab, and everyone else he came in contact with got the same information, including Rugger.

Apparently all went well until they got to Harrison Hot Springs and the drinks were poured. They were poured prior to the business meeting. At the meeting a discussion of fees came up, and there was a lot of bellyaching about assistant's fees for a specialist surgeon who assisted in a case at the same time as a general practitioner, because the GP got paid and the assistant surgeon didn't. Howard rose to his feet.

"Well, I'm from Ontario, and we don't bellyache about fees like this. We just concentrate on getting a good job done, whether we get paid for it or not."

That didn't contribute to his popularity. Subsequently, he grabbed one of the surgeons he'd worked with before, a man who was skilled and well known.

"You don't know shit about closing a belly after surgery," he said.

The surgeon, who was a powerfully built man himself, had bruises on his upper arm from where Howard had grabbed him. These lasted several weeks.

All the way home from the meeting Farab reported, Howard was pounding the car dashboard and shouting, "Those incompetent money grubbing assholes, what an unethical bunch of shits."

Since he had been taken as a guest of Farab's everyone who heard felt this was somewhat inappropriate behavior. The story was all over St. James the following morning, and Laxton got a first hand account from Farab himself. Although reluctant to do so, Laxton asked

Howard how the meeting had gone, and that brought a fresh tirade about the idiots who were there, which more or less confirmed Farab's account.

"Well, I'm glad I checked this out carefully," Rugger said. "Clearly he has to go back to Ontario. We can't have that kind of behavior here. It's going to save us a lot of trouble to keep that kind of crap off our doorstep."

Most of the time Howard was likeable, and Laxton was sorry to see that happen, but he felt Howard had an alcohol problem, which was beyond acceptability. So Howard returned to Ontario. About six months later the practical nurse, who was half his age, followed him and he divorced his wife and married the girl.

Laxton was somewhat sensitive about this situation because he had been living with Diane for a number of months, and they were spending a lot of time together, but Laxton was dubious about marriage. He knew too many people who considered Diane to be rather cheap, despite her good education. He had not picked Diane up out of St. James Hospital so there wasn't any gossip.

Rugger had instituted Saturday morning grand rounds which were an expose of his own work and difficulties. Rugger had that great characteristic of all good teachers in that he would tell everything about his own patients, his own difficulties, and would accept advice and input from others. The residents brought the rest of the cases to the rounds, sometimes to the embarrassment of the surgeon they were working for, but eventually it became an exchange of teaching information and all participated in the sessions.

It became clear to Laxton during the late sixties there was going to be a National Health Insurance Plan despite anything the Canadian Medical Association or any of the local medical associations could do. As usual, organized medicine went about everything the wrong way. Laxton was anxious that the profession indicate they were willing to look at new methods for delivery of health care, because it was clear that the rearguard action being fought by the profession, and the way in which it was being fought, would result in complete government control of all services.

At the time of the physicians' strike in the Province of Saskatchewan, Laxton had been heard because he had written an article for The Yorkshire Post in England, expressing how those in Canada felt about the temporary import of British M.D's who were used to break the strike. That had brought tremendous radio and television coverage for him in British Columbia. But at that time what he was saying was

32

popular, because the socialist government of Saskatchewan had made a total mess of the medical services there and people actually suffered as a result of the activities of Tommy Douglas' government. Laxton's own view was there had to be some changes, but that the profession was setting itself up for a clandestine takeover.

British Columbia basically had three health care plans. One was set up by Physicians, one by Employers, and one by Unions. However, there were other players in the field, and there were no restrictions on who could write health insurance.

From Laxton's perspective it seemed that the best thing that could be done was to have the government assume ownership of the hospitals and wrap into existing plans every person who didn't have coverage, including the native Indian population who had been so poorly treated by the federal government.

The profession put up a barrier against the whole concept of any kind of government intervention in health care. Their position was that the only people not covered were indigents, which was untrue. There had been no chance of health care services getting anywhere during the conservative Diefenbaker years, but with the Pearson government being on record as being in favor of a National Health Scheme it seemed to Laxton this was inevitable. It was against Rugger's better judgement that Laxton went public on several issues and became identified as an authority, if not an expert, on what it means to deal with government. What he knew was about to happen made a great change in Laxton's personal life as well as his future.

CHAPTER 6

PERSONAL RELATIONS AND POLITICS

Laxton would not let his personal problems interfere with his work. A sort of immaturity had lived inside him in personal relationships with women. Diane, though not the first woman he had bedded, had seemed to be more serious than others he had temporary relationships with previously. While friends seemed to marry and divorce time and time again, Laxton had some sort of consistency in trying to conduct a relationship in which he could show loyalty. But he fiercely guarded his independence whenever his work was concerned.

For her part Diane was a nurse who worked shifts and seemed to want someone as a companion. She denied being in love with him, but she was not interested in leaving the co-habitation. Well educated, she sold herself short and behaved with characteristics more worthy of a cheap uneducated menial worker rather than a professional.

"Let's do a pub crawl and come home and screw," she would say to Laxton.

He would look at her and wonder if this was some sort of joke, but it wasn't, and he eventually realized this. At times he would enter into the physical relationship with gusto, often being rather the worse for drink.

"You wanted it and you're going to get it," he'd say.

"You'll be exhausted and dried out by morning," Diane would say.

And he was. Still, the passion was not deep. It was violent and physical. He never thought of her at work and often failed to call her if he was going to be late, so that dinners cooked were often ruined. It didn't really seem to bother her. It was a weird domestic situation and yet they were used to each other. They were able to go out together and appeared at parties and functions together, but others always referred to her as his date, and the fact they lived together was ignored. He had provided a beautiful home in an exclusive area, but in an area where neighbors don't converse or get together, which served to isolate them even more.

His friends told him she wasn't the person for him. Even Rugger said to him: "It's nice to have something flexible to work your energy off on at your age, but don't make the mistake of thinking a life long companion is just a screw and they'll fit into other situations in your life."

"I suppose you mean Diane," Laxton said. "She's all right for the time being, but I have no plans to make this permanent."

Around mid January there was a sudden change. Diane was unwell and it didn't take Laxton long to realize she was pregnant. He knew abortions were illegal so the option wasn't viable. He thought about it a lot.

"Diane, the right thing to do is to get married, and before the child is born."

"Oh, really," she said, "I haven't asked for it. It's your fault anyway because you were drunk and forgot to use a rubber."

"I'm not trying to place fault. We did something together, there wasn't proper planning, we both knew we were taking a risk at the time, and it happened. I'm just saying I'm willing to try to make a go of it. I come from a country where men accept their responsibilities."

"A fuck's a fuck, and you're cut off now until the kid's born and then we'll see what's to be done. You can be sure I won't be going to St. James Hospital for delivery, either."

"Why do you want to cut off sex now when it's safe?" Laxton said.

"Because that's the way it is."

The following months were ones of turmoil at home. Laxton was fed and turned out of his own house after supper. He became distressed with the conversations.

"I want to make an effort so that our feelings become more meaningful, deeper somehow," Laxton said. "I don't know how to talk to you. What can I do?"

"Who wants to talk to you? Just shut up ass hole."

When Laxton tried to get psychiatric help for her, it was rejected after her first visit.

"Is it the pregnancy?" Laxton asked the psychiatrist.

"I believe it goes much deeper than that. It doesn't seem to me it's anything you have any control over and at the moment I don't believe there is much you can do to help."

Diane became vicious, particularly if he tried to show any affection. He suffered snarling remarks.

"Get yourself downtown and get fucked," she said on more than one occasion.

Laxton compromised by becoming involved in the political situation that was also in turmoil. Since Diane now refused to go anywhere, claiming her pregnancy as the reason, Laxton took his office

35

nurse to the political events whenever he could. She was married but her husband was out of town all the time, traveling, and she welcomed the political functions, dances, and strategy sessions. Diane had stopped work and Laxton supported her as he always had anyway. She claimed she was getting care and would disappear for two or three days and then return without comment. He knew she was near term and was not surprised when she was gone quite suddenly one Friday. Laxton didn't know where she'd gone and was upset and tried to locate her for the next two weeks. She suddenly re-appeared baby and all. She had named the boy Sasha.

Laxton wanted to make a fuss of the boy, but he was allowed limited access. He had some hope one day when she referred to him as "Daddy" chortling to the baby. But the contact was superficial, and he was not allowed to bathe or even change the baby. If he picked the child up she would snatch the infant away from him. He also felt he had no one to turn to for advice. He did discuss the situation with his office nurse, but this didn't help much except to get his problem off his chest.

One day he caught Diane alone at home with the baby sleeping.

"Something has to be done about this situation," he said.

"Given time I will do something about it," she said.

It was the week of the surgical convention in Chicago Laxton received a call from his office.

"You'd better get back here. I found out Diane is packing all the stuff in the house and moving out."

"How could she," Laxton said. "Nothing there belongs to her, except for one single bed no one uses."

Laxton flew back to an almost empty house. The bed they had both used was there as well as a table and chair in the kitchen. To his surprise Diane was still there, but no baby. Her mother was also in the house. She was a fat woman with rugged features, a mole on one cheek and she had an asperic tongue. Later Laxton found everyone called her Maggie. There was to be no talking to Diane while Maggie was around.

"You've been fucking everyone in town including your office nurse," Diane said. "And I'm out of here right now."

"This is your home," Laxton protested. He knew it was useless to dispute the lies.

"Not now, it isn't," Diane said.

"Screwing the help and all the whores in town," said Maggie.

Protest was useless and the two took off.

"Where will you be?" Laxton asked.

"I'll send you an address when I'm good and ready," Diane said.

"What about money?" Laxton said.

"Don't worry about us," Diane said.

Laxton was incapable of dealing with the situation. Upon reflection, he felt he must have taken the whole relationship too casually. He found it hard to find deep feelings about Diane, and he couldn't cry about her or the baby. He felt guilty. Rugger, and Laxton's office nurse, both told him to wait. He was bound to hear soon. He believed this until he discovered Diane had withdrawn all the money, including their savings, which he had kept in a joint account, and taken it with her. She would be able to live for sometime on that if she was careful. When he found out she wasn't in the city he felt the only course to follow was to wait until she wrote.

The political situation was such that the government had an overall plan to guarantee no one would go without health care if they needed it.

"From the cradle to the grave," was the cry of all the cynics in the country. The government was called everything from big brother to a series of impolite names that were meaningless. The first critics were the doctors who had a vested interest and who were able to stir up big business and all the other conservative elements who felt they had a lot to lose by the introduction of a scheme that was bound to raise taxes. Big business only supports taxation to make guns and bombs, because the nervousness in the world in such an economy fosters the economic nests of the entrepreneurial rich.

Lester Pearson, Canadian Prime Minister, was dubbed a great peacemaker. He won the Nobel Peace Prize, but that did not endear him to big business. The policy of dramatic reform, which would provide all people with good health care, made big business nervous. That was why the Prime Minister's majorities in the House of Commons were always so small. Laxton toured with Health Minister Judy LeMarsh who was sent around the country to sell the health plan to Canadians. The opposition cry that only the indigent were not covered, but were well provided for, was a perfect chance to tell a not too unlikely story. The advocates of the Health Plan would say:

"It's not the indigent population I'm concerned about. I'm concerned about the man who has a family, and he and his wife both work so they can own their own home and drive a car, when suddenly illness strikes one or other of them. Then the mortgage can't be paid, they worry about their food bill because thousands of dollars are demanded by doctors, demands which have to be met to ensure the survival of the loved one. It's not the rich who suffer, not the indigent, but the blue collar worker, the little man."

Laxton saw that this appeal had most thinking: "That's me!" and for many indeed it was. There was not much said about hospitals because they were already coming under government control which was probably the greatest step ever taken anywhere, for whoever owned the hospital came under intense scrutiny, so hospitals became places to treat the sick rather than make money for crafty businessmen. Laxton was popular with the public but statements that he made such as, "I can't see why anyone should profit from the ill health of others," were not popular with his colleagues.

In any case he saw the legislation pass and each Province of Canada scramble to meet the new laws. At first hospital care in British Columbia was about a dollar a day, which included everything, and was supposedly paid out of Provincial sales tax revenues. In the meantime Laxton's colleagues were screaming about the watering down of health services and the decline in the quality of care.

The objective of the British Columbia Medical Association was to keep the three insurance plans in place and maintain private practice. This way they visualized the insurance payments as a bottomless well. The President of the Medical Association wanted to develop an agreement with the government to protect the physicians so that government intervention would be minimal. He signed an agreement on behalf of all physicians with the three insurance companies.

"The physicians have been sold down the river," Laxton declared publicly, "and within three years there will only be one insurance company run by the government, under the control of the government, and everyone will face unbearable pressures."

"Our friend here maybe right," Rugger said to two of the other surgeons, "but just watch out. The referring doctors think they have such a good deal he's going to pay for what he believes is the truth."

Laxton was feeling the heat of the whole scenario. People were asking slyly why Laxton was saying what he was saying, because the money was so good. He lost referrals he would ordinarily have had and he felt the pinch of their anger. He was wrong about one thing. The government rolled all three plans into one plan under their control within one year, not three years, and the physicians were forced to negotiate directly with the government.

The focus of criticism changed. Although work came back to Laxton on a regular basis, there were those who blamed him for being right, as though somehow he had caused the government's moves. At that point it mattered little what they all thought anyway, for the government had the authority and power to do whatever they wanted, and the medical association representatives were pathetic pawns of their Provincial government masters.

Rugger had become rather ill and was not working at all at this time, although he came to the hospital for coffee some mornings. Laxton had to develop an association with another surgeon for coverage, but financial arrangements were not included. Dave Hubbard was a very pleasant man and had so many great attributes that Laxton laughed off the strange stories he would tell in the surgeon's room, despite many asides about Hubbard directed at Laxton by others. In any case Rugger's heart problem had put a stop to his usefulness in looking on for Laxton if Laxton had to be away. This was why Dave Hubbard was very useful when the word finally came to Laxton from Diane. She wrote from the deep interior of British Columbia describing where she was and what she expected of him. He knew he would have to make a trip to see her and his son.

CHAPTER 7

THE FAMILY

Laxton's statements and overall appeal for the national system had created a great deal of publicity and his name was in the newspapers and on radio. He was interviewed on television. His reservations about the way the government were going about the transition troubled him sufficiently that he was motivated to approach the Federal Health Minister.

"We seem to be missing one aspect of care," he said.

Judy Le Marsh was very bright and was committed to doing what she believed best for health care.

"What's missing?"

"Well, you know physicians are bellyaching about watering down the quality of care, we need to do something to see it goes up rather than down, even if it means surveys of quality of care."

"We'll just concentrate on quantity. Let's make sure everyone gets coverage first and then let's worry about how good it is. You're doing your own work, you're working for us, and you're just worrying too much. Take a few days off."

Laxton took this opportunity to make a trip to the interior of British Columbia to see Diane and the baby. It was his second trip. He felt the first one had gone well and he had asked Diane to come back, but didn't obtain a reply to that question, although she was happy with an intimate dinner and a sexual encounter. He went prepared, hoping to entice her back to Vancouver this time.

In addition, Diane's mother Maggie had become very cordial and had called to say that the next time he came he should stay with her and her husband. When he got off the plane and obtained the rental car he went directly to Diane's rented house. It was a shadow of what she'd been used to in Vancouver. Laxton hoped he'd be able to stay there this time as part of the plans he'd laid to get her back.

"I hear you're going to stay with my mother," Diane said. "It's just as well because I want to introduce you to my husband and we don't want you here."

"What the hell are you talking about," Laxton said. "I was here less than three months ago and we had a great time and I thought -"

"You thought I'd sit on my ass waiting for you while you were running round the country with those stupid government people shooting your mouth off about the health services. I told you I'd solve my problem and I have. You can meet him this afternoon and then you'll see how much you're needed around here."

Laxton got his stuff down to Maggie's house and found he had been given the upstairs room and Maggie and Alf were sleeping in the basement. Apparently they slept down there all the time. Maggie had children around every day. They were Diane's sisters' children from one of the two families. Laxton felt they were brats and that Maggie indulged them.

"You didn't meet Abs yet," she said to Laxton.

"Abs," Laxton said quizzically, "what kind of a name is that?"

"Wait till you see the suntan," said Maggie. She gave a nasty laugh.

The afternoon meeting was almost a legal event. Laxton was shocked when he saw the short, bearded, East Indian who introduced himself as Abdul Athwal. Laxton noticed that both he and Diane wore wedding rings. The name Abs was some sort of nickname.

"How long have you been married?" Laxton asked.

"We were married nine weeks ago," Athwal said.

Laxton realized they got married very shortly after his last visit, which made him angry, anger he controlled so well he was certain the others hadn't noticed.

"We have had much sexual intercourse to make sure there's a brother for Diane's baby, and I'm sure this will be soon."

"I would like to see our baby," Laxton said.

"We will allow you to do that the day after tomorrow," said Athwal, "tomorrow we will be gone for most of the day."

"I presume you have some kind of a job," Laxton said.

"As you know this is a small town and there are five of us here who are general practitioners. I have no reason to tell you this but I have one son already who is with my mother today. My wife died last year."

"I'm sorry to hear your wife died," Laxton said.

"That's over and I have a new wife now."

He put his arm around Diane's waist.

"Let's say noon tomorrow then."

He stuck out his hand which Laxton was tempted not to take, but reluctantly he shook hands, turned and left.

"This is a great shock to me," Laxton said to Maggie. He didn't expect much sympathy.

"I've had to get rid of so many husbands the girls had it would make your head whirl," Maggie said. "There was that husband of her sister Mary's who was a crook. Slippery Herman I called him. He left after I hit him on the head with an old iron frying pan. Never came back. Now she's got someone who works for the city who seems all right. I'm looking after their daughter."

Maggie looked after every relative's child. They loved to come to see her in her relaxed home atmosphere. Laxton wondered if he was one she got rid of, although he hadn't quite made the husband status, and having Diane in town made sure Maggie would be raising her children.

Maggie exerted some dominance over all her daughters.

"I told Athwal that if he was going to be around sticking it into my daughter in this town he'd better make an honest woman of her or he'd regret it. They got married the next week."

"So you really like him," Laxton said.

"You want me to describe him I'll tell you what I think. I think he'd climb over a pile of coonshit just for a smell of her ass. Frankly, he's a prick."

"No, that's not quite right," she continued, "a prick has a head on it."

Laxton had no comment. What was there to say? He thought she was vulgar and yet somehow it seemed natural coming out of Maggie's mouth.

The whole scene had upset him much more than he was willing to admit and he felt he needed to grieve, wishing he was alone in a hotel room.

"I wonder if I shouldn't go to an hotel until I get my head sorted out," he said.

"Laxton," Maggie said, "my place is cleaner than an hotel. I really got myself into gear when you were coming up here. A person needs a feather duster in a mechanical ass-hole to get this place cleaned up for visitors."

She wasn't ready to let him go to bed after one of her beautifully cooked but plain suppers.

"Athwal's own kid will be down here tomorrow. Cheeky little brat I'm taking in hand to try to knock out the bullshit his father puts in his head."

"How did Athwal lose his wife?" Laxton said.

"She committed suicide with an overdose of sleeping pills."

"How awful for him."

"They fought like cat and dog, and you know in a town of two thousand everyone hears about stuff like that, particularly if it's a doctor's wife. If it had been anything else I'd have been sure he'd knocked her off."

"I suppose the autopsy showed what kind of sleeping pills they were," Laxton said.

"Autopsy? A doctor's wife in this town, are you kidding? He just got one of his colleagues up there to tell the cops it was an overdose and issue a death certificate."

Laxton's sympathy for Athwal's loss of his wife began to dissolve when he heard this story. Maggie was a mine of usually accurate information about goings on in the town, of that Laxton was sure. It was too late for anything Laxton thought to himself sadly, but he knew that he had some responsibility to the child and wondered how he was going to deal with this.

He didn't feel he could talk to Maggie about it, and certainly Alf, her husband, only had a grade four education, so he wouldn't be of any help. Laxton had only met him recently and grasped they had nothing in common. His appearance at the house that evening as he came back from a mine union meeting was Laxton's excuse to escape to bed.

"A hell of a committee meeting that was Mag," he began.

"Sit down and tell me about it."

"Evans didn't want to go after higher wages and told us to shut up. I told him I didn't like his altitude."

"The word is 'attitude,' not altitude," Mag said.

"I'm going to let you two talk this over," Laxton said, "I'm headed for bed."

He escaped.

In the early morning, after bacon and eggs and pancakes, in came Athwal's nine year old. Laxton could see what Maggie had meant. He constantly referred to his daddy and how smart daddy was compared to everyone else. This culminated in a remark to Maggie when he suddenly informed everyone, "My daddy told me you were an ignorant old woman."

"Let me tell you something. If they took your daddy, stripped him, and hung him upside down his bum hole would be browner than anyone else's," Maggie said.

The kid was speechless and stomped out.

With some relief Laxton drove to Diane's house only a short distance from her mother's place. Both Diane and Athwal were there with Laxton's son. He was shown the baby but not allowed to hold the child.

"We have a document here for you to study," Athwal said. "You

43

might want to go somewhere and read it and then it will be clear to you just what we intend to do."

"That's right," Diane said, "I agree with everything in there."

The document was from the court. That's what they'd been up to yesterday. It gave Laxton twenty-four hours to give notice to appear before the court to dispute their claim for adoption of Laxton's baby. It was filled with inaccuracies such as the statement he "failed to support the child economically or in any other way." The fact he'd been denied access and not been asked for any support was ignored. The order not only gave total custody but also denied Laxton any further access to his child.

Laxton left the house with the comment that they would hear from his attorneys. Numerous phone calls later he had learned that although he might be able to get visiting privileges to see the baby, there was no way he was going to able to get anything more than that, and since Athwal and Diane were not asking for child support, were legally married, and were adopting the child and accepting full responsibility, there were no good counter-arguments.

"Visiting a child under these circumstances is going to be very painful for you, particularly since the child is too young to recognize you now, and will probably be given a poisoned view of you if you persist in visiting. It is probably in the child's best interests for you to back away from the whole situation," his attorney told him.

There was no one at the house when he got back to Maggie's. Laxton packed his stuff. As he drove to the airport tears rolled down his cheeks. He had never abused Diane; he had catered to her every whim and given her all she wanted. He had offered marriage. He tried to think of the negatives. She had not understood his dedication to his work, but there had never been any arguments about that and she had never made demands that he give up anything he was doing. Everything had been all right until she got pregnant and after that she wanted his child. He could not understand why she would not accept the togetherness he'd offered. Did he love her? He had certainly told her so, but within he wondered if this was really true love. Laxton felt cheated, lied to, and felt this had been done because taking his child would hurt him.

He brushed the tears from his eyes but felt sick inside, a feeling he couldn't get rid of. As Laxton climbed on the plane to Vancouver he made an extra effort to control his feelings so others wouldn't see his distress.

"Poor Sasha," he said to himself.

CHAPTER 8

REASONS FOR CHANGE

After the first week Laxton knew he missed Diane and still felt an interior pain he'd not experienced before. It wasn't that women didn't present opportunities to him, but he had lost all interest in relationships. He threw himself into his work, both the clinical work at which he was so good, and the political work at which he was still a novice. Perhaps he wasn't the novice the other physicians were, particularly those who held elective office in the Medical Association or the College of Physicians and Surgeons which issued licenses to physicians and was responsible for disciplinary action, but among the professional politicians he was a novice.

"Now the scene has moved from the federal to the provincial government," said Rugger, "and watch the abuse. A dollar a day to be in the hospital - we'll never get anyone out."

"What about these right wing egomaniacs who control everything," Laxton said, "people are too afraid of the left wing opposition to ever elect them, and I'm sure the leader of the present provincial government will screw the doctors into the ground."

"You'll see all that," Rugger said. "I've got my own health problem and I don't know how much I'll see."

Indeed, Rugger's heart condition had deteriorated significantly and he was doing very little work. Laxton had to get someone else to look on for him, as Rugger wasn't available to assist him when he needed a specialist assistant. He had Dave Hubbard.

Dave Hubbard was a very pleasant man and had many great attributes. The strange behavior others had hinted at became visible to Laxton suddenly when he entered an office he shared with Hubbard and another surgeon. All the light fixtures were hanging from the ceiling suspended by string, leaving the bulbs clearly visible.

"What the hell is going on here," said Alistair, the other surgeon. "I know you didn't do this, what in Hades was Dave thinking about?"

"Dr. Hubbard said too many light bulbs are getting burned out and it's getting too expensive," the office nurse said.

"It sure looks like hell," Alistair said. "I don't care what it costs, we can't leave it like this."

"Do you know how much we've spent on light bulbs over the last year?" Laxton said.

"As a matter of fact I do," the nurse said. "It was just over seven bucks."

"Get the fixtures put back against the ceiling the way they're supposed to be, and tell Doctor Hubbard neither of us could stand the sight of the string," Laxton said, as Alistair nodded vigorously.

Two days later Hubbard raised hell with the nurse, and wanted to know why the fixtures were back where they were supposed to be. He was informed Alistair and Laxton had made the decision.

"Right, then I want a graph prepared to show the number of light hours per bulb and its relationship to the cost of bulb replacement," he said.

With that he went about his work as usual. Well, not quite as usual, because Laxton became further alarmed one day when his secretary had called him to tell him Hubbard had started an operation but failed to complete it, as it was after six on Friday and he had theater tickets, and would Laxton go back in on Monday and finish the work as he was taking off next week.

Laxton was thunderstruck, and at first didn't know what to do. Obviously he had to get the patient taken care of, and then deal with the Hubbard problem next. This second problem was taken care of for Laxton when Hubbard was admitted to hospital with an emergent surgical problem which made Laxton busier but fortunately gave him control over everything, at least until Hubbard was ready to come back to work.

This problem served to add to Laxton's discomfort. He was trying to put Diane and Sasha out of his mind. He was seeing turmoil in the health care system. And now he had his new pinch hitter behaving in a peculiar manner.

Laxton further embroiled himself with the provincial government's plans. He held no position with them and became a critic from the outside and this affected his practice.

"Everyone should be aware," he told his colleagues, "that the government will not renegotiate this contract annually as they promised they would. The income you get now is what you are going to have to live with because this government will do anything they can to keep costs down, and they'll do it at your expense."

"The Medical Association has an agreement with the government to meet with us again this year," declared the president of the association, "and such talk is irresponsible."

This time several of Laxton's referring doctors were skeptical about what the Medical Association could do, but there were still

46

those who felt he was a rabble-rouser. This view was rapidly dispelled when the government provincial leader initiated a campaign the week following the meeting to prevent physicians renegotiating their agreement. Initially a low key effort, it became more violent when the medical association asked in public when face to face meetings would take place, and this material appeared in the newspapers.

Eventually the government leader hit both television and the newspapers crying out that the province was in serious financial difficulties.

"One of our principal expenses is the exorbitant fees paid to the fat cats of the province. I mean the doctors. In two days time I shall have our insurance company publish the incomes of all physicians in the province."

The incomes were published and, although this was not fair, it was effective. Not fair because it was pre-tax income, because those physicians employing others were listed as being sole earners, because radiologists who had to purchase and maintain their own equipment seemed to be earning exorbitant amounts. One radiologist was shown earning seven point two million dollars but he employed eleven other radiologists and had seven offices with equipment in each. His take home pay was just under a hundred thousand dollars. The government leader declared a moratorium on health care costs for at least a year.

Laxton's credibility increased to some extent but the physicians were suspicious of one of their own tinged with a political brush. Laxton knew that eventually the government would negotiate, but on their own terms. It seemed unlikely there would be anything but discontent on the part of the doctors.

Laxton was elected to the College of Physicians and Surgeons. He had promised to set up a proper quality of care program.

"I have got myself into deep shit again," he told Rugger, "all they want to talk about at the meetings are allegations of overcharging the medical plan and who might be having sex with a patient. They wanted to strike off a family practitioner who was screwing a twenty two year old patient. It was based on her mother's complaint to the college."

"Sounds like there was a good case for it," Rugger said.

"Not much of a case from my perspective," Laxton said, "he'd married the girl before the complaint was even filed, and there was no evidence he'd been messing with any other patients. As far as I'm concerned he covered his rear quite well and if they tried to lift his license and he went to court it would cost the college a fortune, and I doubt they could make it stick anyway. When I brought up quality of care issue no one wanted to listen. The chairman said there were some other issues that were more important. It seems that it's more important that Morgan is screwing his office nurse than people like Jamestown are doing real harm."

"I told you that the only control we have is in our own institution," said Rugger.

St. James boasted one of those popular gynecologists who had the absolute support of the Sisters and the church. He appeared to be a good fellow at heart, but had built his reputation in the Catholic community. Bernie Costogolo was well trained and certified in his specialty. Unfortunately he came to Laxton's attention because of his pattern of practice relating to hysterectomies.

Bernie developed an uncanny knack of tying off, crushing with a clamp, or putting stitches through, the tube which leads from the kidney to the bladder, which is called the ureter. After innumerable occasions of repairing serious damage to that structure, Laxton suggested to Bernie that they insert tubes up the ureters before he did the operation so that he could feel the tubes and identify them then they wouldn't get injured. The request was refused which led Laxton to the Sister who was the Hospital Administrator, informing her of the difficulties, and suggesting that the Medical Executive Committee would have to be told about this.

"You may safely leave this with me," Sister said. "Don't worry about it again."

Laxton felt the problem had been easy to solve. A month later the only Chinese urologist on the staff informed Laxton he was getting the same kind of cases, damaged ureters, and they were difficult to repair.

The last straw came when a colleague of Laxton's opened an abdomen filled with yellow fluid and couldn't find anything. Eventually she was sent home still leaking through her belly and ended up in Laxton's office. He found a totally disrupted ureter with a blocked kidney. The yellow fluid had been urine. It was terrible trying to repair this mess.

The next trip to Sister was less pleasant, as Laxton felt he had to remind her that had her protégé not previously been Brother Costogolo, who taught at a Catholic College, he would likely be long gone from the hospital.

"Just leave it to me," Sister said. "I didn't realize it was still going on."

Bernie continued his complications, although none of the other surgeons knew it for several months, until a friend of Laxton's from

48

another Catholic Hospital in the city brought it up.

"Why can't you guys take care of the fucked up ureters one of your gyne people is creating?" he said.

"What do you mean?" Laxton said uncomfortably. "I used to repair a lot of them, but I raised hell about them and I thought it had stopped."

"Then that's why they're transferring them to St. Mary's to get them fixed. We must have seen six or eight in the last three months."

"He's getting worse," Laxton said gloomily. "But I can't stick my neck out any further."

"If you do you might find yourself out on your ass."

Ruminating on the power of the church did nothing for him. He was acutely aware that at that time you could end up without a hospital to admit your patients and be in dire straights. Since the problem was no longer affecting him directly at St. James, Laxton put it out of his mind. Rugger was too ill to bother about something of that nature but Laxton remembered Rugger's words about controlling poor practice in their own institution and wondered whether even this was going to be accomplished with Rugger out of the picture.

At last the government met with the medical association and announced what the terms would be. They came up with a global budgeting plan. This gave the physicians an overall budget and told the medical association to distribute the funds among the various groups as they saw fit. Not only did this lead to a delay in implementation, but it also led to a dog-eat-dog attitude amongst the physicians.

"You surgeons need to take a cut," an Internist said to Laxton. "We're the ones who have to get up at night all the time."

"What I can tell you," Laxton said, "is the government knows its business, and everyone who was so keen to make a deal with them got themselves into this mess."

At an association meeting an ophthalmologist had a lot to say about competence. Many were amazed, because they felt sure it would affect his referred practice.

"In the highly trained specialties like ophthalmology," he said, "we deserve much more money than the ordinary doctor who is just a jack of all trades. I put more mistakes right than I do doing what is supposed to be done in my own practice."

Despite hissing and booing he continued in a loud voice.

"There are a lot of people going blind because they are diabetics being improperly treated by general practitioners."

McLuster was a general practitioner of the Catholic self-righteous group and he was on his feet at once. He was a malicious and lying conniver and it subsequently turned out he was the one who had protected Costogolo from what should have been the wrath of the Sisters.

"All ophthalmologists should remember, as should other specialists, that it is we the general practitioners who send them their patients."

Three weeks later the ophthalmologist temporarily closed his office because he had psychiatric problems. Undoubtedly they were present when he made his speech at the meeting.

Laxton now faced the bitterness of the disruption of his almost sealed family life, the disappointing troubles within St. James, troubles he felt were going to recur and become worse, and the unfortunate internal battle created within the profession by the government's global budgeting program. Laxton decided there had to be a better way.

CHAPTER 9

GOING SOUTH

All the setbacks Laxton experienced, together with the political climate in the Province of B.C., led him to look south for other opportunities. There were others who were escaping to the United States, but most of them came from Ontario. Just what triggered Laxton's desire to move on was not clear. His recent personal disasters were accompanied by his disturbance at the lengthening waiting lists specialists were experiencing. This made him feel the patient's chances of cure were affected in a detrimental way.

The American Consulate in Vancouver reminded Laxton of an old British railway station because of the long line of opaque windows made of corrugated glass, seated side by side, which would be lifted from the inside, invariably by a female representative.

"I want to make application for entry to the United States to work there," Laxton said.

"There are very limited opportunities for immigrants," a tall, angular woman with sharp cut features said. It was clear she had no intention of making eye contact.

"I'm a physician," Laxton said.

She walked away to a counter behind her and consulted a book on the counter.

"It appears you could be eligible," she said. "You need to fill in these application forms. Take them with you and look them over carefully before you fill them in and then bring them back."

She pushed the forms toward him and then slammed the sliding window shut. The information sheet with the forms listed the acceptable occupations and there were not that many on the sheet. Laxton wondered why she consulted a book.

The forms were not difficult to fill in. He listed no dependents as he was now convinced he had none. It was not difficult to swear he was not a communist and also that he had not committed adultery in the United States, nor had he a criminal record. It was difficult to get back to the Consulate because the first time he tried was a Monday and he was barred from entry because that was a day you had to have an appointment. He went down on a Friday just before they closed. He knocked on a window. Ultimately another window down the row shot up and a gravelly voice said, "Yes."

This time the lady was fair and fat with cheek jowls and a wisp of gray hair in front.

"I have completed the application forms I was given and I have them here."

The woman took them without much enthusiasm and glanced at them quickly and then said, "What's your occupation?"

Laxton was about to respond it was on his form when some sixth sense told him not to.

"I'm a physician, surgeon actually," he said.

The woman walked away to the counter behind and consulted a book on the counter. After a few minutes she came back.

"You might be eligible," she said, "leave the forms with me and come back and see us in a couple of weeks."

"Should I see you?" Laxton said. But the window was already down.

After two weeks Laxton returned and this time went to the window where he had been seen on his previous visit. After a moment or two another window further up the row was thrown open so he moved quickly up to the open window.

"My name is Laxton and I have applied for a visa and was told to come back today."

This time the reception person was small in stature and slight in build. She had a limp.

"When did you file the application?" she said.

"It was filed two weeks ago."

"Oh, it usually takes a lot longer than that. I can't imagine who would tell you to come back so soon."

She looked at Laxton as though he was a liar.

"Can you tell me what stage it's at?"

"Do you have relatives in the States?"

"No, I'm afraid I don't."

She walked over to the counter behind and Laxton was able to see there were many filing cabinets. It did not take long before she returned with an index card, which Laxton could not really see. She studied it for a moment or two.

"Yes, we have your application, but we haven't any word yet. Come back in a week."

And slam, down went the window.

It was actually twelve days before Laxton got back to the consulate. This time he went to the closest window and was surprised when it was opened almost immediately. He did not recognize the dark-

52

haired girl who stood before him. She was tall and thin and he decided older than she looked, about forty-five he judged.

"Name is Laxton," he said, "Doctor Laxton. I have applied for immigration to the United States and I was told to come back to check on the status of the application."

Again the index card appeared. The official looked at the index card, put it down, went to another filing cabinet and came back with his application forms.

"These are incomplete," she said, "we have no records of your qualifications. We need notarized copies of your certificates attached to the forms."

"All right," Laxton said, "while I'm here, tell me, is there anything else you need?"

"Not at the moment. I really couldn't say what they might ask for."

"Who are 'they'?" Laxton asked.

"The authorities, of course. We'll hang onto your form and you bring in your certificates. Good afternoon."

Laxton wondered if he took a day off he could accomplish all the paperwork at one fell swoop. When he talked to Rugger about it, Rugger shook his head and said, "If you're really serious about all this you'd better get writing and get yourself a job somewhere. If you've got some American raising hell to get you down there, you'll improve your chances."

It had not occurred to Laxton to get a job before he had permission to enter the country, but it made a lot of sense to him.

"My photos will be out of date before I get a visa the way these people operate," he told Rugger.

Laxton had contacts. He had given papers at meetings. After drawing a couple of blanks he found a urologist in Burbank, California who offered to help and made him a definite offer of a job.

The certificates were all notarized and he had his job offer letter tucked in his pocket when he next visited the consulate.

"These are all very well," a woman he'd never seen before told him, "but we need to see letters of confirmation of your training."

"You know I do have a job to go to," Laxton said. He was somewhat abrupt. He produced his letter.

"We shall need that later, but we need these other documents first."

"No one told me I needed proof of training. You can't get these certificates without training. I'll get you the letters, but I should have been told they were needed when I was here last time."

"They change the rules all the time," the woman said.

Laxton's next visit brought him almost a sigh of relief. It was the lady with the cheek jowls and wisp of gray hair.

"It's nice to see you again," Laxton said.

"I don't remember ever seeing you before," said the woman, "how can I help you?"

When his forms were produced and he handed over his letters certifying he was trained, she went through the documents.

"There isn't a license here to practice in the United States. Where's your certificate from the examination board for foreigners?"

"I'll get a license to practice in one of the States to you as soon as possible," Laxton said.

This proved to be a marathon task. Laxton eventually went to the Licensing Board Office in California and was told he could get a license there by reciprocity with another State but not with Canada. A trip to Iowa got him a license there through the recommendation of an old friend who had come from England and practiced there. California's board then said as soon as he took up residence in California he could get his license. He would be subject only to an oral examination.

The consulate was adamant he must have the license before he would be given a visa and he must also have a job in the same State. Laxton proceeded to do what he could to get a job. He had no desire to go to Iowa and went through a month of agony obtaining a license in Tennessee, passing their oral without problems. After some searching he found there were two possibilities. He could get a job in Memphis or take a position at the University of Arkansas in Little Rock. In any case he could now go to the consulate with the job and his Tennessee license.

When Laxton presented his Tennessee license to yet another person he had never seen before, the employee took the material into the back somewhere and returned after a few minutes.

"This isn't what we needed. We need a certificate from the Board of Examiners for foreign graduates."

Laxton was angry at last. He knew that meant taking examinations and that these were only designed to enable a person to take the State examinations.

"If you don't find this State license acceptable," he said, "I want an appointment with the Consul, and if this can't be resolved at this level, I shall have to go to Washington."

"Just a moment," the girl said. "Please sit down and I'll be right back."

Laxton sat down and waited. He had assigned the time and he was feeling militant about this issue. Eventually, up went the window and there stood gray streaked hair and jowls.

Laxton got up and approached the window.

"We just checked with the Consul and this license is quite acceptable," she said. "There are some other things which have to be done. We need a certificate from the police in each country in which you've lived to say you haven't pursued any criminal activities, and you have to make a date after that to be finger printed here and we also take a photograph."

"Maybe I can make an appointment for finger printing," Laxton said.

"Just a moment," the woman said, "I'll get you an appointment."

When she returned, he was given an appointment about a month away. The woman actually smiled.

"Here's a form for your employer to fill in. He'll have to go to the labor department to finalize this," she said.

Subsequently Laxton found out that the form and the visit to the labor department were to determine he was not taking a job away from an American citizen, or that they couldn't get an American citizen to take the job.

Laxton was able to obtain a clearance from the Royal Canadian Mounted Police within a few days but it was a month before he heard from the British police. The letter came from the Wakefield and District Municipal Police Department and read:

It is not the policy of police authorities in England to give information or to issue clearances at the request of persons or foreign governments.

Laxton took the letters to the U.S. Consulate when he went for his appointment to be finger printed. There was a door at the far end of the room that was divided like a stable door. Laxton was admitted, once again by someone he'd never seen before, and taken along a short narrow corridor to a room with a camera and apparatus for fingerprinting. Two photographs were taken and two sets of fingerprints. When he tried to give his letters to the girl she said, "You must submit those at the front. Go to one of the windows."

Laxton reflected he had never yet seen a man anywhere in the office. He went through the usual routine, knocking on the wrong window and the usual routine of seeing someone he'd never seen

55

before. He presented his two letters to the angular lady, thin as a rail with sunken eyes and hollow cheeks. She looked at the letters.

"This is what we expected from the English police," she said. "Please sit down and wait a minute."

When she returned, she said, "Your paper work appears to be complete. Since you were born in England you will fall under the English quota for immigration and we will contact you to give you an appointment for an interview with the Consul as soon as your name comes up."

"Exactly what does being in the English quota mean?" Laxton asked.

"At this time it is favorable," she said.

It was two weeks before Laxton received a letter telling him to report on a Monday at eight a.m. for an interview with the Consul. He had to wait two weeks for this event. On the day in question he went down to the consulate being sure he was dressed in a smart business suit. When he arrived there was a sergeant at arms guarding the entrance.

"Name," said the sergeant.

"Laxton."

The sergeant looked down a list, found his name and ticked it and said, "Find a seat. You'll be called."

The room was indeed full of people but there was room at the front and he took a seat. Looking around he noted all the windows were closed but the upper half of the stable door was open. From time to time the loudspeaker blared out someone's name.

Laxton sat in his seat until after ten when eventually the speaker blared out:

"Doctor Richard Laxton."

It was the first time anyone had used his name and title in the consulate. He went to the stable door where the lady who had taken his fingerprints waited.

"We have to do the fingerprints again," she said. "They got misplaced."

Following this process he waited another hour when the loudspeaker blasted his name out again. Laxton felt they were enjoying the doctor bit in front of all these people. He thought he must be getting paranoid.

"That will be twenty five dollars cash for the visa," said the girl at the door, "in American funds."

Fortunately Laxton had read all this on the original instruction form and he handed over the cash.

"Please be seated and I'll get you a receipt."

He went back to his seat and waited fifteen minutes before he was called again and given a receipt.

"Please be seated and the consul will see you in a few minutes."

About half past noon one of the glass windows was raised and the first man Laxton had seen appeared at the window. He was tall, about forty, with a small moustache and glasses.

"Richard Laxton," he called out, without the aid of the loudspeaker.

Laxton went to the window. With barely a glance at him the man said, "Is there anything you want to change on this form."

"No," Laxton said.

"Raise your right hand."

As soon as Laxton was sworn in, he was told to sit down. It was almost two o'clock before the lady with the gray streak in her hair appeared at the stable door and without the aid of the microphone shouted, "Richard Laxton."

She had a sealed package in her hand. She looked straight at Laxton for the first time and said, "Take this package. You'll need this when you cross the border. You must cross the border within six weeks from today or you'll have to go through this paper work all over again."

CHAPTER 10

CHOOSING A DOCTOR

The Memphis surgeons who had promised Laxton a job told him he must obtain a license in the State of Arkansas because they practiced in West Memphis, which, although on the state border, was in Arkansas, and there was no courtesy reciprocity for physicians and surgeons practicing in either state.

He had written to the Arkansas State Board of Medical Examiners and received a very discouraging form to fill in with an information sheet which stated foreign graduates were not eligible for licensure without full examinations, but he was invited to fill in the form anyway. Laxton reflected this probably happened because the University had expressed an interest in hiring Laxton and the Professor had talked to the Secretary of the Board.

The application form was followed by a letter that stated that the board required a certificate from the consulate that affirmed his medical training and certified it to be correct as he had reported it. Clearly, Laxton thought, there was no way the consulate could do this for him, and had they been able to he didn't believe they would anyway. It was a tremendous surprise when he obtained the certificate without any difficulty and it turned out to be the most impressive looking document in his package.

He had almost made a decision to go to Memphis because his experiences in Little Rock had been most disconcerting. His friend Jim Green was a radiologist at the University there and wanted Laxton to locate in Little Rock and had prevailed on him to pay a visit. The clubs were very impressive, and he liked the University atmosphere. He liked the professor, although Laxton was amused when he asked the professor how he felt about an ex-Englishman from Canada coming to teach in the south.

"It's better than a damn Yankee anyway," the professor said.

The thing which upset Laxton was when he asked his friend Jim about the black people and where they lived.

"They stay in their part of town and we stay in ours," Jim said.

"I'd like to see where they live," Laxton said.

"Since it's daytime we can get in the car and lock all the doors and I'll drive you through that part of town."

Laxton saw the refrigerators and coke machines on porches,

wrecked cars in the gardens, and general litter. But it looked clean to him and the people he saw on the streets looked normal.

"What is the real difference, Jim?" he asked.

"You'll find out a negra is closer to an animal than we are."

Laxton was rather disgusted with this attitude and perceived a serious type of prejudice existed in Little Rock and that was the factor which made him decide he did not want to live in Little Rock. Memphis appeared more cosmopolitan.

His new buddies, Hazeltine and Milton, seemed so open and moved about freely.

"Why don't you call the Board of Examiner's secretary in Arkansas while you're here ?" Hazeltine said. "He lives in a town not too far away and you could drive over there."

It came about that Laxton found himself, one Saturday morning, at their choice, in a small town with wooden sidewalks. The town seemed to be composed mostly of churches and bars. There he stood, dressed as though he had stepped from the New York Hilton, the object of staring and ogling from locals, whose dress was of an extremely casual nature. Laxton was certainly out of place. Years later he supposed he should have had serious doubts about what he was doing, but having determined a course of action he was not the type to turn back. He began to rationalize why he was following this path.

He found the Health Board Secretary's clinic office. It was a building that looked like a barn, painted red with a typical barn roof. Inside was a large waiting room with those wicker chairs, so commonly seen in the south, having the huge oval back at the top of the chair, but not usually seen in a doctor's waiting room, and in this case they were made comfortable by rather large dirty cushions. Lounging in some of the chairs were black patients, clearly waiting for the doctor.

Laxton approached the desk that was built into the wall, the top of which was at least six to eight feet wide. It seemed to be supported by a hefty girl in white, who could have been mistaken for a nurse, sitting sprawled over this structure that gave uplift to her sagging breasts.

As he approached her he saw she was skimming through an article entitled "Medical Ethics", but doing it in such a way that it was at once obvious to him that she was not actually paying any attention to the contents of the publication.

"I have an appointment with Doctor Volt," Laxton said, "I'm Doctor Laxton."

She put the magazine down at once and hurried into the back.

Within a few seconds an older man, five feet seven, graying hair, medium build, peering over half moon glasses, and decked out in a dirty greenish Hawaiian style shirt with an open neck, casually wandered to the desk. His stethoscope hung around his neck and he fiddled with the end of it as he said, "Come on in doc, is that your paper work you have there?" He had a thick southern accent.

Laxton handed the envelope to him and followed him down a very wide corridor from which sprung many examining and consulting rooms. What Laxton found unusual were the double louvered half doors, the type seen at the entrance to bars in those old western movies. Volt made a sudden right turn into one of these rooms and sat down at the desk inviting Laxton to sit in what clearly was the chair usually occupied by the patient. He opened the envelope and took out the many documents.

"Show me the certification from the Canadian Board of Medical Examiners," he said.

Laxton found the correct page which Volt scrutinized briefly and said in a shocked tone, "Why, it's writ in his own handwriting! Who is this fellow? Writ in his own handwriting!"

"That's the signature of the College Registrar," Laxton said weakly, nervous and shocked by this unexpected development.

"This is very irregular, it's not even typed."

"The one from the medical society is," Laxton said, "it's on the adjacent page."

"That don't matter. It's this certificate, isn't even typed. What's his name?"

"Maybe you can't read it because of the notary stamp," Laxton said quickly.

"That's right, it is notarized." Volt interrupted him.

"What's this?" he asked, turning another page.

"That's a letter confirming I'm a Fellow of the American College of Surgeons," Laxton said.

"That don't matter," Volt said as he began to turn the page. Laxton wasn't surprised because it was a form letter.

"Just a minute," Volt said, looking at the page once again, "it's signed by Frank Padburg. An Arkansas boy. I must read this."

There was a short pause.

"So Frank Padburg says you're all right, eh? Well, if you're good enough for Frank Padburg, you're good enough for us."

With that he stood up and said, "Follow me to the State Board office."

They walked down the long, wide corridor at the end of which was a conventional door. Above the door was a small hand painted sign which said: "State Board of Medical Examiners."

"We has reciprocity with Canadian trained physicians," Volt said.

"My original training was in England," Laxton said. He was afraid of any kind of deception.

"Canadian trained, I said, and that's what you are," Volt said, "and we has reciprocity with Canadians."

The State Board office turned out to be a converted kitchen; the sink and cabinets were still there. In front of these were two desks face to face. At the first desk was seated a young southern miss with a frilly dress. She had sharp features, slightly crooked teeth, but a nice smile.

"This here's May Belle," Doctor Volt said. Just then a door on the right opened and a slightly plump, red-faced lady entered. She had a long full dress, which was designed to conceal her ample hips. Although her face was red and wide, the skin was tight and unwrinkled.

"And here's my wife Brenda Jo," he added, and this here is Doc Laxton, a Canadian doc, here to escape socialized medicine they have in Canada."

"Now, Brenda Jo, look at what the fellah what 'as the licensing did on his form, writ in his own handwriting, it is, it's not even typed."

He handed the documents to her and she shook her head.

"What's this thing with blue ribbons?" She said.

Volt took the papers back and glanced at them once more and then, looking over his half moon glasses, he said, "That document is the great seal of the United States Government."

He handed the documents back to her.

"What's all these papers at the back?" she asked.

"Them's his certificates," he said.

"One, two three, four, five, six, seven, eight, nine, ten, eleven; ought to be enough there to give him a license," she said.

"He's Canadian trained and we has reciprocity with Canada," he said with some finality.

"Now what I need is a certificate from the basic science board then I can give you a license," he said, turning to Laxton.

Laxton's heart sank because he knew that if he had to take chemistry and physics exams after all these years the chances of passing were not good.

"I hope I don't have to take their exams," Laxton said.

"You've been in practice over ten years so you won't have to take exams," Volt said.

"What do I have to do to get the Certificate?" Laxton asked.

"Their office is in Little Rock. You should write to them."

After a moment's silence, he looked at May Belle and said, "Call Allie in Little Rock, she should be home Saturday morning, and let me talk to her."

May Belle dutifully dialed the number on an old rotary telephone and after a few moments there was an answer.

"That you Allie?" May Belle said. "Was you doing your washing?"

Laxton could not hear the reply.

"Did you get that dress you was going to get?"

After a pause May Belle said, "Well, here's Joe. I don't rightly know what he wants, but here he is."

"I've got a young fellah here from Canada, a Canadian graduate, and we has reciprocity with Canada and you all got reciprocity with Canada too," Doctor Volt said. "Now what does he have to do to get a basic science certificate so's I can give him a license?"

"Writ this down," he said to Laxton, and then dictated the request for a basic science certificate.

"Oh, and you need a note from his licensing board saying he has a license up there. Take this down," he added, "and you need a cashier's check for a hundred and fifty dollars."

He covered the mouthpiece of the phone and said to Laxton: "They won't take your personal check, it's not good enough for them, that's the government for you, we'll take your personal check, of course,"

As he finished his conversation with Allie he looked at Laxton and added significantly: "And make sure that letter isn't written in his own handwriting; it should be typed."

"Now write me a check for ten dollars, that'll cover the medical license and paper work, a personal check is all I need."

After a moment he said: "Would you like a temporary license right now ?"

Laxton remembered foreign graduates could never get a temporary license so he paused and then said, "Well I need it by January, but not before."

"Takes three months to get the permanent license," Volt said, "they have to be printed up proper."

After this ordeal Laxton asked Doctor Volt if there was anything else he needed to do.

"Where will you practice?" Volt asked.

"Memphis and West Memphis," Laxton answered at once.

"Used to be a nice town Memphis," Volt said, "highest crime rate in the whole United States now. You'll soon find out who's responsible for that. It's them negras, that's who."

"I'll tell you what you can do. You can come and talk to the State Medical Society about the evils of socialized medicine or national insurance or whatever they call it."

When Laxton got back to Memphis Hazeltine asked him how he made out.

"They came to the right conclusion for all the wrong reasons," Laxton said.

CHAPTER 11

LOOKING FOR IDENTITY

"What a pleasure it is," Laxton said to a colleague in Vancouver in a subsequent phone conversation, "I can pick up the telephone anytime and my patient can be hospitalized."

It was the standard of care which Laxton believed essential for good service to patients, and he decided the main reason he had moved away from Canada. Physicians were happy and hard working and Laxton felt the standard of practice was very high and he was unable to see the criticisms of the American system, criticism that he had heard levied by Canadian government officials.

It was soon apparent to him that anyone who had not been born in Memphis, and whose family had not lived there for two hundred years, fell into one of two categories - a Yankee or a foreigner, which the locals pronounced "ferriner." He soon discovered it was better to be a foreigner. His colleagues were quite different from each other. Hazeltine was a small, round man with a shiny baldhead and had an enforced joviality about him. Although it was hard to discern, he was basically a manipulator. He was the one who made sure much money was made out of Laxton for the first six months, and he paid his staff low wages and refused to hire any blacks.

Milton was also short, but trim, with a bald patch at the back of his head. He was the first one to have hair implants, which gave a fuzzy appearance over the area, but did little else to hide it. He swayed slightly as he walked and he indulged in rather cultist activities. He was a devout Baptist who did not believe in smoking, drinking, or promiscuity, but secretly smoked, drank and had an apartment in two places which others, and particularly his family, didn't know about. Despite this he spent a half hour studying the bible daily, when he really had other work to do.

Although he was miserly, Hazeltine was supportive, and eventually made sure Laxton had a satisfactory financial deal. There was no shortage of patients, of which at least thirty percent were black, and Laxton had his share of them. Laxton found the rural white population to be dirtier and more ignorant than most of the urban black population, and wondered about discrimination.

All his colleagues told him there was no discrimination in Memphis, that it was much worse in Chicago.

He found West Memphis to be different in that the majority of the population was black, so most of his patients were black. On an early occasion Laxton took a girl friend who was visiting from Canada on rounds one weekend, and left her in the lobby of the West Memphis Hospital until he had completed rounds. His friend needed to go to the bathroom, so she entered the closest at hand. As she exited from the bathroom a local white lady assailed her.

"You mustn't be from round these parts."

"No, I'm from Canada."

"Well, you'll find the bathroom at the other end of the corridor much nicer. This one is used by those people."

Laxton had further evidence of that attitude when he had lunch one day with one of the black nurses who worked with him in the operating room. About a week later Langley, the beefy, heavy set, tall, chief of the Medical Staff caught him in the corridor.

"You can't date the black girls, don't matter whether they're nurses or whatever. You being from Canada and all mightn't know that," he said.

Laxton, amazed, was quick to deny the allegation.

"You were seen," Langley said, "in the company of the nurse who works for you all in the O.R. in the lunch room. Now, you're doing well here. We wouldn't want anything to happen to your practice, so you should watch it."

Laxton thought it was worse than his experiences in Little Rock. He made no comment.

The hospital had a hard time getting nurses so they advertised in England. The Administrator was sure they would get some of their own people if they could license girls from the U.K. After going through an intensified process to get three nurses he was eventually successful. When they arrived they were all black, having their origins in the West Indies.

"Well, you all know what happened to us in our nurse recruitment," he told the internal staff at a subsequent meeting. "I suppose we have to live with it. See you all in church on Sunday."

When two patients jumped from an upstairs window in the hospital, and there were several serious medication errors in the Institution, Laxton began to distance himself from the West Memphis hospital. It was clear the care was worse than in Canada. It was generalized too, not limited to one physician. It was an institutional problem.

In Memphis things were better, care was good overall, and the

65

hospitals were of high quality, although he had reservations about the reason one of the institutions would have eight hundred medical staff members and only four blacks on the medical staff.

There was one other Canadian at that hospital and he was a vascular surgeon. There was such good control in the institution he was thrown off the medical staff after he had killed four bypass patients.

The town was still socially divided, so that blacks did not mix with whites, except in Whitehaven, where there was reputed to be an invasion, and Memphians began to refer to the area as Blackhaven.

"It's not the blacks who worry me, it's the white niggers," a radiologist said to Laxton.

That was the time of an election for mayor, and there was a black candidate, and he was referring to any whites who supported him. Strangely though, his group did not discriminate against East Indians.

One difficulty for Laxton was that he wasn't a churchgoer. Everyone in Memphis belonged to some religious creed, the most popular being Baptist. As long as you were in church on Sunday to do penance, and you were wearing a smart suit and tie, you could screw like hell the rest of the week and no one cared.

This became an issue later though. An emergency room physician who was about Laxton's age approached Laxton. Milliner was a heavily built man with a head that seemed rather small and disproportionate to the rest of him.

"I want to get you into a private club we have," Milliner said.

"Where is it located?" Laxton said.

"In an old house on Summer Avenue. We don't have to have licenses and it is pretty exclusive. Being single, I thought you'd appreciate it, it's kind of swinging."

Laxton was polite. He felt all he needed at this point was to get mixed up in what he suspected was an illegal drinking and swinging club. He suspected that it really wasn't as Milliner described it.

"Whose in the club anyway?" Laxton said.

"We keep the membership quiet, but there are several attorneys, accountants, and doctors. Girls are from society mostly, some are wives."

The club's downfall occurred when the local clergy became aware of the club. They pressured the police to do something about it. They told the police there was a whorehouse operating on Summer Avenue.

The police staked out the house for nearly two weeks, and this took a lot of manpower. Eventually they raided the place finding two prominent attorneys, two doctors, and a prominent banker in some sort of swing session with blondes.

During the same period two nurses were murdered in the hospital parking lot at three fifteen in the afternoon. There were no police around, and the criminal was never caught. Nevertheless, the swinger's club got buried, as did the nurses.

Laxton's relationship with Nicki, the black O.R. nurse, had progressed more by accident than design. At the completion of one list in the operating room Nicki had asked Laxton if he would be having lunch in the cafeteria.

"Not today," Laxton said. Then, after everyone had gone, he looked for Nicki.

"I would like to have lunch with you," he said, "but I can't do the cafeteria thing, and I wonder if we could go out to lunch somewhere one day. I really don't know where to pick."

"Why, yes we could, and I know where we could go. That Holiday Inn on the hill in Memphis would work."

Laxton trusted her and they made the arrangements. It was clear that this was the one place in the area which turned a blind eye to black men mixing with white women and vice-versa.

When they finally went for lunch it wasn't long before Nicki said, "What was all that stuff about the cafeteria?"

"Langley advised me not to be mixing with any black girls," Laxton said.

"It's none of his business," Nicki said.

"True, but he could cause a lot of trouble for me."

"Hazeltine is screwing that girl who works in dialysis," Nicki said, "why doesn't Langley say something to him?"

"The girl who works in dialysis is white." Laxton said, "In this part of the country you don't see black men or women out on the street with white people, either as a group or as a couple."

"What about where you come from?" Nicki said.

"It wouldn't make any difference," Laxton said.

It wasn't long before the inconvenience of lunch led to the convenience of dinner, and this led to the issue of sex.

"I'm not in the business of taking a chance on pregnancy," Laxton said.

"I had my tubes tied years ago." Nicki said, "I'm curious and it's time."

She had the most wonderfully smooth skin. She approached sex with enthusiasm and enjoyed it. After a number of months Laxton began to have doubts about the relationship. He could never find any

67

grounds for a permanent relationship. Their backgrounds were so very different and he knew they could never get out and about in the south.

"I feel so bad about taking advantage of you when I know I can't offer anything in the way of a public and more permanent relationship," Laxton said as he sat up in the bed one evening.

"White people have such a funny attitude about sex." Nicki said, "To us sex is a physical thing. Love may go along with it, but more often it's just fulfilling a need, not making a commitment."

"Do all black people think that way?" Laxton said.

"Most of them do."

Although Nicki had talked many times about moving to Canada or California where things were different, Laxton knew she was a creature of the south and believed she always would be.

Somehow Hazeltine became suspicious, probably because he heard some rumble from the nurse who formed the partner in his own illicit affair.

"You know," he said to Laxton one day, "that black girl who works for us in the operating room is very pretty, but if she was the last woman on earth I could never stick it into her."

Laxton refrained from saying: "What would you do, stick it up some white ass?"

After a year it became obvious to Laxton he couldn't continue on a permanent basis in Memphis. It was not the medical care or the standard of medicine that posed a problem, so much as the cultural shock of a society still embroiled in the Civil War. It was dangerous to mention the war at a cocktail party unless you were prepared for an hour of educational rationalization. It seemed the Yanks had won the war but the south had all the best generals, best troops, and the best songs.

The white man's world was protected in that part of the south and it required an effort to get on the wrong side of the law if you lived there. However, woe betide the unwary traveler from the north who fell foul of the police in the south. People were locked up in jail for speeding.

Perhaps the blacks suffered more. Close to Memphis was a town called Tupelo, Mississippi, probably the most red neck and bigoted place in the area. They were still burning crosses on lawns in that town. The most ignominious stunt was the arrest of a black man from Memphis who was visiting Tupelo and got drunk. Mysteriously he hanged himself in his cell. The only problem was that he did so with his hands tied behind his back and his feet tied together. The inquest found it to be suicide.

Laxton was disturbed by a conversation he had with Hazeltine one day.

"You see a lot of women with inflammation of the bladder, the chronic sort," Hazeltine said.

"That's true," Laxton said, "a lot of the chronic ones respond to conservative treatment."

"Well, why don't you slip a cystoscope in them and take look around the bladder every three months, just to make sure there's no cancer?"

"If they ever bleed, or the symptoms change, that's exactly what I do, but if the symptoms are the same, and the urine is the same, I don't do that."

"You should do them every three months," Hazeltine said with conviction.

"Why?"

"Just remember we get a hundred bucks plus the office visit if you scope them."

But Laxton refused to do unnecessary procedures. He wasn't like the gastro-enterologist who was their neighbor who felt no patient had been adequately examined until the patient had three office visits and had a scope shoved up his rectum and down his gullet.

"I don't find much usually," said Bigelman, "but they sure get reassured."

Laxton thought he was a pompous ass but never said so. It was important to be polite. Another trait which irritated Laxton was the general belief it was all right to stretch the truth. It was all right to lie if expedient but if the person got caught it was rude to call him a liar.

One of the physicians, Nikki, constantly gave false information. He'd been around show business people so long it seemed he didn't know right from wrong. He got into trouble so often because of his empathy with them. One time he saw a rock drummer with a broken toe in the emergency room. He did all the right things including getting an orthopedic surgeon who had a long conversation with the character. It seemed he had to do a rock concert that night and couldn't stamp his foot because of the broken toe.

After much discussion the orthopedic surgeon decided to put local anesthetic in the toe and have the drummer come back the next morning to get the thing taken care of by splinting with a cast. After about ten minutes Nikki came back and wrote out a prescription for Demerol and Quaaludes, in a significant quantity. He was very popular with the show biz crowd.

"What did you give him?" the Emergency Room physician asked.

"I did nothing really. The orthopod looked after him."

Preliminary investigations in California looked promising. Laxton had not been able to conceal his intentions from Nicki.

"Carry me there with you," she said.

This was not Laxton's intention. He had spent almost eight years in a place he didn't hate but the hypocrisy, the phony southern charm, the language barrier, and the absolutely foreign aspects of the people, all contributed to his discomfort. He had not found his niche and he was having a hard time trying to come to terms with whom Laxton was and where he was going.

CHAPTER 12

CALIFORNIA

When Laxton decided to leave the South it didn't take him long to get on with it. His years in Memphis, while profitable, had made him feel he was marking time. Yet he had done good work but had stayed on the outside of everything and not allowed himself to become involved. Laxton wondered if this was really true or if his feeling of being excluded from the south was because he was a foreigner.

His parting from Nicki was less traumatic than he expected. He had imagined she would be angry and possibly cruel, but Laxton found none of this. She reacted as though it was an everyday event, a passionless separation. Laxton concluded it was a cultural difference that existed between the races. Privately, he was probably more upset than he cared to admit to himself; because he was not the cold fish he led others to believe. In any case few of his colleagues, if any, knew of his relationship. Overall he sensed there was not the warmth at the time of his departure which had been present at the time of his arrival, so there were no parties and there was no kind of farewell supper.

The southerners, with their great reputation for friendliness, behaved as though he was no loss to them.

"They behaved as though they had done me a great favor, whereas they actually basked in my sunshine for a while," Laxton said subsequently.

Laxton had submitted a resume to a Health Maintenance Organization in California who had contacted him when he put his name in the available column in the California Medical Association. His first meeting with Dr. Voltran, the Medical Director of the whole large organization, was revealing in that Voltran emphasized he was being taken into the organization because his reputation, which had preceded him, was that he was an excellent care giver.

"I want you to start in charge of our department, but I envision that you will be able to do a great deal to improve the quality of care in the organization quite soon, and it's possible we may need you to be doing that on a full time basis," Voltran said.

"I don't consider I have more expertise than the next man in quality of care," Laxton said.

"I heard all about your efforts to clean up a Vancouver hospital several years ago," Voltran said, "and I believe you were very effective."

So the matter of Jamestown had followed him here and was known. Not that he minded because he knew he had done the right thing, but it was discomforting that Voltran knew so much about him.

As a Department Head Laxton sat on the Council of the HMO and soon found that utilization of services was more important to them than quality of care. At least he formed that opinion, although quality was always emphasized.

Memorable to Laxton was a meeting where Voltran listened to a pediatrician, John Sunu, who presented and discussed the care of a critically ill newborn. The birth had taken place at the Queen of Angel's hospital with which the HMO had no contract.

"Of course I moved the patient into our system, to our contracted hospital, as soon as possible. Children's hospital is so superior anyway," Sunu said. "The strange thing is that it cost us seventeen dollars more there than it would have to have left the infant at Queen of Angels."

"Well," Voltran said with a leer, "you'll know what to do next time, won't you?"

Such petty attention to minor fiscal advantages for the HMO irritated Laxton, but not so much as the moratorium on elective surgery imposed by Voltran for fifteen working days.

"We just have to improve our cash flow," Voltran told the Council members.

Around Easter time one of Laxton's major cases, who he had moved to the intensive care unit, developed chest pain. Laxton wrote appropriate orders and then returned to the HMO clinic, which was located less than a five-minute drive from the hospital. It was late afternoon. Laxton knew that the pain might be the onset of serious heart disease so as soon as he reached the clinic he dropped into the adjacent office of an internist, Doctor Salil.

"I have a post-operative patient with chest pain, and I'd like you to drop by ICU and see him on your way home," Laxton said.

"But I'm off at five o'clock and it's five to five now," Salil said, glancing at his watch. "You're going to have to get Marlene. She's on call."

"Where is she?"

"Oh, she went home an hour ago," Salil said.

"But she lives thirty miles away and it's rush hour."

"Sorry, I just can't make an exception," Salil said with finality. "I have the freeway to face myself and I don't want to be late for dinner."

This cavalier, apathetic attitude irritated Laxton, because he would respond to calls anytime, whether he was on or off duty.

His devotion to duty became a problem for Laxton when word spread through the HMO system. Two family practitioners at a peripheral clinic were overheard discussing a patient.

"Every time I send him up to the main corporate clinic, they just give him pills. You know what? He's right back with the same problem the following week. He needs surgery. Even I know that much."

"If you want to get him properly looked after, send him over to Laxton," said the other.

That's how Laxton's waiting list grew, although at first he couldn't understand how it was happening. In trying to communicate with referring family doctors for continuity of care, he found that patients seemed to change their doctor all the time. Later he learned that patients had major problems trying to stay with the same family doctor in the HMO system.

At ten to five one day Laxton received a phone call at his clinic office asking him to wait after five to see an emergency. The patient would arrive in a half hour. Although he was not on call he agreed to wait.

The clinic closed at five except for the remote twenty-four hour emergency room at the other end of the building. Laxton's room was a concrete block corner hole with no windows. The concrete was painted a sickly green. The HMO was not catering to the carriage trade. Laxton put his feet up on the utilitarian desk which was pushed into a corner. It was twenty to six.

The patient arrived at six. Aside from drunkenness, there was nothing wrong with him. Although Laxton was a calm, deliberate person, he felt a surge of anger at the dumping to which he had been subjected. That led him to lay out in writing the tests which had to be done, and the kind of diagnosis which had to be made before he would see a referred patient on an emergency basis. The patient had to fall in his specialty, or he wouldn't be seeing the patient. Laxton was sad about the necessity of pursuing such a rigid course of action. It was not an irritation from the company, but the inadequacy of his colleagues which caused him distress.

Laxton was relieved to receive an offer from the corporation to take charge of the quality of care program. Although he despised Voltran, he was unable to hide the inward satisfaction he felt with the offer of this position. He believed that moving into the business and management section of health care would be better than struggling in what he discerned to be a second rate system. He resolved to make a difference to the system. If he accomplished this goal it would enable the organization to become a class operation for superior care. In this new position he wouldn't be constantly on call and would get weekends off, something he had given up the moment he became a physician.

Laxton's new office was a marked contrast to his clinic office. It was on the ninth floor of a modern building. The oak desk was placed centrally in a large room with paneled walls, built-in bookcases, and extensive windows on the exterior wall which rendered a panoramic view of Orange County when you could see it through the smog.

At first the outer office had two secretaries and two utilization review nurses. The function of the nurses was to ensure the patients were in the hospital the shortest time possible. Should the patient end up in a non-contracted hospital it was the nurses' responsibility to get the patient into the system as soon as possible. Laxton was disappointed to find he was expected to participate in this process as a heavy when the nurses failed. The twice-monthly meetings with Voltran were an unwelcome part of the job because Voltran was so focused on saving corporate money.

Everything was going reasonably well when the corporation decided to change the physician remuneration system. Physicians were to be encouraged to set up their own organizations to contract with the HMO to provide care. The corporation could see more money for their shareholders if they put the doctors on contracts where they paid so much per head per doctor per month to cover all services. The pernicious part of the scheme was that the doctor was put at risk for hospitalization of the patient. If everyone stayed well, the doctor was in the money. If many patients got sick, the doctor was out of pocket. The HMO promised to get patients, to contract hospitals, and send money as they were billed for services. Had the physicians known this was simply a copy of the capitation system (so much per head per month) introduced into Great Britain in 1911, they might have been unenthusiastic.

Laxton was suddenly made responsible for recruiting physicians and helping set up the new system in addition to his monitoring quality of care in which his first success had been to stop an older surgeon from performing surgery because of incompetence. Unfortunately the hospital surgical committee had a brief hearing and decided the surgeon was all right. The physicians owned the hospital. Voltran told Laxton that the doctor would not be operating on HMO patients anyway; Voltran would stop that.

"You were quite right," Voltran said. "He's costing us too much

74

money with all the complications his patients get."

Since his contractual obligations were to the HMO the doctor couldn't operate or he wouldn't get his pension when he retired. He was sixty-four. He was not allowed to do private practice because he had contracted full time with the HMO.

Laxton was on a recruiting trip to try to enroll hospitals into the new system. His disadvantage was he didn't know much about the hospitals he had to deal with and the corporation didn't seem to know too much either. The company frowned on doctor-owned hospitals, presumably because they were in the business of making as much money as they could for their M.D's. The corporation was an insurance company in the business of making money for its shareholders. Both parties were driven by the profit motive. Health care was a by-product.

The state required the HMO cover every area before they would license the HMO to give care in this manner, so hospital recruitment was a very important but marathon task. Laxton was having a difficult time getting some areas covered. He welcomed a phone call from a Doctor Aysgarth who explained they had a large group of doctors and an excellent hospital.

Laxton drove up the freeway, first passing the Vietnamese, Spanish, Korean and Chinese signs of Santa Ana, then the clay brown, dry hills north. It was a hot California day, hotter because he was further from the beaches at Newport, and he finally looked down on the toxic fog overlying Pomona and Ontario as he drove to Flashing Rod.

The clinic was a low-slung attractive building, with adequate outside parking for which there was no charge. Climbing from his car Laxton noted the intense, dry heat of the day as he entered the cool foyer of the clinic, which bustled with activity. He introduced himself at the front desk and was immediately shown into an office. The office consisted of two adjoining rooms with a common toilet between them. The room he first entered had a comfortable sofa and armchair, and a coffee table with ornaments. Tasteful pictures hung on the walls.

When Aysgarth entered Laxton noted he was of medium height, rather heavy build, but not grossly overweight. He had a slightly pale round face, which may have appeared paler because he was wearing a white coat.

"I have so many patients," Aysgarth said, "I'm sorry to keep you waiting. Come into the other office and sit there for a short while longer."

The office contained a large, highly polished desk with many files and papers on the desktop. Also in the room was a glass cabinet containing many curios. There were shallow windows with Venetian blinds, outside of which were well maintained shrubs.

"Now," Aysgarth said when he returned, "I've looked at the material you sent so let's discuss the contract."

"The basis of the contract," Laxton said, "is provision of a payment of an overall sum per patient per month to cover physician and hospital services. It is set up in such a way that if utilization of hospital services is low, the physicians are rewarded and share any profits generated with the hospital."

A discussion of the insurance, profits generated, reinsurance methods, stop loss, and other benefits ensued.

"I see," Aysgarth said at last. "Your corporation stands to lose nothing, whatever happens."

"That's true except they lose the whole ball of wax if it doesn't work."

"I'll sign the contract," Aysgarth said, "but we don't want to cover as far as Pacoima."

"Very well. Let me see what I can do about that."

Aysgarth extended his hand and Laxton shook it.

"Come and see me anytime," Aysgarth said. "I'm sure this will work at our institution. Take this down to Mr. Stein, the Administrator at the hospital, and have him sign it."

Laxton's first entry into Valley Hospital took him to the Administrator's office, which had no windows and was separated from the outer office by a secretary.

The matter of Pacoima was settled by a trip to Doctor Gambolini. It was a very different experience. The clinic, although large, was almost utilitarian in nature, filled with apparent Medicaid patients. Laxton had to wait until he was taken to the rear of the building, and then had another wait on the corridor outside Gambolini's office. Ultimately the doctor rescued him, extracted a key from his pocket, looked furtively around, and unlocked the door. As soon as he and Laxton entered, he locked the door behind them.

"You can never be too careful," he said to Laxton with a smile.

They discussed the contract.

"The group must agree to this first, so we'll go to the Board room," Gambolini said.

As they left Gambolini once again locked the door and led Laxton up a flight of stairs that opened into a paneled room with thick woolen carpets and a lengthy boardroom table around which were seated several physicians. Apparently the whole thing had been orchestrated, for they were already waiting for Laxton and Gambolini.

Gambolini sat at the head of the table. He was a man of about five six who was starting to show signs of flab in some areas. His face had leathery skin and wide dry lips, between which he thrust an expensive cigar.

"Give us the pitch," said Gambolini.

He waved towards a short, dark skinned man and looking at Laxton explained.

"Mario is our hospital signatory."

As Laxton discussed the system Mario interrupted him.

"The hospital part --."

"You shut up and let him speak," Gambolini snapped.

Mario sat back.

Laxton, slightly embarrassed, continued. When he had finished Gambolini, in a tone that implied the meeting was at an end, said: "If there are no questions, we'll vote."

The others seemed to be studying their reflections in the glossy tabletop.

"So everyone is in favor?" Gambolini said.

Everyone nodded approval in unison, and the document was signed at once. Gambolini and Laxton descended the stairs.

"You go out this door, it will put you straight in the parking lot," Gambolini said, "you don't need to go through the waiting room."

Laxton found when he exited he had only about fifty yards to walk. He passed several cages containing chained, snarling Dobermans. The first part of the parking lot was clearly the physicians' area, loudly proclaimed by gaudy painted signs, but rather obvious from four Cadillac Eldorados parked side by side, with two Mercedes and a Ferrari. The rest of the parking lot was filled with beat up Fords and Chevy's, and the occasional pick up truck.

Laxton learned the clinic had at one time been under indictment for Medicaid fraud. In this clinic every Medicaid patient had a urinalysis every visit whether they needed one or not, and the question arose whether the tests were actually performed.

Laxton was sure the group could spend the government's money, and equally sure they would not spend their own.

CHAPTER 13

DISMEMBERMENT

Laxton had put the system together for the HMO but the corporation had decided he was too valuable an employee to waste on the California operation and should be at the corporate office on the east coast. This appalled Laxton. He told them firmly he had no wish for this appointment, whatever money they wanted to give him.

"I wish I had your opportunities," Voltran said, "and I would advise you not to upset these people at the top. This organization is run by people of Sicilian extraction and you don't want to get the kiss."

It seemed to Laxton that a period of harassment started at this time. He had an administrative assistant, or so he'd been led to believe, but it turned out that perhaps the assistant had a great deal more power than Laxton had been led to believe. Suddenly, at the daily meetings, the Administrator, whose name was Sanders, became both aggressive and offensive to everyone, but especially to Laxton.

Sanders was a mental cripple from the Vietnam War and had arrived at Laxton's Section from headquarters about a month after Laxton had started. Laxton suspected he had been hired to get rid of some of the administrative personnel because they came under attack every time there was a meeting. It was only since the offer Laxton received to go east that he heard any criticism of himself from Sanders. Laxton reflected that the corporation had been very lenient with Sanders in that they had rented accommodation for him and tolerated the appointment of his live in girlfriend as an Operations Officer in the section. This was strange in that she had no knowledge of the operation, medical matters, fiscal matters, or anything else that might qualify her for such a position.

"This Sanders is a pain," Laxton told Voltran. "He is rather irrational."

"He might be psychotic. He was in Vietnam." Voltran said.

"What can we do about it?"

"There isn't much you can do about any Administrator in the organization, but if you want a tip from me, it would be a good idea to do what HQ is asking of you. Off the record, I think Sanders is a hatchet man, but I'm not sure why he was sent out here originally," Voltran said.

"He's got the corporate sales guy under the gun, and the figures aren't that bad. It's not just the firings, it's all those quitting who are bothering me. Do you know his own secretary quit to find another job?"

"I know," Voltran said, "she found one with the finance director at headquarters here."

"I think Sanders is a very bad influence."

"Look, they're offering you twice what you're getting paid now, and you'll be traveling all over the country evaluating the various operations. Listen to me and take the job."

"The job is not just quality control although they claim that's part of it. The bottom line is how much money they're making and where expenses or services can be cut," Laxton said.

"The bottom line is money, money, money."

Laxton reflected on his year-end with the corporation which was rapidly approaching. He had not had much social life during the year and had concentrated on corporate matters. It was true he had been to a number of the corporate dinners, but Laxton found them excessively dull events in which supposedly inspirational company speakers would pontificate to the physician employees of the HMO.

About a week after his discussion with Voltran he attended a meeting in his own region at which Sanders got into a shouting match with the sales manager, the finance officer and one of the utilization nurses.

"I knew this would be a mess today," said the sales manager later, "I saw Sanders polishing his desk before he came to the meeting. That always means trouble."

It was true that Sanders had a fetish for polishing his desk. In fact Laxton thought he didn't do much else in his office. Also, Sanders had started insisting that anyone who wanted to see him make an appointment with his secretary. This was really a waste of time because he wasn't busy.

The sales manager phoned Laxton and wanted him to come to an after hours meeting with several of the others. Laxton was surprised to find when he arrived that there were almost a dozen people there.

"How do you feel about Sander's behavior?" asked the sales manager.

Everyone was silent awaiting Laxton's words. He felt on the spot. He didn't want to be involved in some clandestine dispute. He didn't respond immediately.

"You must agree," the sales manager said, "the meetings are out of order and destructive. As a matter of fact I recorded the

79

last shouting match without Sander's knowledge, and I think we have enough evidence to do something."

"I don't know how to approach it," Laxton said, "because I'm not sure about Sander's state of mind. I hope you're not recording this meeting."

"We are not," said the finance officer, "but we wanted you here to help and we want you to tell us what we say here will be off the record."

"That isn't a problem," Laxton said, "the problem is it's my belief, based on discussions I've had with more than one person, that Sanders is some kind of hatchet man sent by headquarters, and he probably can't remove you without cause, but he can make your life damn uncomfortable so that you leave of your own volition."

"We're each going to file a letter of complaint against him with the Chief Administrative Officer and copy the Personnel Manager with the letters and see if that doesn't fix his wagon."

"Just what do you expect to achieve?" Laxton said.

"We expect to get the son of a bitch replaced," the sales manager said. "If everyone writes a letter I don't see what else they can do."

Everyone murmured assent.

When Laxton made no comment both the sales manager and finance officer tried to persuade Laxton to join the crusade.

"All I can do is to tell you is I will think about it," Laxton said, "and most certainly no one will hear about this meeting from me. I should add that I'm not convinced that this corporation is what I believed it to be when I joined, and Sanders has not done anything to make me more of a company man. I've been involved in dealing with poor surgeons and physicians in the past. Worse, we have them in this organization. I call them "the killers.""

Laxton knew that the real question was what the company might wish to achieve by appointing Sanders to his post. He had grave doubts that letters would have a major effect, and if so such an effect would be temporary in nature. The whole question of complaints was very complicated in a corporate environment, but Laxton recognized that those at the meeting should know more about corporation politics than Laxton knew.

The fact that the corporation was run by some sort of Sicilian controllers explained to Laxton why there hadn't been any problem getting Gambolini's group accepted, which was something he'd worried about after their contract was signed.

He felt surrounded by problems at work and he wasn't too happy

80

to receive a request to visit Aysgarth at Flashing Rod, particularly as Aysgarth's secretary told him that there were some serious problems for discussion. He was invited to lunch.

CHAPTER 14

ENTER AYSGARTH

Aysgarth sat in his office after everyone except the emergency physicians had departed. They were in another part of the building so he was unlikely to be disturbed. Aysgarth often sat in his office alone at night if he had a problem. It was a time for reflection and he had much to reflect on.

Aysgarth came from a background which had innumerable facets. He had not started as a rich man, but had worked his way up. Starting out with his doctorate in osteopathy, D.O. degree, at a time when D.O's were regarded as rather inferior, he had first worked in an institution which favored doctors of osteopathy over doctors of medicine. After purchasing land he had collected around him a small group of other D.O's and all of them put up money and Aysgarth developed a hospital on the land. He was smart enough to know he needed at least token M.D's as well as osteopathic doctors and he had concentrated on building an institution widely based enough that making money would be the primary goal and giving health care a by product. For Aysgarth it was clear which was the primary goal. Aysgarth's appearance to patients and to other physicians was that of a loving and dedicated provider of quality care. From the first day Aysgarth had portrayed the hospital as a quality institution so that the community thought well of it. All the initial members of the medical staff ended up with shares in the hospital so they had much to gain by admitting people to the institution.

At first there were some strange practices because when a doctor admitted a patient to the hospital, he would find a sealed envelope pasted on the front of the chart which contained a check for fifty dollars, so if one could admit ten patients a week, it was possible to make an extra five hundred bucks a week, which wasn't too shabby in those days.

None of that impacted on the hospital's profit, as such simply jacking up the charges to the patient hid practices. Aysgarth became a powerful financial entity in less than five years. He ultimately owned two ranches, a marina and a yacht. Disposal of one of the ranches turned him into a millionaire, and started him on a career which was unprecedented in the medical profession of Southern California and eventually led to his name becoming a household word in the Los

Angeles medical community.

Aysgarth chose the Hospital Board. There were no elections. In general the Board consisted of people who had put their money into the kitty. He devised a Development Corporation which held the money and the shares, separating the Hospital Board proper from the fiscal aspects of ownership. He kept the land in his own name, in case he ever needed to strong arm the Board.

In structuring the medical staff, membership was almost by choice and choices needed Aysgarth's approval. He made Gotcher chairman of the Board, and himself Chief of the Medical Staff. This gave him immense power at that time. He went over his Board members to see if he thought anyone there would be capable of dealing with the recent problems to get them off his back, but it wasn't just that he didn't want to lose any control, he despised the capabilities of any of them. He had made Gotcher Board Chairman years ago. He was one of the few D.O's who came out of the Osteopathic school with an M.D. This was when the California State Government made osteopaths illegal but gave all those osteopaths who wanted M.D. degrees, M.D. degrees, and turned the Osteopathic schools into regular medical schools. Gotcher was a tall, gray-haired general practitioner who walked the hospital corridors with his hands behind his back, a faint smile on his lips, giving an air of the father of medicine. He was very clinical but not very business like.

The other members, Smiley, a partner of Gotcher's, who fancied himself as a business man, but was basically stupid, was supposed to be treasurer. Greenman, who had a large practice, considered himself the legal expert on the Board but never knew the answer to anything, and was not very interested in the running of the hospital. That left Devises, a nice slow-witted, plethoric individual with a flabby face whose hobby was playing with model trains.

Aysgarth knew he had the Board he had wanted, who could be controlled and manipulated, but wouldn't contribute anything that meant real work.

At an early meeting Smiley said: "Just think of the money we can make out of neurotics."

"If we're talking about making money surgical complications are the way to go," Aysgarth said, "and I know just who to invite to join us."

Herbert Trevellian was such a man. He had gone to Europe where he had supposedly been trained in surgery, but the training was operating on the dead, which generated him a certificate as a surgeon.

83

When Trevellian got back, he operated on everything. If there was an organ in the body Trevellian thought it was meant to come out. His lack of expertise led to a series of horrendous complications that increased hospital lengths of stay beyond imagination, and led to multiple surgeries which generated a lot of money.

It was thus that a Doctor Trevellian joined the hospital staff as a surgeon, or more realistically as a General Practitioner surgeon. The money he made for the hospital did not go unrewarded by the Board and he developed a large practice as well as supportive side ventures.

Physicians and their relatives never ended up in his hands. Trevellian was encouraged to bring as many cases as possible to the hospital. The complications and surgeries only created more wealth for them, and the loose committee structure in the hospital did nothing at all to control practice. In an institution where the norm was incompetence, Trevellian had risen to the peak of the system, but his generation of wealth for the institution and its owners made him a popular figure.

Many wondered why Trevellian had never been sued for malpractice, for there were glaring cases, but Trevellian had a unique method of dealing with people. He would take the oldest woman, someone's grandmother, knowing all the time death was more appropriate than surgery, and address the relatives in a whining voice.

"You don't want to see grandma die an uncomfortable death, do you?"

"But what can we do for her?"

"The only chance is surgery and it's very risky, but I've done a lot of these cases and saved a lot of grandmas. There are no guarantees at this age but you wouldn't want to see your grandma suffer if we could do something for her, would you?"

Inevitably the family would plead for surgery, which would take place prior to death, maybe prolonging a few more days of agony. In the best cases it was a month of poor quality life with many hospital bills.

"We tried so hard," Trevellian would say in the end, "and no one need have anything on their conscience. She was a great lady, and she told the nurses just before she died how much she appreciated all that had been done for her."

Trevellian didn't have a macabre interest in attending funerals. The American culture didn't demand that much effort. Sometimes he sent flowers. Since the hospital condoned his type of treatment and did nothing about it, the public tended to accept it as the standard of care. Although Trevellian was the Jamestown of that hospital, there were no controls and no interest in anything but making a buck.

Aysgarth knew all this and had attracted a good surgeon to the hospital to keep Trevellian away from too many deaths. He had him assist Trevellian. Aysgarth thought it was unfortunate this individual had been caught with possession of cocaine and become a user and had to be let go, because this had left Trevellian to his own devices and which led to further problems. Aysgarth was wondering about Trevellian now that times had changed. An attempt to ensure the quality of care Aysgarth had paid lip service to for so long was underway throughout the state if not the nation. It was not a subject he cared to address at the present time. After all, Aysgarth remembered the time he had been left on call while his partner had the weekend off and he had been down at his yacht in Long Beach for a very immoral and unusual two days, only to return to the hospital to find one of his partner's patients seriously ill. They had operated on the seventeen-year old girl that morning to find a perforated appendix which she had developed in hospital. Neither the operation nor the penicillin had been enough to save her, but a good story saved them all.

The yacht had been a great boon, Aysgarth reflected, especially since he had filled the hospital ancillary posts like Administrator and Pharmacist with strange men who spent time with him down in Long Beach. He hadn't made the same mistake again in clinical practice.

He had become more cautious while Trevellian seemed to have become bolder. In fact Aysgarth had given up the Chief of Staff job when hospitals were required to become more organized and accredited. This was shortly after that episode where Trevellian had booked and started an operation to remove the lower colon and rectum on a patient without bothering to empty and prepare the bowel. The nurses had demanded Aysgarth go to the O.R. He was horrified because the abdominal space was filled with feces.

"Get all that shit cleaned out as well as you can," Aysgarth said, "and fill him up with antibiotics and hope for the best."

It was at this moment the news of Kennedy's assassination came through which gave Aysgarth an excuse to leave. Before doing anything Trevellian had said, "Let's all stop a moment and say a prayer for a great man."

Aysgarth dominated Board meetings where he manipulated his colleagues to obtain whatever he wanted. He had engineered appointments to the staff for unqualified self-styled specialists who were performing surgical work beyond their capabilities.

Aysgarth knew this wasn't the only problem and reflected that since Medicare had come into being, and there were HMO's, the government was getting more militant. Aysgarth was smart enough to know that the medical climate was changing and tonight he had stayed in his office to study the correspondence the hospital was getting from the Peer Review Organization which the government had established to oversee care in the Medicare program. The Hospital Administrator, A.N.L. Stein, who everyone referred to as A.N.L., had done a magnificent job putting the information from the peer review people together. It formed significant criticism of the hospital without actually laying any charges. Aysgarth wasn't sure how powerful the Peer Review Organization was, but clearly they couldn't be ignored. Aysgarth could see from the receipts, which were going down, that something had to be done. Medicare would only pay for so many hospital days and he realized it was now urgent to get lengths of stay of hospital patients down.

He knew this would be unpopular and that for it to be effective he needed someone to point to so he could announce to everyone he had hired an expert.

Aysgarth had been impressed by Laxton but thought that it would be very difficult to get him away from the HMO. Aysgarth had learned one thing; that was that most of the time you could entice people with money. The only problem for once might be the Board who had difficulty recognizing what was happening in the world outside Valley Hospital.

As he left the office he turned out the lights and resolved to firm up the meeting with Laxton.

CHAPTER 15

LOOKING AT VALLEY

Aysgarth's call caught Laxton listening to the usual morning diatribe by Sanders. The note handed to him suggested some urgency and Laxton realized he hadn't responded to Aysgarth's previous message. He was glad to leave the meeting.

"Could you possibly manage lunch today?" Aysgarth said.

"Where would you like to meet?" Laxton answered.

"If you could come to the Flashing Rod Clinic I know an excellent Chinese restaurant close to here, and the treat's on me," Aysgarth said.

"I'll be there about noon if that will work for you," Laxton said.

"That's just fine; see you then."

Laxton didn't waste anytime getting himself on the road. It wasn't that far up there but Laxton thought he'd take a cruise around the area and see what was there. He tried to recall any problems which might have come across his desk, but there hadn't been that much HMO stuff going through Valley hospital. He hoped to God Sanders hadn't aggravated them in some way; it was exactly the kind of thing he would do.

Although it was hot he sat in the car a few minutes with the air conditioner running until it was noon and then went into the clinic. He was taken to Aysgarth immediately. Aysgarth was out of his white coat and putting on his jacket.

"The restaurant is just across the shopping center," Aysgarth said, "we can walk over there. I've got a nice corner spot for us."

Laxton realized a nice corner spot must mean somewhere quiet because there was no view possible in a restaurant in a shopping center. It was supposed to look authentic with bamboo enclosed alcoves for tables and chairs, but the chef, who Laxton could get a glimpse of now and again, belied the name. He was a long-haired, scruffy looking white of nineteen or twenty who one would have expected to be at work in a fast food joint. The food was very good though, if you like the Americanized version of Chinese food, which Laxton didn't. Aysgarth just talked in generalities all through the meal and Laxton wondered what it was that was taking so long to get to the point.

"How are things really going at the HMO?" Aysgarth asked at last.

"About what you'd expect for an HMO."

"I heard they paid for people who would throw patients out and several people left because they got fed up with the system."

"We've lost a few, but the big bone of contention is our Administrator. Anyway, HMO's are here to stay."

"The Medicare program is here to stay too," Aysgarth said, "and they are getting pretty vicious cutting costs and very critical of care in the hospitals. It's no longer what the patient needs that matters, it's get them in and get them out and as far as I can tell cut back on care."

"How do you go about combating that?"

"It has taken me sometime but I think I have an answer. You see we are a private hospital and contrary to what HMO's and others feel we have always been dedicated to giving good care and pampering the patients, particularly the sick ones. I've kept our equipment up to University standards, and we have kept an eye out for good physicians. We have to tighten up if we are going to be able to maintain high standards and pamper the patients. So what I need is an expert who can oversee the quality of care, make suggestions for improvement, oversee our utilization doctors and help them, and I need one on a full time basis who is not going to practice. That will leave him independent to help with decisions."

Laxton sipped the Chinese tea he hated and sort of looked at the tabletop. There was a short silence.

"You'll find it tough to find someone like that," Laxton said at last.

"What do you think such a person would have to be like to be effective?"

"He'd have to have an extensive knowledge of surgery as well as know a lot about other areas, he'd have to know what the Peer Review Organization people are looking for, he'd have to be willing to go to all the committee meetings, and if necessary come down hard on the miscreants, if there are any." Laxton paused and added, "He would have to have complete support of the Administration, the Board, and the majority of the medical staff, and -"

"And?" Aysgarth prompted when Laxton paused.

"And you'd have to pay him a lot of money. I don't know anyone who could fill that spot."

"I do," Aysgarth said.

Laxton knew he was invited to comment on this remark but wasn't sure what to say. He assumed Aysgarth was referring to him or someone he knew. He wasn't sure which but it wasn't as though he was looking for a job. He looked at Aysgarth and with a crooked grin said, "All right. I'll bite. Who do you have in mind?"

"You could do the job. If you think about it for a minute or two you'll come to the same conclusion. How busy are you this afternoon and how long can you be away from the office?"

Laxton thought about the office and its lately unpleasant atmosphere. He supposed he could be away all afternoon for that matter. He'd just have to have a good explanation as to why, if anyone asked him. If they needed him, his secretary knew where he was anyway.

"I can take time," Laxton said, "what do you want to do?"

"I'd like to take you down to the hospital, show you around, let you see the way the hospital operates and what we have. You're not married, are you?"

"I'm not married and right now I have no ties," Laxton said.

"Well, we could go down and you could have dinner with me and we could stay on my yacht at Long Beach afterwards, if you'd like."

Laxton never knew why until a long time later but something told him this last suggestion wasn't a good idea.

"I might be able to have dinner but I couldn't go down to Long Beach and I certainly need to be home tonight."

"That's just fine, let me take you to dinner after we've had a look around the hospital."

It seemed to Laxton this would be an early dinner because he couldn't see how it would take very long to look around the hospital, unless Aysgarth had work to do in the office which hadn't been mentioned yet.

"I would like to think you might be interested and it seems to me proper we should talk about money."

"I certainly don't want to waste your time," Laxton said, "and frankly I don't believe you could pay me enough because I don't think the Hospital Board would pay the kind of money I'm getting now."

Aysgarth already knew what Laxton's income was although he was sure Laxton didn't know he had the information, so he didn't even express an interest in what Laxton was making, which made Laxton think Aysgarth was probably rather naive.

"It's over a hundred thousand," Laxton said.

Aysgarth smiled. He knew it was exactly a hundred thousand plus some benefits like medical insurance by the HMO and pension benefits. His face remained, as always unreadable.

"Let me tell you about the fringe benefits you'd get with us. You'd get complete medical coverage by a doctor of your choice and free hospitalization. We'd prefer in our own hospital, but if you needed to be somewhere else we'd pay for it even if you were away on vacation. We'd give you a month's vacation a year and pay for any trips you felt you needed to take to find out about what the government was up to or what the PRO was doing and we'd give at least one educational conference a year. I didn't mention accident, sickness and life insurance. You'd have them too."

"How much life insurance?"

"You're an executive and we give a million dollars worth and pay the premiums. We take ten per cent of your income and match it and put it in a pension plan for you. You have to stay three years to recover it, but if you moved after that you'd take it with you. You know all that and a couple of hundred thousand a year should be very attractive."

"Yes, it is," Laxton said, "I guess I'd better listen and take a look at it."

"You'll be your own boss reporting to me and I have a hunch we can find some bonuses once in a while. Shall we go?"

Laxton nodded and they walked out to Aysgarth's Cadillac Eldorado.

"I believe you're married," Laxton said, "is this going out to dinner going to be all right with your wife?"

"You know I have a daughter, a son, and an adopted son and I live there part time. Barbara is very understanding and knows I'm busy and have to be away quite a lot."

It did not seem wise to pursue this line of questioning for very long and Laxton was not one to pry if it wasn't his business so the drive to the hospital, which only took ten minutes, was over quite soon.

The hospital was built on a standard plan which had been used in many California hospitals. The physicians had separate entrances, one on each side of the hospital. Aysgarth always used the one closest to the physicians' private dining room because he could park his car almost at the door. It would have been more impressive to take Laxton through the front door, but it required a longer walk which Aysgarth probably thought unnecessary. The main hospital corridor ran in a square, across the lobby in front and across the back of the hospital with an exit to physicians' offices. Corridors off the side of the square led to the emergency room, the X-Ray department, the operating and recovery room, the medical record department, the intensive care unit on one side, and the lab, the gastric lab, the pharmacy, the main cafeteria and physiotherapy on the other side. The center of the square contained the

90

wards and in the very middle the Administrator's office and accounting department where billing and financial matters were handled.

Aysgarth took Laxton all round the hospital, proudly announcing each section or department as he showed them off. He made no introductions. Of particular interest were two private rooms which could have been from a first class hotel. These rooms were for special patients, and that included physicians, Laxton was told.

The hospital was pretty well filled with patients and Laxton noted very modern equipment. The smell of the place did something to him.

"All your meals here will be free. None of our physicians pay for their meals," Aysgarth said. "You can have breakfast, lunch and dinner here if you want. I hired the best gourmet chef to cook for the physicians."

This was the sole introduction made. The mid-European chef looked very authentic and Laxton found out that dishes like filet and chicken cordon bleu were typical luncheon examples.

"Most institutions don't treat their doctors worth a damn," Aysgarth said, "that's why we get some of the best."

Laxton kept his thoughts that freeloaders didn't guarantee quality work to himself and reminded himself he was being cynical. He was thinking it really was time for him to get out of the HMO atmosphere.

Just before four Aysgarth took Laxton to the Administrator's office where he met A.N.L.Stein. He was a much shorter man than Laxton had imagined. He had hollowed cheeks, which belied his chubby figure, and he offered a small flabby hand with finely manicured fingernails. There was an odor of some type of perfume, and his suede shoes seemed expensive but a bit out of place with his business suit. Aysgarth seemed to have an easy relationship with him, and after a few moments chat asked if the others were there. Laxton was led into what was clearly the Boardroom, but it was plainer than he had imagined it would be.

He was introduced to Gotcher, the Board Chairman, and Smiley. Aysgarth then launched into, what was for Laxton, an embarrassing description of Laxton's accomplishments and enlarged on Laxton's qualifications in a rather flowery way. Laxton kept his mouth shut.

"And salary?" Smiley said suddenly.

"The way we talked about it," Aysgarth said.

"I'm sure you'd like to start in a month's time," Aysgarth said to Laxton.

They were all looking at him.

"I would need a contract," Laxton said.

"With us all you need is a handshake. We're honorable men and live up to our promises. We've never signed a contract with anyone we employ and there are no unions in this hospital," Aysgarth said.

"I will confirm that," Gotcher said.

"Me too," Smiley said.

Each offered their hand to Laxton and he shook each hand in turn.

"I have a dinner engagement and I think you do too," Aysgarth said to Laxton.

They left together.

CHAPTER 16

LEAVING AND JOINING

Laxton was often called to Corporate Headquarters for what he would term relaxing but time wasting meetings in which he listened to the latest cost cutting measures the HMO had, or was going to, invoke. When Sanders announced at his stormy meeting that morning that he would see the Sales Manager, Accountant, and one other executive in the early afternoon, and then expected to meet with everyone else again afterwards, Laxton told him he had been called to headquarters and would have to leave at noon hour. Clearly Sanders was displeased but offered no resistance.

Laxton had not been invited to headquarters and did not plan to arrive there until late afternoon anyway, but he saw no purpose in attending yet another unpleasant meeting with Sanders. Sanders wasn't privy to what went on in the medical end of things and was rather afraid of the Corporate Medical Director anyway, so he was sure Sanders wouldn't be doing any checking. He went out and had a leisurely lunch on his own and mulled over the future and planned the afternoon. He drove into LA and arrived at the head office about half past three and walked up to Voltran's secretary.

"Oh Doctor Laxton," she said, arching her eyebrows a little. They wouldn't go up very far because they had been severely plucked. "You didn't make an appointment and you know that means you'll have to wait."

Laxton nodded and sat down. It was half past three and he knew very well it was unlikely Voltran was doing much but he'd make Laxton wait to give Laxton the impression he was very busy. Laxton was sure he'd be seen because he was sure Voltran was waiting for him to say he'd go out to the job in the east. It was about four o'clock when Voltran appeared at his office door.

His secretary had made a couple of trips into the office while Laxton waited.

"Come on in, come in," Voltran said cheerfully, "what's new down your way?"

"Things are in about the same state of turmoil in the office, but my end seems to be under control. That is when I can get at it between Sander's meetings."

Voltran sniggered. "Are there any new developments," he asked.

"Not really."

Laxton noticed Voltran looked surprised, but let it go anyway. He couldn't think of anything to report unless Voltran expected him to discuss the complaint the others had made about Sanders. He didn't know whether Voltran knew about it or not, but he wanted to keep his distance from the whole thing and he had given his word he would do nothing about it.

"Tell me a bit more about the job in the east."

"You're trying to get me to be specific about money?"

"Not at all," Laxton said, "just where would my headquarters be and how much time do you reckon I'd be there."

"Clearly, you'd be in Hartford Connecticut as your headquarters and I'm told you'd have your own office and support staff. As far as I can tell they'd want you to go out to areas where they perceived there were problems and deal with them. When there were no problems you'd go off on your own and look around the operations and write reports. You'd spend a lot of time on the road all expenses paid. You're ideal for it, you're not married and not really tied up, are you?"

"No, that's true, but why out east when we have so many operations in the central part of the country and out west here, it doesn't seem to be an economical way of doing things."

"My boy," Voltran said, "you'll be at the heartbeat of the company. Don't knock it. I'm so glad you've really given this some thought. Why don't you take a couple of weeks holiday and a week to clean up and then come by here and I'll have your airline tickets ready. You're entitled to two weeks vacation and since you'll be moving I'll get you a week extra to get your stuff in order. The company will supply you with a car so you can get rid of your own."

"I've got to run now," Voltran added almost immediately, "have a good vacation."

When Laxton was sure Voltran had gone he wandered over to Human Services. The guy who ran the office handling personnel was about twenty-eight, 5' 11" and had curly brown hair with cheerful features, although he always seemed to Laxton as though his cheerfulness meant waiting to face the next crisis. Jamie Thomas was always happy and nothing seemed to upset him.

"Take a pew," he said.

Laxton sat down and faced him across the desk.

"Heard you were bound for the big city," Jamie said.

"It was an option," Laxton said, "but I'm due two weeks vacation which I'm taking, which will make my last day here two weeks from

94

today, a Thursday. I have this letter for you."

Laxton had taken some time over the composition of the letter, which was brief. He had addressed it to Human Services with a copy to Dr. Voltran. It was dated that day.

Dear Sir:

I have enjoyed my work with the Health Maintenance Organization, but I feel I have to move on to new endeavors. I would like to thank Dr. Voltran and my medical colleagues for all their support and understanding.

Sincerely,
R. Laxton M.D.

Jamie looked at the letter for a few minutes before he said anything. He registered no surprise.

"I have to set up an exit interview," Jamie said.

"Now," Laxton said.

"It is a bit late, so I need to look at the calendar."

"If you want an exit interview, it will be now."

"Does Voltran know about this," Jamie asked, although he had to know the answer was no.

"He will when he gets the copy of the letter," Laxton said.

"Was this anything to do with what happened today?"

"What happened today?"

"I can't believe you didn't know the other executives in Orange wrote a rather damaging letter of complaint against Sanders."

"I don't know what that has to do with me," Laxton said.

"Sanders fired them all today."

"I didn't know," Laxton said, shaking his head.

"I'm finding it hard to believe this didn't have something to do with your decision to quit," Jamie said, "because there has been some tension up there. Can you comment on that?"

"I haven't seen any letter but I can tell you I'm sure whatever they said was correct in every aspect. I refuse to say more than that."

"So where are you going to work?"

"I'm just going to have to take a good look around," Laxton said.

He stood up and held out his hand which was taken somewhat

reluctantly.

"Goodbye."

"Where can we reach you?" Jamie asked.

"You can't. I'm going out of town."

Laxton walked out of the office slowly. Jamie called after him: "I know Dr. Voltran will find you. He'd counted on you to go down east. He won't give up easily."

Tomorrow, Laxton thought, everyone in the HMO would know he was leaving and no one would know where he was going. Both he and Aysgarth had agreed not to reveal what he was going to be doing. He thought of the letter of complaint and what had happened and eventually decided he should call the sales manager and the accountant at home.

After the calls he drove back to Orange County and met them in a bar. The accountant had a wife who worked and they hadn't any children, but the sales manager had a small child and a pregnant wife who had no job.

"So you heard what that prick Sanders did to us," Jeff, the sales manager said.

"I got it at the corporate office," Laxton said, "but I'd like to hear how he approached it."

"He said it had been in the works a long time and everyone in the company knew how incompetent I was and I was to clean out my desk today and get out. I told him he was a prick, a liar and a psychopath and he'd end up in a nut house and I walked out and slammed the door."

"I just listened to a similar kind of thing but I made no comment and walked out," the accountant said.

"What are you going to tell human services?" Laxton asked.

"We're supposed to go tomorrow, but as far as I'm concerned the letter said it all," Jeff said, "I'm just not going to show up."

"I shall show up because I can say a lot more to Jamie Thomas and you know the books were just audited and they got a glowing report which I have a copy of in my pocket," the accountant said.

"You might have a real case against them if you wanted to go after them," Laxton said.

"I wanted to get you guys here for a drink because I wanted to tell you I saw Voltran today for one of his chats but after he left I handed in my resignation to Thomas," Laxton went on, "Voltran will have it tomorrow, and I expect everyone will know, but I wanted to let you know ahead of time. I think they're going to close that office down; I really don't know why, but I suspect part of the operation is being

96

sold."

"I can't see them keeping that fucking idiot Sanders on if it's closed down," Jeff said.

"They brought you out from Ohio, I believe," Laxton said, "where are you going to look for a job?"

"I won't get one here but I only came on condition I get two months severance pay and I'm just going to move us all back to Ohio and forget I was ever here or ever worked here."

If anyone could pull that off Jeff could, Laxton thought. He'd probably say he had to take a long vacation for family reasons or something. Laxton was sure he was competent and had probably done a pretty good job. He was a victim.

"So what are you going to do?" Jeff asked Laxton. "I know being a physician you can always get some kind of job."

"I have something in mind but I'd rather not talk about it," Laxton said, "but first I have a vacation coming to me."

They shook hands and Laxton went home to his apartment. He had never felt the loneliness he felt now. If the phone rang he wouldn't answer, it could be Voltran. He had no girl friends, no responsibilities, no one would need him and he just had to do something. He tossed and turned but couldn't sleep. He had a deep foreboding about the future but could find no reason for such thoughts, and when he finally slept he had fitful meaningless dreams. He was awakened by the ringing telephone and almost picked it up until he remembered there was no one he wanted to talk to, and he had no clinical responsibilities. He decided there and then he would go back to Vancouver and take a look at what was happening there. He got up, packed a bag, called American Airlines and took a cab to the airport.

On the previous Saturday Aysgarth had decided he would have a vacation and take his wife with him. On the Sunday they flew to Acapulco via Mexico City and stayed at one of the hotels on the beach.

Aysgarth had problems he knew were about to hit his clinic. When he had split his office off from the main hospital he had brought out a Texan family practitioner called Golliman. Golliman was a short gray haired man with dandruff which he didn't treat, so his jacket shoulders were always covered with bits of white scale. His face was a bit flabby but still somewhat brown from the sun. Aysgarth put him into a general practice at the hospital and put him in his Aysgarth's own office so he could collect rent on it while he got the Flashing Rod

97

Clinic under way. He made Golliman Chief of Staff at the hospital, taking Aysgarth's place. Aysgarth had pressured the specialists to each spend a day a week at Flashing Rod, but this hadn't worked well because Aysgarth had only one other GP working at the clinic and the two of them couldn't feed enough patients to specialists on a weekly basis. He had especial trouble with general surgery, and finally the surgeons had just flat out refused to come up to the clinic any more. Aysgarth had kept the surgical patients "on hold," determined to somehow get his own surgeon for Flashing Rod.

He needed a break to strategize for the clinic because the Board had already made some remarks about the clinic being divorced from the rest of the hospital. This was true in that Aysgarth had his own Administrator for the clinic, a Terry Card, who was certainly an Aysgarth man and knew how to button his lip. The staff there had expanded with Aysgarth's external contracts, a sales effort at which he was very adept. Since he had made the clinic a twenty-four hour clinic with an emergency room, he had new practitioners and semi-retired practitioners attending on a part time basis, so it wasn't difficult for him to get away. Aysgarth had also tied up the emergency room at the hospital by insisting at the outset he have the contract himself, so he did the emergency room hiring and paid for it out of the contract. It was profitable for him. He had one highly qualified emergency room physician but otherwise used doctors who were trying to establish a family practice as back up in the emergency room. This led to many problems due to their lack of knowledge about emergency procedures, but Aysgarth didn't worry about it as long as no one sued.

The holiday was occasioned by many of the pressures that had recently been brought to bear on Aysgarth, not only over the Flashing Rod enterprise, but also over one of his other businesses. Aysgarth had done a favor for a friend a couple of years before. This had been to pick up some cargo from out in the harbor at Long Beach and to pass it along to some Afro-American businessmen. Aysgarth didn't think much about it at first but later he became suspicious when he found he was getting huge sums of money just for transportation. There had been so many goods he had set up a warehouse in Long Beach and used it for temporary storage of the cargo. He had sort of backed into this enterprise but having done so found it unlikely he could get out of it without a great deal of difficulty and had become very nervous about the whole business. Actually, a businessman called Giocomani had visited Aysgarth on the yacht and ultimately Aysgarth had smelled an organized crime connection relating to the whole business. Aysgarth had taken many steps to make himself as remote as possible from the whole operation, including the warehouse, but had continued to take the cash profits.

It was a strange coincidence that on this trip Aysgarth ran into an older Canadian surgeon vacationing in the same hotel, the meeting occurred because he found himself seated next to Jamestown in one of the sleazy Mexican nightclubs. Both Aysgarth and Jamestown had gone to see the show, which was interesting and unusual. It was probably the only redeeming feature of the place. The breasted tassel queen, with luminous hands painted on her buttocks, rotated with erotic gyrations.

"Quite a show," Aysgarth said.

"Certainly graphic," Jamestown said. He shuffled closer to the woman sitting next to him, who was with him but was not his wife. Aysgarth's wife had moved away from Aysgarth. In the interlude that followed they all sipped Mexican beer.

"I brought my family for a break," Aysgarth said as he introduced Babs to Jamestown.

"Where are you from?"

"I'm from a hospital in Southern California and that's where I live."

"How interesting. I'm surgeon myself, from Canada."

Aysgarth concealed any interest in the information. He determined that since Jamestown was staying at the same hotel, was going to be around another week, he assumed Jamestown and his wife were alone on this Mexican vacation.

Subsequently Aysgarth determined the Canadian was on the staff of a major hospital in Canada. Aysgarth made some telephone calls. Aysgarth hadn't any Canadian contacts, so he had to rely on the Board of Licensure and the hospital, both of which gave brief but excellent reports on his new acquaintance.

In Aysgarth's mind the issue was settled. He had to recruit the surgeon. Here was a man of his own age, well respected, with an acceptable wife, white, and North American. Aysgarth knew everyone had their price, and there was the surgeon he needed so badly at Flashing Rod.

Being kindred souls in a foreign land, there was no way the two were not going to collide again. Almost by accident they met at the poolside at breakfast time. Eventually Aysgarth asked his newfound friend to dinner with the family. At that time he managed to arrange a meeting at the bar. He was one of those few who could separate sex from business, even on vacation, and he could see in the Canadian a business opportunity.

In the bar Aysgarth came to the point quickly. He had no intention of wasting time if the project proved useless. His description of Flashing Rod was glowing, his promise of hospital privileges complete, and to a Canadian, his promise of income outstanding. He gave his newfound friend twenty-four hours to make a commitment.

To a Canadian M.D. income in the United States looked immense. In 1974, when Canadian surgeons were making two hundred and thirty-five dollars for taking out a prostate gland, American surgeons were pulling down at least nine hundred US.

Aysgarth left Acapulco with a committed Canadian surgeon. The only remaining problem was to get him through immigration and licensure. California licensure was not corrupt, which was more than could be said for many other states, but Aysgarth's new recruit had most of the paperwork anyway. Canadian trained, certified, well recommended, and able to speak English, he passed the oral exam easily.

Immigration was another matter. Dealing with the most incompetent department in the US government was most demeaning and frustrating. It seemed any idiot without training, capability, or track record, who came from Russia, Asia or India had priority, although they would end up in the welfare system of the State. They would soon bring in relatives who would also end up in the welfare system of the State. There were also added complications of which Aysgarth was not immediately aware. All were eventually overcome.

In the interim Aysgarth continued to put all elective surgery on a waiting list to ensure immediate income and returns for his new surgeon. Over four months the waiting list became significant in size. Those general surgeons connected with Valley Hospital must have wondered why there were only emergency surgeries, but Aysgarth never had to explain himself to anyone, and questions were never vocalized.

Aysgarth should have noticed that the accounts for the Flashing Rod Clinic fell under the auspices of the Afro-American accountant hired by Gotcher and Smiley, but he ignored that and believed it was unimportant. He knew the operation was destined to be profitable anyway.

Prior to Jamestown's arrival, while working diligently at the clinic, he spent weekends on the yacht with Lense and others. He made up for what had been denied to him in Mexico. There were other arrangements to make, and Aysgarth felt a responsibility to his new protégé. Housing had to be arranged. The eternal pursuit of the dollar had to continue, and the pillars of the clinic concept had to be in place. Aysgarth knew by his own calculations he had established another gold mine. This time it stood alone, and was his own endeavor, and every employee would be part of it, even if it was a subservient part. It was a project that was his to hold and manipulate, because he had built it alone. When Jamestown arrived, there would be no problems. It was unlikely he would ever move. He would be comfortable.

Aysgarth's power was such that his protégé was already a member of the medical staff with full privileges before he arrived in town. Whatever he was or had been, he would have a new start, one with powerful support and a massive amount of work awaiting him, not to mention a generous stipend.

Thus it was that on a bright sunny southern California day the Jamestown couple, Jamestown and Marion, arrived to become part of the Flashing Rod community, and Jamestown became a member of the Valley Hospital surgical staff.

CHAPTER 17

GETTING OUT OF TOWN

Laxton's awakening by the persistent ringing of the phone had told him he had no need to answer. It was the first time he really had not to face an emergency or an urgent situation. He also realized he was really alone in the world. He had not overcome his experiences in eastern B.C. nor had he come to terms with the fact most people needed some kind of contact with others on an ongoing basis. He told himself he was a loner. He had packed a bag and called a cab to the airport. He went to Los Angeles rather than John Wayne because he felt he had a better chance of picking up a flight to anywhere at LAX. The call to American had not been definite enough. There was little difficulty in getting a flight to Vancouver and he got a reasonable rate on the ticket by standing by for a seat. He had no idea why he was going back, not for family reasons, and not to return. It was morbid curiosity. He was tempted to stay in the Richmond area, but since he had rented a car he drove downtown to the Vancouver Hotel and stayed there. It was raining and rather miserable, nothing new.

The next day he drove to St. James' Hospital, walking in as he had always walked in, and wandering to the cafeteria to idly join the surprised group who used to surrounded Rugger.

"I was surprised you didn't come up to the funeral," Farab said.

"No one let me know Rugger had died," Laxton said. "He must be missed."

"He was a feisty old bastard," Farab said, "but we've got along without him."

"Do you still have Saturday rounds?"

"We stopped those and have rounds - well, now and again during the week."

Laxton recalled how Rugger always had said, "If they can't give up making a buck on Saturdays to come to rounds, they aren't worth a damn."

"You heard the latest?" Farab said. "They're trying to make everyone pick one hospital to attend and give up all the others."

"Sounds like financial suicide for physicians to me, especially specialists," Laxton said, "and it's not going to do this hospital any good. It will destroy the diversity of services here. How long are waits for admission here?"

"About four or five months. Even with connections you can't do better than that."

"You do all right if you're the one being admitted, if you're a doc, that is," said one of the other practitioners at the table.

"Even the nurses have no priority anymore," Farab added.

"How are the fees?" Laxton asked.

"Terrible, hardly changed since you left. If you'd come next week, I wouldn't have been here. I've got myself a job with Workmens' Compensation Board. A check every month and extra retirement benefits."

"You're giving up surgery?" Laxton said, but he privately wondered if Farab had any surgery.

"Whose doing surgery around here now," Laxton said.

"The damn catholic guy the sisters favor," Farab said.

"Hush," one of the others said, "you might be leaving but we're not. These walls have ears."

"You want to know something funny?" one of the G.Ps. said. "I have a waiting list to see me. I can't see any more patients than I do. People are waiting three weeks to see me and six weeks to see a specialist and they have to see me before they can get to a specialist, total waiting about three months, even for cancer."

"Yes," sneered Farab, "and you're making over a hundred thousand a year."

"It must be that the receipts as far as money is concerned have shifted," Laxton said.

"You can make a lot of money as a G.P.," was the reply, "but I do work ten to twelve hours a day."

"We have a committee now," Farab said, "which determines what the hospital's needs are, and they take it to another committee set up by the government to see how much can be taken away from it. We also operate on the old military standards. The hospital is paid only part of what they bill and the government budgets for us for the following year cutting our estimated receipts to last year's expenses which were allowed. That's why we always come in over budget and then the amount allowed, the cut down amount, is always almost as large as we need for the following year."

"What an interesting concept," Laxton said, "now I know why I left."

Laxton toured former friends and colleagues. His meeting with his radiologist friend was an eye opener.

"We're making it, but it took a lot of doing, and we are under a threat that the government will move all radiology into the hospitals and make us close our offices."

"But that will lengthen the waiting lists," Laxton said.

"Of course," was the reply, "but you don't think the government gives a damn, do you?"

"There's an election coming up," Laxton said, "who do you think is going to make it?"

"The damn socialists will make it, and they will be much worse, they already said that they would cut the health services and spread them over the Province to make them more efficient. That means they'll cut them down and that's all it means."

"This is a really dismal outlook," Laxton said, "and you're telling me it won't be any better. When are you moving south?"

"My wife won't move, even though she's an American citizen, so I'm stuck."

Laxton abandoned what he decided was a crazy pursuit, something he'd predicted, and concentrated on vacation, but the loneliness began to overtake him. He did the sky ride to the top of Grouse Mountain and noted the food hadn't improved. He even took the train ride up the sunshine coast, but it rained that day and the views of Howe Sound were less than spectacular.

Laxton began to feel that people were probably more important than the environment, and he didn't feel he had developed deep friendships or relationships with anyone. He would not admit this was due to fear reinforced by his former Vancouver experiences. Now he was not in the hospitals, not in practice here, and thought he was tolerated but unimportant to former colleagues.

Laxton heard that there was a party at the tennis club for Jamestown, but of course he couldn't have gone. He wondered why Jamestown was retiring or going somewhere else maybe.

"I don't know what I'm going to do," said one family practitioner, "he was my dumping ground for anything I didn't want."

Laxton took his flight back to California with some satisfaction. He felt he had made the right decision to move. The Canadian health system was going to become North America's killing fields.

When he returned his first trip was to his old office where he copied some papers.

"Come into my office before you do any more copying," Sanders said, appearing suddenly.

Laxton had finished anyway, so he followed Sanders to his

office.

"You just can't come in here and start copying when you've left the company," Sanders said, using his hectoring tone.

"I haven't left the company. This is my last day," Laxton said.

"So your position is that this is your last day?"

"No, that's the company's position. And while I'm here I picked up my stuff from my office. I'd like to know who had the authority to go through all the drawers."

Sanders became red faced and looked very uncomfortable. He went to his office door and called in a junior accountant to join them, practically the only qualified one left in the office. Laxton ambled through the office door and headed for the outside.

"Just a minute," Sanders said.

"Have a nice chat," Laxton called as he walked out.

CHAPTER 18

A NEW BALL GAME

Laxton returned to take up his post at Valley Hospital with renewed energy, believing that Aysgarth's description of the philosophy of the medical staff there should make his job less difficult than anything he had done before in a managerial role.

His office was across the corridor from the Administrator's office and next to the one occupied from time to time by Golliman, Chief of Staff. It was a small, indoor office with no windows, but had a connecting door to the utilization and discharge planning office and beyond that was the medical record library. The utilization nurse and a secretary were housed close to Laxton, two people who would have much to do with his immediate future. Laxton's entry to his new office gave him considerable satisfaction which was short lived. He walked out into the corridor and with a shock spotted Jamestown at the far end of the corridor. Jamestown appeared to be on his way out of the hospital.

"Is this a new surgeon?" he asked Veronica, the Utilization Review nurse.

"I know nothing about him; he just arrived," Veronica said.

Laxton asked Golliman about Jamestown.

"An Aysgarth appointee," Golliman said. "Of course I had to approve him myself and then he just sailed through the committee - just like you did. Do you know him?"

"I seem to remember him from somewhere."

Laxton had too many problems to sort out for him to worry about a new staff member who was apparently already ensconced in the hospital. He knew he had to look at the whole surgical staff, and to this end he decided he would do a computer evaluation of the surgeons' complications. There were not a large number of surgeons in the same specialty but it was possible to study variations like bleeding, infection, returns to the operating room, and patient length of stay. It took some time to set this up and longer to evaluate charts for the last two years to determine any trends,

The most obvious aberration among all the surgeons was Trevellian, who showed up both numerically and graphically off the page. Laxton hadn't the authority to do much about poor quality. His mandate was to decrease utilization of services to save the hospital money. Trevellian's complications would be very expensive on the Medicare program, but not that expensive in the private sector, not yet anyway. Over the year that changed significantly as insurance companies began to comprehend how the government was saving money by pressuring physicians to discharge patients from hospital earlier, and limiting the kind of surgery being done, as well as requiring justifications for each surgery. Companies began to require second opinions before some procedures were performed. Private industry was following the government in cost containment, but their motives were significantly different. Private insurance was interested in saving money within the system, to enhance profits for shareholders, whereas Medicare was interested in saving money so they could keep down overall costs.

The contrast between the government's methods of performing the task, as compared with that of private insurance, was profound. Whereas the insurance companies hired one physician and a couple of nurses to do the job, the government expanded the peer review system with clerks, physicians, nurses, and other disciplines, and paid practicing physicians a fee to review charts so that both hospitals and eventually physicians could be targeted by the payers to deny payments for hospital days and hospital visits. The elaborate and expensive system was set up to drive a wedge between physicians and hospitals, because the hospital would be targeted and the physician's billing ignored. It was a serious disadvantage for nonprofit hospitals, but was not much of a disadvantage for hospitals like Aysgarth's, because physicians were in on the action and had to protect the institution. The monthly check each physician drew from the hospital, his "profit sharing," would be reduced if there were inappropriate admissions or long stays.

It was strange that neither the government nor the private insurance companies had done anything to educate the physicians about the system. Of course the HMOs had been on that track a long time and their physicians didn't need much education.

Laxton knew his job was to educate physicians who didn't want to bother trying to fit into the system, because their own direct receipts were unaffected by the process, and they couldn't see the impact on their hospital paycheck because they never saw the actual accounting and probably couldn't have understood it had it been given to them.

After Laxton had presented each physician with his profile, some tried to improve and conquer each problem immediately, and others just went on as usual. Laxton spent time talking on an individual basis with the physicians, and had the strong Quality of Care\Utilization Review

Chairman do some of the talking for him. It was very important to have a chairman who couldn't be hurt by the process. Where a hospital had a surgeon or internist as Chairman of the QA\UR committee, colleagues might subject him to economic warfare. This they accomplished by simply not referring patients to him, so that he faced a reduced income. Laxton had a radiologist as chairman, someone the physicians couldn't get around. The physicians all needed X-Ray services, and they couldn't choose which radiologist would be used as the radiologists were contracted by the hospital, and it was a gross inconvenience to use some radiologist outside the hospital. Aysgarth tried to introduce regulations which required patients who were going to be admitted to have their X-Rays done at the hospital prior to admission, not by some outside outfit, and although at first he failed to make it stick, the message became clear to many physicians on the staff who knew it was in their own interest to do what Aysgarth wanted them to do.

Laxton took trips to San Francisco, headquarters of the California Peer Review Organization – the PRO, to learn from them first hand what they were looking for, so that he could carry the knowledge back and tell his employer how to get around the regulations, or at least how to maximize income. He came to know the bureaucrats well. Some were retired physicians, others were making a career out of pushing paper for the quasi-government organization, and a few really didn't care what was going on one-way or the other. Since the government reviewed their savings for the system, the main thrust of the PRO was always to get the government to agree to next year's contract so they would all have enough money for their pockets and to pay their underlings.

The Chief Medical Director for the whole PRO, Doctor Montpellier, was an ex-navy man who tried to run the PRO rather like a ship.

"I can see you're doing a good job; you should come and work for us, we could use you."

"I just got started where I am," Laxton said, "but I might be interested later if I could do some good."

"I heard about some of the stuff you did in Vancouver. Very courageous in that backward, decadent medical environment. They'll run the Canadian government out of money before another year is out."

"Sooner or later it will happen," Laxton said, "but Canadians accept mistreatment and malpractice and it will get worse."

He didn't tell Montpellier that Montpellier wouldn't understand why it would happen, nor did he tell Montpellier that there were much worse things going on in the United States as far as quality was concerned, even if they weren't dying waiting for treatment as in Canada. The fact the Canadian governments were setting up lay boards to make decisions about patient care didn't come up either.

It was on one of these visits that Laxton learned the PRO was targeting Trevellian. A few of his charts had come to their attention and he was under an intensified review. The PRO had set up a system where they graded their perception of the errors performed by physicians as small, grade one, moderate, grade two, and inexcusable, grade three. The physician was required to respond to these criticisms in writing and ultimately Laxton was writing the letters for a great many of them. This had accelerated because a few found Laxton could get them off the hook fairly quickly, and there was no delay in receipt of their Medicare payments. There were those who ignored the PRO's letters and those who wrote offensive replies to the PRO. It was not wise to write rude letters to the agency.

When Laxton found out that the hospital was getting penalized fiscally because of the work done by Trevellian, and when he had been unable to get Trevellian to do anything about the letters from the PRO, he started to look at Trevellian's charts.

"This last case is a mess," Veronica said, "he found a patient with a hernia on the left side and operated on the right side. When the anesthesiologist told him he'd done the wrong side, he just redraped the patient and did the other side."

"I wonder what he told the patient," Laxton said.

"I know what he told the patient," Veronica said, "he was overheard."

"So?"

"He told the patient when he did the hernia he found he had one on the other side, so he did that as well."

"I'd wonder if the patient wouldn't question that," Laxton said.

"Nothing will come of it. The patient is one of his nursing home cases."

"The PRO might catch onto it," Laxton said.

"They've sent for it for review," Veronica said.

It was a day or two later Golliman got himself into trouble in the operating room. Laxton had found out that Golliman had problems with his vision and had seen an ophthalmologist who had found severe retinal problems. He had some laser surgery for the problem, but his vision was really poor. These were clearly not the conditions under which he should be taking out childrens' tonsils, but it was a surgery he would not give up.

The child was bleeding profusely from one tonsil bed, the suction stopped working, and blood was pouring out of the mouth onto the operating room floor. Trevellian was nearby and was called in to help. He took a stitch on a huge needle and blindly shoved it into the child's throat, grabbing something and tying a knot. When they got the suction back in service it was clear that Trevellian had stitched the soft palate to the tongue.

"I've got blood coming," the anesthesiologist said, "I ordered one pint, do you think we need two?"

"I've lost lots more blood than this in a child," Trevellian said, "you may not even need what you ordered."

"Her pressure is down and I'll certainly give what I ordered," the anesthesiologist said.

"Get hold of Laxton," Golliman said, "I want him to look at this."

"A good idea," the anesthesiologist said, "this child is still losing blood, and it's clear we need all the help we can get."

Laxton got into the OR as fast as he could because the OR supervisor told him she feared they might lose the child.

Although Laxton stayed calm, he was annoyed when he saw the stitch, which wasn't doing any good at all and shouldn't have been put in. He first removed the stitch and then got a swab of gauze and cotton and put direct pressure in the hole the tonsil came out from. This temporarily arrested the bleeding.

"We'll wait now until you have the blood pressure back up," Laxton told the anesthesiologist.

"Thank you, I've asked for another two units of blood, and I have another IV of dextrin started."

With the two intravenous lines it took about ten minutes before the blood pressure was stable. Trevellian had already departed with the remark, "Should be quite straightforward now, I'm not needed."

Laxton got a tonsillar clamp on the vessel and inserted a fine catgut stitch to tie off the artery which was bleeding. The problem was solved in less than a minute.

"The bleeding area was a little difficult to see," Laxton told Golliman after the surgery.

Golliman was silent for a moment or two and then sighed. He looked at Laxton and finally said: "It isn't your job to bail people out. I know that but there wasn't anyone around. I just did my last tonsillectomy. I have a vision problem."

The child was in hospital for nearly a week but was fine thereafter. Laxton wasn't too pleased to find the Chief of Staff was partially blind and still doing surgery. He took the statement that Golliman would give up doing tonsils with a pinch of salt because he'd heard promises like that before.

CHAPTER 19

SEXUALITY AND RELIGION

Laxton looked at the figures showing Trevellian's major area of admissions for surgery and was not surprised to find most of the patients were on Medicare. Trevellian's complications on the Medicare program would be very expensive for the hospital although they would not be expensive in the private sector. Ultimately it was made clear to Laxton that the PRO would take action against both Trevellian and the hospital itself. Golliman had been sent up to San Francisco to a PRO seminar where he learned the PRO was unhappy with Trevellian. Laxton had not mentioned he knew this.

"Shit," Golliman said to Laxton, "they're after poor old Trevellian now. Can you do anything about it?"

"What do you want me to do, you know Trevellian's work is substandard."

"Maybe you'd better tell Gotcher, protect yourself anyway."

Golliman didn't give a damn about protecting Laxton and knew Gotcher probably wouldn't do a thing about Trevellian anyway. Laxton had already figured this out too, and intended to tell Aysgarth who was the only one who might do something, so he said: "That's a good idea. Gets it off your back and mine as well."

Whether Golliman believed this or not didn't really matter, but as Chief of Staff it was his direct responsibility and Laxton was fully aware of this. This conversation also raised other questions, whether Golliman knew his responsibilities - Laxton suspected he did not - or whether he was a puppet who danced at the pleasure of the Hospital Board and not the Medical Executive Committee.

Laxton knew the PRO would not move for three months, a piece of information to which others were not privy, so he decided he would choose his own time to discuss this subject with Aysgarth.

An in depth review of Trevellian's charts was carried out. The medical librarian pulled them and Angie, Laxton's secretary now, typed up Laxton's evaluations. Angie was a Mormon girl who was divorced and had two children. Although she announced her restrictive religion at the outset she did not appear bound by it, nor did she follow the modesty called for by their bishops. She dressed smartly, albeit with significant brevity. She would appear daily in a different outfit yet always with something quite noticeable about the outfit. Soon after Laxton acquired her as his personal secretary, she appeared in very tight fitting pants which showed off her slender and shapely legs and, because she wore a blouse which was tucked into her pants, her buttocks might as well have been naked.

"Hello," Laxton said, "you look as though you were dressed for a special occasion; the outfit is so smart."

Angie laughed.

"I don't know there's any law in showing off a bit," she said.

"Please continue to do so," Laxton said, "anyone would be proud to be seen with someone who looked so smart."

As the work progressed on a daily basis Angie sported even more noticeable outfits. She finally came into Laxton's office with a dark muslin type of dress, the base slightly wide and ascending like the apex of a triangle to encompass her slender hips, but below running straight across the pubis making it an eye popper to any man. Laxton decided to take her out for lunch. He never knew then or later why he did this, but it might have had something to do with the declared sexuality of the dress. The waist sported a gold chain and because the neckline was gently curved and the sleeves were transparent, becoming dark at the shoulder, the whole upper part of the dress lent itself to a hint of pointed rather than round breasts. Angie's long hair was blond, not the platinum kind, sort of darker, more natural looking, unbleached, and it trailed onto her shoulders. Every once in a while she would take both hands and run them through her hair flinging it backwards with a little shake of her head and then smile through thin lips which revealed even, white teeth. Seen in profile her nose and facial features had a smooth perfection never marred by scowls or other evidence of displeasure.

Contrary to the popular belief of some, physicians do have a personal curiosity about women who are not their patients, and we have to admit some of them are curious about women who are their patients, so Laxton's curiosity was not an unusual male phenomenon. Later, he mused about it quite a lot. He knew screwing had not been in his mind. At that moment it came to him rather suddenly that the simple innocent beauty he believed he was seeing was a shell of chicanery. Such overt sexuality in a proclaimed Mormon surprised him.

At lunch he told her he was going to have a drink.

"I need a drink. I deserve one," Laxton said.

"I guess you know my religion stops me drinking tea, coffee or alcohol," Angie said, her seemingly innocent blue eyes looking directly at him.

"I'll get you whatever you want. You can order juice or something.

113

Anything you'd like to have."

"Just water will be fine."

"Are these restrictions tough?" Laxton asked, although he was sure he knew the answer.

"You know I don't mind the not drinking tea, coffee or alcohol. I don't mind not smoking either."

After a moment she said, "There are no restrictions on sex. Well, not many."

"Your divorce is through," Laxton said, more as a confirmation of what he had heard as well as thinking she might like to talk about it.

"Ah yes, I can perform without complications from there."

Somehow Laxton got through lunch without further reference to sex, but he was uncomfortably aware that Angie was giving him eye signals that he didn't feel were appropriate. They returned to the hospital in his car.

Veronica, who was a stable married woman, had often laughed at Laxton's private remarks to her about Angie. She entered his office with a pile of charts for them to go over together.

"So, you took Angie to lunch?" she asked, expressionless.

"Well, she worked overtime several times without pay, so I thought I should do something."

"What kind of a dress would you call that thing she's wearing," Veronica asked, not expecting a reply.

"That's a jet skirt," Laxton said.

There was a pause. "Just what is a jet skirt?"

"It's one that comes up to the cockpit," Laxton said.

"She's a Mormon. They don't think about sex."

"I'm not convinced that's true," Laxton said.

Another chart from Trevellian. This time he'd treated an old woman by putting a tube through her belly into her stomach through a big incision. In this day and age this is almost invariably done by gastro-enterologists who look down the throat into the stomach and are able to identify where to make a tiny incision in the belly and slip a tube through into the stomach. They are very skilled at this and rarely have complications. Laxton had seen three charts where Trevellian had made large incisions to stick tubes in elderly patients, and two had developed peritonitis caused by stomach contents leaking into the surrounding area. This condition is serious in anyone, but in an eighty-nine-year-old woman, probably fatal. It was an indication of unacceptable incompetence.

"These reviews are simply awful," Laxton said, "what are we

114

going to do?"

"Originally the hospital didn't care, but now they're losing money they care a lot," Veronica said, "and I don't think you can expect much out of Golliman. He lives in his own world and as long as he collects his pay as Chief of Staff I don't think he cares."

"I know he won't be likely to do anything, but I didn't know he was paid. You'd think that would make him do a good job, wouldn't you?"

"I think he just wants to impress the Board and make them think he's doing a good job and think there aren't any troubles."

"But he's elected by the medical staff," Laxton said, "and he's responsible to the Medical Executive Committee, not the Board."

"Oh, come on," Veronica said, "no one else will take the Chief of Staff job which is manipulated by the Board anyway. Golliman seems to control the medical staff although he can't even control who gets on the staff. If a Board member wants someone on the staff, he'll get on."

"Whoever got on that way?" Laxton asked.

"I never said anyone did and I'm not going to name all those I think got on that way, but the last one who got on I suspect was put on by someone you know very well."

"Come on," Laxton said, "spell it out for me."

"I never said this but I suspect Dr. Jamestown got on that way. He's been doing a lot of surgery from the clinic, and it seems to me he'll have to be watched very closely."

Laxton didn't let on he knew Jamestown or anything about him. He looked as though he was studying what Veronica had said. He sat a few moments before getting back to the discussion.

"You'd better tell me, what seems to be wrong with him."

"It's the vascular surgery he's doing."

Laxton kept a straight face. Jamestown had no training in vascular surgery.

"We'd better look at that real soon," Laxton said softly.

Laxton knew he was in a situation where he was unlikely to win. Perhaps he couldn't even do his job. Obviously Aysgarth had brought Jamestown in and probably he knew zilch about Jamestown's background, and he might not want to know.

Time to face all that when the complications were rolling into the PRO and they would become obvious in the hospital before that. Laxton would have to talk to Aysgarth at that time. He did not look forward to telling Aysgarth his Flashing Rod surgeon was a dangerous liability.

As the pace of the reviews increased he was thankful Angie could work overtime and help them all to get the reports up to date. They had busy weeks and Laxton worked until eight or nine at night. One afternoon he was surprised when Angie slipped him a note.

'We haven't had lunch lately. Why don't you call me at home and come over late one night after I've put the kids to bed. You can bring your pager in case you get any calls during the night.

Signed: Angie. xxx"

Laxton filed it in his pocket and forgot about it. He acted as though he'd never received it. He remained courteous and friendly, continued to remark on her beautiful dresses and other seductive apparel she displayed, and smiled a lot but he didn't invite her to lunch again.

His weekly report was sent in confidence to Aysgarth, but to no one else, and it usually brought nothing but a phone call, but on Friday Aysgarth arrived in Laxton's department in his usual hyperactive state.

"I have a great idea for the weekend," Aysgarth said, "I'm going to have a little intimate party down on my yacht and I want to include you in on it."

It was true Laxton had made other plans for the weekend but they were going to be dull and boring, but he decided he'd stick with them. The following week, when he mentioned the invitation to Veronica, she said: "You didn't go, did you?"

"No," Laxton said slowly, "I had something else to do."

"I hope it didn't involve Angie. I don't really know, but there are rumors about some very funny things going on, on the yacht and I don't think, if they're true, you'd want to be involved in them."

"Why not?" Laxton said.

"I think you're just too busy ogling girls to be going down there," Veronica said.

"It wasn't hospital business as far as I know," Laxton said.

"I suppose you know ANL is leaving because he's sick and Aysgarth wants another friend to take to the yacht. ANL was down at the boat all the time," Veronica said.

"I didn't know ANL was leaving, where did you hear that?"

"It was the talk in the cafeteria. Molly let it slip. It was supposed to be a secret but Molly couldn't keep it."

"That might cost her, her job," Laxton said.

Veronica smiled. "She might be the Administrator's secretary but Dr. Gotcher would never let that happen."

116

Little by little Laxton got the picture. He was astounded when A.N.L.Stein was quietly replaced as Administrator by the hospital maintenance man. He never found out why, but Duchemp was not an Aysgarth decision, although Aysgarth hadn't opposed him.

He would never be invited to the yacht, and he would never venture an opinion on anything anywhere at any time. Sometimes he made announcements at the behest of the board, its chairman, or Aysgarth. His deputy was appointed and was a bright young man with a B.A. degree in Administration. They had breakfast together every morning, but nothing much seemed to be accomplished. It wasn't Laxton's problem anyway.

From time to time the Board would ask Laxton to attend at the beginning of one of their meetings, which was almost invariably to ask if he needed anything more in the way of help. It was no surprise when he was asked to attend the next meeting. He was never invited to the gourmet dinner which went with the meeting.

This evening started with the usual pleasantries and it looked like the usual sort of meeting.

Suddenly, Gotcher said:

"We can't identify the person, but we've had a sexual harassment complaint against you."

Laxton said nothing. He was shocked.

"We don't think anything will come out of this, but we wanted to warn you how serious this is," Gotcher continued, "of course you have our complete support, but please keep your hands to yourself. I don't expect you have anything to say?"

"I don't know who this could be and I can't think of anything I've done to warrant this accusation," Laxton said.

He was excused and went to his office. He must have sat there for a couple of hours. He began to figure who must have made the complaint. There was knock on the door. Aysgarth walked in.

"Off the record it was that secretary bitch of yours," he said.

Laxton fiddled in his jacket pocket until he found the note. He handed it to Aysgarth.

"That's it," Aysgarth said, "and she's a Mormon too."

"I don't want this note used," Laxton said.

"It won't have to be used," Aysgarth said. He smiled. "Forget all about it."

Laxton was surprised that Aysgarth knew anything personal about his secretary. It really didn't help the sickness he felt within. He wasn't going to get a good night's sleep.

Although it was late when Aysgarth returned home he went to a special file he kept with special contact numbers. He phoned the Mormon Bishop responsible for Angie's spiritual welfare.

"This is Dr. Aysgarth, sorry to be calling so late but I am an admirer of the sincerity of your church. We employ one of your flock, Angie Summers, and I wanted to inform you and do you a favor. For sometime we have been concerned about her very immodest dresses, which have been flaunted in front of many, but most prominently, in front of our Medical Director. Worse than that she has sent a very, let me say to put it mildly, a very suggestive and seductive note to him and when he failed to respond complained of being harassed, which we all know to be untrue. I'm sure neither of us wants a mess out of this; we don't want the hospital involved and I don't want any reflection on the church because of the outrageous behavior of one of your members. I will find her another job if you can get her out of the hospital at once. Also, we'll see she's paid until the arrangements have been made for the other job. Bishop, I've prayed earnestly about this and I do need your help. Do you need her telephone number?"

"No, I have it," the Bishop said, "and she won't be at work in the morning. It's not essential you get her a new job."

"It's the Christian thing to do," Aysgarth said, "have her phone my Administrator at the farm in a couple of days and we'll see how we can help, I know you'll keep all this as confidential as possible."

"We handle these things in our own way," the Bishop said, "and please don't be concerned."

CHAPTER 20

ENTERING HOT WATER

The following morning Laxton came in late. Angie was not at her desk. Laxton decided it would be perfectly normal to ask Veronica what had happened to Angie.

"Is she ill?" he asked, nodding toward her desk.

"I'm not sure what's going on," Veronica said, "but I understand she has either resigned or been fired, but I think she resigned."

Had Laxton known what had happened he would have been uncomfortable, but not knowing didn't help a lot either.

"Anyway," Veronica said, "they are looking for a replacement."

Laxton had been thinking some rather ugly things about Angie most of the night.

"The bitch," he thought, "just because I didn't stick my prick into her when she wanted it, she pulls this shit off. I should have fucked the ass off her and enjoyed it."

He didn't know what he had to do about secretarial help, and worse Veronica asked him what he was going to do to find out about Angie.

"The bloody nurses," he thought, his English background affecting his thoughts, "they're all the same, they want to know every bit of gossip and they certainly have a nose for scandal."

He had shrugged and decided to play a waiting game. He didn't have to wait long. The next day Veronica told him Molly had told her Angie had written a letter resigning her position and said she had a new job. In fact Aysgarth already had her employed in his "warehouse" down in Long Beach where she dare not wear short skirts whatever the Bishop might have said. She was wearing loose jeans and an unattractive top, hoping this would cut down on the risk of rape.

Laxton didn't know this and he was never to see her or hear from her again.

"Perhaps they found out about her shenanigans," Veronica observed slyly one day, "although I think her resignation came too quickly for that. You were lucky; she might have become a nuisance to you, given time."

"She was the wrong person in the wrong place at the wrong time," Laxton said, "let's forget her and get to work."

"The new secretary will be in this afternoon. She's just going to

119

work afternoons, but I'm sure she won't be any trouble."

Veronica was right. She wouldn't be that kind of trouble anyway. She must have been about five three and weighed close to three hundred pounds. Laxton knew he should be generous but he didn't feel it. His experience of fat women had led him to the conclusion they were invariably slow, sluggish workers. Worse than all this she had ill-fitting dentures which clicked when she spoke, which wasn't often. Her face was floppy and sagged and she had narrow, colorless eyes and graying drab hair. She was an unopinionated stenographer who couldn't spell very well. Her name was Kittybel.

"What do you think of the new secretary?" Veronica asked at the end of the first week.

"She has an unusual name," Laxton said.

"She seems lazy to me, and we have a hell of a lot to get done."

"Whether we like it or not that's what we have to live with," Laxton said.

Close to the end of the week Laxton received a call from PRO headquarters in San Francisco. He was surprised to find himself talking to the Chief Medical Officer. After initial pleasantries the reason for the call was made obvious. Rumor and gossip time was over.

"We are thinking of taking steps against one of your doctors," Montpellier said.

"Which one?" Laxton said.

"Why don't you guess?"

"I don't suppose it would be Trevellian," Laxton said. It was more a statement than a question.

"I'm not really supposed to tell you," Montpellier said, "but the real thing I can't guarantee is that the hospital won't be sanctioned if we catch him out, and you know what that means. The place might get closed down. You know we closed down a psychiatric unit in southern California."

"I know about that, because some people I know have been trying to improve the place and get it reopened."

"That'll be the day," Montpellier said, "usually it takes HCFA (he pronounced it as "HICKFA", the way most professionals referred to the Health Care Financing Administration) so long there's usually no money left to reopen when the time comes."

"If the hospital will do something about this, it might take us longer to get to him."

"How long do we have?" Laxton asked.

"Not very long," Montpellier said.

Laxton knew that was all he was likely to get out of the PRO, but he thought if something was started within thirty days there was a good chance of forestalling the PRO process. Now it became essential to see Aysgarth. Laxton saw him in his office at the clinic in Flashing Rod at the end of that afternoon. He didn't relish what he had to say. He showed Aysgarth all the printouts from the survey that had been done on the surgeons, keeping the details back until the end. Aysgarth wanted to know who had, had so many complications that the bar on the bar graphs wouldn't fit on the page.

"That's what I came to talk to you about. The PRO has let me know, off the record, they will target him, but more importantly they may target the hospital, and the doctor is Trevellian."

Laxton sensed Aysgarth seemed slightly relieved. He wondered if Aysgarth was beginning to get a whiff of what Jamestown might do to them. Aysgarth said nothing for a minute or two, and then he said:

"There's an attorney we used to use who is up in the San Fernando Valley and we need to get him involved. Just let me get his name and address and you can give him a call and alert him. We must have a meeting about this. I'll get Gotcher and Smiley and you and Golliman together for lunch with the attorney so we can set up a plan of action to get rid of Trevellian. Introduce yourself to the Attorney and tell him I'm going to be calling him."

Laxton thought that it was fortunate Aysgarth was going to get on with this himself; obviously he had experience in these matters. Laxton hadn't been involved in such a dramatic private disciplinary action and was relieved it looked as though Aysgarth would mastermind it.

The luncheon meeting was set up for a Friday and was held at a restaurant about ten miles from the hospital. Aysgarth opened the meeting.

"Our Medical Director has come by some privileged information. The Peer Review Organization, Health Care Financing Administration, and God knows who else are about to launch an attack on all of us because of all the complications and deaths that Trevellian is having on Medicare patients and Laxton's bought us some time but we have to get rid of Trevellian. If we don't get rid of him we'd better stop him doing surgery and put him under strict surveillance."

Gotcher looked down at the white cloth on the table and said nothing.

"Have you seen the statistics?" Aysgarth said, looking at Gotcher and giving him a jab to make sure he understood the question was for him.

"I didn't realize it was so bad until I saw those," Gotcher said, "but I stopped letting him do any work for me quite a while ago."

"Just a minute now," Smiley said quickly, "if we're going to do anything let's just stop his surgery so we still have him sending patients into the hospital from his nursing home. No reason why we should lose any business, and we can have someone else operate on them."

"At this moment that's not quite the issue," Aysgarth said, "you'd better tell them in vivid technicolor what you know."

He looked at Laxton who got the message right away. Aysgarth wanted an overkill.

"There's enough stuff for them to get Trevellian and, if they do, two things will happen. The first is that the Board of Licensure will look at lifting his license to practice, the second is HCFA will definitely go after the hospital to get it closed for allowing substandard work to go on for years."

Aysgarth knew the rest of them didn't want to hear this, but he wanted a worst-case scenario painted, and now he had it.

"There's no question he has to be suspended from doing surgery anyway," Gotcher said, "and that's the Chief of Staff's job."

"Let's hear what our Attorney has to say," Aysgarth said.

Pat O'Hara was tall. He must have been six three anyway. He was thin and had brown hair, which had not yet started to show gray. His narrow face had two vertical wrinkles above his nose at the inner end of his eyebrows. Otherwise his complexion was smooth and he had rosy cheeks. He wore a suit but pandered to the California style of going without a tie, something that Laxton found irritating in professionals. He had a rather high-pitched voice for someone so tall, but it sounded authoritative.

"I have a copy of your bylaws here. As long as you go by your bylaws there really isn't any way you can go wrong. Of course you've already broken them by having this meeting."

"We have to plan this properly," Aysgarth said rather sharply, "how can we be in violation of our bylaws when nothing has been done?"

"To put it simply there's something called due process. You intend to do something as a result of this meeting, and there are Board members here who are his last in hospital court of appeal if he demands a hearing and the Hearing Committee recommends a suspension. He would then appeal to the Board and here you are, several of you members of the Board, plotting the suspension. It's very

122

irregular and if he found out it might become very detrimental to the hospital. Let me go on as to how this should be done. Doctor Golliman as Chief of Staff can suspend Doctor Trevellian either by going to the Medical Executive Committee and having them vote for suspension, or if serious enough he can do a summary suspension and go to the Board afterwards and ask them to confirm the summary suspension. If the doctor requests a hearing you have to appoint a Hearing Committee consisting of people who are not in active competition with the doctor. Also, you'd be best advised to have your Medical Director present your case if that happens. That's because he's independent. Hopefully, it won't come to that. But you'd better be sure there are no more meetings like this."

Aysgarth paid the bill.

"Golliman knows what he has to do," he said, "and this meeting never took place. Let's go."

About a week later Aysgarth handed Laxton copies of the letters Golliman had sent to Trevellian exercising a summary suspension.

"I told him to stop sending this shit to Board members and to copy you on everything," Aysgarth said, "then of course you can slip me a copy."

Laxton realized this meant Aysgarth trusted him but didn't trust Golliman. Laxton thought Golliman a fool not to have sent him a copy anyway, and it might have been a good idea to discuss tactics before jumping the gun. A summary suspension is meant to be used when someone suddenly does something in the hospital or operating room, something which is totally inappropriate and such a suspension is usually exercised within a few days of the event.

Trevellian had been on vacation skiing in Switzerland for the last two weeks.

CHAPTER 21

GOLLIMAN MOVES

Quoting the bylaw correctly and adding a few phrases Golliman thought appropriate simplified the letter sent to Trevellian done by Golliman.

> Dear Doctor Trevellian,
>
> In accordance with the bylaws of Valley Community Hospital, Article 6, Paragraph 6.1 through Paragraph 6.2, you are hereby notified that your hospital privileges are suspended for a period of 90 days. This suspension means that you may not serve as primary surgeon or assistant surgeon on any cases. If you desire to admit surgical cases, they must be admitted to the chief of the surgical department. Your medical privileges are likewise suspended for a period of 90 days and any medical patients must be admitted to the chairman of that department.
>
> Furthermore, any patients you are currently treating at Valley Community Hospital shall be assigned to another physician, taking into consideration the wishes and desires of the patient.
>
> Copies of this letter are being sent to the Medical Executive Committee, the Board of Directors of the hospital, and the Administrator. If you choose to respond to this letter, it must be in accordance with procedures outlined in Article 6 of the hospital bylaws.
>
> Signed: James E. Golliman, Chief of Staff.

Trevellian's office staff, who called Trevellian in Switzerland and read the letter to him, opened the letter. Trevellian had no idea what Article 6 said. The article spelled out that all he could do aside from meeting with the Medical Executive Committee was to ask for a hearing before his peers in the hospital. He left Switzerland as he had originally

124

planned and returned home at the time he was expected.

The Medical Executive Committee met a week later. Laxton was present to hear the discussion. Golliman read his letter to the committee.

"The PRO has sent for a number of Doctor Trevellian's charts and this was drawn to my attention," Golliman said. "After I reviewed these charts, I realized we had a serious problem on our hands."

Laxton knew that Golliman had neither reviewed the charts nor did he understand the contents anyway. As Golliman made numerous errors in describing the content of the charts sent to the PRO, Laxton surreptitiously passed notes to him to get him somewhat on track. The committee was shocked because nothing like this had ever happened in the hospital before, and they felt threatened and angry.

A committee member, Doctor Adilman, intervened. "Mr. Chairman, I believe you can confirm we'll all lose money if we don't take this step."

"Yes, and we might lose the hospital too," Golliman said.

A motion to support what had been done was passed unanimously. A list of the charts requested by the PRO, with summaries of the problems, was attached to the minutes. Trevellian was allowed to appear before the committee but this didn't take place until after the decision was made.

"I have never had any problems with any patients," Trevellian said, "this is clearly a vendetta and I shall get to the bottom of who is behind it."

The committee appointed Laxton to represent them if Trevellian should ask for a hearing.

The following day Trevellian came to Laxton's office about the charts.

"Why don't you look at them," Trevellian said, "and then I can come back so you can tell me what possible problem there could be?"

"I will look at them and give you the worst case scenario," Laxton said, although he already knew the answer.

Laxton told Aysgarth by telephone that he thought Trevellian would be looking for a deal.

"I don't want him in surgery," Aysgarth said, "and outside of that he needs supervision."

Trevellian's return to Laxton's office was quick.

"You know I think you'd better make a deal with the committee," Laxton said.

"So, what do they want?" Trevellian said.

"If you'll give up doing surgery and assist an approved certified surgeon in cases needing surgery, they might go for something like that."

"I won't do it," Trevellian said, "I'm a better surgeon than most of the people here, and I've been doing it a lot longer."

He got up and walked out.

Laxton sighed. He was sure Trevellian would ask for a hearing and speculated it would not be easy. First, they had to find physicians who were not competitors, they couldn't have anyone with a vested interest, and a strong chairman was essential on a hearing committee. Then there would have to be an independent hearing officer, some attorney to make sure the case couldn't be overturned in court if Trevellian subsequently appealed. Laxton knew his work was cut out and that his reputation and future depended on a successful conclusion to the business.

Laxton made one more attempt to talk Trevellian into a peaceful solution, but his stubbornness and militancy only confirmed he would not even look at any negotiation at all.

It took two weeks to get a hearing committee together. As always, Aysgarth was in the background, although no one knew it, so that aside from one member of the hearing committee, Aysgarth had approved them all. They weren't in his pocket, because there had been a lot of difficulty in obtaining those without pecuniary interest and those who were in no way in competition with Trevellian.

The committee chairman was Bill Rekuf who, being a radiologist, had no possible competitive interest and had no monetary interest in the hospital. The other members were Herman Shickelhurtz, an anesthesiologist, Bill Yakamoto, a neurosurgeon, Bill Sanders, an orthopedic surgeon, Michael Tan, an otolaryngologist, and an alternate was a family practitioner Joe Biggerstaff.

The Hearing Officer was James P. Buck, an attorney. No representation by attorneys was allowed at the hospital hearing, but the accused was allowed to bring fellow physicians to help him. He brought Mark Polo, a gynecologist of questionable repute, and Benson Rao, an East Indian physician who had assisted with a number of his cases.

Laxton was there on behalf of the Medical Executive Committee, and of course Golliman was there as an observer. The hearing officer was not going to let him intervene.

The first meeting was held on a spring evening, and after a preliminary statement the hearing officer had each committee member introduce himself so that the court reporter could make a record

126

and had each member establish they had no prejudice or bias against Trevellian. He then asked Trevellian if he had any objection to any member of the committee and if he thought they could reach an impartial decision. Trevellian voiced no objection to any member. To Laxton's surprise the hearing officer then made a statement that he had originally been contacted by Trevellian to look into the matter for him, but that he had not been retained and had not discussed the case with Trevellian.

"The chairman of this committee knows about this and does not feel this would bias my position as hearing officer," Buck said. "I also asked Doctor Trevellian and he has no objection."

"I am represented by Doctor Rao and Doctor Polo," Trevellian said.

"Does this mean we would be any different from being witnesses?" Polo asked.

"It certainly does," Buck said.

"We are just here to be witnesses for him, and for no other purpose," Polo said.

There was vigorous nodding from Rao.

"It is not my intention to commence with the gynecological cases anyway," Laxton said, "so Doctor Polo might not want to stay tonight."

"I expect this whole matter cleared up in the next couple of hours. You would expect that could be done, wouldn't you," Trevellian said, turning to Buck.

"I believe it's very doubtful we could get through all these cases tonight," Buck said, "but your witnesses will be heard, I assure you."

"You mean it wouldn't be convenient to start with the gynecological cases," Trevellian said.

"No, it wouldn't," Laxton said firmly.

"The Medical Executive Committee can decide the order in which they will take the cases," Buck said, "especially since the onus of proof lies with them."

"Have you received all the letters listed here," Buck asked Trevellian, "including the one to the Board of Licensure?"

"Let me explain what I received. I received a phone call from Doctor Golliman while I was skiing. Actually, I called him and Doctor Golliman said he hated terribly to give me a suspension, but the PRO was investigating some of my charts and it was necessary to suspend me for ninety days according to PRO rules. I told him something to the effect that the PRO didn't need to be notified unless a person was suspended for more than forty five days, and he said he had to make a ninety-day suspension in my case."

"Well," Buck said, "you can start with a preliminary statement."

The hospital hoped if the PRO saw what was going on they would halt proceedings against the hospital and if Trevellian was stopped at least the hospital would be all right.

"I believed the reason for the suspension was to protect patients so I didn't know what it was about and I only got a copy about this when I asked for one."

"Did you discuss this with anyone," Buck said.

"Doctor Golliman. He said he reviewed the charts, and although he's just an ordinary family practitioner, he thought he knew enough to suspend me."

"Have you had adequate notice so you can defend yourself against the charges?"

"I can defend myself based on the charges," Trevellian said.

"Do you know what the charges are?" Biggerstaff said.

"I met with Doctor Laxton, who went over the charts with me but wouldn't write anything down so it couldn't be used at this meeting."

"Doctor Trevellian, when we met did you know this meeting was going to take place?" Laxton said.

"No, I didn't," Trevellian replied.

"Then what meeting are you talking about?" Laxton said sharply.

"I understand what you said, but I wanted something in writing subsequently."

"I don't have a problem with the Medical Executive Committee putting on its case tonight," Buck said.

"Fine," Trevellian said. "Let's get the show on the road."

"To give Doctor Trevellian due process we should be in a situation where he has a copy of the charges in writing," Laxton said.

"Do you need that?" Rekuf asked, reasserting his authority as chairman.

"If you give me my privileges back, even if I have to have another surgeon assist me, that will be fine. However, at this point, I've already suffered financial loss and personal stress, so I want to get this situation cleared up," Trevellian said.

"Can you get the charges to him a couple of days, Doctor Laxton?" Buck said.

"Certainly," Laxton said. "I do want it understood, to be fair to

Doctor Trevellian, that if I go into the problems of each chart tonight, we won't end up examining each chart in detail."

"That's all right," Buck said.

"Then the meeting will end with the reading of charges and problems with the charts, and at a subsequent meeting we'll have to go through each chart in detail," Laxton said.

"Well," Buck said, "you can start with a preliminary statement."

Laxton went through his own background and explained his role in this process.

"One thing which needs clarification is the misapprehension that the PRO is totally responsible for the suspension. The suspension was not based on the PRO calling for charts; it was based on a review of those charts which were sent for by the PRO. There were some other factors involved. First, Doctor Trevellian's surgical work has been under scrutiny for many years, and concerns about his work were expressed since nineteen seventy-seven. Secondly, for many years each Chief of Surgery has made some personal request for Doctor Trevellian to reduce his requests for surgical privileges, but he always reapplied anyway, and their requests were ignored. Third, several surgeries done by Doctor Trevellian in previous years show many deficiencies. A review of these cases is indicated and several of these may be included for the committee to assess."

"I think we shall just have to stay with whatever charges are brought, and the things which made Doctor Golliman reach his decision, not whether the committee felt there had been questionable work going on for years. That's not very significant," Buck said.

"I think Mr. Buck means it's not very significant at this hearing," Rekuf said.

"That's right," Buck said. "We have to be legal. The fact is that the committee can only consider charges related to the suspension. What may concern the Medical Executive Committee otherwise is not of any concern to us."

"Since nothing was given to Doctor Trevellian in writing, I think it's only fair to him for us to give him those charges in writing within the next day or two, and then we can proceed, and he knows exactly what problems were perceived by the Medical Executive Committee," Laxton said.

"I tend to agree it's really unfair to Doctor Trevellian to have to respond to something he really doesn't understand," Buck said.

"That's how it all began, being unfair to me and stopping me help humanity," Trevellian said. "I want to get going so I can get back to

129

practice medicine the way I've been doing it for the last thirty years or so. I'm the one who is disadvantaged."

"I agree with you," Buck said, "but you need a fair evaluation and you might want to go on now, but--"

"Of course I want to continue," Trevellian snapped. "I want to continue so I can get back to practice the way I'm used to practicing, and I want him to continue and make specific charges if he can find any, and if he doesn't, don't make them."

"I'll see the charges are presented to you in writing," Laxton said.

"I'll agree you should have these charges in writing, Doctor Trevellian," Buck said. "I suggest the chairman of the committee adjourn for a week when we can all get together again with written charges."

"I want to make a statement and I want to make it now," Trevellian said.

"Fine, go ahead," Rekuf said. "I have absolutely no objection."

Trevellian stood up and looked awkward until he spotted Golliman, when he assumed an expression somewhere between cynical and aggressive.

"I've been practicing at Valley Hospital for fourteen years, or from whatever time the hospital opened. I admit about a hundred and sixty patients a year, so I'm the one keeping the place in business. Many of my patients require a wide variety of surgeries. I haven't had any malpractice suits, and I haven't been before the medical and surgical committees in all these years. The letter from the PRO in San Francisco asked to review six charts - two vaginal hysterectomies with A and P repairs, two suprapubic prostatectomies, a cholecystectomy with common bile duct exploration, and a permanent tube gastrostomy. These were elderly patients who did well except for one who fell out of bed and fractured her pelvis. I've talked to the head of the PRO who told me they review two hundred and fifty thousand charts, and up to thirty charts of any one physician. Since I'm the one sending patients here and holding the place together, it's not surprising they sent for my charts. I believe Doctor Golliman's response to the PRO requests for charts by suspending my privileges was hasty and improper, as was notification of the Licensing Board. I was judged guilty of medical and surgical mismanagement by an ordinary general practitioner, even though a surgeon had not looked at those cases. If the PRO hadn't sent for the charts I wouldn't have been suspended. I expect this committee to find me all right, and that Golliman shouldn't have taken

130

my privileges away. I am requesting reinstatement of my privileges, and that the Licensing Board be told I'm all right. I demand there be no reviews of my charts over the last fifteen years, and that the Hearing Committee get on with the job and decide for me so I'm not suffering from financial losses like I am."

"Do you want to comment?" Buck said to Laxton.

"I'm sure the committee understands that I shall bring factual evidence from the charts and I shall quote, and if necessary produce, fully qualified specialists who are surgeons, including those specializing in the urinary tract called urologists, those specializing in women's diseases of the uterus, ovaries, reproductive system who are called gynecologists. On the medical side I shall quote or bring medical specialists – that is internists - as well as medical specialists who have gone on to become specialists in bowel diseases called, as you know, gastroenterologists, those who have gone on to specialize in heart disease called cardiologists, or lung disease called pulmonologists, and I shall show how they were not used or were used inappropriately. The evidence will show that Dr. Trevellian's privileges in surgery have to be removed permanently."

"What about including those of us who are putting his patients to sleep?" Shickelhurtz asked.

"Yes, I will include anesthesiologists," Laxton said.

"You people are ridiculous," Trevellian said, and he walked out.

"We'll reconvene in a week's time," Buck said.

CHAPTER 22

TREVELLIAN'S DISASTERS

A day or two after the meeting Trevellian reappeared at Laxton's office to ask if the committee would accept a compromise. Trevellian's idea of compromise was that he should give up urology, assist in surgery, but still perform gynecology and general surgery himself after having a consultation on each case. Aysgarth had certainly told Laxton this was not acceptable and Golliman confirmed this. Laxton knew it wouldn't be looked on with much favor by the PRO, because he had told Montpellier that the hospital would stop Trevellian's surgery. In return the PRO had said two things would happen. First they would hold up the reviews of Trevellian's charts until the matter was resolved by the hospital, and secondly there would no sanctions against the hospital if that course was followed.

Only Laxton and Aysgarth knew that and knew they couldn't tell anyone else. Strictly speaking it was not correct for the PRO to be doing that for the hospital, and had it leaked out it could have caused a major scandal, except there was nothing in writing. The only thing Laxton was doing which made him feel uncomfortable was sending copies of the transcripts to Montpellier. Worse, he had a visit from a representative of the Board of Licensure who also managed to get an agreement that they would also get a copy of the transcripts.

Trevellian's proposal was not acceptable, and Laxton told him so. He told Trevellian what was acceptable. Trevellian then went and saw Golliman and followed this by going to Rekuf and some of the other Hearing Committee members. He tried to discuss some of the cases which were likely to come up with each one of them. It had a rather negative effect, and each member phoned Rekuf to complain about the harassment.

When the Hearing Committee resumed the following week Buck, the hearing officer, was clearly furious. "In a conversation I had with Doctor Rekuf, I was told that Doctor Trevellian had contacted him and other members of this committee to discuss matters related to the case. I say here on the record that must not be done. This is a formal matter, and anything related to it must be discussed in this room at a meeting. I'm telling Doctor Trevellian he must not contact members of this committee related to any cases which are the subject of the hearing. I don't suppose you wish to comment, Doctor Trevellian?"

"Yes, I do," Trevellian said. "I don't recall discussing specific cases with anyone. I was told that if I would forgo surgery I could assist in surgery, and ultimately reapply for surgical privileges. I've decided I won't do urology so I don't think it's necessary to review the urology cases. I want privileges to do gynecology and general surgery. Of course I won't do high-risk cases. I've changed my mode of practice because I had ten Medicare patients in the hospital this weekend, and I had two or three consultants on every case. I would like to compromise with the committee on those terms. I want a stop put to this ongoing review of my surgical charts over the past fifteen years at Valley Hospital. This is what I discussed with Doctor Rekuf and Doctor Golliman."

"Very well," Buck said, "but even this type of discussion should not be held outside this hearing room. Is this an offer you're making to this committee?"

"Yes," Trevellian said.

"First let me ask the representative of the Medical Executive Committee if this an offer they could accept."

"In my view," Laxton said, "it's not the prerogative of this committee to make deals."

"No-no, we won't make a deal," Buck said quickly, "what I really meant was, is this an acceptable offer to the Medical Executive Committee?"

"No, it isn't," Laxton said.

"You are free outside the hearing to meet with Doctor Laxton and members of the Medical Executive Committee, Doctor Trevellian, should you wish to make a compromise. You should not meet with members of this committee to discuss anything related to this hearing."

"For the record," Laxton said, "Doctor Trevellian came to my office with these same proposals and I told him at that time these proposals were not acceptable and then he brings them to this committee, which has no jurisdiction to make a deal."

"Do you deny," Trevellian said, "that I approached you to ask if I could be reinstated to assist in surgery?"

"I don't deny you approached me to plea bargain your case, but that was not the sole content of your proposal, as you indicated here today. You were told if you totally give up your surgical privileges that the Medical Executive Committee would consider allowing you to assist in surgery."

"Let me say this," Buck said, "it's important these conversations take placc outside this hearing."

"All right," Trevellian said.

"Now let's get on with the job we're here for."

"I would hope that we can go over the gynecological cases first, so my witness can leave," Trevellian said.

"That's acceptable," Laxton said. "But it is not acceptable that the urology cases are excepted from the hearing, because they show a pattern of practice that is common to all Doctor Trevellian's cases, and this aberrant pattern will show up in other cases we consider. Having said that, I will proceed."

Laxton was very annoyed and wondered how many of the consultations Trevellian had asked for over the weekend were necessary. He was just as likely to over-utilize as he was to fail to call a consultant when he needed someone.

"The charges on the first case are that a totally confused patient signed her own consent form. That the woman had no preliminary studies of any kind, and that because her bladder was half full of urine all the time anyway, a suspension operation was improper surgery. There was no consultation of any kind and the surgery made the patient worse. Then she was not properly controlled, and fell out of bed and fractured her pelvis. She was admitted walking from her own home and was sent out of the hospital to a nursing home with a tube in her bladder, unable to walk. She should not have had surgery anyway. So, in summary, this was an eighty-five-year-old woman with Alzheimer's disease who was totally confused, looked after by her husband, was wearing a diaper, had her uterus removed, and a repair was done and ultimately she fell out of bed, broke her pelvis, and was sent to Doctor Trevellian's nursing home."

"I'm going to tell you about her," Trevellian said. "She was able to take care of her own things and she just had a poor memory, not Alzheimer's disease. Her husband was blind. When she got to the nursing home she was better off with a catheter. She just got confused after surgery because of her cerebrovascular disease. Well, she did fall out of bed and fracture her pelvis."

"That's not my fault."

"Was she in restraints?" Rekuf said.

"No, the nurses forgot."

"You didn't order restraints," Laxton said.

"Do you want to question Doctor Trevellian, Doctor Laxton?"

"You operated on a patient with her bladder half full. She couldn't empty it. She had residual urine," Laxton said to Trevellian.

"That's because her bladder was sitting down by her knee,"

134

Trevellian said. "I don't even know if it was a residual."

"Yes, it was. It's here in the nursing notes," Biggerstaff said.

"In your own history you say the patient had Alzheimer's disease. Now you just told the committee she didn't have Alzheimer's disease. Did she or didn't she?" Laxton said.

"I don't really know," Trevellian said. "Her husband said she had."

"Her blind husband told you she had Alzheimer's disease," Laxton said.

"If she had Alzheimer's, or might have had Alzheimer's, don't you think you should have found out before you had her sign a consent for surgery?" Rekuf asked.

"Well, I thought an operation would improve her," Trevellian said.

"I thought you were asked if she could sign the consent," Biggerstaff said.

"It's not my job to ask who signed the consent."

"But," Biggerstaff persisted, "you made a diagnosis of Alzheimer's and asked her to sign a consent for surgery."

"I didn't ask her to sign," Trevellian said.

"Don't you think it's the responsibility of the surgeon to see that the consent form is appropriately signed?" Laxton said.

"I didn't look at the consent form," Trevellian said.

"You mean you do surgeries without looking to see if the consent form was signed and who signed it?"

"It's the nurse's job, not mine."

"In a court of law," Laxton said, "it would be held to be your responsibility. Isn't that so?"

"I don't know. I haven't had anything to do with malpractice. I'm learning a lot from this review."

"Did you call a neurologist to see her?" Laxton asked.

"No, I didn't."

"So, she's a confused old lady who didn't have the benefit of a neurologist, correct?" Laxton said.

"Well, she didn't have any sensation losses."

"Did you have her bladder examined, or do any X-Rays?"

"No," Trevellian said. "I could guess what they were like."

"Based on the work you did, you couldn't conclude this would be a successful operation, could you?"

"I just felt it would be okay."

"I'd like to hear from Doctor Trevellian's witness. He's a

135

gynecologist," Biggerstaff said.

"I don't know all the ramifications of this case, but I think if I was asked how to handle this case I would say some consultations ought to be done," Doctor Polo said. "But he did a good job. There wasn't a lot of blood lost."

"Are there any other conditions that could have caused the patient to be leaking urine which would have made you not do the surgery?" Doctor Rekuf said.

"Oh, I didn't say I would have done surgery in this case, because there are some other things. Since there was a question of Alzheimer's disease she probably should have been seen by a neurologist."

"Could she have had conservative treatment?" Rekuf said.

"She could have had a pessary and a catheter through an incision in her bladder," Polo said.

"What about an ordinary catheter and a leg bag?" Laxton asked.

"Nothing wrong with that," Polo said.

"I discussed this case off the record with Doctor Polo," Trevellian said, "but if it was today I'd have four or five consultants."

"I want to comment that if you just talk to someone in a locker room about a patient, you can't call that a consultation, and I don't think anyone else would," Polo remarked.

"Doctor Trevellian, if you had this case all over again now, would you proceed in the same way?" Rekuf asked.

"In view of everything I've heard I would have six or seven consultations on every patient."

"Thank you," Rekuf said.

"Whether they were needed or not," Trevellian added.

"To go on to the next case," Laxton said, "here's an eighty-three-year-old woman with no kind of preoperative studies, no consultations of any kind, who walks into the hospital from her own home, is operated on by Doctor Trevellian and he removes her uterus and the pathologist can find nothing wrong with it. She becomes confused in hospital and is subsequently discharged to Doctor Trevellian's nursing home with a tube in her bladder."

"This woman is better off in my nursing home," Trevellian said. "Also, she had her bladder hanging down by her knees. She left hospital with a catheter in her bladder but it kept her dry."

"I don't see why she would need a medical consultation, why would she need that?" Biggerstaff said.

"Is there any surgeon here who would operate on an eighty-three-year-old without a medical clearance?" Rekuf asked.

136

"Before anyone answers that," Laxton said, "just note the fact that it's documented she had heart disease and lung problems."

Every surgeon on the committee affirmed that he would have had medical clearance.

"We just have to remember she walked in thinking clearly and was carried out confused," Laxton concluded.

"Let's go to the next case," Rekuf said.

"I'm presenting this urology case to identify an overall pattern of incompetence in the management of surgical cases by Doctor Trevellian," Laxton said.

"But I said I'd stop doing urology," Trevellian whined.

"Hopefully you'll stop doing any surgery. However, this patient came in for an operation on his neck and then Doctor Trevellian took out his prostate. The documentation showed the patient had no urinary complaints at all but his prostate, which was quite small, was removed through an incision, and he was in hospital twenty-five days. No tests or work up were done and there is no record of a rectal examination to feel the prostate."

"Oh yes, I did one," Trevellian said. "I just didn't write it down. He was eighty-one and all old men have prostate troubles, so I didn't write anything down, like he didn't void like a young man. I knew all about him because he was in my nursing home. The X-ray that was done says prostatomegaly, which means he needed his prostate out. He had residual urine on the X-Ray report as well."

"Do you usually discuss the X-Ray reports with the radiologist before you do surgery?" Rekuf said.

"Yes. Always."

"Do you remember I was the radiologist on this case, and I told you that I didn't think the residual meant anything because we had just taken out the catheter?"

"I don't remember that."

"Don't you remember I told you there was insufficient evidence of obstruction in this case? I remember because I was so frustrated you insisted these things be placed in the report."

"I don't remember this at all."

"You've said you can remember every detail about this man's surgery and his symptoms, but you can't remember talking to the radiologist about his X-Rays?" Laxton asked.

"No."

"Have you ever considered that if this man needed his prostate out, a small gland like this could be removed through an instrument?"

"Oh, you mean ream it out - no incision. Well, I don't do those, so I cut it out."

"Let me go to the next case," Laxton said. "A seventy-two-year old male who could not pass urine. He was on a drug that often causes this condition, and Doctor Trevellian had him catheterizing himself, which led to a bladder infection. In addition, he was a diabetic and legally blind. He had heart disease, high blood pressure, and shortness of breath. Doctor Trevellian operated on his prostate and there was so much bleeding a specialist had to be called to salvage the patient - to save his life."

"The man took his wife's pills," Trevellian said. "That's what caused all the trouble. When I did the operation on his prostate, the urologist was just finishing a case in the next room, and he just came in. I didn't send for him. He said he'd help and when he came into the room he just took over. Before all this the patient was catheterizing himself, as you've been told. He was--"

"How does a man who is totally blind catheterize himself?" Laxton interrupted.

"Well, he could walk fine, and he had Braille. Maybe his wife catheterized him. I don't know. Let me go on. When the urologist came he just took over."

"I can call him as a witness, Doctor Trevellian, so I caution you to answer correctly. Didn't he tell you that this was a near disaster and you shouldn't be doing this kind of case?"

"No-no."

"Then I will call him, because that's what he told me was the situation."

"He did tell me this was a serious case and he felt he needed to be there, but if he hadn't been there I'd have fixed it myself."

"But he told you, you shouldn't be doing this kind of case, didn't he?"

Trevellian looked at Laxton. "Those weren't his exact words."

"But that was the gist of what he said, wasn't it?"

"He told me I shouldn't be doing urology."

CHAPTER 23

MEGAN

A few days later Trevellian went to X-Ray and invited Rekuf to come to an oboe recital that was being held at the Villa, Trevellian's nursing home. This type of thing was arranged from time to time because Trevellian claimed it was put on for the residents and that made it deductible. Rekuf refused because he saw through this as a gimmick to influence him.

"You have to watch him," he said to Laxton confidentially, "he'll use anything to get this thing dropped."

"I was going to ask you," Laxton said. "He's invited me to go to his facility again and see how it's run and what improvements he's made."

"You're not on the hearing committee, and you represent the Medical Executive, so it wouldn't matter and might be quite useful to take a closer look at what kind of an operation he's running up there."

"I don't think I've anything to lose," Laxton said.

One Thursday Laxton accompanied Trevellian to the Villa nursing home. It was a class operation, but Laxton found out there were only two Medicaid patients there. The rest of the patients had money. He also confirmed that patients admitted there who had other physicians as their family doctor changed doctors within the first month of their arrival. They became Trevellian's patients.

"I have to leave," Trevellian said, "but I want you to come over to Administration first, and you can see what has to be done to run a place like this."

As they entered Administration there was a large executive desk behind which sat Trevellian's wife.

"I want to introduce you to my wife," Trevellian said, "She acts as the Administrator."

Laxton was surprised to see that Trevellian's wife was about twenty years younger than Trevellian.

"Megan's been here a few years. She has good training for this job. She's not a nurse, but she is trained in psychology, and started counseling before we met. When she gave that up she took some accounting, so she's a great asset. I'm going to have her show you the offices, and she'll answer any questions. I have to run over to my office for a couple of hours."

"Thanks for the tour," Laxton said sincerely.

Megan Trevellian was a tall, slender girl with dark hair which fell onto and below her shoulders. She had casually tied it back with a bow, but it was loose, full-bodied hair, which was straight. Her face would have been more appropriate for modeling than administration or secretarial work. She had carefully made up lips, soft and full, which parted in an inviting smile revealing white, even teeth. Her thin, dark eyebrows surmounted clear blue eyes enhanced by long eyelashes. Her high cheekbones gave her a Nordic appearance. She seemed to constantly wear an expression which exuded friendliness. As she came round from behind the desk Laxton saw she was almost his height. She was wearing a white dress, tailored and obviously expensive. It fell immediately above the knee, leaving much to the imagination. Her very thin waist was partially hidden by the looseness of the dress, but it was obvious she had a slender waist. In the same way there was that hint of shapely buttocks above long slender legs. Her breasts appeared firm, but the dress didn't make them provocative. All in all this was a classy lady, Laxton decided.

"Why do you think Herb brought you up here?" she said.

Laxton felt awkward. Megan laughed. "Do you think he thought it would stop the hearing?"

It was not the kind of conversation Laxton wanted, and he said nothing.

"I know a bit about you, and I know it won't make any difference," she said. "Herb brought this whole thing on himself, and he's only got himself to blame. I don't expect you to talk about it, and I won't either."

"Have you been married a long time?" Laxton said.

"Over ten years. I'm almost thirty. And no, it wasn't a great romance. I'm comfortable with it and wouldn't change after the way it's now set up. I'm frank enough to admit that with what I've gained, and since Herb has more than three million dollars, I don't want to make changes."

She paused and looked at him. "I don't know what I can show you here, because I don't do that much anyway. I just keep everything under control when he goes off skiing, or to a meeting, or some vacation. We go away together about once a year."

Laxton was puzzled by her frankness, but he knew he should say something. "Maybe we could go and have coffee somewhere," he suggested rather feebly.

"Let me take you up to the apartment here. It's never used unless

140

I stay over when Herb is away, but it's nice, and we can have coffee there."

Megan led the way to the elevator and they rode up to what turned out to be a penthouse apartment. The living room was furnished in an old world style with dark cherry wood tables and large comfortable armchairs, one on each side of a long curved sofa. The room was done in magenta colors, which gave it almost a Victorian feel.

Megan went to the kitchen, which had very modern appliances and was a contrast except for the dark wood cabinets which continued the theme. She made coffee in an automatic coffee maker and started to place mugs on a tray. Laxton had followed her into the kitchen. "We could just drink coffee here," he said.

"I suppose you take cream and sugar," Megan said as she opened the refrigerator.

"How did you guess," Laxton said.

He didn't feel the least awkward around her, and couldn't get over how comfortable he felt in contrast to the feelings he had around Trevellian. He leaned against the long counter while Megan perched on the edge of a freestanding island. The kitchen was large, even for a penthouse. He looked at her quizzically.

"There are three bedrooms with full bathrooms, and a small dining area just off the living room," she said.

"You don't have children," he said.

"No, we don't."

"This is a large place. Why do you have a house as well?"

Megan laughed. "You haven't seen the house yet," she said. "It's much larger. Besides, it's at the beach. Why don't you come down and visit so you can see it?"

"Maybe sometime, but it wouldn't be appropriate right now."

There was a pause.

"I don't see why this stupid hearing business should stop you visiting me," Megan said. "You know the hearing is delayed two weeks. Despite all this talk about wanting to get finished, he still has to go off out of town to look at some business deal. Herb's gone tomorrow for this week and part of next. Come down Saturday. No one's going to know but the two of us, and I'm a good cook. I'll draw you a map, or I'll pick you up if you want."

"No, no, no," Laxton said. "Not a good idea."

"But the visit is." She seemed to be scribbling on a square of paper which she thrust in his hand. It had the address on one side and a map sketched out on the other side. Laxton looked uncomfortable.

141

"Remember, you're coming to see the house and me, and we're not going to talk about hospitals, hearings, or nursing homes. We're going to walk on the beach and you're going to get the best meal you've had in a long time. Bachelors get neglected, particularly if they're all work and no play, so I'll expect you at seven. Don't let me down."

She had already opened the door and hustled him to the elevator. In less than a minute he found himself on his way to his car. He drove back to his office at the hospital.

"What was Trevellian's operation like?" Veronica said.

Laxton shrugged. "It's a nursing home. They seem to be nearly all private patients. A couple of Medicaid perhaps. It must be a money maker."

"He's greedy. He doesn't need to do surgery at all with all the money he's making up there."

It had already occurred to Laxton that he was never going to be influenced by Trevellian's whining about economic hardship again. He had responded to Rekuf's inquiries similarly and indicated to Rekuf that there was no way Trevellian was suffering from shortage of money.

Laxton had grave doubts about the Saturday invitation but didn't have much to do and knew he needed to stop working nights and weekends. The hearing had put pressure on him because he had to catch up on his other work in his own time. He looked at the scrap of paper he'd stuffed in his pocket and saw the telephone number there. At about three on Saturday he called.

There was no doubt whose sultry tones answered the telephone. He paused for a moment. "Laxton," he said abruptly.

"You don't have to be so formal. Where are you, and why aren't you here?"

"I don't know whether this is a good idea."

"I'll expect you in half an hour."

The phone was dead. Laxton looked at the receiver and replaced it. He reflected she had said seven, and wondered why he'd called so early. He had originally thought he would find an excuse not to go, but realized that wasn't the real reason. He wondered why he was dressing carefully, but decided he'd go with an open neck shirt anyway. It was late spring and California was hot and dry. He decided to take nothing, despite the temptation to take a bottle. Flowers would have been overkill, and Trevellian was loaded anyway, and his wife probably had everything she needed.

He followed the map on the square of paper she had given him and drove right past the place because there was a high walled entrance concealing the house and grounds, and he missed the number until he had driven past. He did a U-turn further down the street and shot into the driveway, which curved around toward the house. The grounds were professionally kept. There was too much for owners to look after anyway. The back of the house sloped down to the beach. He rang the doorbell.

Megan answered at once. There were no live-in servants, and it was clear she was alone and had kept her promise. She looked even more startling than at their first meeting, although her dress was elegant and casual, very much shorter than her business dress, and her legs were bare.

"Let me show you the house, or would you rather have a drink first?"

"It's fine. I'd love to see your house. I'm impressed already."

Laxton had entered the spacious hallway with a high ceiling leading to a large living room with windows front and back. The front windows had mesh drapes, but those at the back were huge and overlooked an Olympic-sized pool on a terrace which ended in a low wall. There were steps down to the beach. There were trees at each end of the pool and a Jacuzzi at one end. The pool and terrace were accessed through spacious French doors. The contrast with the apartment was immense because the house was very modern and very California. There was a floor to ceiling fireplace, the ceiling being cathedral and light cedar. The floor was tiled. The house was enormous because a corridor led to an adjacent part which was two stories. A curved staircase from the hallway could also access the upstairs part of this. There were too many rooms on the main floor to absorb the floor plan in one visit. The upper story was also large but the bedrooms were immense, the main one had a king size bed, an adjacent bathroom with a tiled octagonal tub. The exterior windows opened onto a narrow deck that overlooked the pool, the beach, and the ocean.

Laxton was impressed.

"The styles are different. I mean here and the apartment. Which do you like best?" Megan said.

"I like the apartment furnishing best, but that's probably because of my English background, although I know this is more - more -"

"Pretentious?"

"I wasn't going to say that, but yes, and it's so California. I think they always end up overdoing everything."

Laxton was too polite to ask how many millions it had cost but he could imagine.

"A drink?" Megan said, as they descended the stairs.

"Scotch, I guess."

Megan went to the bar, which was on the wall under the stairwell. She made the drinks.

"Give me your jacket," she said suddenly. Laxton complied and Megan dropped his jacket on the sofa. They sat together at the bar.

"There isn't much personal contact for me. We have all these musical events at the nursing home, and a bunch of people come who haven't any relationship to the nursing home or its residents. They're mostly friends of Herb--or business acquaintances."

"And friends of yours," Laxton said with a smile.

"It's not true. I was born in the eastern states anyway and when I came out here I developed friendships in university but soon after marriage most of my friends were put in the unacceptable category, so they drifted away. I go out alone quite a lot."

"Where do you go?"

"Theater, opera, orchestral shows. Sometimes even revue type shows."

"And which bars do you frequent," Laxton said, and then immediately regretted the question because of the look of pain which crossed her face.

"I don't visit any," she said coldly.

"It was a totally inappropriate question and I apologize. I just thought that maybe you needed to get out into some kind of company."

It was a weak explanation and he knew it. He turned his glass round on the bar, rotating it slowly with his right hand.

"I don't do that, and I don't go the church route either, and I'm not a very good charity worker. As far as the hospital is concerned, I want to stay away from that because it has become a very strange institution, if you don't mind me saying that."

"What makes you say that?" Laxton said.

"The original idea of the hospital was to keep most of the earnings as profit for the doctors. That's all right except, now the whole thing seems to have become a money-grubbing exercise at any cost."

Laxton could see the irony in sitting talking to the wife of one of the most incompetent members of the medical staff and hearing complaints from her about the poor quality of care.

"I don't think medical staffs today are getting any better," she went on, "in fact I wonder how many of them have ethics left."

"There are too many killers out there," Laxton said.

144

"I know you think you can clean the place up," Megan continued, "but in the end it isn't likely to make much difference. They want you there only to help them collect money, because it's all the Valley people think about. Well, there may be one or two who are there for other reasons, but not very many. We made a lot of money out of the place but that's when they were treating nervous break- downs, people they can't admit nowadays. We make a lot out of the nursing home and Herb doesn't need the hospital, but he needs to go on with his business deals and he uses the hospital to feed his ego and he won't give up. Money has been a bad influence on him. Our whole marriage became oriented to money. He even had me sign a separation agreement for tax purposes."

Laxton looked shocked.

"You don't need to look like that. I made sure I had control over a lot of money before I consented to that one. I'm worth over half what Herb is worth."

Laxton knew Megan had only partial insight, because the hospital had profited from Trevellian's complications until Medicare came along. He wanted to change the subject.

Megan stood up. "How about a short walk on the private beach and maybe a dip after that?"

They walked together on the beach barefoot for the best part of an hour, walking through the incoming water which broke over their ankles and lower legs. Laxton felt refreshed when they returned to walk around the pool. Megan led him to the change room.

"Here, there's lots of trunks. I'm sure you can find a pair. See you at pool side."

With that she skipped out of the room and went upstairs.

When they met at the poolside later, she was wearing a wide striped black and white two-piece which emphasized her attributes. The pool temperature was seventy-five, but seemed cool enough, and the refreshed drink helped. The scotch and water had been made in a tall glass so the strength was the same, but there was more water as a thirst quencher. Laxton sat on the edge of the pool and sipped the drink. They exchanged small talk and then she asked him about himself. He found it easier to talk to her than he had to any other woman.

It was cooling off, but Laxton still felt warm. He thought it might be the scotch.

"Let's go inside," Megan said. "I have a cold dinner, and the air conditioning will help us cool off."

She gave him a terry cloth robe and they went to sit at the bar because Megan told him she would bring the food there so that it would be quite informal. They had another drink before they ate, and then out came a good white wine to go with the meal. The sun was going down as they finished eating.

"You're getting drowsy," she said.

"I know," he answered wearily. "It's the sun, the booze, the good company, and the food."

"Come," Megan said, taking him by the hand. "Let me show you the sunset."

She led him upstairs through the bedroom and onto the outside balcony overlooking the pool and ocean. The sun was a deep red glow reflecting on the ocean, but it was still very warm outside, which caused Laxton to take off his robe as they stood on the balcony together.

"I think I'm going to call you Laxy," Megan said.

"I don't mind. I had it all through school."

"And you're still drowsy. Come inside."

She led him to the bed and he found himself falling on his back onto it. Megan's robe had slipped to the floor and suddenly she was on top of him. He held her as he received a violently passionate kiss. Then they were on the bed unclothed, and she was on top of him, kneeling with her legs on either side of his body. He found himself struggling to hold on as her buttocks moved up and down and then rotated, first to one side and then the other. He rolled her over and pounded her until she cried with ecstasy and he could hold on no longer.

Afterwards they slept, creeping beneath the sheets and clinging to each other. He thought of nothing but Megan as he fell asleep.

Laxton woke to find Megan standing beside the bed with morning coffee and toast. She sat on the bed and they ate and drank. They looked into each other's eyes until he took her in his arms, standing, and before long was pounding her against the wall, ultimately leading her to the bed where they continued until there was a mutual explosion once more.

It was still very early and they slept again. Later she brought him a razor and toothbrush, and he went into the bathroom and shaved and showered before he went back and sat on the bed next to her.

Laxton left early on Monday morning and dropped by his own place to change. He was at the hospital sooner than usual, which brought Veronica into his office.

"I see you had a weekend where you got some peace. You weren't obsessed by Trevellian," she said.

"I certainly wasn't obsessed by Doctor Trevellian."

146

CHAPTER 24

ARROGANCE BEGINS

Laxton spent the week sending out copies of Trevellian's charts, being careful to obliterate the hospital name, the physicians involved, and anything which might give away who and where the care had taken place. The charts were sent to well-recognized authorities so that these would be blind, unbiased opinions and he wanted to see how his views compared with those of others. He managed to get the process accelerated and limited the reviewers to seven.

The first chart back was from the Professor of Surgery who had written, "Why is this man allowed to continue this incompetent butchery on innocent people?"

Others had written comments, if not as blunt, certainly not complimentary. Of the seven surveyed not one of the accepted authorities found excuse for the work done by Trevellian.

Laxton planned to present this to the committee and felt it would wrap up the process and he would be rid of the matter. It was an early June evening when the committee next met. Laxton had told Rekuf about the blind study and he agreed this should be a fast way to get the matter completed and finalized.

As had become usual Buck opened the meeting and handed over to Chairman Rekuf.

"Mr. Chairman," Laxton said, "as soon as we have been through the cases I will present a blind study done on all the cases by well-recognized specialists and present their conclusions on each case to the committee members. These opinions were obtained without the specialists, who are not in any way connected to this hospital, being aware of who was the physician involved and which hospital was involved."

"Very well," Rekuf said.

"I'm not sure we can allow that," Buck said, "Doctor Trevellian should have the right to cross examine any witnesses who express an opinion on the cases, and unless you identify these doctors and bring them here so he can question them I don't think it would be appropriate. How do you feel about this Doctor Trevellian?"

"I object. It's not fair to me. I should be able to question them."

"If this was allowed, and Doctor Laxton was to read these into the record, I think the committee should give very little weight to them."

"It would be possible for me to give the names of the reviewers and their qualifications," Laxton said, "and I know these people have a lot of credibility and the committee would recognize that."

"I don't believe that hearsay evidence should be introduced," Buck said.

"You know our bye-laws allow the introduction of such evidence in hearings like this," Laxton said.

"Why can't you bring the reviewers here?"

"This was a blind study without identification of the hospital and we had the cases reviewed on that basis. It is not unusual to get such reviews done in medical circles," Laxton said.

"Do you object to this Doctor Trevellian?" Rekuf asked.

"Yes I do. This whole thing is unfair to me and this is another example. I'm being held up here when I should be seeing patients. Let him bring these people here so I can ask them questions."

"It's perfectly all right for you to bring witnesses here," Buck said, "and we don't want to deny fairness to Doctor Trevellian."

"It's already unfair," Trevellian whined.

"If you are ruling that blind studies cannot be submitted, I shall have to call witnesses," Laxton said.

Laxton was annoyed because presentation of evidence by independent witnesses based on their evaluation of the charts would have clinched the matter and shortened the hearing process. Obviously Trevellian was afraid of this and he suspected Buck knew very well it would all be over very quickly. Laxton suspected Buck had denied this presentation because it affected the massive amounts of money he was putting in his own pocket. Laxton knew Buck was getting a thousand bucks a night for each session.

Trevellian had his own little surprise. He presented photographs of patients whom he claimed he had cured and how they looked today. When asked where the photographs had been taken he admitted they were taken in his own nursing home.

"I will refer to these later," Laxton said, "and I believe little weight should be given to this kind of evidence."

"Do you want to pick up from last time and proceed," Rekuf said.

"In summary," Laxton said, "we were dealing with a patient with urinary retention. He was on a drug notorious for causing retention and there was no documented reason why he was getting the drug. According to the chart the patient catheterized himself and got an

148

infection. The chart says he's diabetic, legally blind, has high blood pressure, heart block, irregular pulse and an enlarged prostate. The bladder examination report had six deficiencies, there were no medical consultations and the anesthesiologist said he was a high risk for surgery. Doctor Trevellian took him to surgery and removed his prostate through an incision and ran into serious technical problems and a urologist had to be called to stop the bleeding and save the patient's life. He had to be given four bottles of blood. Doctor Trevellian's operative report suggests the specialist was just an assistant, but from the operative report he dictated it's clear that wasn't the case. This surgery, which ordinarily takes the best part of an hour, took three and a half hours. We are going over old ground, but in detail."

"Is this an accurate copy of the report?" Buck asked.

"Yes it is, and I can explain everything," Trevellian said.

"Do you want to go on?" Buck asked Laxton.

"If Doctor Trevellian wishes to discuss the case, let him go ahead first."

"This patient started taking his wife's pills and that's why he got into trouble. I catheterized him but he kept a catheter at home and continued to catheterize himself after that. Anyway, I decided he needed his prostate out because it was enormous, and the urethra got torn so I put a tube in above and below and a drain as well. At the end of the procedure when I tried to irrigate the catheters everything came out of the drain so I knew I had to open him up again. The anesthesiologist said the urologist was in the next room finishing a case, and did I want him to come in. When I opened the patient up again the catheters had come out and there was blood pouring out of the bladder. The specialist came in and asked if I wanted help, and I thought it wouldn't hurt. I expected him to step across the table from me but he stepped into my place and I watched over his right shoulder. He dictated his own operative note. The blood loss was about one bottle. The procedure only took two hours."

"Excuse me," Shickelhurtz said. "The anesthetic record says there was an estimated blood loss of four or five bottles. Also, the surgery was listed as starting at twelve-fifty-five and finishing at sixteen-fifty-five. That's four hours. You didn't put down who assisted you."

"I always dictate who my assistants were. Don't you do that Doctor Trevellian?" Yakamoto said.

"No, I never do that."

"You don't put in your operative report who assisted you?" Laxton asked.

"No."

"Don't surgeons usually list who helps them in surgery?" Biggerstaff said.

"I always do," Yakamoto said. "I believe it's required for legal purposes, and the name doesn't get on the chart if you don't dictate it."

Laxton looked at Trevellian and asked, "When you put the catheter in originally, was it meant to stay in and did you use a catheter with an inflated balloon to make sure it stayed in?"

"Yes," Trevellian replied, "but the bag became deflated and he catheterized himself with the same catheter, I think."

"Well, you wrote down he catheterized himself in February, is that correct?"

"Yes."

"You have documented he's blind, you told us at the last meeting as well, and I find it difficult to understand how the patient catheterized himself if he was blind. Can you tell us that Doctor Trevellian?"

"Well, he walks fine but I don't know whether he did it himself or his wife did it."

"But you recorded his wife suffers from Alzheimer's disease," Laxton said.

"It's just a little bit of Alzheimer's."

"Did you find the bladder normal when you did the cystoscopy?"

"It was quite normal."

"Doctor Trevellian, why did you cut a piece out of the bladder and have it examined by the pathologist if the bladder was normal?"

"There was a pathologist around, so I thought I might as well give him something to do and have it examined."

"The pathologist said it was normal. It was normal bladder wall, wasn't it?"

"Yes, it was."

"I don't see any reference in your operative report to the tear in the urethra," Laxton said.

"No. It's not there. I didn't put it in the report."

"So you admit your operative report doesn't say what actually happened."

"I always tear the urethra when I take a prostate out."

"You dictated a report which reads as though you did the whole procedure alone and had no help from a specialist." Laxton said.

"Well, I dictated my report and he dictated his."

150

"The patient lost a lot of blood and was in a serious state when the specialist came in, wasn't he?"

"We fixed it."

"In fact the specialist told you this was a bail out from near disaster, didn't he?"

"No."

"He remembers this case very well," Laxton said, "and I will call him here if necessary. He told you that you couldn't salvage the situation and shouldn't be doing such cases."

"He told me it was serious, and I think he felt he needed to be there, but if he hadn't been I'd have been all right."

"But he told you he thought you were not capable of doing the surgery," Laxton said sharply.

"He didn't use those exact words."

"Let's be simple. That was the gist of what he told you, wasn't it?"

Trevellian took a deep breath. "He felt I shouldn't be doing any urology at all."

"Let me summarize," Laxton said. "This patient had a suprapubic prostatectomy done by Doctor Trevellian, who got into serious trouble, and a urologist had to come in and bail him out, stop the bleeding, repair a torn urethra, and stop the patient being killed, and the urologist told Doctor Trevellian he shouldn't be doing urology."

"Have you anything to say?" Buck said to Trevellian.

"No."

"Doctor Laxton's last statement is very serious, and is really hearsay, and I want to know if these are the true feelings of the urologist. Do you agree, Doctor Trevellian, with what Doctor Laxton is saying, that the urologist didn't think you were capable of this kind of surgery?" Dr. Yakamoto said.

"The urologist doesn't think ordinary surgeons should be doing this. He had mentioned this to me."

"Don't you want the urologist to go on the record, or do you just accept what Doctor Laxton said and say it is correct?" Yakamoto said.

"I don't think he thought I should be doing this kind of surgery. He felt that way and had told me so before I did this case."

"You mean you knew," said Rekuf, "that in his opinion you were not competent to do this kind of surgery before you did this case?"

"Yes."

"Let's go on to the next case," Rekuf said.

"This is a lady who was seventy-two, bedridden, a schizophrenic,

151

and she had several strokes and couldn't talk or move. Doctor Trevellian had booked her for him to put a tube in her stomach to feed her, but he canceled this surgery because when she arrived at the hospital she was seriously ill with an infection. After treatment another surgeon said she should have her gall bladder removed because it was the cause of the infection but Doctor Trevellian sent her home. Five days later she came back even more seriously ill, and at that time Doctor Trevellian took out her gall bladder and stuck a tube in her stomach. Four days later the wound fell apart and she was taken back to surgery again. Right after the operation she died. His judgement in this case was very poor." Laxton sat back and waited.

"This patient had jaundice before," Trevellian said confidently, "And I cured her. At that time she was very ill, but she got better with antibiotics so I sent her home. When she came back, she was worse, so I took her gall bladder out, put a tube in her stomach and then the wound fell apart, and though I stitched her up, she expired."

"But you were told the best time to do the surgery was when she was better, but you ignored that advice," Rekuf said.

Trevellian shrugged.

"Don't you remember," Shickelhurtz said, "I talked to you about this case when she was readmitted. I told you that if you insisted on operating on her we should do the minimum possible to save her life. You took three hours and stuck a tube in her stomach. I told you several times during surgery that you needed to do as little as possible, but you insisted on putting a tube in the stomach."

"I don't think it took all that long to do the gastrostomy."

"You took an hour," Shickelhurtz said.

"Are you aware you have done five times as many of these gastrostomies as all the other surgeons in the hospital put together?" Laxton said.

"Well, most surgeons don't do sigmoidoscopies..."

"That's a lower bowel procedure and you know it. We're talking about the stomach," Laxton said.

"They don't do the same procedure as the gastroenterologists..."

"You're not answering the question. Do you want me to repeat it?" Rekuf said

"The patients come from my nursing home, and I can decide what happens to them," Trevellian said belligerently.

"These are very sick old people who can be done by the gastroenterologists under a local anesthetic, and you gave them all a general anesthetic," Rekuf said.

"I'm as good as anybody," Trevellian said.

"Here you admit a woman who has had jaundice on several occasions, positive tests for gall stone on several occasions, and you want to stick a tube in her stomach. How did you conclude she needed that?" Laxton asked.

A long discussion followed in which it became apparent that Trevellian was unable to justify any kind of surgery on the stomach.

"One thing's bothering me," Biggerstaff said. "You signed the consent form for surgery. Wouldn't it be better to get a family member to sign it?"

"This wasn't an elective thing. It was an emergency, and if you can't find a relative, usually two doctors can sign the consent form."

"Did two sign the form?" Biggerstaff said.

"I don't know. I'll have to look."

"You just signed it by yourself," Biggerstaff said.

"How did this patient become designated for no resuscitation?" Shickelhurtz said.

"My consultant did that."

After a long discussion it was clear Trevellian had written the order, but the family had not been consulted.

"Would you like to summarize this?" Rekuf said to Laxton.

"Here is an elderly lady admitted with a severe infection diagnosed as acute cholecystitis, with a surgical consultation recommending cholecystectomy and with medical clearances which were ignored. The patient was returned to a skilled nursing facility and was readmitted a few days later with peritonitis. At that time, against the advice and judgement of others, the gall bladder was removed and a tube placed in her stomach. The wound fell apart and she had to be re-operated on, at which time the tube was removed from her stomach, and after this operation she died."

"No one is recognizing I wouldn't do high risk cases anymore. I would limit myself to low risk cases. You can get complications with a hernia or appendix or hysterectomy. I've never had any, but you can get them. That's the kind of case I'd do."

"Today's meeting is closed," Rekuf said.

The failure to get the blind studies admitted irritated Laxton, but there was nothing he could do about the decision. It simply meant he'd have to go through many more days, because he'd have to get witnesses to support the Medical Executive Committee's viewpoint unless the hearing committee would vote for what was needed.

"What a mess," he said to Golliman after the meeting. "Now it

153

looks like we have to get witnesses called."

"It's all over for him," said Golliman. "Whatever you do, it's all over."

The following day Laxton got a call from Aysgarth to come up to the clinic. He went up at lunchtime.

"I heard by the grapevine we have a couple of problems on the Hearing Committee," Aysgarth said. "There's no doubt we can get a conviction and some suspension of privileges, but I want to see a unanimous decision to stop him."

"What do you suggest?" Laxton said.

"You'd better get witnesses to knock him off the surgical business. Here's a list of people to use as witnesses. Just remember, you didn't get it from me."

CHAPTER 25

TREVELLIAN BLUNDERS ON

During the following week Laxton was sitting in his office when the private line rang. He had given his private number out to few people, so he was surprised to hear Megan's voice on the phone. He knew Trevellian didn't have the number, but he couldn't remember during the wild weekend if he might have given it to her.

"It's me," she said.

"So I see," Laxton said. "What made you call?"

"You know there's a fourteen day delay in your proceedings, and guess what?"

"I can't guess," Laxton said.

"Herbie is going to be away for four days."

"Listen," Laxton said. "It's just too risky. I can't come down there when there are short periods like this. It's a chance I can't take."

"Who said anything about coming down here?" Megan said. "I'm not stupid either. I'll take a cab to a neutral point, and you can pick me up. That way the cab driver will only know I went to some shopping center, and you will control the rest."

"But where do you want to go?" Laxton asked.

"I want to come to your place. I know, I know, you're going to say it isn't good enough for me to see, but that's not it. I want to see you."

"You must have done this before," Laxton said. "It seems like you have it down pat."

"Laxy," she said, "you know very well I've done nothing like this before. You are the very first one I've ever been spending time with, and I know we can't do the kind of things we'd like to do together because of the risks, but I want to see you again, and soon."

As Laxton made the arrangements he thought he must be a sucker to risk so much, but he was obsessed with her and they certainly could do things together which were very interesting and ultimately very relaxing. He decided to follow her plan of action. He nonchalantly found out in the hospital that Trevellian was indeed going to be away. Rekuf told him he was relieved not to have to see Trevellian for a few days, because Trevellian had been coming to X-Ray to ask about every report sent to him, and it was a confirmation for Laxton Trevellian was going away because he had told a disinterested Rekuf about his trip.

"I've kept my mouth shut," Rekuf told Laxton, "but there have been some strange looking men spying on my place lately."

"Oh, come on, you're not going to tell me Herb has people watching your place."

"I'm going to tell you one of them was driving Trevellian's car."

Laxton had arranged for Megan to call him before she left for the center. She called from the center.

"How do you know we won't be followed, or that you haven't been followed? He could hire someone to do that," Laxton said.

Megan laughed. "I know I'm not being followed, and you're not being followed, but I do have something to tell you about one of your committee members and being followed. Trust me."

He did trust her, but didn't know why. He picked her up and took her to his condominium. He was sure they weren't followed.

"I hear the noose tightens," Megan said, flippantly.

"What's this about one of the committee members?" Laxton asked. He was put out.

"Herb thought that if he hired a couple of mean looking guys to watch over the committee chairman, it might frighten him. I told him he was crazy, and it was a waste of money. I asked him why he didn't hire someone to look on you or the Chief of Staff who has the poor eyesight and heart problem, but he said you were just a hired hand of the hospital and Golliman had no power. He said it would be dangerous to mess around with you because you were too square and too straight."

"Christ," Laxton said forcefully, "I need a drink."

"So do I," Megan said.

She had brought a small bag and put some things away in Laxton's bedroom, and then started idly to tidy the place, but not for long. They couldn't keep their hands off each other.

"I've never been an orgasmic person until I met you," Megan said.

"You're kidding."

Megan shook her head and smiled. "I'm not kidding."

"I've never had it so good," Laxton admitted.

After a meal they began to talk of things they might have been able to do if circumstances had been different.

Megan suddenly changed the subject. "I know we try to keep off the hearing business, but one thing you should know is that Herb is planning to call some witnesses in his defense and he'll probably parade them before the committee. You need to beware, because they're con artists, but the committee might listen to them."

156

Laxton didn't show surprise, but he felt it. He just couldn't see anyone of value testifying for Trevellian. "Where are they coming from?"

"You see, he has a lot of old cronies from outside the hospital, not on your staff, but they've been around a long time, and I guess he just gives them the charts and tells them he wants them to say everything he did was okay. Since he wasn't sure who might come he's got a list of witnesses as long as your arm."

"I'm tired of this business," Laxton said. "He really shouldn't be doing surgery."

"I know," Megan said. "You wouldn't believe it, but there's more than enough money pouring in from the Nursing Home."

"Do you have to phone him, or is he going to phone you?"

"I'm going to contact him on Monday from the nursing home. I can retrieve any messages here from my answering machine at home, but he won't call. Just let's relax and enjoy the time together."

The time spent with Megan was even better than it had been previously and Laxton realized it was not an environmental reason they got along so well. He wondered if she was really forward and others would consider her to be a hussy, but he dismissed any such ideas because of the comfort and tenderness she offered him.

When the committee reassembled to hear further evidence, Laxton presented a forty-five-year old lady who Trevellian operated on and performed a facelift. Trevellian was not a plastic surgeon. The poor woman had suffered a terrible infection following the surgery, had not been given antibiotics, and had ended up with tremendous scarring.

"Pus was coming out of the incisions and no cultures were performed. No antibiotics were given," Laxton said. "The husband complained to the hospital and is threatening to sue both the doctor and the hospital."

"The suit is not relevant to this hearing," Buck said.

"Doctor Trevellian, do you have any explanation?" Rekuf asked.

"She got her infection just before she left hospital, and it's true she had no antibiotic in the hospital."

"The charges from the suit allege no antibiotics were given for a week after infection developed," Laxton said.

"We can't admit things into the hearing which happened outside the hospital," Buck said.

"I don't know what the husband is complaining about. She was as ugly as hell before I started on her," Trevellian said.

157

Laxton had only wanted to bring the committee's attention to the type of work Trevellian was doing with skin problems and he followed up with a case which had happened in the hospital.

Laxton presented a ninety-year-old woman who had a skin graft performed on her heel, and a month later he removed part of her stomach and put a tube in the stomach. The skin graft had been done on an infected surface, and anyone with any medical knowledge knows quite well that a skin graft will not work if the area to which it is being applied is infected.

Trevellian was charged with grafting in the presence of an infection and cutting out pieces of the stomach where there turned out to be a benign tumor, sticking a tube in for no good reason, without the benefit of adequate investigation.

"No one seems to know the nursing home could be fined ten thousand dollars if this heel wasn't taken care of. It's true I had to operate on the heel twice. I did it the second time when I operated on the stomach."

"Does this patient have any evidence of hardening and narrowing of the arteries?" Rekuf said.

"Oh, yes. She had a stroke a year or two ago."

Rekuf's face took on the kind of expression one might see in a teacher about to lecture a small child about something that should have been obvious. "She had a stroke because she had greater than ninety per cent blockage in both her carotid arteries. A consultation from a neurologist says she had Alzheimer's and severe senile dementia. He also made recommendations, but the son thought her quality of life was so bad surgery wasn't warranted."

"She was doing fine on aspirin a couple of years later," Trevellian said.

"Don't you agree there is significant danger giving an anesthetic to a patient like this?"

"She survived the surgery."

"If you were going to give her an anesthetic for that, couldn't she have had something done to her carotid?"

"The family didn't want that."

Laxton was shuffling his feet and looking annoyed. "I find a considerable lack of credibility in your argument that her son wanted her stomach operated on when he had said he wanted no surgery previously."

"That was two years before."

"Did you have a consultation to reevaluate her two years later before you did this surgery?"

"Well, we knew she had all that stuff anyway." Trevellian looked quite smug as he said this.

"Don't you realize that if she had blockage to the arteries going to her brain there was probably blockage of the arteries going to the legs, and that's why the heel was falling apart," Laxton said.

"I think she was better after the operation."

"But the skin graft didn't take, did it?"

"No. It didn't take."

"Then how the hell could she be any better?" Laxton said in conclusion.

"Is the state pretty hard on the nursing home if you don't take these cases to surgery?" Yakamoto said.

"When I've been coerced by the nursing home I've responded, so I've had no trouble," Trevellian said.

"It's your nursing home. Who coerced you?" Laxton said.

"The Administrator."

"Is the Administrator a nurse, or medically qualified?"

"No."

"Have you ever turned a patient down for surgery who was in poor condition?" Yakamoto asked.

"At this time, I can't recall."

"Would you do such a case now?" Rekuf said.

"No. I'd get someone else to do it."

"What changed your mind? Why not do it anyway?"

"Some of this pressure has changed my mind."

"But what about the pressure from the state?"

"But I'd make someone else do it."

"This could have been a malignant tumor, couldn't it?" Laxton said.

"I suppose so."

"This is just another case where a ninety-year-old woman was brought into the hospital and subjected to surgery with virtually no indications. She was confused and had Alzheimer's disease and senile dementia and she signed her consent form herself. She couldn't have known what she was signing. In addition, she was overloaded with fluid after the procedure, and went into congestive heart failure and the anesthesiologist started emergency treatment so she didn't die in the recovery room. Also, Doctor Trevellian, you treated this patient with tobramycin and there were contraindications to using this drug."

"The pharmacist wrote the order," Trevellian said. "They know more about these things than I do. Eventually I stopped the drug."

Rekuf's face showed his disgust, a disgust which he was unable to keep out of his voice. "Let's go to the next case."

"This is an eighty-five-year old woman who had a series of admissions to this hospital. The first admission showed she had a polyp in the colon, but there was a suggestion of malignancy in the tip of the polyp. There was no malignancy in the colon itself. However, from then on it was referred to as cancer of the colon. Her second admission five years later was because she was dehydrated, and a year after that she was admitted again and a tube was placed in her stomach for feeding. A month later she was admitted because she had an infection in the bladder and kidneys. Doctor Trevellian said he had done a hemi-colectomy on the patient, which generally means half the colon was removed. However, he really only took out four inches of colon. The dehydration admission showed no dehydration at all. The admission where the tube was placed in the stomach has a note on the chart which reads, 'Patient confused, does not respond when spoken to, has mittens on both hands. She signed her consent form.' The reason given for making an incision and putting the tube in the stomach was that family members asked for a gastrostomy. There was no reason given for the procedure. The last admission for bladder and kidney problems showed a germ sensitive only to furadantin and not sensitive to tobramycin. Doctor Trevellian ordered tobramycin."

Laxton's summary was succinct and clearly had made an impression on the committee.

"Let me tell Doctor Laxton this woman didn't come from my nursing home at first. I did a great operation. I got all the cancer out-"

Laxton interrupted. "Didn't one of the other doctors tell you he could get that out through an instrument without any cutting surgery?"

"Certainly he said that. But I said no, because it was my patient, so I cut open her abdomen and took a big piece of bowel out."

Laxton was getting irritated. It seemed obvious to him that Trevellian was totally incompetent.

"You see, Doctor Trevellian, she was admitted with dizziness, vertigo, headache, right earache, and you wrote she had Meniere's disease, heart disease, high blood pressure, possible stroke, and finally a polyp in the lower colon. What kind of tests did you do for all these other serious illnesses this poor woman had?"

"I looked at the polyp through an instrument and I did a barium enema and I had a gastroenterologist see her."

160

"But, Dr. Trevellian, you didn't do any tests for all these other complaints, did you?"

"No, I felt her problem was her polyp and I wanted to cut it out."

Shickelhurtz became agitated. He stood up and in an angry voice he said, "You never did a rectal examination on this patient either. You also deferred a pelvic examination. Explain."

"I did them," Trevellian asserted, "I just didn't write it down."

"Your operative report says you did a left hemicolectomy, but the pathology report describes this as an anterior resection and that's what it was, wasn't it?" Laxton said.

"No. I did a hemicolectomy."

"Then how come in your discharge summary you wrote that you did a low anterior resection?"

"Oh, all right," Trevellian said with resignation. "Call it whatever you want."

"What did you bill for? You get more for a hemicolectomy," Rekuf said.

"I billed for a hemicolectomy," Trevellian said. "I think these terms are just colloquialisms."

"The pathology report also said this was a polyp, and there was no malignancy in the sigmoid colon which you took out, and yet you labeled this woman with cancer of the colon from that moment on."

Trevellian shrugged. "I took her into my nursing home and no one was going to see her but me after that, so it didn't really matter. I didn't have any X-Rays done for putting the tube in her stomach because I didn't need any. They'd have shown she couldn't swallow barium anyway, so why try."

"Doctor Trevellian, this patient was brought to the hospital because she had cut her arm about three days before your admission, and at that time she had barium studies done. She swallowed the barium just fine, and the findings were normal. Will you comment on that?" Laxton said.

"Well," Buck said, after a pause, "do you have any comment Doctor Trevellian."

"None."

"You'd better go to the next case," Buck said.

"This was a ninety-year-old patient who had a tube put in her stomach through an incision because her family asked for it. Yes, another one. There was no other reason given for the procedure," Laxton said.

"This old lady couldn't swallow anything, and the nurses couldn't get a tube down her throat," Trevellian said.

"But she was admitted with a tube down her throat," Laxton said loudly. "You wrote that yourself."

"Also," Rekuf said, "she had an X-Ray with barium a week before, and the report says the barium passed easily into the stomach."

"Don't you recall this examination?" Laxton asked Trevellian.

"No, I don't recall this, but I think you can induce a patient to do anything you want, but you can't sit around looking after the patient all day. I stick a tube in and they can just shoot the foodstuff in through the tube directly into the stomach."

"Had this patient lost weight?" Sanders asked.

"I don't weigh patients," Trevellian said.

Biggerstaff looked sympathetic. "Perhaps Doctor Trevellian didn't know about the X-Ray."

"Why wouldn't he?" Shickelhurtz said. He still looked annoyed. "The whole chart is given to him on admission. The inpatient notes are on the right side of the folder, and the outpatient notes are on the left side."

"I never look at the left side," Trevellian said. "I thought those were social workers' notes or something like that, and weren't very important."

"All the copies of the X-Ray reports, whether inpatient or outpatient, are copied and sent to your office, aren't they?" Rekuf said.

"Yes. Sure."

"Why don't you look at this chart?" Shickelhurtz said, persisting.

Trevellian took the chart and studied it a few minutes. "I guess there are some things I'm just not too aware of as far as the hospital procedures are concerned."

"We just can't pursue this case any longer. I'm sure there are no more questions. If the committee will allow, I'm going to ask Doctor Laxton to get on with the next case," Rekuf said.

"This is an eighty-five-year old patient from the nursing home. This case is an absolute disgrace--"

"Doctor Laxton," Buck said, "I don't think you should express opinions like that. Just give the committee the details and let them decide whether it's improper or proper handling."

"This is another patient Doctor Trevellian brought in to place a feeding tube in the stomach. However, when she was admitted she was jaundiced and was found to have a stone in the bile duct. The gastroenterologist drained the duct and the jaundice disappeared.

The gastroenterologist felt that the duct should be looked at through an instrument, and that the stone should be removed through the instrument if it was still there. The patient was a high risk to take to surgery for other reasons, and everyone in contact with her thought she might die if open surgery was done. Doctor Trevellian disagreed and changed his surgical booking now to removal of the gall bladder instead of putting a tube in the stomach, refused to listen to the gastroenterologist, and ordered the patient to surgery. On her way to the operating room she went into heart failure and his surgery was canceled. Three days later he took the patient to surgery when there was still fluid in the chest from the heart failure and the surgery showed no stone in the duct and the gall bladder was normal but was removed and then a tube was put in her stomach as well and brought out through the incision. The patient ultimately had her wound burst open and had to be operated on again and this time the tube was taken out of the stomach, and she expired after surgery."

Trevellian leapt to his feet. "It's a lie, it's a lie," he shouted his face becoming red. "Yes, she died, but I had X-Rays, CAT scans, and all sorts of tests. I canceled the surgery when she wasn't fit for it, and she only had a little bit of heart failure anyway, so I rescheduled her when she was fit. The gastroenterologist didn't know what he was talking about and neither did the internist. He's a young black guy who came from an HMO originally. I shouldn't have canceled the surgery the first time around. She had great care and the family was pleased."

"You were uncomfortable with the internist?" Rekuf said in a quiet way.

"He was a young black guy who's in Zinfeld's group and he knows nothing."

"You said he was with an HMO," Laxton said. "He was an Associate Professor at the University, wasn't he?"

"He was black and ignorant."

"I don't think that's the way to refer to a certified specialist with that background," Sanders said.

"Mr. Buck criticized my characterization of the case," Laxton said, "but I don't hear him saying anything about the way this specialist was described."

"I think there's far too much hearsay stuff going on," Buck said. "Although it can be admitted, I think you should refrain from such comments unless they can be proved."

"There wasn't anyone who would give this woman an anesthetic when she was going into heart failure the first time around," Shickelhurtz said.

"Doctor Trevellian, did you discuss this case with all these people before you canceled surgery?" Yakamoto asked.

"Yes. I did."

"So you knew she wasn't fit for surgery, but you didn't think she was a risk?"

"Oh, no. I thought she was a risk, but she was in optimal condition at that time."

Trevellian had taken on a lecturing posture and stared at the committee members unashamedly.

"If you take a patient to surgery and they die during surgery, then that's the greatest risk of all," Yakamoto said. "We have the anesthesiologist telling us he wouldn't risk an anesthetic."

"The way I do surgery there is almost no risk, but delaying until she seemed better was a bad idea."

"The day you wanted to do surgery she was put in the Intensive Care Unit and on a respirator," Laxton said. "Not too many people thought she would survive even if the surgery was canceled. She did. Everyone else wrote the surgery might be a terminal event for her."

"I don't remember that," Trevellian said.

"Look at the chart," Rekuf snapped.

"Has anyone got any more questions?" Buck said.

There was silence. All the committee members sat staring down at the table they were seated round.

"The committee needs to decide whether they wish to hear witnesses relating to the cases, or whether they have heard sufficient evidence to make a decision," Laxton said.

"If you will let the committee meet alone for a few minutes, we'll let you know," Buck said.

After waiting outside the room for five minutes, Laxton, Trevellian and Golliman were called back into the room.

"We need to hear what witnesses have to say," Rekuf said.

CHAPTER 26

ON THE HOT SEAT

"The time is six twenty-five p.m. and we are ready to continue the hearing in the matter of Dr. Trevellian," Buck said.

The committee members were seated around an oblong table with Rekuf at the head and Buck seated next to him. Laxton was on one side and Trevellian on the other and Golliman was relegated to a chair behind everyone. The court stenographer had her own desk with the equipment set out on it.

Laxton drew attention to the fact that there had been errors in the transcripts, and asked for corrections. One related to something Trevellian had said and Buck looked at Trevellian and said, "Do you recall this Doctor Trevellian?"

"No, I don't," Trevellian said, "and I can see no reason for keeping all these people waiting while we go over this matter. I object to the untimely way you're all conducting this hearing, wasting my time and preventing me from leaving town ever since this business began. I'm a prisoner in my own house, waiting for you to decide when the next session will be. I haven't been able to get away at all."

Laxton knew better than to dispute that, and he sat silently while Buck addressed the matter.

"This hearing will not go on forever," Buck said. "But the evidence has to be heard, and you have to have an opportunity to respond."

"What I want everyone to know is I cannot leave town. I cannot go on vacation or do anything until the hearing is completed. I'm under great strain. I haven't been able to leave my home, and my wife is trapped there and miserable as well, and she's not getting any pleasure."

"In any court of law," Buck said, "there are certain protocols to follow, and this is a similar process. One thing comes to mind, and that is I admonished you previously about trying to talk to members of this committee outside this room, and it has been brought to my attention that you have discussed certain matters with committee members outside this room. I'm telling you again not to do that. The next matter of business relates to witnesses, and I would ask you if you've received the list of witnesses Dr. Laxton is going to call."

I have, and I object to Doctor Silason who is biased against me.

I have an abrasive relationship with him, and I object to him being called."

"Let me tell you that the Medical Executive Committee can call whomsoever they want to call, whether they are biased against you or not."

"We shall also call Doctor Lime, who is a partner of Doctor Silason, and I note Doctor Trevellian has referred cases to him," Laxton said.

"Yes, but who knows what Silason may have told Lime to say," Trevellian said.

"In that case, it maybe necessary to call several surgeons," Laxton said, "just to be fair to Doctor Trevellian."

"Don't you have anything better to do with your time?" Trevellian said, raising his voice.

"Doctor Trevellian, when will you give us your list of witnesses? We need to know whom you will call on your behalf," Buck said.

"I won't call any, why should I?"

"There are one or two more cases to consider before we go to witnesses. The first one is a patient who was admitted to rule out a heart attack. He was ninety-six, and was put in the intensive care unit at a weekend. He had severe irregularity of the pulse, and Doctor Trevellian never bothered to see the patient, but he did order drugs over the telephone all weekend," Laxton said.

"I knew him for six years, so I didn't need to come to the hospital to see him," Trevellian said.

"Didn't you realize you gave drugs which caused his blood pressure to fall, and he was rescued by another physician who was in this hospital seeing another patient?" Laxton asked sharply.

"He didn't die, anyway," Trevellian said, smiling.

"I have to say that's true," Biggerstaff observed.

"You discharged the patient from the hospital when he was unstable. He died outside the hospital two days later."

"The charges reflect Dr. Trevellian was called before the Quality Assurance Committee here in the hospital," Shickelhurtz said.

"Yes," Laxton said. "Two things come out of that. First he was warned, and secondly he was given the exact protocol to follow on each future admission of this kind."

"Doctor Trevellian, is this correct?" Rekuf said.

"Essentially so." Trevellian said.

"This brings me to the next case," Laxton said. "But I should remind the committee Dr. Trevellian was told that the patient must be kept in hospital at least twenty-four hours and he was given a list of tests that should be done. He admitted a fifty-two-year old woman the day after his appearance before the Quality Assurance Committee. She was said to have suffered a possible heart attack, but she was discharged in fifteen hours. The tests were not completed, and some of the results were not back at the time of her discharge."

"This patient was a Medicaid patient," Trevellian said. "So I treated her like a Medicaid patient, and we didn't need to keep her as long. I was told the hospital doesn't want Medicaid patients coming here or admitted here. They don't have any money."

"If they are to be transferred somewhere else there is a minimum wait of three days," Laxton said. "You know that very well, Doctor Trevellian."

"We don't get paid much for Medicaid patients, and neither does the hospital, so I examined her and she said she was okay. I called an internist and he agreed to discharge her."

"There was nothing in the chart about this," Laxton said.

"I have a letter. I have a letter." Trevellian sounded jubilant. "There was no coercion either. He wrote it without coercion. It says, 'At the request of Dr. Trevellian I am making a note regarding a conversation we had on the care of patient -- relating to her admission two years ago. He telephoned me to tell me he was going to discharge the patient, and I raised no objection.'

So he discharged her, not me. She's just a Medicaid patient anyway. I wouldn't have cared if she'd stayed another six days. I'd just have billed Medicaid for whatever I could get."

"Wasn't the letter written after you heard the case was coming up before the Quality Assurance Committee?" Laxton said.

"I asked him to write the letter so the Quality Assurance Committee couldn't sanction me because he was the one who discharged the patient."

"You haven't written anything about this in the chart, have you?"

"She was only Medicaid, so I didn't write much," Trevellian said.

Laxton expected someone on the committee to raise the issue of the standard of care received by this patient, but it seemed everyone was ignoring this.

"Why should there be any difference between the treatment received by a Medicaid patient and any other patient admitted here?" Laxton said after a short period of silence.

"That's hospital policy. They don't want Medicaid patients here.

It's nothing to do with me."

"The policy is and always has been that a patient admitted with a suspected heart attack must be admitted, and can be transferred when stable, but cannot be thrown out," Laxton said.

"That's the law also," Buck said.

"You're correct," Laxton said.

"I didn't know. My experience has been that other patients who were Medicaid were discharged. This one of mine just slipped through the woodwork. I go as to what is hospital policy."

"Do you really believe you can treat Medicaid patients in this fashion?" Laxton asked.

"I'm going to rule he answered the question," Buck said. "He believed Medicaid patients should be discharged as soon as possible."

"It's not really his fault then, is it?" Biggerstaff said, looking at Laxton.

"If you think it's all right to treat Medicaid patients this way, and if you think that written protocols shouldn't be followed, and if you think that a written order by Doctor Trevellian was written by someone else and that there was no reason for Doctor Trevellian to follow guidelines verbally given to him by the Quality Assurance Committee the day before he admitted this patient, then I think you might conclude he could be excused," Laxton replied.

"I think this should be a warning to all of us. People are people, whatever their insurance might be," Rekuf said. "I wouldn't have thought there was much to say about a case like this."

"Nor would I," Yakamoto said.

"Is your first witness ready?" Rekuf asked Laxton.

The first witness, Doctor Clearsil, was a certified specialist in obstetrics and gynecology. He was rather a square sort of man physically, and his face had a rugged appearance, with fine lines on his face, showing he had been around awhile. He was given a seat opposite Trevellian.

"I believe you reviewed this case for us," Laxton said, handing him the chart.

"I have."

"Would you comment on the case for the committee?"

"Actually, as I view these cases, I think I can make the same point on both, as there are many similarities, so we can look at them together. The way I see them, there are two issues involved. One is the procedure itself, and the other one comprises the factors of age and the medical condition of the patient. The preoperative evaluations for this condition, regardless of the patient's age, were inadequate based on present day knowledge of what stress incontinence is, what conditions have to be ruled out, and the type of procedure that has to be performed to correct the condition involved. If I was going to perform this operation, I would need to make sure the patient didn't have a neurological disorder, that she doesn't have urge incontinence or overflow incontinence. These questions have to be answered and they weren't. If I felt this patient had stress incontinence, I would choose an operation from above. You can't accomplish this by doing what Doctor Trevellian did. I would certainly not take a patient like either one of these to surgery without a cardiac evaluation."

"The second case showed a bladder almost always full of urine."

"Wouldn't this be a contraindication to doing a suspension operation?" Laxton said.

"Of course it would."

"Listen Joe," Trevellian said, "if you have a patient with her uterus hanging down her thigh, what would be your operation of choice?"

"I would have to know what kind of stress incontinence she had, and I would have to have an opinion to make sure this person was able to withstand a major operation."

"Look at this picture," Trevellian said. "Here's what she had."

"Stop," said Buck. "What is the picture, and where did it come from?"

"It's another of my patients who had the same--"

"I object to the introduction of photographs of another patient, because we have no evidence they represent the same problem," Laxton said.

"This is on another patient and not relevant to this case," Buck said.

"Doctor, I felt the work up you did on this patient didn't justify the procedure," Clearsil said. "Did you know the type of incontinence she had?"

"The patient was wetting her pants all the time," Trevellian said.

"How did you know she didn't have a neurological bladder?"

"From the result," Trevellian said.

"Is that the way you do it all the time, see if it works?"

"Yes."

"You need to establish the cause before you do the operation," Clearsil said.

"Do you get all these consultations, because if you don't, you're

169

just like me?" Trevellian asked.

"You need to separate the cases, because one had Alzheimer's disease and the other became confused after surgery," Laxton said.

"She doesn't have Alzheimer's disease," Trevellian said, "it was the husband who told me she had Alzheimer's. And the results were great."

"When I looked at these cases, I didn't look at the result. I'm glad they turned out all right, because if you did a hundred cases like this I'll guarantee you wouldn't get good results on most of them," Clearsil said. "I look at these cases in the light of today's knowledge. Have they been properly evaluated? I conclude your cases weren't."

"But you feel there is an increased risk going through an incision from above, so what I did is better?"

"You're not listening. What did the patient have? What was the diagnosis?"

"Water was running out of the bladder and the bladder neck was not held up."

"How do you know that? What tests did you do?"

"I stuck my fingers in the vagina and pushed up and she was dry."

"That's not an acceptable test and you know it. There are a lot of simple tests I do on my patients all time."

"But I got a good result," Trevellian said.

"You seem to have missed the whole point," Buck said. "There is, as I understand it, the question of why you operated on these patients at all. What Doctor Clearsil is saying is that you didn't have a good reason to do what you did."

"Do you think Doctor Trevellian should be doing gynecological surgery?" Laxton asked Clearsil.

"I can only tell you what I know based on these cases, and based on these I would have real doubts about whether he should be doing this kind of surgery or not."

"Okay. Thank you," Buck said.

"The next witness is Doctor Silason," Laxton said.

"Are you going to call any other surgeons?" Trevellian said.

"Oh, yes."

After Doctor Silason had been recognized as a certified specialist and expert, Laxton asked him to comment on the cases he had reviewed.

"The first patient had surgery canceled, and then it was done later. She was discharged with everything going wrong, on the wrong diet and with a high temperature."

"How do you feel about placing a tube in the stomach?" Laxton asked.

"This woman didn't need a tube in her stomach. She was not malnourished. She was obese and in fact had gained weight. Why cut her open to feed her through a tube?"

"There was no consultation with gastroenterologists before surgery was done. Do you think this was incorrect?"

"We must all work together these days, and it's my practice to have them see such patients prior to surgery," Silason said.

"What do you conclude about the patient who had the skin graft?"

"There was no way this graft could have taken with all the infection present and without the use of antibiotics. I would not have chosen to apply a biological dressing to an area like this. As far as her stomach operation is concerned, there was no work up, no indications for what was done to her, and then a tube, which was not indicated, was stuck in her stomach and brought out through the incision. You could almost predict disaster."

"If you wanted to get a stomach tube put in, would you have it done by the gastroenterologist rather than doing full blown surgery?" Shickelhurtz asked.

"Yes, I would. It's preferable and a lot easier on the patient."

"You are ridiculous," Trevellian said, "I'm sure all the consultants in the world would have agreed with me."

"You're not listening," Silason said. "In this day and age we work together, we work with others. We must give the patients options where they exist, and use consultants when they do a procedure we do but do it with less trauma."

"No one knew about the infected heel until later," Trevellian said. "The necrosis was dry necrosis, so nothing was lost by putting on a graft."

"Do you agree with that?" Buck asked Silason.

"I believe that statement shows the doctor is not up to date on knowledge regarding necrosis, dry or wet, and knows nothing about modern methods of skin grafting. His methods are below practice standards in the community."

"What about the patient who had the colon operation?" Laxton said.

"This is the lady who had a tube put in her stomach, a gastrostomy, because the family wanted one. That is never a reason for a gastrostomy.

171

The patient should have been seen by the gastroenterologists."

"She was seen a year ago by one," Trevellian said.

"That is not appropriate."

"Would you comment on the use of tobramycin as an antibiotic?"

"That was quite serious. Doctor Trevellian gave the antibiotic to a patient with renal failure, which became much worse as a result of the antibiotic."

"Would you comment on the jaundiced patient with the common duct stone?" Laxton said.

"This patient was subject entirely to the whims of Doctor Trevellian. He didn't avail himself of the advice of other consultant specialists who could have prevented the surgery. I don't think he's kept up with the times. I don't think this patient was ever a candidate for surgery. With today's technology such stones can be removed through an instrument."

"Do you think Doctor Trevellian should be doing general surgery, Doctor Silason?"

"I reviewed four charts thoroughly. We all get older, and I feel Doctor Trevellian is in decline. He has not kept up to date but could perhaps be rehabilitated if he was to take three years training as a resident in surgery, or if he took a two-year family practice residency he could have his primary skills brought up to par. He's not capable of writing orders on patients, not capable of performing surgery on patients, and shouldn't be assisting in surgery."

"I knew you'd be biased," Trevellian shouted. "It's a waste of everyone's time you're being here. Get out you bastard. Get out."

"That's quite enough of that," Buck said. "I'm the Hearing Officer, and I will make those decisions. If you can show the committee that the doctor is biased, feel free to do so."

"Let me ask you, Silason, do you recall me assisting you in surgery?"

"I don't remember you ever assisting me in surgery."

"Let me remind you I told you how to do the case because I knew and you didn't. I didn't agree with what you were doing and I shouted at you."

"I don't remember ever working with you," Silason said adamantly.

"Well, that's why you're biased. I may have old fashioned mannerisms and talk to myself and look slow and bumbling, but I'm not in decline."

172

"I wish to state I don't know Doctor Trevellian personally, we don't work together, and as I said previously, I don't base my opinions on a doctor's personality or whether he talks to himself or not or whether he appears bumbling. I read the charts and it's from the evidence in the charts one can determine a doctor's knowledge, his degree of knowledge, and his state of knowledge. On that basis I judged Herbert Trevellian incompetent."

"It's very late," Buck said, "I think everyone is tired. Doctor Silason has given us a lot to think about and we need to set up the next session."

Trevellian jumped to his feet, his face red with anger. "I will tell you this," he shouted, "I shall bring witnesses and show you what fools all these people are."

"I think you intended to all along, didn't you," said Laxton.

CHAPTER 27

MORE TROUBLE FOR TREVELLIAN

The atmosphere was tense. Everyone now took the same seat round the oblong table in the small room with three buff colored walls and floor to ceiling glass at the one end which contained the only other door in the room, and led to the outside. It was rarely used and the glass looked out only on shrubs, which obscured any view. This increased the claustrophobic atmosphere of the room. Laxton's witness was directed to a seat next to him, and he faced Trevellian across the table.

Dr. Frizman, the gastroenterologist, was a slender young man of thirty with dark, curly hair and a pale sharp-featured face. He appeared nervous as the session started and he was qualified as an expert witness.

"Give us your opinion about the charges on the case where the lady had jaundice," Laxton said.

"The first charge that non surgical treatment was inadequately pursued is correct. From the time we were consulted we continued to bring up time and time again doing everything through an instrument. The second charge that looking in the duct through an instrument would have been proper treatment in this case is correct. The literature is replete with such an approach. I trained to do these procedures at Yale and at the university in Japan. My complication rate is zero, and the success rate is ninety per cent. There are other doctors who also do these procedures, and they are qualified and available. I would have handled this case quite differently."

"Is there anyone in your group besides you who does this procedure?" Rekuf said.

"No. There is not."

"I didn't know he was the only one who did the procedure," Trevellian said.

"But you wrote in the chart you discussed this with Doctor Frizman," Laxton said. "In any case, how many of this kind of case have you had in the hospital in the last six years?"

"Fifteen common duct stones, I guess," Trevellian said.

"And you did surgery on all of them?"

"Yes. There was no one doing stuff through an instrument until a year ago."

"I have been doing them here for the past five years," Frizman said.

Trevellian shuffled his feet and leaned forward looking at Frizman. "It's all the complications they have, and I have to operate and straighten them out."

"Doctor Frizman, tell us your complication rate again, would you," Laxton said.

"The national average is six percent, but I haven't had any yet."

"They are the only people I can use," Trevellian said. "There aren't any others in this hospital."

"That's not true," Frizman said.

"There aren't any practicing here."

"That's not true," Frizman said again.

"You say there are other gastroenterologists?" Shickelhurtz said.

"Yes, there are two and--"

"And they are both active and come to this hospital?"

"They do, and they are very good."

"Do you use general anesthetics for this procedure?" Shickelhurtz asked.

"No. We don't."

"Doctor Trevellian, it appears you were concerned about the complications of polyp removal on the lady you operated on with the colon problem. That is, if you had let Doctor Frizman do the endoscopic procedure," Doctor Yakamoto said. "But this patient was at great risk for a general anesthetic. Can you comment on that, Herb?"

"Well, I use these gastroenterologists all the time, and I was worried about a complication."

"You got one anyway," Rekuf said. "What about putting tubes in the stomach? Do you have a high complication rate from that, Doctor Frizman?"

"No, we don't."

"I sent you a case like that today, didn't I?" Trevellian said.

"You sent a patient who may or may not need a gastrostomy," Frizman said.

"What is your point?" Buck asked, looking directly at Trevellian.

"It was Doctor Silason who said I was never involved in gastrostomies with the gastroenterologists. I have come around to accepting their opinion."

"In other words you are telling us that you're willing to accept different methods of treatment that--"

"That I might not have accepted before. And one question Doctor Frizman, are you aware that the surgical method I use for gastrostomy has a very low complication rate?"

"I don't know how that relates to me," Frizman said. "The cases you should be doing your procedure on are quite different from those we do. We do our cases mostly on elderly people who are high risk cases, and the literature supports the way we do them on a population of this age."

"Well, I'm doing them on the same population," Trevellian said.

Laxton looked up toward the heavens and rolled his eyes, and even Biggerstaff shook his head. Rekuf could be heard muttering to himself, and other committee members shuffled uncomfortably.

Laxton cleared his throat and said, "Based on what you know, Doctor Frizman, do you believe Doctor Trevellian is capable of this kind of work?"

"Just a minute," Buck said. "How many charts have you reviewed?"

"I reviewed all the charts I was given, but I don't think it's fair to Doctor Trevellian for me to comment on the basis of a few charts, and I don't think it's fair to the committee."

"I think that's fine," Biggerstaff said.

"Do you want to comment on my other cases you've handled with me over the last five years? You've seen my practice and you were here when Dr. Silason made his statement. Do you think I know what I'm doing?"

"I think Doctor Silason criticized the method of practice more than anything," Laxton said.

"I shall allow Doctor Trevellian's question anyway," Buck said. "I think Doctor Frizman's opinion might be valuable."

"I'm willing to give an opinion on over a hundred cases of many kinds I've worked with him on over six years. In the past he's done what he wanted to do many times, and I often felt it was not the correct course of action. When he listened to us I felt he had as good knowledge as many family practitioners, so to single him out would be unfair. Many times I disagreed with him vehemently, but it was his patient and he has a license to practice, so I couldn't do anything. I found him very difficult to work with."

"It was suggested some updating might be an appropriate course of action," Laxton said. "Do you think that's a valid observation?"

"Probably so."

"Let me ask a question," Buck said. "When you talk about disagreements are you talking about medically uncalled for decisions?"

"That's what I'm talking about."

176

"Was this on numerous occasions?"

"On very many occasions."

"More than with other physicians?"

"Other physicians worked in a symbiotic relationship with us. Doctor Trevellian often didn't, and I think that was detrimental to his patients."

"Would you say then that other physicians worked within community standards, and Doctor Trevellian didn't?" Laxton said.

"At times."

"Did you ever feel pressured to support decisions you disagreed with?"

"Sometimes I did. More recently I've been more aggressive."

The witness was excused without further questions and Buck called a short break.

After the break Laxton called his next witness, Doctor Sinclair. Sinclair was a young man with a handlebar moustache and rather long hair, but he had a distinguished past record, and his rather casual appearance hid a very sharp mind.

After his credentials had been established, Laxton asked him about the gall bladder duct stone case, and the circumstances in which he was involved.

"A great deal has been said about this patient being a high risk case. That's what anesthesia said. How did you feel about the case?"

"I felt this was a high enough risk almost anything should be done to avoid surgery," Sinclair said.

"Did you discuss this with Doctor Trevellian?"

"I told him the patient should be managed without surgery if at all possible, but he said he was taking the patient to surgery despite my opinion."

"Have you ever felt pressured by Doctor Trevellian to just clear a patient for surgery rather than do a full evaluation?"

"He can only answer based on these cases, not others he may have handled," Buck said.

"I definitely felt pressured on cases I handled in this series," Sinclair said.

"Did you get pressure like this from other surgeons?" Laxton said.

"No, I didn't."

"Wouldn't you say that your job is to get patients ready for surgery and see them through the post operative period?" Trevellian said.

177

"Yes, I would."

"So it wouldn't be wrong for me to ask you to get the patient ready for surgery?"

"That's correct. But I want to add something. The fact is, I knew a colleague of mine thought this patient shouldn't go to surgery."

"Haven't you been in a situation where your colleagues felt one way and a surgeon felt another, and the surgeon proceeded?"

"Yes."

"I'm fed up with this whole process," Biggerstaff said suddenly. "I see what the doctor means when he says it's unfair. I have a practice, and I don't like this whole thing, and I feel like I want out."

"No one likes this," Shickelhurtz said. "But we do have a responsibility to patients and to the doctor here, and I, for one, will not do him the disservice of walking out."

Biggerstaff began to pout and the others stared at him.

"I want him to stay," Trevellian said.

"Let's get on with this," Rekuf said.

"Doctor Sinclair, what do you think of the management of the patient with the rapid heart beat who was treated over the telephone?" Laxton said.

"He thought the weekend resident had seen the patient, but the one problem I had with this was Doctor Trevellian gave an order after nine at night and must have known at that time that the weekend resident was not coming to see the patient. He issued five orders over the phone and was making assessments on a patient he hadn't seen that day."

"I know of a case where the Chief of Surgery treated an arrhythmia over the phone and he didn't come in and see the patient," Trevellian said.

"What other doctors do has nothing to do with this hearing," Buck said. "There should be disciplinary--"

"I'm saying it's an acceptable standard of care," Trevellian interrupted Buck.

"If you want to ask the witness that question, go ahead, but you can't just be making statements. In fact, I'll ask him. Is it within the standard of care not to see your patient or not to ask if another physician saw your patient for you while you're giving orders throughout the course of the day?"

"It's all very well to treat the patient over the telephone if they're doing all right, but I come back to the same thing which is that the patient wasn't seen at all that day," Sinclair said.

178

"I think he's saying the patient should be seen daily," Biggerstaff said.

"You bet," Sinclair said. "It's also in our bylaws."

"Would it also fall below an acceptable standard of care if the doctor didn't ask if another physician had seen his patient that day?" Buck said.

"In my humble opinion I'd say yes, because of the whole series of phone orders that went on all day."

"I was watching television, sixty minutes actually, and I forgot to ask," Trevellian said. "Anyway, the five orders were innocuous."

"I would say four were active intervention orders," Sinclair said.

"Are you trying to say changing the verapamil--"

"He's seen your orders and answered your question, and I'm telling you as the Hearing Officer you might not agree with the answer but you can take that up in your summation, not waste everyone's time now."

"The patient was ninety-six," Rekuf said. "Do you think it's all right to treat a ninety-six-year old over the phone, and in fact would you have done that?"

"I don't think that's an appropriate question, Mister Chairman," Buck said.

"I want him to answer," Trevellian said.

Buck shrugged.

"If I had seen the patient that day I might have treated him over the telephone," Sinclair said. "The key is I would want to see the setting he was in, and how he looked."

"So you wouldn't blindly treat the patient," Rekuf said.

"Definitely not."

"Did he see the patient the day before?" Shickelhurtz said.

"The patient was admitted by the Emergency Room physician, and he didn't see the patient," Laxton said.

"Another problem I had was that Doctor Trevellian wrote a note he dated the day he didn't see the patient, to make people believe he had seen the patient that day," Sinclair said.

"Falsifying the records," Laxton said.

"That comment wasn't called for," Buck said. "Let's go to the next case."

"This next patient was the one who was admitted the day after Doctor Trevellian had been told what protocols must be followed to rule out a heart attack and failed to follow them. Did you review this chart Doctor Sinclair?"

"Yes."

"Did you see the patient was discharged in fifteen hours, and do you recollect he wrote a retrospective note on the last case? Were you aware he asked the consultant to write a retrospective note on this patient?"

"Yes, I saw that."

"Did you see the consultant suggested several tests and Doctor Trevellian ignored them?"

"Yes, I saw that."

"Also, the consultant saw the patient the day of discharge, and wrote notes saying there were still tests to be done, and then Doctor Trevellian discharged the patient and in fact wrote the discharge order himself. The tests weren't done."

"That's correct. He did that."

"Therefore he broke all the rules for care. Are you aware Medicaid patients must be treated the same way as anyone else, and the rules can't be bent because they're Medicaid."

"Everything you've said is correct, and all the rules were broken."

"I want you to read the consultant's letter," Trevellian said. "Then you'll see I had every right to discharge the patient, and in any case this was a Medicaid patient."

"As you well know," Sinclair said, "it doesn't matter whether the patient pays cash or is a Medicaid patient. If they're sick, they must be treated."

"I want to shoot some rapid questions to Doctor Sinclair," Rekuf said. "In the case of several consultants, was Doctor Trevellian given the feelings of all the consultants?"

"I was frustrated and angry about the case you're talking about. I don't know whether the others told him what should be done, but I did."

"Secondly, does he stay within the confines of his expertise when compared with other physicians?"

"It's my feeling he frequently extends beyond his capabilities, trying to be an expert in everything. I think if he was in Central Africa or somewhere it might be very appropriate for him to be doing what he's doing, but here in southern California where there are all sorts of specialists, it isn't. I found it frustrating and dangerous that he doesn't know when to step back and ask for help."

"I want to say something," Trevellian said. "I don't think any of these people are competent."

"I want to see what kind of courses you take to stay up to date, Doctor Trevellian," Rekuf said. "Please bring what courses or instruction you have taken over the last five years, and we want to see the type of courses, because you've been doing almost everything."

"Have you asked for the courses of all the physicians in this hospital or on this committee?" Trevellian asked aggressively.

"You are answering a question with a question," Rekuf said. "We can't force you to bring the material, but it would be in your interests to do so."

"I want to know if Doctor Sinclair is aware I had a surgical consultation on the case he just discussed, and is he aware that the surgeon agreed with me?" Trevellian said.

"Yes, I'm aware of that surgeon and his opinion, and I've seen you use him many times, and I've never seen him disagree with anything you ever said or wanted to do"

"If no one has any more questions, I think we can excuse Doctor Sinclair," Rekuf said.

"Let's try to get through the other surgeons," Buck said.

Laxton told the committee he didn't wish to go through the whole series of cases again, and with the permission of the chairman and the Hearing Officer he would have each make a brief statement. All had reviewed the cases and Doctor Silason's testimony. This brought a look of relief to the faces of some members.

The first surgical witness was a partner of Doctor Silason, and Trevellian alleged he was biased.

"You have to show that to convince us," Buck said.

Trevellian didn't respond.

"Does Doctor Trevellian send patients to you for surgery?" Laxton said.

"Yes. I've had at least eight or ten in the past two months," the surgeon said.

No one commented so the surgeon went on, "I reviewed all the cases and the testimony, and I think Doctor Silason was very generous to Doctor Trevellian. I expect the Board of Licensure will look at him, and I think they'll wonder if he ought to have a license to practice."

Trevellian was on his feet once more shouting, "No one likes a snot, and that's what you are. You nasty shit."

"I think that's quite enough of that," Buck said, his distaste showing on his face.

"Has any committee member any questions?"

"It's late," Rekuf said. "I think we'll wrap this session up now. We don't need to hear any more of your witnesses. Doctor Trevellian, we need a list of your witnesses at least forty-eight hours before the next meeting, and Doctor Laxton needs one as well."

"It will be done," Trevellian said.

Laxton was sure no one on the hospital staff would appear for Trevellian so he knew the witnesses would be external. He went to his office. It was now eleven at night and he sat for about fifteen minutes and was surprised when the phone in his office rang.

The sultry tones at the other end told him who it was immediately.

"Herb just called me. It mustn't have gone too well for him," Megan said.

"I don't think it did. Why doesn't he just quit? He's only getting himself in deeper."

"He has too much time on his hands. I really called to tell you he's going to be away again before the next session, and I'm going to call you as soon as he's gone."

"Okay, but be careful."

"Of course I will. You know how I feel."

"I'll wait for the call. I could use seeing you soon."

"Wait, I hear the car--"

"Bye, doll."

Laxton walked into the bedroom. He was carrying tea. He looked at Megan lying face down on the bed with only her legs covered. She had sensuous buttocks, and he always felt a stirring even afterwards. She turned and sat up, pulling the sheet up to cover her breasts when she heard him.

She had just rolled up unexpectedly at the apartment. He had upbraided her gently for not phoning before, but she knew him too well and knew he would be alone. They had rolled around his bed in evident desperation, and the conclusion had been long in coming because both had wanted to prolong the experience.

"I'm going to talk shop for a minute or two," Megan said. "You know Herb is going to call witnesses, and I know under ordinary circumstances it wouldn't matter much, but he's paying a lot of money to a Professor of Gynecology to come to the hearing and say what Herb wants him to say."

Laxton realized he should have expected something like that.

"You have a name?" he said.

"His name is Professor Gard from UCLA and he's not that

182

old."

"It will pose a problem, unless it can be shown he's being highly paid."

"There was one part of the conversation I overheard."

"I don't think anything you heard in private will do me much good."

Megan smiled mischievously, continuing to sit on the bed with her legs bent up, her arms around them, and her chin resting on her knees.

"Come here again," she said.

"What are you holding out from me?"

"They were worried because Gard had some sort of problem with the Licensing Board. Something to do with fraudulent records, but it won't come out for another month. I said come here."

"I can handle you again," Laxton said.

CHAPTER 28

FIGHTING BACK

Buck opened the session in the usual way, and inquired whether or not the chairman and Doctor Laxton had been given notice of the witnesses Doctor Trevellian intended to call on his behalf. No one had seen the list except Buck himself.

"I'm going to wave objections to this irregularity, provided Doctor Laxton will agree, because Doctor Trevellian's witness is here. I also see you have a list of twenty people, and I think this is most unreasonable and I want to see you cut the list down. The Medical Executive Committee kept their list quite short, and you should do the same, so I want you to tell me which of these witnesses you will call by the end of this session."

"Very well," Trevellian said.

The first witness was introduced to the committee as Doctor Gard, and he had impeccable credentials. He was tall but rather overweight, and he carried an assured self-righteous look on his face. He had slightly graying hair and bushy, gray eyebrows. His eyes were cold blue and hard with no glimmer of sympathy.

"Have you reviewed the gynecological cases?" Trevellian said.

"Yes. I have," he said.

"Would you discuss the cases, please?"

"The first patient had a cystocele and an enterocele, and she was losing some urine as well, but that was incidental. She was admitted and had surgery which was appropriate for the condition, was slightly confused after the procedure, and was then discharged in excellent shape."

"Was the procedure done appropriate?" Trevellian said.

"I reviewed your operative note, and I consider the standard surgical procedure you did to be well within the standard of care as therapy for this patient."

"Do you think a urological evaluation was necessary in this case?"

"No, I don't think most gynecologists would request that, because the patient's primary condition was gynecological."

"Do you think a neurological examination was necessary in this case?"

"I see no reason for one. The standard of practice doesn't require it."

"Do you think there should have been a second gynecological opinion on this type of patient?"

"No, that's not the standard practice."

"In view of the fact this patient was oriented and cheerful when she was discharged, and that her gynecological condition was cured by surgery, would you feel this patient had a good result, and that the community standard of care was met?"

"Most certainly."

"Finally," Trevellian said rather pompously, "would you recommend leaving a patient like this with just a catheter, that is a tube in her bladder forever, and do no surgery?"

"I think that to leave a patient who wanted surgery herself to have to wear a catheter all her life is not acceptable practice."

"Doctor Laxton," Buck said. "Do you have questions of this witness?"

"It's absolutely clear this patient had an enlarged heart, chronic disease in the lungs, and had to be given aminophylline in the hospital. The reason was not documented. The final diagnosis was coronary atherosclerosis, serious heart disease, and she was eighty-four years old. Do you think it would be unreasonable to expect a medical clearance on this patient before surgery?"

"The anesthesiologist who evaluated this patient should have done that. Since she tolerated the procedure very nicely, the outcome speaks for itself. After all, she had been seen by three physicians before surgery."

"Three physicians were not involved," Laxton said, "Doctor Trevellian was the primary care physician as well as the gynecologist. She was not a referred patient."

"I misunderstood that," Gard said.

"The patient had Parkinson's disease, according to Doctor Trevellian, although he said he wasn't sure about that, but he treated her with a drug for Parkinson's disease anyway. Wouldn't you think that it would have been appropriate to obtain a neurological consultation?"

"I'm not sure Parkinson's disease is a reason not to do surgery."

"Doctor Trevellian said his reason for surgery was incontinence. The cause of this was not established. Wouldn't a neurological examination have been a good idea?"

"What good would a neurological examination do to determine incontinence," Gard said.

"Wouldn't you think that under these circumstances some

185

knowledge of the way the bladder contracts and expands, that is the urodynamics of the bladder, would have been useful?" Laxton said.

"Oh, you must mean a urologist. I don't think the major reason for surgery was her loss of urine."

"Couldn't the loss of urine be due to the neurological problem?"

"Oh, sure," Gard said.

"Under these circumstances, wouldn't you have done some studies?"

"I guess the pertinent question is not what I would have done, because I'm at the University and I run a teaching practice. I think the question is what do the rest of the people in the community outside the University do with these cases."

"What knowledge do you have of the standard of practice in this hospital?"

"I don't practice here, but the standard must be the same as nationwide, and I know what goes on nationwide."

"You are not answering my question," Laxton said sharply. "You don't have any knowledge of what goes on in this hospital, do you?"

"That's correct," Gard admitted rather stiffly.

"In your practice at the University, you're telling us you would do these tests, aren't you?"

"Yes, at the University we would do those tests on a patient like this."

"Is an anterior repair a good operation for this?" Biggerstaff said.

"Yes it is," Gard said.

"Do you do Kelly repairs for these people?" Laxton said.

"No, I don't."

Bill Sanders had been silent through this whole process suddenly leaned forward. "How much time do you spend in professional testimony?"

"Probably one percent," Gard said.

"Are you paid for that?" Sanders continued.

"Yes, I am."

"Are you being paid tonight?"

Trevellian shuffled his feet and leaned forward to try to catch Gard's eye, which came to Buck's attention.

"Doctor Trevellian, I don't want you instructing witnesses in anything. Don't interfere with the process."

"Doctor Trevellian suggested I submit a bill for this," Gard said.

186

"Thank you," Sanders said.

"Doctor Gard, I see you were at UCLA a long time, but now you're with UCI," Rekuf said.

"That's correct."

"You must belong to a lot of organizations."

"I belong to the gynecological-urological association, and when I was president I polled members about managing incontinence, and most said they would do a cystourethrogram before doing a case like this."

"Would you, Doctor Gard?" Rekuf said.

"I always do, but then I've written a text book on the subject, so I might be called biased by some."

"Do you have other authors in the book?"

"Yes. I edited it. There are seventeen others."

"And did they espouse the philosophy that such an evaluation should always be done?"

"Yes, they did. But it might not be a community standard."

"But you would always do one, right?"

"Yes, I would."

"So, in conclusion, we can say patients you see have a full work up, don't they," Laxton said.

"That's correct."

"In a patient who had all sorts of medical things going on, what would you do personally?"

"I'd ask her about them."

"And if she was confused, what then? Would you have consulted an internist?"

"If I felt I needed one."

"Put yourself in Doctor Trevellian's place, and pretend you're not at the University and you inherited a patient with medical problems and you're about to operate on her and couldn't obtain information from her, would you, or would you not, have an internist look at her?" Laxton said.

"The question is being asked in a vacuum. There are a lot of ifs ands and buts, so in my personal situation I would have asked for a consultation."

"This isn't important, because I would always have two or three consultations now," Trevellian said. "So we'll go to the next case."

"You have to wait until all members of the committee have asked all they want to ask," Buck said.

"Are you aware most of these cases come from Doctor

Trevellian's nursing home," Laxton said.

"No."

"I have a letter from the patient's husband," Trevellian said. "I want to admit it as evidence."

"Doctor Gard, did you rely on this letter to make your evaluation of this case," Buck said.

"I did not. I haven't seen the letter."

"Then I see no reason to admit the letter."

Laxton had a copy of the letter because Trevellian had started to hand them out. "This letter is written in medical terminology anyway. We don't even know who wrote the letter."

"The letter gives the symptoms and the patient's complaints," Trevellian said.

"Yes, but those things should be in your chart," Buck said.

"I forgot to put them in the chart," Trevellian said.

"Judgement has to be made on what you put in the chart, and about you as a physician," Buck said.

Dr. Gard related the history on the next patient, who had signed her consent form but was said to have Alzheimer's disease. Trevellian asked all the same questions he had asked on the first case and obtained the responses he presumably wanted.

"What about her falling out of bed and breaking her pelvis?" Trevellian said.

"That's the fault of the nursing staff," Gard said.

"Is it the standard of practice anywhere for a patient with Alzheimer's disease to sign their own consent form?" Laxton asked.

"No, it isn't," Gard said.

"If you had a patient you suspected had Alzheimer's disease, would you make that diagnosis without a work up?" Laxton said.

"If I had any doubts, I should have to get a neurologist."

"This patient had dribbling all the time. Do you see any tests to determine why?"

"We do these tests at the University all the time because we are top quality but I don't think the people in these smaller institutions bother."

"So in your institution you would have done an evaluation."

"Yes."

"Do you think, based on these two cases, that my surgical privileges should be taken away from me?" Trevellian said.

"I think you did a great job. Very good surgery," Gard said.

"Does that conclude the questions?" Buck said.

"Do you know anything about Doctor Trevellian's training?" Laxton said.

"No, I don't."

"Let me ask you about the termination of your relationship with UCLA," Laxton said.

"Just a minute," Buck interrupted. "What is the relevance of this question?"

"It speaks directly to the credibility of the witness," Laxton said.

"If it appears not to do so, I shall tell the committee to ignore it."

"I resigned," Gard said.

"Why did you resign?"

"I don't see this is going anywhere," Buck said.

"It certainly is going somewhere," Laxton snapped. "Had it anything to do with the fact that a disciplinary action was taken against you by the Board of Medical Quality Assurance of the State of California?"

Committee members were suddenly all attention, staring at Gard. Gard was silent.

"Do you want to tell us about this or do you want me to read the indictment to the committee?" Laxton said.

"It was related to my records," Gard said stiffly.

"The indictment alleges you were falsifying medical records for the purpose of performing unwarranted surgery and experimental surgery on patients, and you were found guilty of that. Is that correct?"

"In essence it is correct."

"I have no further questions of this witness," Laxton said. "I'm sure the committee will know what weight to give to his testimony."

"It's all right for you to go," Buck said quietly.

Trevellian looked crestfallen. Laxton guessed he must have wondered how Laxton had obtained this information when it hadn't even been published yet. What a wonderful invention the telephone is, Laxton thought.

"You can call your next witness," Buck said to Trevellian.

"Could we have a few minutes break first?" Trevellian said.

A fifteen-minute break was taken, and Laxton took a short walk outdoors. He had not intended to see anyone but he ran into Sanders.

"I know we're not supposed to talk about the hearing, but what a waste of time we've had tonight," Sanders said.

"What did you think about Gard's testimony?" Laxton said.

189

"When you hire a whore you get fucked," Sanders said. He walked away smiling.

Back on the record at last Trevellian introduced a surgical witness, Doctor Kent.

"Have you read the record of the patient who had a colon resection and five years later was admitted because she hadn't been eating?"

"Yes," Kent said. "I did that a week or two ago."

"Did you think it was appropriate to put a tube permanently in her stomach?"

"Oh, yes."

"In your hospital how many of these are done by surgeons rather than gastroenterologists?"

"A hundred percent are done by surgeons."

"Is it all right to bring the tube through the incision?"

"It can be done that way."

"In anesthesia, do you use a local and supplement it with a light general anesthetic?"

"Believe it or not," Kent said, "we do them all under general anesthetic."

"Do you think I gave appropriate care?"

"Certainly you did."

"That's it," Trevellian said.

"Are you a member of the staff of this hospital?" Laxton said.

"No, I'm not."

"Do you know anything about the standard of care here?"

"Not much, no."

"Do you know anything about the percentage of stomach tubes inserted in patients in this hospital?"

"No, not much."

"And all the gastrostomies done in your hospital are done by making an incision."

"Yes, they are."

"How do you do them?"

"I make a little stab wound and bring a tube through it."

"In the kind of gastrostomy Doctor Trevellian does, are you aware that it's recommended the tube be brought through a stab wound?"

"Well, you're right, but some people bring it through the primary incision."

"You don't do the same kind of a gastrostomy. Wouldn't you

190

admit that in the type Doctor Trevellian does, there is a chance of infection in the tissues?"

"I don't think so, but I've never done one like that and I'm envious of Doctor Trevellian being able to - well, I mean, I don't know how to do them that way."

"If you don't know how to do them, do you feel you can comment as an expert?" Laxton said.

"No, I don't," Kent said.

"In the case where I took the gall bladder out," Trevellian said, "I want to admit a letter from the pathologist showing the gall bladder was acute, not just chronic."

"Just a moment," Buck said. "Is this an original letter?"

"Yes, it is. I got it today."

The letter was read and only added more confusion to the situation.

"The letter should have no weight at all," Rekuf said. "It doesn't prove anything. It's just a smoke screen."

"I'll get it clarified," Laxton said. "But I can't get the pathologist to come and testify. I do think I can get a clearer letter."

"I don't see any objection to the surgery anyway," Kent said. "I think the post operative care was all right."

"Have you any experience with endoscopy? Do you know of people who look in the duct with an instrument and take out stones" Trevellian said.

"We have the best in the area," Kent replied.

"What about that in this case?"

"He would never have done that in this case. The gall bladder was infected."

"You can't testify in that way," Buck said. "You don't know that for sure. You may give your opinion, but not that of someone who isn't here and can't be cross examined."

"I say it shouldn't be done," Kent said.

"Do you do the endoscopy instrument procedures?" Buck said.

"No, I don't."

"Do you think that the charge that I was wrong not to try this procedure is correct?" Trevellian asked.

"No. I don't."

"Is this procedure done in your hospital?" Laxton asked.

"Yes."

"How many cases have been done in your hospital?" Laxton said.

"None."

"So you have no experience of it."

"Well, I've heard about it."

"Do you know the national complication rate from this procedure?"

"It's very low. About one percent."

"No," Laxton said. "It's higher than that. It's six percent. Do you know the rate in this hospital?"

"No, I don't."

"It's zero percent. So, if our gastroenterologist felt that surgery could be avoided in this case, do you maintain that was not a correct assessment?"

"I think you could get the same result with surgery and get the gall bladder out as well."

"Do you believe that the best time for surgery was her first admission?"

"I agree with Doctor Trevellian. That was the best time."

"So you would have operated on her with septicemia, would you," Laxton said.

"What? Was a blood culture done?" Kent looked nonplussed.

"It's in the chart. I thought you said you reviewed the chart."

Trevellian was waving his arms around.

"Stop trying to instruct the witness, Doctor Trevellian," Buck said. "I want to hear an answer."

"It wouldn't have been a good time to do this if the blood culture was positive. But I suspect the organism came from the bile, so surgery might have saved her."

"You said you reviewed the chart. What about the same organism found in the urinary tract. Could it have come from there?" Laxton asked.

"But if the culture from the bile was positive --"

"There was no culture from the bile duct."

Kent didn't reply. He sat at the table with his chin supported by both hands and stared straight ahead.

"Do you believe if you did a hundred cases like this you'd get a hundred percent good result?" Laxton said.

"I object to you saying that, because the result wasn't that bad."

"Doctor Kent, are you one of those people who believes if the result is good that the decision was right?"

"I haven't experienced a case where a doctor was faulted when the surgery turned out all right."

"I've handled hearings where the physician lost his privileges, although the results were good, and he lost them because he failed to do the tests he should have done before surgery," Buck said.

"In this case there was no stone in the duct. This patient may have been able to be treated conservatively. Isn't that correct, Doctor Kent?"

"Maybe so."

"Let's go to another case," Trevellian said impatiently.

"One moment," Rekuf said. "The committee has questions. Why haven't you availed yourself of the gastroenterologist doing this type of procedure in your cases?"

"I have," Kent said.

"You just testified that you had no experience of the procedure, and hadn't used it," Laxton said.

"I did use it occasionally. You misinterpreted what I said. I meant I wouldn't use it on an occasion like this."

"The next case was the catatonic schizophrenic who had gall bladder problems and was admitted twice." Trevellian was pushing to get to the case and started without an okay from the chairman. "Do you think this patient was a good patient for the permanent stomach tube?"

"Yes," Kent said. "I think she needed it."

"Even though the abdomen burst open, you agree she needed it."

"Yes."

"Do you think the burst abdomen hastened her death?"

"Not really."

"Thank you," Trevellian said with a smile.

"You just stated this woman needed this tube," Laxton said. "Couldn't she just have been handled with a tube down her nose or throat?"

"No. I think she needed the permanent tube."

"You are aware, Doctor Kent, that when her abdomen burst open the tube was removed."

"With the kind of operation which had been done it had to be removed."

"Are you aware another one wasn't placed?"

"Doctor Trevellian decided he'd use one through the mouth or nose."

"You have just told us she needed a permanent tube, and that one by the nose or mouth wasn't any good in this case, and now you're

193

saying it's all right, aren't you?"

"Well, she had the brain disorder."

"That doesn't answer the question. You're avoiding it. Answer the question." Laxton was annoyed. The constant, continuous toll he felt had been imposed by Aysgarth was getting to him because he wasn't sure the result would be the way Aysgarth wanted it. He knew Biggerstaff was already fed up and might cause a split vote.

"I haven't really looked at this for a month, so I might have forgotten some things," Kent said. "But truly he would have had to discontinue the permanent tube if he'd not done the operation the way he did."

"According to you, this patient needed a permanent tube."

"Yes she did."

"Do you think I should be stopped from doing surgery, Doctor Kent?" Trevellian said.

"That's why I'm here. I can't believe anyone would want to take your privileges away on such flimsy evidence."

"I take it you are basing your opinion on these cases we have discussed with you," Laxton said.

"These cases?"

"You can only base your opinion on these cases," Buck said.

"Oh," Kent said.

"I'm going to close this session," Rekuf said. "We'll hear your other witnesses next session, Doctor Trevellian. The committee is going to call the anesthesiologist who gave the anesthetic to this lady who died."

"I object," Trevellian said. "The chairman is biased against me, and has been working with the Medical Executive Committee and Doctor Laxton to gang up on me."

"You had better substantiate those charges," Buck said at once. "They are serious charges."

"The chairman is always asking tough questions of all my witnesses, and he also helps Doctor Laxton by asking questions he forgot to ask. Also, he was on the committee that brought the charges against me. I want him disqualified."

"The committee will meet immediately and others are to go out of the room. Your request will be considered."

When nonmembers had left, Buck asked each committee member what he thought.

"I don't think there's anything wrong with what Rekuf is doing," Biggerstaff said. "Laxton is really hard on poor old Trevellian, and he's not such a bad fellow."

"Whether he's an angel, a saint, or a devil is irrelevant," Buck said. "Your job is to look at his work. I take it you think Doctor Rekuf should stay on the committee?"

"Yes."

The other committee members agreed.

"I found it offensive he brought that whore in here, and he has tried every trick he can think of to get this thing dissolved instead of over with, and he's just playing for more time now, just hoping we'll all go away and it won't happen. I won't sit on anything like this again, but I will see this one through," Sanders said.

The committee called the others back into the room.

"The committee has decided that Doctor Rekuf has no bias at all, Doctor Trevellian, and I must point out to you that you can expect tough questions from any committee member. There is no evidence of collusion of any kind, and Doctor Rekuf was not a member of the committee that brought the charges against you."

"Very well," Trevellian said.

CHAPTER 29

EVIDENCE

"As Hearing Officer I want to notify everyone that the committee chairman has decided to call the anesthesiologist who gave one or more anesthetics to Doctor Trevellian's cases," Buck said, "and we are now ready to continue the hearing related to Doctor Trevellian's privileges."

Laxton knew about the anesthesiologist Rekuf was going to call, but more importantly for him he knew that the witness Trevellian had brought was from USC.

When the last session was over Trevellian had disappeared, or so Megan had told him, and he had established for himself that someone else was taking Trevellian's calls in his medical practice. Megan didn't seem to know where her husband had gone, but she had been able to arrange for Laxton to meet her at a friend's house.

"Mary is away," Megan said, "and I'm supposed to look after her place, and I want to meet you over there."

Again Laxton protested that it was too dangerous, but she had him attuned to her desires and he hadn't needed much persuasion. She told him that night that Trevellian had entertained his witness at the house, and that the witness had drunk too much.

"Although he's a professor at USC it seems to me he's pretty stupid. I'm not sure, but I don't think he's a certified specialist anyway, and he seems to think disjointedly. He's an old friend of Herb's, a classmate from way back. I don't think he knows what he's getting into."

"What else is weird?" Laxton said.

"He hasn't given anesthetics for anything but obstetrics for the last five years."

Laxton found this difficult to believe, because although he saw Trevellian as a surgical menace, he didn't think he was totally stupid.

"I present Dr. Freidlander, Associate Professor of Anesthesia at USC Medical Center, who is teaching anesthesia residents," Trevellian said when the committee reassembled. "Do you see that the original anesthetic evaluation on this patient was two days prior to surgery, and do you agree the patient might have been a different grade of risk on the day of surgery?"

"That's quite possible," Freidlander said.

196

"Do you see the article we submitted that states that the complication rate in young women for these endoscopy procedures is much higher?"

"Objection," Laxton said sharply. "This man is here as an anesthesiologist, not a surgeon or gastroenterologist, and was listed to comment on anesthetic matters, not surgical."

"He will testify about examining the duct through an instrument as well," Trevellian said.

"This man can't be an expert in endoscopy unless he does them," Laxton said.

"We'll see," Trevellian said.

"You have every right to find out if he knows anything about it," Buck said. "But I'm going to advise the chairman to let him continue, although any member of the committee can question his credentials at any point."

"Doctor Freidlander, have you or your colleagues monitored patients having this procedure and anything related to it?" Trevellian said.

"We are quite frequently present, and we are responsible for the anesthetic in these cases."

"Does the hospital require you to be there when these are being done?"

"Always."

"Have you had serious complications in these procedures?"

"Yes, yes. I've had respiratory arrests when these were being done."

"Before you answer the next question, at which hospital were you monitoring these cases?" Buck asked.

"I work in several hospitals."

"Which ones did you monitor cases in?"

"They were downtown Los Angeles hospitals," Freidlander said. "We did ECTs in those."

"That's electro convulsive therapy," Laxton said. "Not ERCPs, examining the gall bladder duct."

"I mean ERCPs, endoscopy. Yes, that's what I mean."

"Do you think it's as easy on a patient to have the gall bladder out as to have an endoscopy?" Trevellian said.

"Certainly is."

"You can go ahead and ask questions," Trevellian said to Laxton.

"Where did you graduate from?" Laxton said.

"The Osteopathic College of Medicine."

"What year?"

"Let me try to remember--"

"Was it the same year as Doctor Trevellian?"

"Yes. Now I remember. We were classmates."

"Are you a Board Certified specialist?"

"No, I'm not. But I'm eligible."

"As of what date would that be?"

"About twenty years ago."

"Board eligible is up to five years after training, or five years after taking the written exam. So are you still Board eligible?"

"I guess not," Freidlander conceded.

"When did you last do anesthetics for endoscopy?" Laxton said.

"Must have been a year ago."

"Just a minute," Shickelhurtz said. "Just what kind of anesthetics are you giving now?"

"I give them for obstetrics," Freidlander said.

"The patient you are testifying about had fluid on the lungs. Don't you think a less risky procedure might have been in order?" Laxton said.

"What kind do you mean?"

"An endoscopy, doing everything through an instrument."

"That's a really dangerous procedure. Now, of course in the hands of real experts like we have at USC you don't worry. But our professor is one in a thousand."

"I think you just said you were opposed to endoscopy except in your professor's hands."

"No, no. In my opinion it's an inherent risk to the patient, but with a very ill patient I like to see them cut open."

"Endoscopy is not necessarily done with general anesthetics," Laxton said.

"They should be. They should be."

"Are you aware we have done two hundred cases here without anesthetics, and without any complications?" Laxton said.

"No, I'm not. That's an excellent record."

"You testified you don't have anything to do with endoscopy now. Who's doing the anesthesia at the university?"

"They don't give anesthetics at the university for endoscopy. They don't use our department."

"How can you say these patients should have general anesthetics when they don't give them at the university?" Laxton asked.

198

"Well I think they should."

"But you're a professor. How do you teach the students?"

"I don't think it comes up in my teaching."

Laxton thought for a moment or two and then said, "Did you completely review the chart on this patient we're talking about?"

"I don't think I did."

"In that case, how do you conclude this patient should have had major surgery?"

"Well, the patient was acutely ill."

"Acutely ill with what, medical or surgical conditions?" Laxton said.

"Either or both."

"Do you know anything about this patient's gall bladder or duct, or just what Doctor Trevellian told you?"

"Just what he told me, and I saw part of a transcript of the meeting."

"Do you know what the findings were in the duct or in the gall bladder?"

"No, I don't."

"I have no more questions of this witness," Laxton said disgustedly.

"Did you review the chart at all?" Shickelhurtz asked.

"Oh, I read it through."

"Did you review the internist's notes?"

"I can't remember."

"How long have you been doing obstetrical anesthesia?"

"At least five years."

"So you haven't been associated with endoscopy for at least five years?"

"Probably not."

"You told us you believed this patient should have major surgery rather than endoscopy," Rekuf said.

"Let me say this," Freidlander said. "If I'd seen this patient that would have been my conclusion."

"Do you review all the charts of patients you get for anesthesia?" Rekuf said.

"Sometimes I do."

"Not all the time?"

"Sometimes you can guess. You get a feel for what's going on."

"What about this second patient?" Laxton said.

"Pretty straightforward if you ask me."

"You examined the chart?"

"In its entirety."

"And you can't see any problems?"

"No."

"Why did the patient have all those respiratory drugs postoperatively?"

"She did?"

"You had the chart, doctor," Laxton said. "And you claimed you reviewed it."

"He was only here to answer anesthetic questions," Trevellian interrupted.

"Please, please, let's go to the next case," Biggerstaff said.

"No. I want to excuse this witness and get to the witness we called here and have him give testimony," Rekuf said.

Doctor Diamond was a slender, young man with delicate features and even white teeth, who seemed to wear a perpetual frown.

"You're also on our staff here, aren't you?" Rekuf said.

"Yes. I am."

"Tell us about yourself."

"I'm a certified specialist in internal medicine, also in anesthesia."

"You called two of these patients as Class four risk, the worst they could be, didn't you?" Rekuf asked.

"Yes. I think they were seriously ill patients who were at serious risk for anesthetics."

"How did you review the patient we've had so much argument about? The one that most wanted to do an endoscopy on, but she ended with major surgery?"

"My routine is to go over the chart and then examine the patient before I give the anesthetic."

There was a glint in Trevellian's eye. "But in this case you just rubber stamped what someone else had written, didn't you?"

"Certainly not. I went and examined the patient in the intensive care unit and she was a very high risk. Class four."

"You didn't write that down though," Trevellian said gleefully.

"She was the same as the previous description--class four."

"Let me see if the nurses made a note," Trevellian said.

"You're calling him a liar," Biggerstaff said. "You are trying to make fools of us as well."

"All right," Trevellian said. "She did well with her anesthetic though, didn't she?"

200

"It wasn't the easiest anesthetic, but we got her through all right."

"Would it be correct to say a large number of patients this ill might not survive surgery?" Buck said.

"They would all have serious postoperative complications," Diamond said.

"I'm finished with him," Trevellian said. "I object to Doctor Laxton being able to sneak in another witness like this."

Buck was clearly furious.

"The committee called Doctor Diamond," Buck said. "It wasn't Doctor Laxton or myself, it was the committee. Doctor Diamond is excused with thanks, Doctor Laxton has submitted the statement you made to the Medical Executive Committee as an exhibit, Doctor Trevellian."

"I object. That was when I was trying to make a deal with them," Trevellian said.

"There is no mention of that. In fact you were rather hostile and said no deal was necessary, so I shall allow it to be admitted."

"We'll now go to the summation," Rekuf said. "Go ahead, Doctor Laxton."

The committee had sat into December and it looked like the end of the road. Laxton had prepared his summation carefully.

"On March thirtieth, the Chief of Staff summarily suspended Doctor Trevellian's clinical privileges initially for ninety days based on review of his medical records."

Laxton then outlined how the privileges were restricted, what the restrictions were, and the fact that Doctor Trevellian had requested this hearing. He spent sometime explaining how the summary suspension had taken place.

"What is not at issue," he continued, "is whether Doctor Trevellian is a partner in this hospital, how long he has practiced here, and how many patients he admits to the hospital, and what happened to the patients before and after their discharge."

Laxton then went over each case in detail, making points as he went along. "The surgeon who does not care who signs the consent, doesn't get consultations when needed, and brings as a principal witness a Professor who was convicted of falsification of records and who has written a book stating that patients should have all the things he denied they needed to have to this committee. Doctor Trevellian's comment now is he would have two or three consultations on every patient, whether they were needed or not. There were patients who, to put it bluntly and clearly, he killed. He could always remember normal evaluations, but rarely could he tell us about abnormal ones."

Laxton went on to discuss Trevellian's predilection for sticking tubes in the stomach in a way that was twenty years out of date, the obvious fact he didn't understand the type of surgery he was performing, did the wrong things so often, and used inappropriate antibiotics. Then he stuck a tube in a woman's stomach because the family wanted it. He operated on a patient for a common duct stone which had passed, and she subsequently died.

By the end of this testimony it should have been clear to all that Trevellian was dangerous.

When Trevellian started he told them he had practiced at the hospital for fifteen years, and the hospital needed his admissions to survive. He constantly referred to Doctor Gard's evidence, which supported almost everything he did, and went on for an hour repeating what Gard had said.

"I have been called nasty names by old ladies when I wanted to put a finger in the bowel or vagina, so that's why I didn't bother."

His statement was interminable, and he referred to Kent's opinion of what a good surgeon Trevellian was, to Freidlander's opinions about endoscopy, and concluded that most of those who had spoken out against him were jealous of his nursing home. As his endless testimony, filled with excuses and lies, went on it was clear everyone was getting bored and some members yawned. When he was finished, Buck asked Laxton if he wished to rebut the remarks.

Laxton responded: "The only thing I would say to the committee is that the evidence is in the transcripts and I would enjoin them to look at the lack of documentation and the documentation in the charts. Look at Doctor Trevellian's statements in the transcripts and at the witnesses' statements in the transcripts. Look at the statements in context, not out of context. Remember we're determining whether Doctor Trevellian meets the standards of practice in this hospital, and I submit he does not. Finally, as it states in the hospital bylaws, the committee should base its decision on the evidence introduced at the hearing, and all logical and reasonable inferences from the evidence and testimony. I have no further comments."

"You can now do your rebuttal, Doctor Trevellian," Buck said.

Trevellian jumped up. "I will now distribute copies of my rebuttal to all members of the committee."

"No you will not," Buck said. "A rebuttal must be based on what Doctor Laxton said, not something you concocted earlier."

"That's what it does," Trevellian said.

Buck looked at the sheet Trevellian was trying to distribute.

"Let me read this section. Here you refer to a physician who had a cocaine habit no one did anything about. That is not a rebuttal."

"Why not just make it an exhibit for members to read later," Laxton said. He knew from a very reliable source it contained a threat to committee members. He was probably the only one not surprised.

"I'm sure when you've read my statement you will all agree with me," Trevellian said with a nasty leer.

CHAPTER 30

TREVELLIAN'S THREATS

Megan called Laxton at his home from a shopping center in town. "It's over, isn't it?"

"No decision has been reached yet. You have to know Megan, we simply can't go on like this because of the risks involved."

"I know, but I have something to tell you. Herb thinks he'll be okay, but whether he is or not he's going to sue everyone."

"Thanks for calling, but you'd better not call again unless he's out of town," Laxton said. "You know how much trouble I'd be in if it ever came to light."

"I know all about that, and trust me to be careful."

Laxton went down and cornered Rekuf right away, to bring him up to speed on what was going on. It didn't really matter, whatever the decision they would be sued, so the threat in his rebuttal was meaningless.

"Can you talk to Aysgarth and make sure if we're sued that the hospital will pay all the bills?" Rekuf said.

"And we need it in writing," Laxton said.

"Off the record, I wouldn't trust the bastards we're working for one iota," Rekuf said. "And this bullshit about gentleman's agreement stuff is just that - bullshit."

Laxton went to Flashing Rod Clinic to talk to Aysgarth. He told Aysgarth that he knew there was going to be a universal decision, and that it would be what the Board wanted, but there was one snag.

"How can you be sure about the decision?" Aysgarth said.

"Because the Hearing Committee members need, in writing, an assurance they will be defended against any action Trevellian might bring against them."

"You can consider it done. I'll see that you and every committee member gets such a letter from the board chairman, but no one must reveal anything about it. I'll get the hospital attorney to draw the letter up. Tell Rekuf to get on with the meeting as soon as possible. We've got Joint Commission coming to inspect the hospital the week after next."

"In two weeks," Laxton said astonished. "I haven't done any work on that."

"That's Golliman's job, and he'd better be ready. I want that decision a done deed before Joint Commission gets here. By the way, you know Lense has gone, I suppose?"

"I heard. It was rather sudden wasn't it?"

"There were a lot of reasons I don't want to talk about, but the new pharmacist is lost, and I hear there are a lot of outdated medications on shelves in the pharmacy. You'd better look into it."

"That's not only going to get us into trouble with Joint Commission, it's illegal as well," Laxton said. "I'll give the new guy a couple of days to clean it up, and then go by and tear the place apart and make sure everything's in order."

Before the Hearing Committee got together with the Hearing Officer they had a clandestine meeting and agreed Trevellian should do no more surgery, and that any cases that were considered serious medical cases, especially any in the intensive care unit, would have to be under the care of a specialist. The meeting with Buck took a couple of nights, and was simply to put the decision in a format difficult for Trevellian to challenge. Trevellian immediately appealed to the Hospital Board, which was his next step. The Board held a meeting in short order.

Aysgarth expected it to go rapidly, and was surprised when Smiley wanted to modify some of the decisions. "Couldn't we allow him to assist and do the odd hernia?"

"First of all, he doesn't know what he's doing, and secondly that'll only land everyone in a lot more trouble," Aysgarth said.

"We must support the Hearing Committee," Gotcher said. "We have to be unanimous."

"He's a really nice chap," Smiley said, "and he helped us a lot in the old days, at the start up."

Trevellian's complications had made money in the old days, but Medicare had changed that with their flat fee system for hospitals. Trevellian himself might have been making more, but the Feds were onto him, and the hospital was being threatened. Aysgarth patiently explained that.

The Board issued a reasoned statement of support, also written by an Attorney, confirming the decision taken by the Hearing Committee. It appeared that Trevellian's goose was cooked. There was so little happening that everyone relaxed and assumed that Trevellian had accepted his restrictions. Words filtered down that he had tried to get into other local hospitals, but the word was out about him.

Golliman wrote a note of thanks to Laxton for a job well done.

About three weeks after the letter there was a knock on Laxton's door, and it opened to admit Megan. Laxton was sure his clandestine folly had come home to roost at last, and all the forms of recrimination and disgrace were racing through his head.

"You are Doctor Laxton, aren't you?" Megan said.

"Yes."

"I'm here to serve these papers for Doctor Trevellian," she said, handing him the documents. "Good afternoon."

She was out of the door before he had recovered. Laxton looked anxiously at the papers. They were a suit for damages for terminating Trevellian's privileges. The hospital, the Administrator, the Board, and twenty nine-staff members were charged with conspiring to terminate Trevellian's privileges and deny him a living. The document was about ten pages. Trevellian was claiming damages of ten million dollars against the hospital, and a million dollars against each member named in the suit, plus his legal expenses. Laxton was relieved to see Trevellian apparently knew nothing of the shenanigans that had preceded the suspension. He was aware that the matter had been reported to the Licensing Board.

As Laxton stepped out of his office, he immediately saw Golliman with the same papers.

"Why would Trevellian have his wife serve the papers?" Laxton said to Golliman.

"That was his Nursing Home Administrator," Golliman said. "He's too cheap to pay a professional to serve the papers."

Laxton took off to Flashing Rod where he caught up with Aysgarth. He felt he needed someone who had connections and knew what it meant before he talked to anyone.

"I don't think we have to mess with trying to fix the Judge," Aysgarth said. "This action of Trevellian's just won't fly."

Laxton talked to the hospital attorney the next day.

"I'm just writing a letter to everyone. We're looking at it at the moment, but what he wants to do I don't think will work."

"But this can go on for years," Laxton said.

"No, he's got it on the fast track and it will be heard not later than a month from now."

If this whole thing wasn't enough to upset Laxton, a call to him at his apartment from Megan was about the last straw. He didn't know whether the call was being monitored, recorded, or what might be going on.

"Laxy," she said.

"Who is this?" he said, although he knew.

"Oh, come on, I'm not taking any risks and I'm not ringing from

206

home. I'm in a department store."

"Give me the number and I'll call back," Laxton said. He wasn't even sure that was safe but he dared not tell her to go to hell, which was the way he felt.

He looked at the number she had given him and guessed it probably was a public phone. He dialed.

"Herb says he has a million dollars and he's going to sue everyone and clean up some more, and I'm sorry I just came in and out of your office like that, but he wouldn't pay to have the papers properly delivered. I had to take them everywhere, but no one knew me anyway."

Laxton said nothing.

"Are you still there?" Megan said.

"Yes."

"I want to phone you and arrange something."

"No," Laxton said sharply.

"I don't want this to make a difference."

"It does," Laxton said. "I have to go."

"Let's just play it by ear and see what happens, please."

Laxton replaced the phone quietly and went out.

Laxton spent more time with Rekuf. Laxton felt he himself was taking the whole thing more seriously than the others. Rekuf seemed to think it was funny.

"I've never heard of anything of this sort," he said. "When I talked to Buck about it, he simply couldn't see how anything like this could work for Trevellian."

"Did he say why?"

"What he said was no reputable firm of attorneys would try to short circuit the system."

"Of course, he's not named in the suit."

"I don't know why you would worry about it. After all, you're just an employee of the hospital who followed instructions, and it's likely you'll be excused at the outset. In any case, the evidence against him is really quite damning and I don't see how he can keep that out of the suit."

"But he's charging there was a conspiracy against him," Laxton said. "He claims we were all involved."

"I admit you might know more about that side of it than I do, and I don't want to hear about it. If I was you and any kind of discovery or anything came up, I'd lie like hell if you had to. Don't think for a minute Aysgarth and the board people will ever admit to anything."

207

Laxton was racking his brains to try to think if there was anything he'd said to Megan which may have hinted at some impropriety, but angrily told himself that when he began to think with his prick, his memory was gone. He began to think of all the famous people in history who had lost out because they hadn't kept it in their pants.

At the height of things he received a letter from Golliman. He always wondered why the stupid son of a bitch didn't just walk into his office and ask him anything he wanted to know. After all, Golliman was right next-door.

"It has come to my attention that you provided the Board of Medical Quality Assurance of the State with copies of all the transcripts of the hearing. I want to hear you did not do this, because you had no authority to do it. We must maintain absolute confidentiality in matters of this sort."

Laxton was tempted to ignore the letter, because all Golliman had to do was to phone their attorney to find out about it. He showed the letter to Aysgarth, who told him he'd already seen a copy.

"He sent a copy to every board member," Aysgarth said. "He's jealous that the board has been giving you all the glory for the hours you spent working your ass off to get rid of that idiot Trevellian, and Golliman doesn't have the brains to accomplish what you did. He's managed to persuade the board that he's the only one who should be allowed to talk to the Joint Commission people when they come to the hospital, so he can regain some glory. It will only take a moron to pull the wool over their eyes anyway, so don't worry about it. Just look after that pharmacy business for me, because if there's anything wrong there it could be a problem for me. Lense was a close friend of mine."

Laxton wished he had Megan to talk to, but he knew he couldn't do it. He hadn't realized how much he'd used her as a sounding board during their many clandestine meetings, and began to realize she had been much more than just a sexual exercise. After he thought about it, he decided to deal with Golliman's letter head on. He had the advantage of knowing Golliman had sent a blind copy to all board members, something Golliman couldn't know he knew. But he also knew he had to protect his source.

Laxton wrote a letter to each member of the board enclosing a copy of Golliman's letter to him.

I am enclosing a copy of a letter which I received from the Chief of Staff, which is exactly the kind of subject which should not be in writing under any circumstances, especially with the current suit filed against everyone. He could have asked me about this matter verbally, or

208

consulted with our attorney. Instead he opened a paper trail concerning this matter which could be subject to discovery. In any case, no damage has been done at this point in time because the copies of transcripts sent to the Licensing Board were sent in response to a specific subpoena. The Board of Medical Quality Assurance obtained a subpoena signed by a judge, which must be obeyed, and which required we send them copies of all transcripts of the hearing, as well as the final determination. This subpoena is in the hands of our attorney, and I have a copy in my office as well. I would suggest that in future materials in writing which may impact the suit be avoided, although this matter is clearly not an issue because of the circumstances under which it was done.

He sent a copy to Golliman, which avoided writing a letter directly to him. Aysgarth telephoned Laxton as soon as he got his copy of the letter sent to all board members. "Good work. I'll roast the stupid bastard at the next board meeting. Just shove the knife all the way in, that's what I'm going to do."

Laxton knew Aysgarth had come to dislike Golliman. Laxton had never cared about the matter one way or the other until then. He decided Golliman was too stupid to be a danger, and not worth a lot of effort.

The pharmacy was another matter, and although Laxton didn't understand about Aysgarth's friendship with Lense, he knew it was vital to keep on the right side of Aysgarth and intended to do so.

The new pharmacist was female. She was one of those rabbit faced women with buckteeth and a frightened manner. Laxton found a lot of drugs outdated, but didn't say much about it. He cleared them all from the shelves and put them in a large bag, which he took and threw into the bottom drawer of a cadenza in his office. He made sure the disposals were listed and had them designated destroyed. He didn't feel he could trust rabbit face to take care of it.

When he next ran into Golliman on the corridor, the Chief of Staff pretended not to see him. Laxton decided with some satisfaction Golliman had got his come-uppance.

The Joint Commission of Accreditation of Hospitals is another of those bureaucratic bodies which determines whether hospitals are doing the right thing or doing good work, and to be turned down by them could have a serious fiscal impact on the hospital. The Inspectors for the organization, usually retired incompetent morons, go to the hospital often accompanied by a couple of docs from the State Medical Association. Also accompanying this motley crew is some Director of

Nursing who somehow got away from her home hospital, based on the belief of the Administrator of the hospital where she is supposed to be working, that having a connection with Joint Commission will stand them in good stead when their turn comes for review. They turn down less than one percent of the hospitals accredited by Joint Commission, and of those who were turned down, ninety per cent were granted accreditation on re-review.

The Joint Commission came and went, the Inspectors dogged by Golliman. After they had gone, the hospital personnel were given a little party by Administration. It lasted for an hour after work.

Trevellian's suit came up in court the following month. The hospital attorneys had filed a response which quoted numerous cases where actions such as the one Trevellian filed, had failed because they hadn't followed due process. The Judge decided the case should be dismissed because Trevellian had not filed a mandamus action to overturn the decision of the Hearing Committee and Hospital Board.

The option open to Trevellian was to file such an action, when all the cases heard would become public knowledge. Of course other cases might come to light and Trevellian might face malpractice suits.

The following week Laxton's phone rang. Aysgarth had been burning up the phone lines because he had found out that Jamestown's work was beginning to create problems with the review organization. But it wasn't Aysgarth this time.

"Don't hang up," Megan said, "Herb's going to drop the whole matter and leave things as they are. Just wait until you're convinced I'm telling the truth. Then I'll call you, or better still call me."

CHAPTER 31

GOLLIMAN'S INTERLUDE

Aysgarth had invited Laxton for one of his lunch deals. On those occasions he was more voluble and let out a stream of information. He was in one of his hyper and expansive modes carrying on about enlarging the hospital, suggesting Laxton needed a better role, talking of how much more money could be made. Eventually he got down to the nitty-gritty.

"Have you looked at Jamestown's stuff?" Aysgarth said, as he put away gobs of Chinese food.

Laxton had a real problem because he knew all about Jamestown from Canada and was pretty sure Aysgarth didn't know he had any knowledge of Jamestown from Canada.

"What about his background before?" Laxton asked. "Do you have a written report on him?"

Aysgarth considered this for a minute or two before he went on. "The reports came out of British Columbia, but not from any specific hospital. There were a lot of personal testimonials by way of letter. I don't know they weren't lies, but his license was all right."

It didn't surprise Laxton that Aysgarth might think they were lies. He was used to dealing with his colleagues in the hospital whom Laxton knew lied to him. What they didn't know was Aysgarth always found out sooner or later.

"My people have been on to me for a long time about Jamestown, and Rekuf has called me and discussed it, but no one wants to go through another Trevellian mess," Laxton said. "Different situation. Entirely different. Jamestown's under contract to me, and I can break it and he can't do a thing about it. Just don't want the scandal. Real question is whether he's losing us money yet, and whether the peer review people at the State level are on to him."

Laxton sighed. It was always either money or power with Aysgarth.

"Bit of a complication is that he hasn't been feeling well," Aysgarth continued, "perhaps the climate doesn't suit him this far south."

"He's out doors playing tennis all the time, or so Veronica said," Laxton said as he finished his tablespoon of cold china tea.

"He's going to have to go somehow. I saw those figures you sent

211

me on the costs, and I've got trouble with that accountant Gotcher and Slimey moved into the board ages ago. I know how well we're doing at the clinic here, and he keeps coming up with figures showing we're either at a loss or breaking even. Fortunately, I've enough on those bastards on the board to keep them under control."

"Something weird is happening with Golliman," Laxton said. "He's been writing around to find things out about my background, and for no good reason."

"Golliman has become greedy and a liability, but there isn't anyone else who'll do his job We're only paying him four thousand a year on top of his practice and he wants more money and power now. Have a talk with Gotcher if you have any evidence of what you say. You'd better wait a week or two because Golliman wants to discuss your position with the board. I shall be there of course, so he won't get away with anything. We might have to take steps to get rid of him."

Laxton started his enquiries about whether Golliman had been writing to places about him, and was lucky enough to get his hands on a response from the American Specialty Board. Golliman didn't even see the letter.

Golliman wrote to Laxton about the quality of care files and charts which Laxton kept in his office.

"I am deeply concerned about maintaining privacy relating to quality of care and I don't think these reports should be kept in your office. I would appreciate receiving them at your earliest convenience."

Laxton could just have copied the documents and sent the originals to Golliman, but he felt to concede anything to him would just open a can of worms. He told Aysgarth that he was going to do nothing.

"I was going to call you. Forget Golliman for the minute. Jamestown just collapsed on the tennis court. They're going to do an autopsy tomorrow. I'm sorry about it, but it does solve a problem."

Jamestown had suffered a cerebral hemorrhage and had died instantly. Aysgarth called Laxton's office to tell him the news, and to let him know Golliman wouldn't get to talk to the board until the next month.

"When is Jamestown to be buried?" Laxton said.

"You know that's the weirdest thing," Aysgarth said. "Someone in Vancouver claimed the body; someone who claims to be his wife. I thought his wife was here living with him."

Laxton couldn't see any harm in telling Aysgarth part of the truth now Jamestown was dead.

"Jamestown lived with a girl who had been his office nurse and he was separated from his wife. I believe he supported her and was just as happy she stayed in Vancouver."

"You knew him then," Aysgarth said quickly.

"He worked at a different hospital," Laxton said. "He was down at the Vancouver General."

"Well, his body's going back to Vancouver for burial. I don't know what will happen when the two women are at the funeral together. I suppose I should go. Someone has to go. Do you want to take the trip?"

"Why not send Golliman or the Administrator or someone else," Laxton said.

He didn't really want Golliman snooping around Vancouver and was very sure Aysgarth wouldn't send him, and the hospital administrator was hardly suitable. He was still trying to think of someone else because it offended his sense of hypocrisy to attend the funeral of someone he'd thrown out of a hospital. He toyed with the idea of going and not showing up for the funeral, but dismissed it at once.

"I know," Aysgarth said. "I'll send the administrator from Flashing Rod Clinic, a most appropriate choice. I suppose we should pay for Marion to go too. She lived with him and they seemed to get on well. I pity her. He probably didn't leave her a penny, but I think we can keep her on here at the clinic and make her full time instead of part time until she decides what she wants to do."

"She made him very happy," Laxton said.

Aysgarth's unexpected flashes of compassion often surprised Laxton.

"You know," Aysgarth said musingly, "I think he killed some of the patients he operated on."

It was the end of the Jamestown and Trevellian era. To Laxton it was the end of two evil men. One had been removed by the hearing process, the other by a higher authority.

During the month following Golliman flooded Laxton's office with letters, since Laxton hadn't replied to the first letter. One of the letters sent by Golliman said that he must see the correspondence on one of the physicians. Laxton sent a note telling him to see the quality assurance nurse.

Laxton got Gotcher to come by the office, and showed him what was going on with Golliman. Gotcher never liked to be caught in any trap or involved in overt conflict, and he didn't want any disturbances.

He knew Laxton had saved the hospital, but he wanted Golliman where he was.

"I'm going to speak to him," Gotcher said. " I think he should stop writing these foolish letters. I suppose he's too proud a Texan to come next door and talk to you. Try to work closer with him. I'll speak to him today."

During the week following problems arose with one of the vascular surgeons, resulting in the loss of a patient's leg. The review organization was already onto it and Laxton called the surgeon, Dr. Grass, to come into his office to discuss the case.

"I don't know who told the review people about this case," Laxton said. "It usually takes them three months to get to anything, so the first question is, how did they get the information?"

"I asked the Chief of Staff, and frankly, he said he was sure you told them," Grass said.

"Doctor Golliman might be Chief of Staff, but he's paranoid because they are looking at his work, and he thinks I'm responsible for that. My job is to protect you people, unless it's so gross as to be indefensible."

"Like Trevellian," Grass said.

"Yes, you know all about him."

"He was a fucking menace. You know, I tried to get information too, but was told it was in the ordinary course of review and there was only one other bit of information."

"And?"

"I brought your name up and they said they didn't know if you were aware of the case, but if not it wouldn't hurt to discuss it with you, so I knew it wasn't you who told them."

"It could have been the patient's family, because if they complain there's a fast review of the case."

"I'm absolutely sure it wasn't them."

Laxton sat lost in thought for a minute or two.

"You don't think it was Golliman himself, do you?" Grass said. "You know he hates Jews, and that's me."

"I do think he might have done the reporting, but not for that reason. We'll just have to wait awhile and see. Now what about the case?"

"It was a disaster. I don't think we should have even operated on the patient, but that's a retrospective view."

"Let me talk to San Francisco and see if I can't get it handled in-house," Laxton said.

After Grass had left Laxton got hold of Montpellier, in San Francisco. He said, "You know that vascular case Golliman reported out of here."

"The amputation after three surgeries?" Montpellier said.

"Yes. That's the one. Will you give me a shot at doing the necessary in-house stuff here in our QA committee?"

"After the job you did on Trevellian I think you deserve that. When are you coming to work for us?"

Laxton laughed. "You don't pay much," he said.

"By the way, Golliman tried to make out he did all the work on Trevellian, but I'd read the transcripts."

"For Christ's sake, don't let anyone know I sent you copies," Laxton said.

"Don't worry. We won't. Good luck with Grass."

The following day another letter came from Golliman.

"It came to my attention you have been attending all hospital committee meetings. Since you are not a member of the active medical staff I do not believe you have any authority to do this and I expect you will stay away from all meetings until this has been clarified by me at a future meeting of the Hospital Board."

Laxton had a letter of authority from the hospital board anyway, signed at the time of his appointment, so he just went to that day's meeting to find Golliman at the meeting, looking as though he might have apoplexy the moment he saw Laxton. Laxton quietly handed him a copy of his letter from the board before the meeting even began, and a few minutes after Rekuf called the meeting to order Golliman got up and walked out.

Aysgarth told Laxton that Golliman had his say at the board meeting, gave Laxton a copy of the minutes, and suggested that Laxton get an appointment with the board to give them a story which had the savings he had engineered for the hospital in it.

"Golliman thinks he can do your job and pick up extra money for himself by having us unload you and let him do the work."

Every year the Health Care Financing Administration published rather misleading statistics based on hospital deaths, and those found their way into the newspaper and caused hospitals a lot of trouble. A hospital had the right to respond before the data was released, and then they had to publish the hospital's response. Valley Hospital had never been in the newspapers, because Laxton had always had the death charts pulled and reviewed them himself and written an explanatory report. That year Golliman managed to see the report never reached

Laxton, and it was only when the Administrator saw what was about to happen that he dropped into Laxton's office. The charts were pulled on an emergency basis, and Laxton hauled them home, working over a weekend, twenty four hours without sleep, to write a suitable response, get it in, in time, to ensure nothing would appear in the newspapers. Worse, he had to beg the Feds for a twenty-four-hour extension for the response. The only thanks he got was from Aysgarth, who got the whole story.

When Laxton went before the board, he pulled no punches. He presented written evidence of what Golliman had tried to do, including the inappropriate inquiries into his background, and the numerous attempts to bypass Laxton with matters that fell in his own area of expertise. The board listened politely until Laxton revealed the attempt to get Grass into trouble. That bit got their attention. Up to that point it had been clear to Laxton that if the board thought Golliman could do both jobs and it would be cheaper for them, they might have taken that route. Suddenly, the hearing was sympathetic to him. Unfortunately Golliman had been told to stay away. Unfortunate because Laxton had questions for him which would have shown him to be the fool he was. The chairman reassured Laxton there was no danger he would lose his job, but hoped he would try to work a little more closely with Golliman.

The following day Laxton went into Golliman's office and kept his temper very well. He told Golliman he would drop by from time to time as the board chairman had suggested, and keep him updated on recent developments in the quality of care field. Laxton didn't feel optimistic that it would be helpful. He discussed Golliman's health with him in a friendly manner. His poor eyesight, the dermatitis from his scalp which led to the gray shoulders, and the heart irregularity Golliman was always boasting about. Golliman, for his part, tried to give the impression he was satisfied, but never once referred to the letters he'd sent, his inquiries, or any of the other sneaky things he had pulled off.

Everything became routine again. The Grass affair was solved by setting up monitoring, which Grass had no real problem accepting for ninety days, and that satisfied Montpellier and the Peer Review Organization.

One Friday Laxton's home phone rang. He was snoozing and answered it rather sleepily. The voice soon brought him upright.

"You must know it's over, and he's gone for several days. You'll think the reason is quite funny when you hear. I want to come up and

216

talk to you anyway," Megan said.

"I don't know," Laxton said with a sigh. "I just don't like the risks."

"Hang on for a minute or two. Trust me."

Whilst Laxton was holding, his doorbell rang.

"Damn," he said, and hung up.

He went to the door and opened it and Megan walked in.

"Where did you telephone from?" Laxton demanded.

"Downstairs in the lobby. I was determined to see you. It's been too long."

"Where's dear Herb?"

"He has a friend in Arizona, and Herb has a license there, so he's gone over to his friend's hospital and he's doing some surgery there because his friend broke his wrist and can't operate."

"How the hell did Herb get privileges at the hospital?"

"Kingman's a very small place, and Herb's friend more or less runs the hospital."

"Is this going to be permanent? I mean, is Herb moving to Arizona?"

"No way," Megan said. "He just wants to prove to himself he can continue to do surgery, and do it without anyone here in the LA area touching him."

"What a hell of a lot of gall," Laxton said, "but it almost runs in the family."

"Don't you want me here?"

"You didn't bring any clothes."

"I left the bag in the lobby. I came in a taxi."

"I'll go get the bag," Laxton said with resignation.

When he returned, Megan had relaxed completely. She was sitting on the sofa, ankles crossed, and her loose blouse hung in a provocative way. She wore a modest skirt which fell below the knee. Laxton didn't think it would stay on that long.

"How have you been doing?" he said.

"Once Herb got his offer from Arizona he decided there and then he could take the occasional trip, and he might as well drop the appeals. I sighed with relief."

"Why didn't you go with him?"

"Obviously you've never been to Kingman."

"So as far as you can see, he won't cause trouble here."

"Laxy, the only thing he's been worrying about is the Licensing Board. He had a letter from them saying they were looking into these

217

cases, but that's a month ago and he hasn't heard a thing. How would they know about it anyway?"

"Beats me," Laxton said. "But any privilege restrictions have to be reported to the Licensing Board."

"If that's all, he probably won't hear any more from them then because they won't have any details of the cases."

"Perhaps that'll be all," Laxton said. "But don't forget the grape vine. You know you really shocked me when you served the papers. I've never heard of anything like that. Why didn't he have it done in a regular manner?"

"To save money he didn't even need to save. But I made sure everyone thought of me as his Administrator from the nursing home. How's everything going at the Valley dump anyway?"

"God, have I had trouble with Golliman. He's an egomaniac."

"What's he up to now?"

"He tried to get my job and his folded into one for himself," Laxton said. "I managed to get the board to cool it for now. He couldn't do my job anyway."

"Watch out for him. He's a mean, dangerous s.o.b, even if he looks benign," Megan said. "You'll never know what's going on behind your back while he's smiling to your face. He hasn't got the guts to come up and tell you what he thinks. Just don't trust him. You know, I suppose, he's been Chief of Staff as long as anyone can remember."

"Well, they do have a general meeting and an election," Laxton said.

"No one else wants the job, so he always gets elected. Also, they're a little afraid of him because they think he's Aysgarth's boy, or else used to be, but he does go to board meetings."

"I know that because he tore what I was doing apart at one," Laxton said.

"Say, are the ground rules still the same?" Laxton said, abruptly changing the subject.

"Of course they are," Megan replied. "And what and who have you been doing since you made sure I was out of the picture?"

"I haven't seen or talked to anyone else outside work. I was a fool to think I could just let you go. I can't, despite the risks."

"What risks? There haven't been any, and I was really smooth when I did the deliveries. Today, I used two taxis to get here, and I wasn't seen in the lobby. I did it all quickly. As soon as I'd punched in the combination and got through the door, I just picked up the phone and got you right away. No revelations will come from me. I want you as much as possible, and if ever there was a hint from Herb, I'd be gone. I want you, and at a different time and different place we'd have been a great team. By the way, I think you should look around for a job somewhere else, close by of course."

"Why do you say that?"

"I just heard, and you have just confirmed, that Golliman is up to something which might lose you your tenure, unless you have an iron-clad contract, and those people don't give out contracts. Why don't you try something in a larger hospital? I can tell you of one or two in the area who are looking. You're too good for those people anyway. They just use you as a tool for their own needs, and their commitment to quality is a joke."

Laxton knew a lot of what she was saying made sense but he wasn't ready to pack it in yet. He really thought he could still make a difference and was doing so, but Megan had put a new spin on stuff and he wondered where she got all her information. He doubted that the rather illegal way Trevellian had been suspended had come to her ears, but nothing would surprise him at this point in time.

"You heard Jamestown died, I suppose," Laxton said.

"He was a worse surgeon than Herb," Megan said, "it was common knowledge after his first month here, and he and that woman weren't married."

"You aren't seeing anyone else from the hospital, are you?" Laxton asked.

"I'm not seeing anyone from there or screwing anyone from there."

"All right, I won't ask where you get your information, and I do believe what you're telling me."

Megan pursed her lips and then smiled that inviting smile which affected Laxton so much. Soon the affection was transferred from lips to hips.

After the hectic weekend Laxton went back on Monday feeling in a joyous mood, confident and ready for hard work. He accompanied Aysgarth to a finance seminar in Los Angeles. Aysgarth slept through much of the seminar. Laxton had noticed his boss seemed much more fatigued recently and had driven off the highway one night when he fell asleep at the wheel. He told Aysgarth he should get a medical check up.

"It's my stomach," Aysgarth said, "and I'm taking Zantac for it."

Laxton went by Golliman's office a couple of days later because Golliman had left a message that a black orthopedic surgeon he suspected Laxton used to know had applied for staff privileges, and he wanted Laxton's opinion.

"Certainly I knew him, " Laxton said. "He was so bad they threw him out of a small, poor quality HMO.

"I shall keep him out of here," Golliman said. "I'll ask for a full written recommendation from the HMO and I know they won't give him one. Oh, by the way, how's Mrs. Trevellian these days?"

"What do you mean?"

Golliman chuckled. "When Trevellian hears how you and his wife have been carrying on, and when the hospital board hears, we'll have an interesting situation. You could save everyone trouble and resign."

Laxton walked out of the office. How had Golliman found out or was it a bluff? Laxton didn't think so. It hadn't come from Megan, of that he felt sure, but he remembered asking Golliman why papers were being served by Trevellian's wife, and he'd given that away inadvertently at the time the papers we served. There must have been someone else who knew something for Golliman to have got hold of the information. Would Golliman use it? Laxton would bet on it. He resisted sharing the information with anyone, including Megan, until he'd had time to think about it.

Golliman became friendlier after this episode and would actually come into Laxton's office.

"You're getting to be pals with Golliman," Veronica said one day. "Maybe he's trying to learn about quality and utilization at last. That's if you think his brain still functions."

Veronica could be vicious, and both she and Laxton were frank with each other.

"I think he's started to be a friend," but Laxton's voice betrayed some doubts.

A day later, during the late afternoon, Golliman burst into Laxton's office carrying an electrocardiogram. "Look at this. I just had it done because I had chest pain last night."

Laxton was horrified to see the auricles were fibrillating, but worse there were some runs of ventricular fibrillation, a terminal event.

"We're going to ICU right now," Laxton said. "Look at that fibrillation."

"I've had auricular fibrillation for years," Golliman said. "I haven't done a thing about it, and look at me, I'm just fine."

"Not with the ventricles fibrillating. You're at great risk."

220

"I'll go to the office next door and collect a couple of items. Will you ask Sinclair or someone to meet me in ICU?"

"Of course," Laxton said. "I'll call him now."

"I don't think I need to be admitted."

"Get over there now," Laxton said as he grabbed the phone.

"I'm not surprised, " was Sinclair's comment, "I've seen him once, and he won't do anything you tell him to do. He's the worst patient. I'm on my way to ICU."

Golliman was admitted. Laxton thought he had better let Aysgarth know because the ventricular fibrillation was very serious.

"Ah," Aysgarth said, " maybe we'll have another stroke of luck. Just joking. Anyway, I'm on my way down there so I'll go see him. Sometimes we have to give our friends a little help."

Laxton went to ICU and sought out Sinclair. "I'm just going to zonk him with sedatives. Obviously, he's had a mild infarction but he's his own worst enemy. It's a wonder he isn't dead already."

Laxton went to Golliman's bedside. He was in an end bed, slightly secluded from others, almost a private room,

"I'll see you later," Laxton said to him.

There was no one on the corridor, and he got into Golliman's office with a credit card. He'd never opened a door that way before, but it was easy. Laxton did a thorough search and managed to even access the one drawer which was locked without breaking the lock. He found his own file and picked it up. There was nothing in it about Megan and himself, but he took it anyway. He searched for a file on Aysgarth. Since Aysgarth was a staff member a file had to be kept in the office, so he purged the file taking out anything that he thought Aysgarth might not want in it. He abandoned the search after about two hours. He left Golliman's office without being seen, and unlocked his own office next door. He sat at his desk for a few minutes and looked through the material. What a devious man was Golliman

The following morning he went in at his usual hour.

"Doctor Sinclair was here looking for you. He's gone to the ER," Veronica said. "Do you know Doctor Golliman died last night?"

Laxton looked at her with disbelief. He turned on his heels and went to the ER. Sinclair saw him and left the patient he was attending and came over right away.

"I didn't want to bother you last night, because there wasn't anything else for you to do. I suppose they told you in the QA department that he'd died. He must have had another massive heart attack. Aysgarth was in to see him and soon after that he went into ventricular fibrillation, and died. He was very lucky to have you do what you did for him; I don't think anyone could have made him go to ICU. It was bad luck he died. He'd neglected himself for years."

Laxton stood with his head bowed for a moment or two. Strange he'd died right after he'd seen Aysgarth.

"Don't feel badly, you did more than enough for him," Sinclair said. "The family doesn't want an autopsy, and there's no reason to do one."

"You know he was the wrong person in the wrong place at the wrong time," Laxton said. "I'd better order a wreath for the funeral."

CHAPTER 32

FROM DEATH TO DISHONESTY

Trevellian was still away at the time of Golliman's funeral.

"You can be sure he wouldn't have gone to the funeral anyway," Megan said. She was at Laxton's apartment.

"One thing we need to talk about is that Golliman knew about us, and I'm wondering how many more may," Laxton said. He had agreed to let her come to the apartment because he needed to get to the bottom of the leak.

Megan went quite red in the face. "No one else knows I swear. The truth is that Golliman's office nurse used to work for me at the nursing home, and I believed she was still a close friend. I see her fairly often. I'm sure Golliman didn't know we were friends, but she had a close relationship, and I don't mean sexual, with Golliman. She gave me a lot of stuff about the hearings when Herb was before the committee, and told me a lot about the hospital and a lot about what was going on with Golliman. That's how I knew Golliman was no friend of yours. What happened is inexcusable. I was telling her something about the hearing and she realized the information could only have come from you, and she asked me if we had been seeing each other. I realized if I lied it might be worse. I didn't know she had let it slip to Golliman until a few days ago, and I didn't know how to tell you or what to do, but I've done one thing. In any case with his background, and I know all about him, I didn't think it would ever come to light. What did he say?"

"It doesn't matter," Laxton said. "You don't know she hasn't told others in Golliman's office or in the hospital. You don't know she won't use it in the future."

"I do know the answers to those questions, because she doesn't work in Golliman's office anymore. She's back working for me, and I'm sure she knows her job depends on keeping her trap shut. She was very upset when she knew what she'd done, and did volunteer the information. She's too well paid now to either move from the nursing home or shoot her mouth off anywhere. That's one thing I think I've done right."

"We don't know Golliman didn't tell someone else," Laxton said.

Megan was almost in tears.

"Let me quote you," Laxton said. "Let's play it by ear."

223

Megan knew how to show gratitude for something she wanted so badly.

Aysgarth didn't hide his pleasure at the recent events and told Laxton he would now move forward to his next strategy.

"We came out pretty well," Aysgarth said, and he was quite bouncy. "Two undesirables died in less than two weeks. Natural causes are always the simplest way. Of course sometimes a little potassium chloride helps. I want you to activate your application for staff privileges, and then I'm going to get your whole portfolio changed and see you get a bunch more money as well. We'll make major changes in this hospital and come out with a larger institution making more money and I'll see you get your share. Just watch me."

Laxton thought it was better to say nothing at that point in time. He really wasn't clear what Aysgarth had in mind, but he allowed himself one question.

"Is the Vice Chief of Staff going to move up?"

"Certainly not." Aysgarth replied. "He doesn't even want to be Chief of Staff, and he's innocuous anyway. I want him where he is. I shall set up the Chief of Staff thing, and you'll get the job by unanimous consent, and you're going to keep the paycheck you get now as well as one for Chief of Staff. You're going into the two hundred and fifty thousand bracket to start, and you're going to help wield power. We've got to take over the board and do what we want to do in the institution."

Laxton was not averse to more money and more power, because he inwardly intended to turn the hospital into a class institution and then hold it up as an example to others. He hadn't forgotten what Rugger had told him. He knew he'd have to get rid of some people somehow, and bring in others. Aysgarth wouldn't stop that, as long as the others weren't sharing the kitty. A good income from patient care, yes. A share of the hospital's profits, no. That was Aysgarth's philosophy.

It took Aysgarth a week to get Laxton on the staff and appointed Chief of Staff and Vice President of Medical Affairs. The Chief of Staff appointment was done by write in ballot of all the medical staff. Since Aysgarth got all the ballots, Laxton wondered about the real result.

"I need to know just how many enemies I have out there," Laxton said.

"Of course you do, but there was only one vote against you."

"Trevellian," Laxton said.

"Funny as it may seem, he voted for you. No, it was Smiley, and we'll take care of him in our own time."

He was only one board member, but he was Gotcher's partner, and that bothered Laxton. "What about Gotcher?"

"He voted for you. Smiley is retiring from practice, but going to stay on the board and he wanted a position. We're gonna give him one. He fancies himself as a salesman, so he can go out and do some recruiting. That'll be on the next board agenda. That will keep him quiet and give him lots to do. I'm sure you can feed him some places to go to look for staff." Aysgarth winked.

The first order of business for Laxton was to go through all of Golliman's notes and files in his office. Laxton concluded Golliman was a mean, incompetent son of a bitch. The notes, materials, and scrutiny he had hidden away on Aysgarth were inexcusable. He had a file with personal letters which were clearly the property of their owners. He was tempted to hand them over to Aysgarth, but could see the down side of that. He decided to take them home, keep them there, and say nothing unless he was asked about the material.

The first board meeting accomplished Aysgarth's first goal of getting Smiley out of the way doing recruiting. It would be a month before he got started as he had to get out of his family practice. The meeting had a lot of routine stuff and Laxton, acting under Aysgarth's instructions, gave a very routine report with little or no hint of who might be coming or going. It seemed incredible to Laxton that Aysgarth had the power to influence the credentials committee to the extent he could get someone put onto the hospital staff with virtually no adequate inquiries into credentials. It was against all protocol, and very dangerous, but in fact it seemed to keep undesirables out.

One of the first things Laxton did, as soon as he found out board members could do almost anything they wanted to do in their own area, was to get the wall taken out between what had been Golliman's office and his own and to get the Medical Staff Secretary behind a partition so she wouldn't hear any conversations in his now expanded office. He left the door to the quality assurance and utilization department in place, but still kept it locked. By closing off the original door to his office, he now had a lot of space and still an escape route if he wanted a back door out.

Aysgarth was getting his Long Beach business better organized, shoving another level of management between himself and the recovery of, and distribution of, the contraband. He felt the more remote he was from actual operations, the less likely he was to run into troubles with authority. He gave a lot of thought of how to insert someone into the hospital organization, but ultimately bit the bullet and used the expertise of Alex "The Wilt" Giocomani, who he had met at one of his parties some years before. For Aysgarth, the influence of Giocomani meant the security of not having to clear an employee because he would know who to hire and how to control them. Aysgarth's meeting with Giocomani was memorable because he was able to discuss something which had been very much on his mind for sometime. It's all very well to make a lot of money illegally, but very hard to keep it hidden. Of course that same problem was a major problem for Giocomani.

"Have you ever thought of using the hospital as a laundering operation?" Aysgarth said.

The Wilt was a large man with jowls and a harsh, almost hoarse voice. He was always suntanned from his many journeys to South America, and he had the appearance of a solid businessman and would have passed as pure American had it not been for the slight Mediterranean accent.

"Not much problem setting up a foundation and corporations for financing, but what about profits?"

"The hospital runs at a profit," Aysgarth said. "That's not a problem."

"We have to have some control over the operation. There isn't a sweatshop I run where we're not on the board of the outfit. I'd like to have two on the board who'll do my bidding."

"I've just made a move where I've pushed a fellow on the board who will do my bidding. Trust me."

"Is he in on your operation?"

"This guy is too honest for that. He has to be kept outside any activities which maybe questionable, because he wouldn't fit. Don't worry. I can manipulate him and he'll do what we need done. In a hospital you don't make a profit if you haven't honest connections and decent quality care, and this is the one man who'll give us that. He doesn't have a streak of dishonesty on him, but he is learning the political smarts."

Aysgarth felt his description of Laxton was rather well done and very accurate and he expected Giocomani to see the rationale of someone honest who was subject to pressure. He wasn't disappointed.

"We have to live with them bums anyway, and you need some on your side. I just got one straightened away in one of our other operations, but you know all them politicians become bent."

226

"Bent?" Aysgarth raised his eyebrows.

"They don't call what they're doing crooked, but sure as hell that's what they'd call it if I was doing it. If he's going to be political, he'll end up being controlled."

"Not a big politician. Just local hospital stuff," Aysgarth said. "Your other operations going well?"

"Arkansas is weird, but when they listen and they see bucks rolling their way, they sure become cooperative all the way from the Governor down. In fact the Governor's in on it all. Let me get our people to set up the corporations and the foundation, and you look at the board seats and getting some control."

"How about compromising one or two of the present board members?"

"That'd work," The Wilt said. "But that's up to you."

The only thing Aysgarth wasn't overjoyed about was that he was compromising himself with people he'd have preferred not to have to deal with, but he had overall plans for total control of the hospital, and he knew these people knew how to help him launder his money, which was becoming an embarrassment.

Aysgarth managed to get both Gotcher and Smiley involved in a business relationship where they first accepted money which was coming directly from the illicit operation, and later managed to get them compromised by setting up a paper trail which led from them right back to the operation. The delightful thing to Aysgarth was neither one of them was really aware of what exactly was going on, and they believed they were in the import-export business, which in a way they were.

Smiley was out trying to sell the hospital so other MD's would use it, and he got to a group in a nearby town. The advantage would have been adding thirty people to the medical staff, mostly family practitioners, but a surgeon as well. They all had well-established practices. Smiley was quite excited about the prospect, but eventually the group themselves began to have doubts. As an added incentive he sent bonus checks to each one of them at the month end, although they hadn't admitted any patients to the hospital. This eventually came out at a board meeting when the group decided they definitely weren't coming. The checks had a negative effect on some of the group, who returned them uncashed. Others, who also didn't come, were not as principled. Probably no one would ever have found out about this operation, but Gotcher and Smiley's accountant asked how the returned checks were going to be handled. And he did it at a meeting of the board. That got Aysgarth asking questions. Laxton had questions too, but limited his questions to asking what the purpose was behind the handout, and Smiley was forced to admit he used it as an incentive to get them to become staff members.

"You have to give them a bit of a push," Smiley said.

"Even if it's risky and dishonest?" Laxton said.

CHAPTER 33

AYSGARTH CONTROLS

Aysgarth had made a point of getting Laxton to his home for evening meals on a number of occasions. The matter of the yacht had come up a number of times, but Laxton had made it clear he didn't want to go down there, particularly at night. His reluctance to visit the yacht day or night had come up after a luncheon with Terry Chart, who was Aysgarth's Administrator for the Flashing Rod operation. Terry had worked for Aysgarth for several years, and had been close to him on all issues. He even came to the hospital for meetings of the physician group Aysgarth had made successful as an Independent Practice Association, and had helped negotiate many of their contracts.

Terry had told Laxton at lunch one day that he had refused to go to the yacht.

"After all," he said, "I'm a family man, and I don't want to do anything to do with the sort of activities which are reported to go on down there."

Laxton had no idea whether the implication of Terry's comment was valid or not, but he wasn't going to let himself be put in any situation which might prove difficult and embarrassing and might alter his relationship with Aysgarth. He had no wish to embarrass or anger someone he regarded as his boss.

Aysgarth had immediately accepted Laxton's position, and all clandestine meetings were held at Aysgarth's home or one of his favorite restaurants. They were only clandestine in that Aysgarth wanted them to be private, and didn't want others to know what he was planning. He shared his ideas with Laxton because he expected and got his support at meetings. In return Laxton got physicians he had managed to contact and select onto the medical staff quickly.

"I think the time has come to broaden the board and get a couple of outsiders we can rely on," Aysgarth said. "This will need some changes to the Development Corporation regulations which I'll draw up and get the boys to adopt."

Laxton wondered how. He couldn't see any of them giving up power unless they had to. But that was Aysgarth's problem, because Laxton didn't sit on the Development Corporation. He wondered why he was being informed.

"I have a couple of names to bring up when these regulations are changed," Aysgarth said, "and I'll need your vote to stick them on the board."

"I can't see a problem," Laxton said. "Whom do you have in mind?"

"I have a couple of business associates. Bright people. One is an international financier who keeps a low profile."

The surgical aspects of care at the hospital were a continued anxiety for Laxton. Some of the older surgeons seemed to forget basic principles of surgery. One well-respected surgeon had operated on a woman with a pelvic abscess which resulted from diverticulitis of the colon. The correct procedure was to divert the flow of fecal material by doing a colostomy, which he did. About two years later the woman returned healthy and happy, but complaining of a swelling around the colostomy site. It was correctly determined to be a hernia, and the surgeon said he would repair it.

"While you're at it, why don't you hook my bowel back up, I just feel great and have no troubles now."

You don't have to be bright to know that if you have a pipe, which is damaged, and you divert the flow away from the damaged pipe you won't get leakage, but if you hook it back up again without repairing the pipe you'll end up where you started. The surgeon didn't even examine the lower bowel with X-Rays or an instrument, he just went ahead and hooked it back up and repaired the hernia. The poor woman didn't even get out of the hospital before she had another diverticular perforation and pelvic abscess. Numerous operations later she died.

It was part of Laxton's job to monitor and counsel such surgeons. That surgeon, who had a great track record, had pulled off something worthy of Trevellian.

"How could you do something which every text book of surgery tells you not to do?" Laxton said.

"It was a mistake, and I know I'll be before the QA committee. I'll just admit I was wrong."

Despite the tragedy, Laxton had virtually no problems with a surgeon who admitted his error, provided it wasn't repeated. It always meant more paper work and discussions at the QA committee, with competitors in the background whispering about the possibility of stopping the surgeon, or restricting his work. It made for an unpleasant atmosphere.

With Golliman gone the staff had accepted Laxton as a wise and benevolent Chief of Staff who would help to protect them wherever possible. Most were grateful for his association with the board, although they hadn't liked it at first, and once they saw the Trevellian situation as an isolated incident they were comfortable with Laxton.

Laxton had a lot more trouble with Ching, a gynecologist, who had five malpractice suits filed against him, and was militant in his attitude despite errors totally condemned by his peers. Laxton knew Ching operated at another hospital and, after discussing the situation with Aysgarth, he sent for Ching.

"Frankly," Laxton said, "you have five malpractice cases filed against you and you're going to lose four of them."

"I didn't do anything wrong," Ching said. "People are just after money."

Although that was usually what malpractice suits were all about, in Ching's case there had been condemnation from his own department and the QA committee, and questions had been asked at the board. The first malpractice case was about to go to court when Laxton summoned Ching.

"You have a choice," Laxton said. "I have here a letter of resignation from the staff of this hospital which, if you sign and leave quietly, will not be publicized or mentioned in any way. If you choose not to sign the letter of resignation, then I shall suspend your privileges for obstetrics and surgery in this hospital, and this will, of course, be reported to the Licensing Board and become a matter of public record in short order. That will mean the other hospitals will hear about it, the State Board of Medical Quality Assurance, who issue your license, will pursue the matter to try to remove your license to practice, and you can be sure your license will be removed. Also, it will most certainly come out in the malpractice suit that you have been suspended from surgery and obstetrics in this hospital, which won't do much for your case."

"I need twenty four hours to think about this," Ching said.

"You haven't got twenty four hours. If you don't sign this letter now, I'll issue the suspension right now and call an immediate emergency meeting of the Medical Executive Committee and it will be in the hands of the licensing people before the day is out."

"I'll eventually get everyone here," Ching said nastily, as he signed the letter of resignation. "I'd like to know why this happened to me."

"You were the wrong person in the wrong place at the wrong time," Laxton said, as he ushered Ching out and prepared to notify all departments of the immediate resignation.

"How did it go?" Aysgarth asked later.

"Maybe I couldn't have done all the things I threatened him

with," Laxton said, "but I could have done many of them. Our strength was he hadn't been here but a year or two, and he had all those malpractice cases filed against him."

"I have complete confidence that all those things would have happened," Aysgarth said. "I have a pretty good idea what you can do when you have to. It's just as well you're so honest. You'd have made a damn good criminal."

Within a month the board took on two lay members, Giocomani and the Reverend Potsweller. Aysgarth knew both. The Reverend was a former catholic priest who had been kicked out of the church a year before and had become some kind of minister to Giocomani and his buddies. He had a great advantage in that in his collar and gown he was able to make many journeys overseas, especially if there was something very important afoot, and his journeys were deliberately limited, and sometimes routed through Rome, so that he had never aroused any suspicions as he went through customs. Aysgarth actually believed that, although the Reverend was associated with The Wilt, he really was legitimate.

Aysgarth got Laxton away for a couple of courses at the hospital's expense, and it just happened the dates coincided with the next board meeting. Aysgarth told Laxton there was nothing much for the meeting anyway, so not to worry about it. In fact it was the meeting where the corporate entities and the Foundation were reported. The hospital accountant was excluded from handling matters related to them, and an attorney's office well known to Giocomani was in charge.

Gotcher smiled with pleasure when he heard about the initial donations being made. Smiley went along happily, even when the hospital accountant felt he should have some control of the accounts.

Aysgarth told Laxton that the hospital now had a foundation for contributions so they could expect money for development and improvement. Suddenly, without a word of support or mention of activity to the board, Aysgarth was rushing round the hospital with an architect planning to redevelop the lab, X-Ray, and expand the hospital. A government certificate of need was no longer required in California.

Laxton thought about all this but said nothing because he hadn't been told anything. Aysgarth also tried to introduce interns to the hospital from the Osteopathic College. He got students from the college into the hospital, but ran into opposition from Gotcher and Smiley. Aysgarth found out they could get more funds if the hospital was teaching. Gotcher and Smiley vehemently opposed helping train D.O's. They wanted an affiliation with an MD University. There was little or no chance of that. It seemed ironic to Laxton who knew that Gotcher and Smiley had been in the last DO graduating class from UCI when California had outlawed Osteopathic Colleges, so with their osteopathic training they had been given M.D.'s.

CHAPTER 34

SECRET LIFE

"Why the hell is Aysgarth staying in an apartment in Long Beach when he has the yacht down there?" Laxton asked Terry.

"It's as much beyond me as it is beyond you. It seems like having two residences in the same town."

Neither Laxton nor Terry had any inkling what was going on, although both had reservations about Aysgarth's lifestyle. Terry had filled Laxton in on a number of Aysgarth's utilization methods, mostly because Aysgarth had Laxton doing it for him for a couple of weeks. Every day Laxton would go to the Flashing Rod Administration office and deal with the requests. Aysgarth had told Laxton he wanted utilization tight, but Laxton couldn't go as far as Aysgarth had with a patient who had landed in another hospital. The ER physician there had called Aysgarth for permission to admit the patient for twenty four-hour observation for a possible heart attack.

"Let me speak to the patient," Aysgarth said.

"Are you having any pain now?" he said when the patient came on the phone.

"No, not at the moment, doctor," the patient said.

"How did you get down there?"

"My car is here in the parking lot."

"Discharge yourself from the hospital and drive to our Emergency. They'll be expecting you. If you get any pain on the way, go to the nearest phone and call 911 for the paramedics."

When the patient got to their ER they found it was his cervical spine and he could be treated as an outpatient. When Laxton heard the story he knew it was impossible for Aysgarth to be sure the patient had a cervical spine lesion, and that twenty-four hours in a hospital with appropriate tests would have been the quality way to go. His own utilization decisions wouldn't be that risky.

"What's he doing there this couple of weeks?" Laxton asked.

"I'm not sure, but I can tell you I think Long Beach is a hell of a place for a vacation," Terry said.

"What does Babs think about all this?"

"His wife is used to it. She's taken to coming to the office to help with the accounting here."

For Aysgarth things were going well. His apartment distanced

234

him from the illicit operation. He had Gotcher picking up money from the yacht, and had told Gotcher he wasn't using the yacht the rest of the time, to give him an opportunity to hold some of his clandestine meetings with Molly down there, should he wish.

The Wilt had insisted on visiting the yacht once, and used this opportunity to question Aysgarth more about the board.

"Who's in our pocket?" he said.

"We have Gotcher and Smiley for sure, and the rest follow along."

"What about this Laxton you put there?"

"Laxton is totally honest, and will clean the hospital up for us to make it a class operation. He wants the best operation in Southern California, and I think we'll get it."

"Maybe we ought to involve him a little more, for extra insurance."

"We'd lose him if we tried. He hasn't the capacity for any activity that isn't a hundred percent above board. This is going to pay off for us. Don't worry about Laxton."

It was eight days later Aysgarth resurfaced at Flashing Rod. He had been having his own kind of vacation in Long Beach, and on that evening he ran into a tall muscular black man and engaged him in conversation with a view to further activities. When the guy made it clear he wasn't interested, Aysgarth changed feet and went over to see an attractive lingerie sales lady who he had visited before. He determined she wasn't expecting anyone, and then started sexual advances. She didn't need much encouragement and they ended up on the sofa engaged in a fast paced intercourse. Aysgarth couldn't hold on the length of time he could with male encounters. It was soon over, and he didn't stay long.

As he ambled toward his car, he ran into the same tall black man he had seen earlier in the evening.

"Hello," Aysgarth said amiably.

If Aysgarth hadn't had training in martial arts he would have received a kick in the crotch, but he saw it coming. Although the black was much taller, he was not afraid.

"You just messed with my woman," the man said. "Now you get yours, motherfucker."

Aysgarth stepped aside as the man came at him, and used the reverse kick to the belly. It was the only kick he got in. His younger and taller opponent had been trained in martial arts as well. He grabbed Aysgarth's leg and twisted it, throwing Aysgarth to the ground following up with a kick in the stomach. While Aysgarth tried to get to his feet his opponent whipped off his wide leather belt and repeatedly beat Aysgarth, following with a massive kick in the face.

"Take whatever you want," Aysgarth mumbled, "Just leave me alone." He threw his car keys out and was trying for his wallet when he received a final kick to the head and his opponent picked up the keys, climbed into Aysgarth's car and was gone.

Aysgarth was semiconscious with blood streaming from his nose. He struggled to get up, which he eventually managed. It was a bad part of town, but there was a sleazy hotel a block and a half away. It took him ages to get there as blood streamed down his shirtfront and soaked the handkerchief he had.

The night porter didn't seem overjoyed to see him, but all Aysgarth could do was to ask for the phone.

"I only want to call my stepson."

The night porter didn't look like he liked it one bit, but he dialed the number for him and Aysgarth asked to be picked up, saying only his car had been stolen and he was injured. Clearly the night porter wanted him out of the hotel.

"Your car was stolen?" he said.

"Yes, I was beaten up and my car was stolen."

The night porter called the police. He didn't know Aysgarth's stepson had to come all the way from the Flashing Rod area to get him. Although the police were close, they took their time getting there. The night porter had not mentioned the injury. Both officers were black men.

"You must have been stopped or something," the officer said. "Not a good part of town for you to be stopped. I'll call an ambulance."

"No, no," Aysgarth said. "I'm a doctor, and I have a broken nose, that's all. My son is on his way to get me."

Aysgarth's stepson arrived in a moment or two and took over as well as he could. He described the vehicle and then got Aysgarth into his own car.

"I'd better get you to Long Beach Memorial Hospital," he said to Aysgarth.

"No," Aysgarth said. "Get me to the ER at Valley."

He was taken to his own institution and was lucky that a properly trained ER physician was on duty.

"I'm going to have to put a posterior nasal pack in, as well as one in front," he said.

Blood work was done and Aysgarth's hemoglobin was down. It appeared the packs were controlling the bleeding though.

"You need to be admitted."

Aysgarth shook his head. "My son will drive me home. I'll get Nukimmi to look at me in the morning."

The ER physician could hardly tell a boss like Aysgarth he had to stay in the hospital, so he was released.

Laxton was told about Aysgarth's nose the next day. The peculiar thing was Aysgarth had only filed a stolen car report. The vicious attack wasn't mentioned in the police report. It was actually Terry who found that out when he took the call that let Aysgarth know his vehicle had been found and it was just two blocks from the site of the assault.

Nukimmi, the ear nose and throat specialist, took Aysgarth to surgery on an out patient basis and straightened out Aysgarth's shattered nose as well as he could, and repacked the nose. Aysgarth said he was attacked as he was on his way from the yacht. The details were very sketchy. He insisted on returning to work. He hadn't allowed the ER physician to do X-Rays, having promised he'd get them done the next day, but it was several days before they were done.

Laxton wanted to know why Nukimmi had operated on Aysgarth without skull X-Rays.

"He told me everything had been taken care of," Nukimmi said. "Stupid me, I believed him. Also, I told him I'd take the pack out in five days. He took it out himself after three days. He was lucky to get away with it. He wouldn't admit he'd taken it out. He claimed it fell out. Nasal packs don't fall out on their own."

It wasn't long after that Laxton's phone rang. It was Rekuf.

"Aysgarth's on his way to your office. He needs a CAT scan of the skull, and we offered to run him over there because he shouldn't be driving himself. He refused. See what you can do with him."

Aysgarth came with a packet of films in his hand. "Look at these films," he said.

Laxton pulled them from the jacket and studied them. "I'm very suspicious you might have some bleeding, a hematoma there inside the skull."

"That's what Rekuf thought. He wants me to go for a CAT scan now."

"You need to be driven over there, and I'll take you," Laxton said.

"No. I've been driving around for a week. I can drive myself there. It's not that far."

Laxton thought for a moment and realized Aysgarth would do as he pleased. He was acutely aware of the fact that Aysgarth had been falling asleep at the wheel, but he knew how stubborn Aysgarth could be.

When Aysgarth left Laxton went to X-Ray and sought out Rekuf.

"I couldn't do much with him, and I thought he probably could get over there, but if they find anything they can stop him driving back."

"I wouldn't count on it," Rekuf said. "But we'll try."

The CAT scanner was portable and served three hospitals, but Rekuf's group read all the scans. The scanner was not at Valley that day.

"I'm going to stay in my office," Laxton said. "Give me a call when you know anything."

It was inconvenient for Laxton, because Trevellian was away again and Megan was due at his place. She had her own key but would wonder what had happened to hold him up. He tried phoning his place and got the answering machine because she never picked up his phone.

"Megan, if you're there, pick the phone up," he said.

He got her on the second try.

Aysgarth walked into Laxton's office an hour later. "Look at this scan," he said to Laxton. "This is why I felt rotten."

The scan showed a significant sized subdural hematoma, a blood clot which was creating some pressure on the brain.

"Where are you going to go to the neurosurgeon?" Laxton said. He envisaged having to get Aysgarth to some university center.

"Bill Yakamoto is on his way over."

Laxton was surprised. Aysgarth would get a lot of extras in his own hospital though, but Laxton thought he'd have wanted a big name surgeon from a university center.

Aysgarth was admitted and Laxton asked Yakamoto what it really looked like. Yakamoto told Laxton that there was a significant blood clot. "But it has to be evacuated, washed out through burr holes, and I'm going to do it in the morning."

"Is he going to have a general anesthetic?"

"Yes. I do most of my neurosurgery under general."

Laxton went home to find a loving Megan with a great meal prepared waiting for him.

"What happened?" she said.

"To make it a short story, Aysgarth got beat up down near his yacht at Long Beach, and he has a subdural hematoma they're going to evacuate in the morning."

"A blood clot on the brain? Come on, what really happened down at Long Beach?"

She always seemed to have a nose for mysteries, but Laxton really couldn't answer the question because he simply didn't know.

"He was the wrong person in the wrong place at the wrong time," he said.

"Yakamoto is his neurosurgeon," Megan said. It was more of a statement than a question.

"That's right," Laxton said.

"I bet you hope he doesn't start yapping as he's coming out of the anesthetic."

The thought had occurred to Laxton. He had been concerned about risk, despite reassurances from Yakamoto that it was really a straightforward procedure, no cause for worry. He suspected a dead Aysgarth at that moment would be a serious problem.

"I suppose there's always a chance of that yapping, as you call it, but it's commoner as a device in movies and books and really doesn't happen that often in real life. How long can you stay?"

"A couple of days. And yes, I did turn the bed down and make it look as if I'd just slept in it in case there was anything unusual. He doesn't look in my room that often anyway."

Megan was always very thoughtful and careful to prevent discovery. They had a great time together despite the drama going on at the hospital, and they were both able to enjoy all aspects of their relationship until dawn.

The next morning Laxton was told Gotcher was looking for him which was very unusual. Gotcher rarely arrived at the hospital before ten.

"I suppose you heard about Aysgarth," Gotcher said.

"Yes," Laxton said.

"I think we'd better be ready for him to be gone a while. He's not going to make the next board meeting anyway."

It was true. The meeting was in two days time. Laxton was surprised it had become some sort of concern.

"If there's anything really special, we want to do, we'd better get on with it," Gotcher said.

"Is there anything?"

"I'll have to think about that," Gotcher replied.

CHAPTER 35

AYSGARTH'S ILLNESS

The surgery went well and Aysgarth didn't reveal anything while under the anesthetic. Megan hadn't been the only one who had remarked on the possibility of Aysgarth talking during induction or when coming out of the anesthetic.

"Maybe we should all gather round the recovery room to find out where the bodies are buried," Rekuf had said. Then he laughed. It was a half jest but it told Laxton a lot of people knew who held the power.

The board meeting had opened with routine stuff. Laxton gave his report which encompassed the clean up operation in the medical staff and the recruitment of new members. It had been easier to stop surgeons from doing procedures when they seemed incompetent and to place restrictions on family physicians using the intensive care unit when it wasn't necessary to do so. It's difficult to know if the way Trevellian had been dealt with had acted as a catalyst, or if Laxton's style as Chief of Staff was responsible. The staff certainly listened to him with respect.

"We do have an item we need to consider tonight," Gotcher said, looking down at the table as he always did when bringing up a problem he didn't like to approach. "We have a report on the finances of the Flashing Rod Clinic operation, and I'm going to call on our accountant to give this report."

The report was lengthy and convoluted, but in essence suggested that the operation had lost over a half million dollars in the last year. Laxton was no good with figures and couldn't make head or tail of the assertions.

"Have we a written copy?" Laxton said.

"We felt this should be kept very secret," Smiley said. "Be really bad if it got out, but you can look at them here."

Laxton couldn't tell anything from the paper work. He remembered that the accountant had been working for Gotcher and Smiley in their office for years, and wondered why someone hadn't felt this to be a conflict of interest.

"Maybe our new board members would like to take a look at this," Laxton said, flicking the sheets over to Giocomani. He remembered Aysgarth had described Giocomani as an international financial expert. He knew Flashing Rod was totally an Aysgarth operation, and close to

240

his heart. To bring it up when Aysgarth wasn't present struck Laxton as strange, and he realized there was something going on he didn't understand. He knew what was being done wasn't right. Laxton had instinctively involved Giocomani, although he only knew what Aysgarth had told him about the man. To Laxton he looked like a businessman who had risen from the other side of the tracks, and if so would spot any irregularity in the paper work. Both Gotcher and Smiley knew that Aysgarth had found this benefactor who was now Chairman of the Hospital Foundation and Laxton suspected that they felt he would not feel kindly disposed to financial loss so that presenting a dismal picture of Flashing Rod would disenchant Giocomani about Aysgarth. Giocomani barely glanced at the papers and passed them immediately to the Reverend Potsweller.

"Here, Reverend, you look at them first."

The Reverend Potsweller merely glanced at the papers. He cleared his throat and spoke with great dignity. "There is a moral issue here. The clinic is run by Doctor Aysgarth who is currently indisposed. He won't be indisposed forever and it would be immoral and unchristian to pursue this without him being here. I have been meaning to say this, but didn't know the proper time for it. Before we go, I think we should say a prayer for Doctor Aysgarth."

"We certainly should do that, and I'll ask you to say a few words at the end of the meeting," Gotcher said. He looked very uncomfortable.

"I feel it'd be wrong for me, despite my financial background, to vote on anything without the gentleman being here," Giocomani said quickly.

Laxton wanted to laugh. This must be the first time the board had ever had a prayer proposed to them, never mind having one said at a board meeting. These two had put a stop to whatever was going on. It was a relief to Laxton, because he knew that Aysgarth would have expected him to fight off anything like this.

"Let's talk off the record a minute. What were you going to propose?" Giocomani said.

"We'd just sell it off," Smiley said. He was never one to know when to keep his mouth shut.

"I'm just appalled," the Reverend said, "I can't believe we're talking about this behind the man's back."

Gotcher clearly looked as though he needed to do a recovery operation. "You're quite right. It was thoughtless to bring this up right now." He looked at the accountant to imply it was his fault, although Laxton knew it wasn't. The accountant only spoke when spoken to.

"I think we should drop it and leave it right out of the minutes."

"Let's just have something written which says the finances of the Flashing Rod Clinic were discussed. That should satisfy everyone for today," the Reverend said.

They could hardly refuse, although Gotcher looked as though he might choke. Laxton silently thanked the Reverend for being a smart cookie. Aysgarth would see the minutes and it would make Laxton's job much easier, because Aysgarth would be bound to ask about it, and he could never be accused of letting the cat out of the bag.

Getting rid of Flashing Rod could only be aimed at reducing Aysgarth's power base, and it would be obvious to physicians in the hospital that someone had ridden rough shod over Aysgarth. That would apply particularly to those specialists who had been forced to go up to the clinic to see just one or two patients, and had resented Aysgarth for this coercion. It had never occurred to Laxton there might be any kind of power struggle going on.

Laxton went to see Aysgarth the next day. He was in a lush private room.

"Have you seen this room before?" Aysgarth said. "We keep it for special people. I could run the whole operation from here."

It was a beautiful hospital room. It had two phone lines, a fax machine, a copy machine, a computer, and an impressive desk. All the hospital outlets were there as well -- suction, oxygen, cardiac monitor, crash cart. It was the executives' ideal for hospitalization. The family hadn't been neglected either, with plush armchairs, a sofa, and a table where four could dine.

"So how did the meeting go?" Aysgarth said.

Laxton asked Aysgarth with a hint of a smile if his doctor approved of him getting back into business, knowing all the time that Aysgarth's surgeon would have no control over Aysgarth if he thought he was fit enough to do business.

"He's going to let me go in a couple of days," Aysgarth said.

"You'll be getting minutes anyway," Laxton said. "It would be preferable if the information I give you looked like you got it from the minutes."

Aysgarth shrugged. "Giocomani came by the room after the meeting."

"Bit late for visiting, wasn't it? There was this weird financial report about the clinic, but we didn't get hard copy."

"As soon as I get a copy of those minutes I'll demand Gotcher give me a copy of their financial statement," Aysgarth said, "In the meantime tell Terry to get a full financial report from our clinic records. I don't want to talk to him about it on the telephone. I might be overheard. That accountant from the valley has been conniving with Gotcher and Smiley on this one."

Laxton took a trip to Flashing Rod and sat in Terry's office with him to go over the meeting content.

"I knew quite a bit about it because the boss left me a note here the night of the meeting," Terry said.

"He must have had it dropped off," Laxton said.

"No, he was here, but don't tell anyone I said that."

"Of course I won't, but no one would believe it anyway, so what have you got to worry about?"

"I don't want to be found drowned in the bay floating off Long Beach."

"You've got me at a disadvantage," Laxton said. "What are you talking about?"

"Remember we talked about the car theft and how that was the only thing reported to the police."

Laxton nodded.

"And how the assault wasn't reported. What you don't know is Aysgarth's wallet and everything in it was delivered here to me at the clinic. It was found in the sofa of some black woman's apartment. There was a note with the wallet, presumably from the woman, claiming she hadn't told her husband about the incident. I saw that the boss got his wallet back, but I destroyed the note. I told him it had just been delivered as it was, with everything in the wallet including his money, but there was nothing else. I told him there was no indication where it came from. He didn't want me to let the police know he'd got it back, although he'd told me it was stolen. I bet it was never reported."

"Was all this before his surgery?" Laxton said.

"That's right. It was the day after he was beaten up, and I'm told a small black guy delivered it. You know he said all he could remember about the black guy who beat him up was that he was enormous. Have you seen the newspaper recently?"

Laxton shook his head.

"Let me paraphrase it. In one section Jack Aysgarth is in a hospital. In another part of the paper an enormous black man was found floating in the bay at Long Beach. And he was very dead."

"I never heard any of this," Laxton said.

"Neither did I," Terry said. "But we'd better watch our backs. As far as I know, he thinks you're great and I think he likes me."

243

"I know that's right. But the less said about these matters the better. Between the two of us, how's the clinic doing? Does it break even, make money, or what?"

"When this was set up the set up was very peculiar. The hospital supplies some of the services and pays some clinic salaries. For example, my salary comes from the hospital. Then there's the Development Company which was involved in financing the building. It is all so convoluted that it's possible someone could produce figures which suggested the operation runs at a loss. The facts are we meet all expenses and they are all paid for out of profits from the clinic. One of the confusing things was that Aysgarth took money from the hospital to study setting up a day care surgery center here, and I don't know what the costs of that were. But if we totally divorced ourselves from the hospital we could get by and make a profit."

"The reasons for getting the clinic sold must be political, as far as I can see," Laxton said.

"You bet they are." Terry replied. "When Doctor Aysgarth came up here it was to prevent the local town from putting up a hospital which would impact on Valley Hospital. That's one reason we have a twenty four-hour emergency room. He told the local council they didn't need to raise the money to build anything, because he'd have a twenty-four-hour service and a hospital connection. It would affect the hospital if this clinic was lost. Anyway, it's not going to happen while Aysgarth has the control he has.

When Aysgarth was discharged from hospital he became as hyperactive as ever. He was rushing round the hospital, an architect in tow, supervising plans being drawn, and talking about expansion. Laxton was sure the next board meeting wouldn't be too bad.

When the meeting was called to order the Flashing Rod Clinic was first on the agenda, but Aysgarth held up a hand.

"Now we'll get the real figures from Terry Chart, who I brought down. Just ask him to come in."

Terry's figures certainly were different from the hospital accountant's figures, and it was clear the business was going nowhere. Both Giocomani and the Reverend had nodded approval all through Terry's presentation.

"You must have padding in there," Smiley said.

"I wonder if you'd like to step outside," Aysgarth retorted.

Smiley was a squeamish little man anyway, so there was no fear he would do that. Laxton was uncomfortable with the tenor of the meeting anyway.

"You're using our Chief of Staff to do utilization for the IPA," Gotcher said, "and I don't think that should be going on."

"Actually, the IPA is a hospital based body and has nothing to do with the Flashing Rod Clinic," Laxton said. "It's just that the utilization stuff goes to an office up there, and it's more convenient to do it there."

Gotcher and Smiley looked displeased, but Laxton wasn't about to let himself become a pawn in their games. The others seemed disinterested.

"Those idiots better not start fooling with me," Aysgarth said to Laxton after the meeting. Laxton took all this in stride and wasn't worrying about anything because his own operation to turn the institution into a class place was going so well. There had been some subtle changes in the patient mix. Some of the patients had come from rather far away, there had been much more private work, but there had been a number of gunshot wounds. Laxton regarded this as changing times. Rekuf said to him one day that he couldn't understand where all the creeps with the money were coming from.

"How do these elements come from Flashing Rod?" he said.

Flashing Rod was a bedroom community of the most stable kind. Laxton found that what Rekuf had been talking about was many of these strange patients were being processed through the clinic up there. Eventually he looked up patient source and type. They all had money and there were no dead beats. Laxton wondered if this had something to do with the attack on the clinic by Gotcher, but dismissed this as ridiculous. All he and Smiley were interested in was money.

The pattern of those admissions looked almost as though the clinic was catering to criminal elements, which Laxton dismissed at once as ridiculous, but he had to admit the patients from Aysgarth's operation had addresses which were remote from Flashing Rod. But Aysgarth himself had always had a widely diversified practice and Laxton reminded himself that Aysgarth had an excellent reputation in southern California and people had always come from places far away to see him as a physician. He actually talked to Gotcher one day and hinted that he thought there were a lot of private patients coming through Flashing Rod Clinic.

"I know," Gotcher had said. "That's one of the pluses of the operation."

Laxton concluded that aspect had nothing to do with Gotcher and Smiley's attempt to close the clinic.

"Where in hell are all these strange patients who come through the clinic to the hospital coming from?" he said to Terry.

"Oh, you've noticed some of the patients we have now, have you?"

"I just thought the pattern had changed."

"You're my friend," Terry said. "So please listen to me. Just back off, all right?"

CHAPTER 36

AYSGARTH AND BAY HOSPITAL

A month had passed, Aysgarth had missed the board meeting, and it hadn't mattered very much. Gotcher and Smiley seemed to have backed down on their demands for closure of the Flashing Rod Clinic. Laxton wondered if it was the private patient load or some other factor. Perhaps Aysgarth had leaned on them somehow.

His own report to the board had been welcome. They had received university recognition because of their medical staff excellence. The university hadn't yet gone as far as to offer any kind of affiliation, but it seemed they were on their way and this was entirely due to Laxton's efforts, which the board recognized.

Laxton had to resist nearly all the people Smiley had tried to promote onto the staff. The State Board had already disciplined two of the specialists Smiley had wanted on staff for deaths they had caused, so Laxton struggled to keep it all clean.

Laxton had to do the utilization for the IPA more frequently, but he saw less of Aysgarth.

"I'm worried because I think he's sick," Terry said to Laxton. "But he won't see anyone. He gave up his place in Long Beach. It's gone. He sold it, but not the yacht."

"I've never been able to talk to him about his own health," Laxton said. "I don't think there's anything I can do to help."

Laxton hadn't seen Aysgarth and it was almost two weeks before he ran into him. He asked him how he was feeling.

"Terrible," Aysgarth replied.

"Why don't you go and see someone?"

"I will," Aysgarth said. Then he was gone.

One night Laxton was about to leave his office when he ran into Aysgarth on the corridor. He could hardly carry on a conversation he was so short of breath.

"Let me get a pulmonologist," Laxton said to him.

"No, I have an appointment. I just have to get there."

Laxton was alarmed. He couldn't find Terry, and he was afraid to call Aysgarth's home. He went home to brood. Megan couldn't be reached so there was no solace there. Laxton was a sensitive man, especially when it came to those he liked and respected. He worried about Aysgarth, but there was nothing he could do. The next day Terry told him Aysgarth had disappeared. He may have known more than he let on because he told Laxton that he thought Aysgarth's stepson had driven Aysgarth to San Diego.

As far as Laxton was concerned the whole business was bizarre, and he got on with his work and forgot about Aysgarth. It was another week before he heard Aysgarth was back home and not short of breath any more.

"He has to have special treatments," Terry told him over the telephone. "He's getting intravenous infusions every day."

Laxton had a difficult time catching up with Aysgarth. It was as if he didn't want to talk to anyone. Eventually he got to talk to him.

"Everything's going to be all right," Aysgarth said. "Just trust me."

Laxton didn't know the details of Aysgarth's medical care, but Terry got his hands on some of the information and copied it and stored it. He was careful not to tell anyone what he knew about the illness, but said enough and asked enough questions to make Laxton wonder.

"I've never known Jack Aysgarth to go anywhere but into his own hospital," Terry said. "Why do you think he went elsewhere?"

"I can only think he wanted to keep the whole thing secret," Laxton said, "but I'm not sure why."

"Think about it, and see if you come to the same conclusion I did. He hasn't told us anything about it either."

The realization of the whole thing came to Laxton during one of his trysts with Megan.

"Is Aysgarth back?" she asked.

"Yes, he's back."

"I know I've been bugging you to get out of there and get another job, but if you can't see his illness as a reason you're not as bright as I thought you were."

"We don't even know the diagnosis," Laxton said.

Megan laughed. "You must be the only person who doesn't at least suspect what it is. You know about the yacht in Long Beach, and maybe you don't know only totally male company goes down there, but you must have suspected. A.N.L Stein, Lense, and the others were going all the time. I'd put every penny I have on a bet that Aysgarth has AIDS."

Laxton was silent for a short time. He sighed. He remembered someone had told him about A.N.L. Stein's sexual preferences.

"I suppose I just didn't want to think about it," Laxton said helplessly.

"You should be thinking about it. He's walking around the hospital and treating patients in the clinic and he's probably got AIDS, and if anyone finds out--"

"Megan, shut up. I know very well if what you say is true and anyone finds out the hospital and clinic will be in deep shit."

Laxton was up at the clinic one day when Terry said Aysgarth was over in a treatment room and wanted to see him. When Laxton got over there he was lying down, an intravenous almost finished.

"Can you discontinue this for me?" he said to Laxton.

"Sure," Laxton said, as he prepared to slip out the needle.

"Just a minute," Aysgarth said. "Use gloves, please. Be careful not to jab yourself with that needle. Give it to me."

Laxton handed him the needle and stepped back.

"I don't want you to tell anyone but I have a lung problem. It's an inoperable tumor, and I'm having chemotherapy."

Laxton had no doubt this explanation was a fish story. He felt a deep sadness inside. It wasn't long after that Yakamoto said to him in confidence that neither he nor Nikimmi were willing to treat Aysgarth again.

"You know," Yakamoto said, "there's a rumor he's got AIDS."

"Where did that come from?" Laxton said.

"He's been gay for years. That much I guessed. But I have a friend down at that clinic on the road to San Diego, and he told me to be very careful in dealing with him because he might have a sexually transmittable disease."

"I hope you don't want me to tell him you won't look after him," Laxton said.

"We'll tell him if we have to tell him."

Aysgarth was off work more. He was losing weight and didn't look well. Terry told Laxton there had been a massive meeting with attorneys at Aysgarth's home, but he hadn't been there. Aysgarth had done something relating to incorporation and family trusts. His will might have been changed.

"He wants to see you here on Wednesday," Terry said. "For your own protection I think you should come and see him."

Laxton thought that was weird. He had never refused to see Aysgarth so he would be there. It was a private meeting.

"You never had any kind of a contract except a handshake," Aysgarth said. "Frankly, Smiley and that bastard Gotcher can't be trusted. So, in case anything happens to me because of my lung tumor,

249

here's a contract for you. You'll see it's backdated and signed by me and Gotcher. Don't ask any questions about it, just sign here and I'm going to keep one copy at the clinic, and I'll get another copy placed where it can be accessed and give this original to you."

Laxton took the contract without comment.

"I know all about your absolute dedication to honesty, but do me a favor and remember you got this contract when you first came on board. I signed it and I got Gotcher to sign it, and that's all you know about it. Don't worry about me. Take care of yourself. If you ever need to use this, I'll be dead."

Laxton became concerned about what might happen if Aysgarth was gone. Already board meetings were taking on a more unpleasant tone, although for some reason the two lay board members made certain that nothing which impacted on Aysgarth was ever an issue. In a way they might as well have been his voice, for he was never at meetings. Maybe Megan had been right, Laxton ought to get out. Problem was, he felt he was within reach of his goal to get the hospital designated a full teaching institution. But almost is not there, and it might be sometime before that was accomplished. In the meantime the undesirables had to be kept off the medical staff, and surgeries that shouldn't be done at the institution had to be shipped elsewhere. It was getting harder to do his job without Aysgarth to back him up.

He sought Aysgarth and ran him down at home. He was sitting in an armchair in his dressing gown.

"I feel terrible," Aysgarth said, as he put his head down on a nearby table. "Just awful. I'm getting to a point where I don't want to live."

"Do you think I should be doing any work outside Valley? Working for others, I mean," Laxton said.

"Yes, you should. I don't know what will happen at the hospital. Those people I got onto the board won't take over the hospital, they can't manage it. Frankly, you're not devious enough to deal with any of them. Those two members who are new--"

"You mean Giocomani and the Reverend?"

"Yes. They have more power than you might think. They won't do anything that will hurt you, but they don't suffer fools gladly. Where were you thinking of going?"

Laxton mentioned another hospital which was looking for his services, and told Aysgarth he thought he could work there part time and play it by ear. It could be full time if he wanted.

"Do it," Aysgarth said. "Your contract provides for it anyway."

Laxton hadn't really read the contract carefully, so he did so later and he saw he had the right to do work elsewhere. He went ahead and met the board at Bay Hospital. The hospital was larger than Valley Hospital, was also physician run, and they seemed to have lots of money. Laxton was told he had a free hand, would be given a written contract for part-time work which would become full time any day he wished. He was to get a hundred and fifty thousand dollars a year part time, and make two hundred and fifty thousand dollars a year if he became full time. Laxton was somewhat uncomfortable about it because he was taking two hundred and fifty thousand a year from Valley for full time employment. He told Gotcher he was consulting for another hospital and hoped it didn't pose a problem.

"I had a phone call from Aysgarth," Gotcher said. "He told me you'd discussed it with him, so I suppose it's all right."

"He doesn't seem to be getting any better," Laxton said.

"I haven't seen him but I believe he's worse, and he told me he won't go back into hospital. I couldn't get any information out of the hospital in San Diego, so I don't know what's wrong."

Laxton wasn't sure whether Gotcher was telling the truth or not.

Laxton spent his mornings, and sometimes his afternoons, at Bay Hospital, and found he was treated with respect and given very nice privileges for his comfort. He didn't become a member of the medical staff.

It was rather like starting at Valley all over again. The utilization was sloppy, and the quality of care left much to be desired. There was an excellent ER and trauma service, which was being exploited by illegal immigrants and was costing the hospital a lot of money. There were so many problems Laxton wondered if he should get an assistant to help with the work. Problem was he would have to convince both places he needed one, even if he paid the assistant himself.

He let his work run into the night and found Valley's ER filled with a lot of strange characters processed through Flashing Rod. He asked the ER physician if it wouldn't be a good idea to send some of these patients to a trauma center. He knew Bay could deal with them much better. And what about the drug cases, shouldn't they go to a rehab center?

"It wouldn't be a good idea. These are all pay patients, and they're under some sort of agreement Aysgarth worked out with someone. We're not sure who."

"I see," Laxton said.

He didn't see, but he had his suspicions that all these people were involved in some illicit business. A few patients had clearly been addicts, and there was some kind of Long Beach connection. It was better left untouched.

He found there was as much lust after money at Bay Hospital as at Valley Hospital. For the board, the bottom line was always the dollar, but many physicians at Bay weren't participants in the fiscal side. The control was in the hands of a few.

"I wish you could just maximize our receipts and forget about quality of care," one board member said to Laxton.

That meant a maximization of utilization at the expense of quality, even though it was almost impossible to work that way. Laxton's conscience wouldn't have allowed him to do this. He was too dedicated to perfecting the system of care, stymied always by those who were in it for the money.

There was another trauma. The hospital had refused to follow many of the Medicare parameters, and they had refused treatment to some Medicaid patients and over billed for others. The Administrator had ignored letters from the Health Care Financing Administration, and subsequently HCFA said they would close the hospital to all Medicaid and Medicare patients. Laxton came up with a plan the medical staff refused to support. The following week it was published in the newspaper that the hospital would be closed to those patients.

The Chief of Staff at Bay hadn't wanted the medical staff told what HCFA could do. At the next meeting Laxton intended to bring out the truth. Fortunately, someone else on the medical staff had seen the notice in the newspaper and brought it up. Laxton then told the staff they had either to go ahead with the correction plan he had outlined, or face closure of the hospital to all government-sponsored patients, and he warned that all insurance companies would soon follow suit.

The staff accepted the plan, and Laxton flew to San Francisco to meet with HCFA officials to get the hospital back in business.

The day after he got back and went into Valley hospital he learned two things. Aysgarth was bedridden and short of breath again. He refused to be hospitalized. There was a suit against the clinic by a nurse who had been giving Aysgarth his IVs. She claimed she hadn't been told she was treating a patient with AIDS. She had a copy of Aysgarth's lab report.

CHAPTER 37

AYSGARTH'S DECLINE

When Laxton got off the plane he was angry to find Megan waiting for him. He had to grind his teeth to control himself. He walked from the plane knowing no one had been told when he was returning. Someone from Bay had dropped him off when he left, but his return date was unknown. Megan must have been the only person who knew the date and time of Laxton's return, and he hadn't told her, so the fact she found out spoke volumes about her abilities to get information. As soon as Trevellian had left, Megan had made it her business to find out when and where Laxton would reappear.

"I don't think that appearing in public together anywhere will improve our relationship," Laxton said rather mildly considering his inner anger, licking his lips with the tip of his tongue.

She had waited until he was walking alone from the plane before she appeared. Laxton felt a hand on his back, turned sideways, and there she was. It wasn't that he wasn't sure whether or not Herb had gone somewhere, it was more than that. He didn't want to be seen with Herb's wife in public, and it disturbed him that it seemed she didn't care.

"It's not far to the car," Megan said. "We're going to be in the darkness the minute we walk through these doors."

Laxton followed her to the car, got in, and fastened his seat belt. "Is there some reason that you simply had to see me tonight?" he said.

"I wanted you to know that things are happening at Valley. I hear Aysgarth is very ill and short of breath. Also, I hear there's a suit against the clinic. Something to do with some nurse treating him who didn't know about the AIDS."

"Don't tell me the whole thing is public."

"No, it's not public information, and forget you heard it from me."

"You can't leave this car parked outside my place," Laxton said.

"You're not so angry I can't stay at your place then. I'll drop you off and be back in no more than a half hour."

Laxton thought what a fool he was, but he wanted her anyway. He needed someone to talk to, if nothing else. Of course that wasn't the only reason he wanted her. He just nodded, took his bag when they reached his apartment, and got out of the car.

"Take my bag in with you please," she said.

The following day he went into Valley and saw the hospital administrator. "Is it true there's a suit against the clinic?"

"I don't know what you're talking about," was the reply.

Laxton went to his office and called Terry Card at the clinic. "What's this about a suit?"

"Where the hell did you hear about it," Terry said. "There's supposed to be a lid on the whole thing. I'm not even supposed to know about it."

"I heard it in San Francisco," Laxton lied.

"What?" Terry yelled in his ear.

"It was a joke," Laxton said. "Never mind how I heard. I guess that's why our good old hospital administrator doesn't know."

"He's the one who does know," Terry said.

"That goddamn frog will lie to me anytime and all the time. I also heard about Jack's condition, and I suppose I'd better go in and see him at home."

"See if you can't get him to go back to San Diego. He says he's going to stay home and die. By the way, he resigned from the hospital board."

"I'd better go in and see him tomorrow."

"You'd better go in and see him today if you want to see him alive."

Laxton took Terry's advice and hastened to Aysgarth's home. A male nurse, presumably hired, let him in. Aysgarth was propped up in bed and short of breath. He was getting oxygen. He groaned.

"I hope this will be over soon," he said.

"Who's looking after you?" Laxton said.

"I've got an internist. I'll need someone to sign the death certificate without an autopsy. That's arranged. I'm glad you came, because I wanted to see you," Aysgarth went on slowly between breaths. "I heard you were away, and hoped you'd get back soon enough."

He turned to the male nurse. "Get those packages for Doctor Laxton."

When the male nurse had gone Aysgarth motioned Laxton closer.

"One package you can open right away. I've arranged for you to have some shares in the Development Corporation and hospital. That way you'll get something out of the place whatever happens. There's a second package to be opened only in an emergency. I can't foresee what might happen. Giocomani is a good businessman, but he won't stand

254

any nonsense. I don't suggest you get tied up with him but you need to help him as far as the hospital is concerned if he asks. He is probably the only one who'll know what to do if things go wrong. If there are real troubles open the second package and don't be afraid to use its contents any way you have to. There'll be enough in there for your absolute survival. If everything is going well, don't open the material up. It's for survival."

"Is there anything I can do for you?" Laxton said.

"I think you should turn into a real mean bugger. You're just too nice, and nice people always get hurt."

As Laxton turned to leave Aysgarth waved weakly, exhausted.

Within two days Aysgarth was dead. Laxton wondered how many people knew the real cause. He knew Aysgarth did, the nurse at the clinic did, Terry did, and Laxton did.

Probably Gotcher did, but then many suspected and few may have known. Aysgarth himself thought no one knew. Laxton couldn't understand why there wouldn't be a memorial service, because Aysgarth was well known and well respected throughout Orange County. Laxton learned that Aysgarth had set things up with a request there was to be no publicity. He was as afraid of the discovery of his sexual habits after death as he had been before. Aysgarth suffered from the illusion that no one knew or suspected he was gay.

At the first board meeting there was a short prayer before Smiley and Gotcher got down to the destruction of the Flashing Rod Clinic. Clearly this did not sit well with Giocomani. He and the Reverend were not pleased but Gotcher introduced some clinical grounds for closure. There was so much general agreement that Laxton just abstained from voting, and the sale of the clinic was to be very soon unless someone from the hospital could be found to go up there and run it for them.

"Unless you can get someone of Doctor Aysgarth's caliber I don't want to see this route followed," Giocomani said.

A few days later Terry called Laxton at his office. "I thought you should know I just received my notice as Administrator here. They fired me."

"Who sent the letter?"

"The hospital administrator. He gave thirty days notice, no reason."

"You should know that either they will recruit a new medical director from the hospital, or sell the clinic. I never imagined they would try to remove you. I know you have a five-year contract in writing with four years to go."

"The only problem is my contract in writing is only signed by Aysgarth. But he was the Medical Director, so I don't think they could do anything about that, do you?"

"I think you have a number of options. You could send a certified letter which says you have received notice clearly in breach of your five-year contract, and you look forward to clarification of their letter. I wonder if you should hold onto the contract until they ask for a copy, or you could send a copy. Alternatively, you could hold onto it until you've seen an attorney. The other option is to consult the attorney first."

"Do you think I'm going to need an attorney?" Terry asked.

"Yes. I don't trust these people at all and you shouldn't either. I think they're going to get rid of Aysgarth's people."

"What's happening with the Emergency Room? Aysgarth had the contract."

Laxton was also uncomfortable about the ER, where Gotcher was trying to take it over. The ER physician, Doctor Blau, wanted the contract and he was certified in ER medicine. Gotcher would be a disaster because he would use the ER as a training ground and income producer for those starting in practice. Aysgarth originally got away with that kind of thing, it was true. He had used Flashing Rod ER for that purpose.

"I'm not sure, but I'm hoping Blau will be appointed."

As Laxton left his office he ran into Gotcher. "I hear Terry Card got his notice."

"We have to get rid of him," Gotcher said.

"Oh?"

Gotcher wasn't going to discuss it and walked on.

Terry received a further letter which said he must be out of his office no later than thirty days from his notice. His attorney filed for breach of a contract. That meant the matter would come up at the next board meeting. This was a time when Greenman got into his element because he fancied himself as an authority on legal matters. Everyone expected him to be vocal, but it Giocomani who was vocal.

"Just a bunch of attorneys involved and this could go on for years," he said. "I've done it lots of times. I had one case I kept going for five years, and the other party got fed up and went away. We're the ones here with the deep pocket and here's a guy who hasn't been paid worth a damn, so what kind of money does he have? How much dough does he want anyway?"

"It's the principle of the thing," Gotcher said. "We can't have employees pushing us around."

"It's dollars and cents," Giocomani said. "And you haven't got six months to piss around. If you want to drag for a week or two, it don't matter to me."

Laxton was irritated by the way they had gone about the whole matter. "Wouldn't it be better to wait until we know what's going to happen to the operation before actually terminating the administrator, or do we already know?"

Gotcher cleared his throat and looked down at the wood table, no doubt looking for inspiration to transfer from the wood to his head.

"It's true we don't know what is going to happen yet, but we need to clean house so we aren't carrying deadwood."

"From a legal standpoint," Greenman said, "I don't think he has much going for him. I think we can--"

"Don't matter what you think," Giocomani said. "I have all the experience in the world with this, and the simple fact is you can either throw him some money and he'll walk happily, or you can drag it out hoping he hasn't a sharp attorney and maybe he'll get tired. Those are your only two options."

It was the first time Giocomani had been so vocal and definitive, and Laxton thought Gotcher and Smiley were looking rather uncomfortable. The meeting was not very long and little else was accomplished except Doctor Blau, the ER physician was awarded the ER contract. It appeared there had been an effort to make sure Gotcher and Smiley didn't get this and everyone on the board, including Laxton, voted to award the contract to Doctor Blau.

Two weeks later Laxton received a letter from Smiley terminating his post as Vice -President of Medical Affairs, a post he was holding in addition to Chief of Staff.

Laxton called an attorney he knew well and showed him the signed contract from Aysgarth and Gotcher and gave him a copy. "Just go ahead and deal with this for me," he said.

"This isn't a problem. They haven't got a leg to stand on."

About a week later Gotcher appeared at Laxton's office. He looked rather sheepish. "I can't remember signing this contract, but it is my signature and I know it is a binding contract, so you've every right to stay. The question of your voting power on the board is another matter. You have to have shares to be a voting member. We never insisted when Aysgarth was there, but we have to run things properly now."

"I wondered if that was an issue," Laxton said smoothly. "So, to clarify matters, here's a copy of the letters relating to shares, plus the number I own. It's all laid out there."

Gotcher looked at the documentation. "So Jack gave you shares."

"Looks like it, doesn't it," Laxton said. "That should clarify my right to vote."

"Well, um, I don't think there's anything I can say."

"I don't think there is either," Laxton said.

Gotcher left.

Laxton was not so naive that he thought that would end the matter. Some way or other incompetent physicians were getting on staff through Smiley's efforts and somehow they had got through credentials without his knowledge. Smiley had dodged him when he tried to catch up with him to discuss this. Laxton knew Megan had been right when she predicted it would be a very different place without Aysgarth.

The real question for Laxton was what he should do to protect himself because he knew there was little he could do for the hospital. He had a call from Montpellier about the problems the Peer Review Organization was coming up with relating to Valley hospital and he had procrastinated. He lost his control of quality, and he knew it.

"You know," he said to Rekuf, "you were asking me about medical staff appointments. I can't veto them."

"Are you telling me that Aysgarth, with all his faults, was the person holding this structure together?"

"Aysgarth was a very powerful man until he was sick, and up to then no one on the board dared to come out in the open against him and his ideas, and he had good ideas. I could get cooperation with staff appointments and getting rid of incompetent people, but now the atmosphere has changed significantly."

"Did you know that the pathologist hasn't been able to get his contract renewed," Rekuf said. "Our contract comes up next year, so I'm going to start on it now."

"Many things are being done without ever coming to the board," Laxton said. "In a way they are following precedent, because that's how Aysgarth operated."

"Maybe they can't touch you, but even so if I was in your shoes I'd watch my back," Rekuf said. "Please don't quote me."

Gotcher and Smiley were holding clandestine meetings that Laxton became aware of by accident. The board meeting had been postponed, and when the board finally met Gotcher outlined proposals for overhauling the system of operation. Smiley sat looking smug but was silent.

"There is the question of quality of care," Laxton said, "we're getting inquiries from the PRO. I have problems with some of the recent staff appointments. Two members were known to be suspended from other hospital staffs and two have been responsible for deaths of their patients. There was a question one of them might have been accused of murder, only it didn't happen."

"The hospital ran before you came on the scene," Smiley said. "Your clean ups have started costing us a package. You don't realize some physicians have to cheat the system to make money, not just here, but all over the State. It is going to be cheaper for us if you aren't here, rather than have you here conniving with the PRO and HCFA to ensure good quality care. I think we can make a lot of money working round the system."

"The problem with that," Laxton said, "is that it is tantamount to killing."

"We understand something you don't. Our job is just to treat patients. We don't have to cure them."

"We decided we don't need a Vice President of Medical Affairs," Gotcher said, entering the discussion at last, "and it seems to us it has become a redundant position, but you do have a contract, so we'll have to make a settlement favorable to you. I'm sure you won't want to stay on the board and remain Chief of Staff after that's all settled."

"You can send such a proposal to my attorney," Laxton snapped, "but be very careful about the terms and conditions of the agreement if you want to get it signed."

"I know how to do these things," Gotcher said. "Doctor Smiley is right. We did all right without this quality stuff--except for Trevellian, of course. But you have become a liability. There's one thing we need to know. Have you got the original copy of your contract?"

"Of course," Laxton said.

"We need to see it. If you've got it at home, could you bring it to my office tomorrow?"

"Very well," Laxton said.

"Who made these decisions without talking to us?" Giocomani said quietly.

"We want to meet with you and the Reverend after the meeting," Gotcher said.

"Let's make that right now," Giocomani said.

After a moment of silence Gotcher said, "This meeting is adjourned."

Laxton immediately went home, took the contract from his desk and met his attorney the following morning. The proposal from Gotcher was already there and his attorney went over it with him. Laxton told him what had transpired.

"It sounds to me as though you'd be better out of there anyway. Their proposal to pay you two million dollars over the next two years doesn't seem too bad, if you can live with their other conditions."

Laxton went over the contract and began to write out the changes. He had a problem with a requirement that he would never reveal to any person or persons the quality of care given at Valley Hospital to any patient now or in the future. Laxton had it changed so that it said any patient who had already been reviewed by the PRO. He rejected the phrase which required his resignation from the board, but agreed not to seek reelection as Chief of Staff. The agreement would be secret, revealed to no one but the parties. Laxton told his attorney he wanted the two million deposited in trust right away. He would not accept two million over two years. His attorney told him he would be better off tax wise taking it over two years.

"It won't be better for me if the second million isn't there next year," Laxton said.

Laxton worked late that night and took all the documents he thought he might need and took them to his home. When he got home he found someone had attempted to burglarize his place. It looked like an amateur job, but nothing was missing. He took a long time to decide to call the police and report the theft. He needed Aysgarth's advice. Eventually he called the police anyway, but they weren't impressed and pointed out they rarely caught petty thieves.

The following morning Laxton found his office had been gone over. Again, nothing was missing. Gotcher called to ask Laxton if he could drop over to his office with the original copy of his contract, and was told he could see it only at Laxton's attorney's office. He was suspicious that an attempt had been made to find and destroy the original contract.

Giocomani arrived at the office unannounced. He came in and closed the door and sat down. He was a smoker and rolled a cigarette between his fingers as he made himself comfortable.

"Doctor Aysgarth and I had a business partnership which you don't need to know the details of so I won't tell you," Giocomani said. "I promised Jack I would look after you without taking you into business, and I shall. For a number of reasons this hospital has to be sold and I might need some help from you later on. Be assured it'll be sold. You got any questions?"

Laxton shook his head.

"Keep in touch." Giocomani got up and left.

There was a tremendous hassle over the termination agreement, but Laxton stuck to his guns and refused to sign until his terms and conditions were met. As soon as the old board members knew Laxton couldn't be removed without acceptance of his terms and conditions they bit the bullet and signed on. Smiley created serious trouble by getting an underground buzz amongst the medical staff underway suggesting Laxton had damaged the hospital, and caused much resentment among the staff. This angered Laxton a great deal, but he couldn't do anything about it.

The day after the agreement was signed Laxton found his name had been removed from his office door and the office was locked. He came back at night and used his credit card to open the locked door. The only things of importance to him were his own personal belongings and pictures, which he removed. When he left he locked the office behind him.

He found out when the board would next meet. He arrived late, avoiding the meal but not the meeting. He faced hostile eyes except for Giocomani and the Reverend whose faces were impassive.

"We have a legal right to exclude you from these meetings," Greenman said. "We didn't believe you'd even show up."

Gotcher was staring at the table. Laxton shrugged and said nothing.

"We have routine business," Gotcher said, "and I believe you came to give your report, so let's have it."

"I'll read it," Laxton said, "and after I shall expect to be excused as I have another matter to attend to."

Laxton gave a low key, inoffensive report and skipped over glaring problems he had seen in the last week or two. There had been three deaths in the hospital under very strange circumstances.

He had work to do. He removed Aysgarth's secret envelope and decided he must open it. It seemed as good a time as any to see what ammunition was in the envelope. Aysgarth had written very frankly, with an instruction to destroy the letter as soon as Laxton had the information. There were photographs he was invited to keep and use, as well as some enclosures. Aysgarth clearly wanted his own letter destroyed. He didn't want his history known.

Laxton was shattered to find that Aysgarth had been involved in a highly dangerous and illicit business which he worked from his yacht, and he concluded immediately who the high financier might be who Aysgarth had worked with in this business. There was a lot of information about Smiley as well as Gotcher. There were photographs of them taken in conditions which were incriminating. Smiley in particular had been photographed moving contraband into the warehouse, and the people who had worked with him were listed. In addition a whole list of physicians he had bribed to join the hospital staff were listed as well as copies of letters he had written. There were copies of letters where Aysgarth had told him to cease and desist from this, and another from the hospital attorney warning him of the illegalities. It wasn't clear whether either one of them really understood what they had let themselves into down in Long Beach. Eventually Laxton felt sure Smiley had a good idea what he was into because he had written to Aysgarth to say he didn't care how illicit the business was as long as he made money. He had written a note that having teenagers sniff a little kept the economy going nicely.

Greenman had been having a torrid affair with his office nurse, and there were letters and a list of places they had been seen together. Aysgarth said Greenman had no intention of leaving his wife. She was the one with all the money. There was similar information on Gotcher and Molly. Aysgarth's documentation was as thorough as it had always been when he was alive.

Laxton copied what he needed to on the hospital copying machine. The originals and the rest of the material he locked in his safe deposit box at the bank. He was shattered at the implications of the material and nervous about what he had learned.

He thought of Aysgarth, what a mixed figure he had been. He wondered about the violence which had eventually surrounded him, and the death--or was it deaths? And even though he had gone, was the information he had given Laxton safe for Laxton to have? Did Giocomani know Laxton knew about the illicit business?

CHAPTER 38

IS IT TIME TO GO?

"Are you going to get out?" Megan said. "I would if it was me. There's no future there and you can leave without blame."

"I'm not sure I shouldn't just sit tight for the time being, and just play it by ear," Laxton said.

"To gain what?"

Laxton hadn't told Megan about his shares, his liaison with Aysgarth, and his knowledge about the culpability of Smiley and possibly Gotcher.

"Let's leave it the way it is at the moment and trust me to work it out."

"I think there's something you're not telling me."

Laxton said nothing. By mutual consent the subject was dropped.

"You are taking a bigger interest in what I'm doing these days, Megan," Laxton said. "I used to think it was because of Herb's case before."

"You knew it wasn't. I'm very interested in what you're doing. There's still that opportunity I told you about at the downtown hospital, if you don't like Bay."

"They all have the same problems and I'm getting depressed with it all. For example, Bay has acquired that Doctor Ching we got rid of from Valley. He's killed a couple of babies down there already."

"Do you have to put it in such a crude way?" Megan said. "You mean he lost two newborns."

"When the physician deliberately goes out of his way through effort or neglect, or when he over treats knowing full well what he's doing isn't called for, it's worse than doing something wrong through ignorance. It's killing, and I've taken to looking at it that way."

"You are too much of an idealist."

"You have been taking so much interest in me lately. Does that mean we need to talk?"

"We always need to talk, but it doesn't alter our arrangement. You know what the score is. Herb and I live separate lives and have an arrangement which works well, and that hasn't changed. Am I in love with you? Probably. But I have it under control and I mean to keep it that way," Megan said.

"And for us?" Laxton said.

"I'm available nearly all the time. You should bless your good luck. I make no demands on you; I give and don't take."

"We get on like a house on fire in private, but neither of us knows how we'd do together in public. We don't have a complete relationship, Megan."

"I want to get you into a decent job you can enjoy and you'll feel more settled then. Maybe we can talk some more at that time."

Laxton wasn't in the mood to talk much anyway. There were too many problems and he hadn't finalized anything. He couldn't complete his relationship with Megan the way he thought he wanted to, and he didn't feel he had completed what he set out to do at Valley. He'd let disaster overtake him.

Laxton was working at Bay Hospital when he received a telephone call from Giocomani.

"I'm going to come down there to talk to you this afternoon," Giocomani said.

When he arrived, Laxton took him into his office and closed the door.

"Let me tell you where we are," Giocomani said. "The hospital has to be sold. Gotcher is on board, Devises is on board, but Smiley and Greenman are not. Smiley don't know what he's dealing with. He's stirring up trouble in the medical staff 'cos a lot of them have shares and he can make them believe sale of the hospital will hurt 'em."

"But it will, won't it?" Laxton said.

"If we don't sell, they'll be a hell of lot worse off, believe me. Since you left, the place is going down the tubes."

"I don't happen to have enough clout with my shares to make a difference," Laxton said.

"There are a couple of ways this can be handled, and I'm going to lay it on you. I don't have no big problem seeing Smiley ceases to be trouble to anyone. If I do that it'll be a permanent solution. He deserves it anyway. But that's a little too simple. The son of a bitch should be punished for what he's done. It'd serve me better if it was simpler. You can do that for us 'cos you have all the necessary info."

"What do you mean by that?"

"Oh, come on Doctor, I know what Jack Aysgarth gave you. Him and me was very close and he told me where to come if I needed this help. Here's what I want you to do. Tell Smiley what you can do by talking to the AG's office about his activities and tell him he'll find out if he just quietly agrees to the sale of the hospital it'll all go away."

"And what do you think will happen if he won't agree to do what I ask?"

"I'm sure he'll agree. He's not that stupid," Giocomani said.

After Giocomani had left Laxton thought about the mess. He realized that if Giocomani acted, Smiley wouldn't be around. He believed it firmly. He suspected his previous conversation with Terry a long time ago about the death of Aysgarth's attacker might have something to do with Giocomani. He wasn't sure what doing nothing would lead to for himself, he knew too much. He didn't want to be a party to any kind of violence, or suffer it, but he didn't want to be involved. He let a couple of days go by when he received another call from Giocomani.

"While you're at it," Giocomani said, "have a word with Greenman too. I'm sure you'll know what to say."

Laxton felt he couldn't let this just go on. He called Gotcher and arranged to meet Gotcher and Smiley at Gotcher's office in an afternoon.

"I don't know what you want to talk to us about," Gotcher said stiffly, "but the sooner we get this over the better. You don't have a place in our plans so perhaps you can explain what's so important."

"I came to talk to you about the sale of the hospital," Laxton said. "I know there's a buyer, so it shouldn't be too difficult for you. I know you have agreed to the sale Doctor Gotcher, but I hear Doctor Smiley has a problem."

"That's what's going to stop the sale," Gotcher said smugly.

"And now you can get out," Smiley added. "We will be running the hospital ten years from now."

"I think not," Laxton said. He dispensed with politeness. "You, Smiley, wouldn't want the drug people informed of your connection with the warehouse in Long Beach. I'm sure you wouldn't want any kind of investigation started. Believe me, they would be very interested in some of the photographs of you down there. I have them in my possession. You were photographed handling cocaine shipments. If any of that got out, the hospital would be gone with a bang. And, by the way, I have some very interesting correspondence and copies of checks which came my way from when you tried to bribe physicians to come onto the medical staff here, which the Department of Justice would be very interested in seeing. You might possibly save the hospital from such a revelation. Its reputation would be tarnished, and you would unquestionably be arrested. You have a way out of this. I wouldn't have to reveal any of this if you just quietly agree to the sale of the hospital.

"You wouldn't dare let the police have that information," Smiley said.

"I think he would," Gotcher said. "I believe we have misjudged him rather badly."

"I suppose you are the one who arranged for your former HMO to buy us out," Smiley said nastily.

This was news to Laxton, he hadn't known who was going to buy the hospital. He kept a straight face anyway.

"I really don't want any part of this, " Laxton said. "My mission is saving lives."

"You haven't the guts to do a goddamn thing," Smiley said to Laxton.

"Go home," Gotcher said to Smiley, "we'll get together in the morning and go over this."

Laxton held up his hand. He knew Smiley had interpreted his attitude as weakness. "I need to hear before you go that what you said is your last word on this, because I have a meeting with the Justice Department tomorrow."

"You can go fuck yourself," Smiley snapped, "I don't believe you've the guts to do a damn thing."

He walked out.

Laxton got up slowly while Gotcher watched him from his armchair. He didn't move when Laxton walked out. He knew he had a problem because Smiley wasn't going to comply. He had to do something.

The following morning he called the prosecutor from the AG's office he knew would be handling the Trevellian case and arranged to see him. He laid out the information relating to Smiley's bribery of physicians, and handed over the documentation. He made no mention of any of the other information he had. He knew that Smiley would only come around when the point had been driven home.

"God. What damning information," the attorney said. "I'll let you know what happens. We'll talk to him this afternoon."

The following day Giocomani called Laxton. "Someone did some very good work on Smiley," he said. "One down and one to go."

"I'm not sure I know what you're talking about," Laxton said.

He couldn't wait to have it all behind him. How the hell had he become mixed up with all these people he didn't want to be involved with? He didn't want to take part in any of it. He thought he was out of it, but he wasn't. He tried to convince himself he was saving lives by

266

what he was doing, Smiley's life anyway, and he knew going to the police would have only made him unsafe, and he might have been accused of being implicated.

Late afternoon he went to Greenman's office and told the receptionist he had business for that afternoon but he could wait until the end of office hours. He wasn't kept waiting very long.

"Doctor Gotcher told me I might expect a visit from you, but he didn't tell me why. I suspect it might be about the proposed sale of the hospital to your old HMO. I know you know that'll put their physicians in the hospital and all of us out, except possibly X-Ray and pathology. Why would I go along with something like that?"

"Your choices aren't good," Laxton said. "I don't like this but I'm a messenger. I chose to be a messenger because the alternative for both of us maybe much worse. Aysgarth and the rest compromised themselves and those left have to go on with the sale to avoid--shall we say consequences."

"I'm not through. I could try to stand up to them, don't you think?"

"No." Laxton said. "Do you want me to spell out why?"

"Try me," Greenman said.

"A certain party is in possession of some correspondence between you and another person. These are copies of letters you or another person wrote about your relationship, which I know you wouldn't want your wife to receive, and I know she will if you don't comply."

Greenman took the letters and looked at them briefly. "These aren't the originals."

"They can be produced if needed," Laxton said.

"Okay, I'll go along with the sale all right, but I would like to get my letters back."

"One step at a time," Laxton said. "Once the place is sold maybe my contact will get rid of the letters, or maybe even return them to you. I can't promise."

He left the office with a sinking feeling. He'd done his part, probably successfully. He could probably never let Greenman have the letters and he knew he must hang onto the photographs for his own protection.

To his surprise Gotcher called him after the board meeting. "It's all gone through," he said. "Do you know anything about what Aysgarth did when the Foundation was set up?"

"Nothing," Laxton said truthfully.

"Funny. All the millions in the Foundation seem to have been distributed and I don't know where."

"Don't know a thing about it," Laxton said, although he was sure the money had been laundered elsewhere somehow.

"I feel bad about Smiley," Gotcher said. "It's almost certain he'll be convicted."

"He had his opportunity, and he made it essential that the point be made. He turned out to be the wrong man in the wrong place at the wrong time."

CHAPTER 39

LAXTON IS SET UP

"I'm going to do you one last favor," Giocomani said to Laxton.

Laxton had not expected to see him again and was distressed when he showed up at Laxton's office at Bay Hospital. He had done Giocomani a favor and in return he expected to be left alone.

"The best favor you can do for me is to leave me alone and forget about me," Laxton said.

"You did us a great favor. Now I know, because Jack told me, you don't want no part of no shady activities, but I'm going to make it even, and then you'll be on your own. I know too that you have a lot on the ball. Jack was a great judge of that sort of shit. He told me we were damn lucky to have you and you should be somewhere where you could really pull strings. We operate out of Miami through Arkansas, and the Governor of that State has been a lot of help to us in our operations. You'll be getting a call from one of his people to make you an offer you can't beat anywhere."

"I've been in the south Mr. Giocomani and I know it's just not for me. I don't want to be in the south. I got out and I wanted to get out. I just need to be left to work things out for myself."

Giocomani smiled. "You gotta believe me," he said. "Listen up real good. You ain't gonna be in the south at all. This man's gonna be President of the United States."

Laxton knew it was fine to do organized crime a favor, but never let them do one for you. He looked at Giocomani and temporized. "No one can be sure of what you're saying," he said, "in fact it seems to me to be very unlikely."

Giocomani laughed. "You know that we put Jack Kennedy there. You must know that, there's been stuff in the papers about it years after. But the bum didn't keep his side of the bargain. And that's what you're worrying about. You think we'll come and ask you for something. Not true. You've already paid us in full, so forget that. No, you can be sure we're going to put this shithead in the White House and I'll bet he'll just be glad to let you loose cleanin' up the health care mess like you want to do. Ain't nowhere like the top to be effective."

Laxton was silent. He didn't know what to say or do. He couldn't discuss the situation with anyone. He assumed that Aysgarth had set this up before he died; he was sure of it. Aysgarth had wanted him to do it, and he'd fallen into this because he did a couple of favors for the mob, because he didn't want to see people killed. That's what they were, he was sure, the mob, and he was sure he knew where the Foundation money Giocomani had been looking after had gone. What would working for a politician who was connected with them be like anyway? Perhaps all successful politicians were involved with organized crime; he didn't know. Some people thought they were.

"I didn't come for an answer today," Giocomani said at last, "and you'll likely not see me again anyway. But you will get a call. Go and take a look at them before you turn it down. This guy's wife is a real sharp lawyer. We helped her make a bundle on the stock market and in real estate. You'll like her, good looking blond with rotten legs, but sharp as a tack. That's all I came to say. Shake hands and I'm outta here."

Laxton shook the offered hand. He had doubts that he would be left alone having been unwittingly involved with them. Also, he'd got in deeper because he didn't want to see anyone hurt, even though those threatened had done significant harm to both Laxton and his cause.

Then there was Megan. She seemed to have set up almost a second marriage situation with him, he thought. Almost bigamous. She was doing business with Trevellian, another kind of crook, and getting her emotional needs from Laxton. In love with him she'd said, but she wanted to keep things as they were and just have him hanging around. If he was to go somewhere else, would Megan follow? Probably not. Laxton reminded himself that when he began to think with that part of his body he was in trouble. But it wasn't that simple, she meant much more than just the physical act of sex. He stopped reminiscing when he realized there had been nothing but talk about all these things. That's all it was talk, he told himself.

It was a long weekend and Megan was alone again. He got home to find her cooking dinner.

"Where has he gone this time?" he said.

"Arizona. There was a problem with one of the patients, so he went. He wants to be sure he keeps that thing in Arizona going."

Laxton didn't want to know any more about it. He looked through his mail and was surprised to see a letter from Trevellian. It had been mailed a week ago. He looked up to see Megan watching him.

"It's nothing," she said, "or at least I think you'll think it's nothing."

Laxton tore the envelope open. It was a letter from Trevellian asking Laxton to defend him before the Licensing Board Hearing.

Trevellian was offering a large sum of money if Laxton would do that for him.

"You know what's in the letter?" Laxton said.

"Yes. I told him it was a crazy idea because you can't be prosecutor and defense attorney on the same case in different settings. He didn't see it that way."

"You're right," Laxton said. "Are you sure there's nothing else behind this?"

"Certain. Herb thinks that you did such a good job stopping his surgery at Valley that you could equally stop them from suspending his license, or whatever else they're likely to do."

"But this isn't even logical," Laxton said, "one of the Valley committee members is on the State Licensing Board, and Herb should know that."

Laxton poured drinks for them while he mulled over this unexpected turn of events in his head.

"Laxy," Megan said, "I know you can't do anything like he wants. You can't even help him and retain any credibility yourself. He's been a really sharp businessman and made so much money he doesn't need to work at all. He can get a good attorney anyway. Tell me, in your opinion, what will they do to him?"

"Frankly, not half as much as he deserves. He was knocking people off Megan, and I don't think he knew or understood what was happening or what he was doing. They'll probably reprimand him, fine him, and send him away with a caution never to do any more surgery. Unfortunately, that won't apply to the Arizona Board who aren't likely to hear about it. You know he shouldn't be going over there."

"You know, Herb means well for his patients. He wants to make them better. If he hadn't been doing surgery all those years we wouldn't have owned the nursing home and a lot of other endeavors like the funeral home. He made a lot of money but he didn't do anything other surgeons weren't doing. That's what the profession is about."

"My God," Laxton said, "you sound just like he does. You might be a parrot."

"That wasn't nice. I'm quite capable of thinking for myself and I came to those conclusions a long time ago. Just think about the people you were working for, supposedly on the other side of the fence. Do you think they're honest in the way they make money?"

"Bluntly, there are killers out there. Not every surgeon is a killer, but there has to be both an incentive and a deterrent to make the system clean. The public, that's the patients, don't know what's going on and

271

they've become trusting and totally dependent on doctors. I've been trying to do something, but I haven't got very far. I thought there was a chance here to do something worthwhile. It's about saving lives and being decent to people."

"The medical profession isn't the place for an idealist," Megan said.

The call from the Arkansas came the following week. It came from an Alvin Malnik who Laxton had never heard of, and had no idea who or what he was. He would later discover Malnik was someone else reported to have mafia connections. He was put in touch with a Jerry Papadopoulus who was involved in the Governor's campaign for the Presidency. Arrangements were made for him to meet some of the people involved. He felt he had nothing to lose by going anyway. He didn't want to explain to Megan so he led her to believe he was visiting old friends he'd known previously when he lived in the south. He didn't take the trip too seriously because they hadn't sent tickets. He stayed in a very nice Hilton in the capital. His meeting with Papadopoulus was invigorating. Just the self-confidence of someone so young who felt he was manipulating the public into voting for this unknown, ebullient Governor was refreshing.

"We are recruiting for the health team which will be our priority once the boss is in office. There's definitely a spot for you. You have great credentials which I went over personally."

This was a shock to Laxton because he hadn't sent them anything. He said nothing but studied Papadopoulus while he talked. He was of medium height, slender, slightly pale, and definitely didn't come from the south. He wore glasses. The campaign was one of those glitzy, bus-tour, save the economy, type of things. There were signs everywhere around the headquarters which proclaimed, "It's the economy stupid." Laxton wondered why anyone should believe this when the economy was already improving under the current administration, but he told himself again he didn't understand politics anyway.

It wasn't long before Papadopoulus pumped him on his views about health care.

"We think health care is a big issue. You're a doctor and most docs seem to be satisfied with practice the way it is. But we think the public is fed up, and our polls suggest we're right. Maybe we need to expand Medicare, but is it organized the way it should be?"

"There are something like thirty-seven million Americans who have no insurance at all. The people who have insurance find it covers only part of their costs. Some physicians just rip the system off, and there are so many standards of care in the country it's sickening," Laxton said.

"How about the Canadian plan; you were there."

"It is clearly headed for disaster and will run out of money and care will be rationed, more than it is right now. The waiting periods are disgusting, and a lot of them are due to the fact that the government has closed down beds that are needed, or built institutions claiming they would have extra beds, and they've been left empty. There isn't much point in having universal coverage if people are denied services or have to wait months to get them. Canada has gone that way. Physicians here say Canada is worse. Worse? It's a fraudulent disgrace. People with 90 per cent blockage of arteries supplying blood to the heart waiting three months for surgery, emergency rooms turning people away, and a government that hasn't the guts to do what really needs to be done. They're a thousand per cent worse than Britain, so I won't be going back to Canada. The British faced the fact they couldn't run a system with Regional Boards like Canada has just adopted. Of course there's a wait in Britain, but you can get around that in that country."

"So you're saying universal care won't work?"

"I never said any such thing," Laxton said. "You have to take steps. First, you need everyone covered and you need equality of coverage. In other words you need the Medicaid patient receiving the same opportunity for care as the Medicare patient, and as the privately insured patient. We don't have that in the United States. You see, you need a health care coverage card which entitles you to health care but doesn't identify the type of coverage you have. That should make services equal to all recipients. Second, you need a standardization of hospital charges. There are such gaps in the billing by hospitals that a private hospital in one area may be charging twice what a similar nonprofit hospital is charging in the same area, and they might be giving less in the way of services. I'm sure the idea of competition between hospitals is counterproductive."

"Are you suggesting that hospitals would be better under the government, or the State?"

"Unfortunately most of them would be better if they were operating under somebody with clear-cut State or National objectives. I wouldn't preclude the idea there should be some private hospitals, but private hospitals should be for private patients who want to pay. There should be other hospitals for the rest of us, and these institutions should all have the same objective, and that objective shouldn't be

273

making money."

"Do you think physicians should be making money the way they do out of Medicare and Medicaid?"

Physicians rarely make much out of Medicare and certainly don't make any out of Medicaid. The problem is, the private sector is picking up the tab for what physicians, and institutions, aren't making on these other programs."

"Well," Papadopoulus said with a smile, "at least we got a Democrat when we decided to take you on board."

"What do I have to do?" Laxton said.

"The campaign is going really well and as soon as it's all wrapped up we'll call you. It sounds to me we need a gigantic overhaul of the health care system and I know someone whose going to love you."

"I've heard that one before, and I'm not holding my breath," Laxton said.

"You'll be amazed at what can be done from the top."

Laxton didn't recollect whom he met during that trip, but he didn't meet the blond who was the Governor's wife. They were on the road campaigning. He wasn't even sure in his own mind they could beat the Republican incumbent who, though dull and boring, was very stable and had the kind of first lady everyone would vote for if she was the one running. True, she was not very political, or very beautiful, but she was Mrs.America.

Laxton called Megan on her private line at the nursing home.

"Which flight, what time and where?" she asked.

"Orange County, supposedly at four thirty, and it's Delta."

"I'll be there."

He pondered long and hard about Megan and this possible opportunity which might come up. She was pressuring him to stay around Orange County but he hated what he was doing at Bay. The PRO had phoned him to go work for them, but seventy thousand a year wasn't attractive when he was making a quarter of a million. From what he'd seen they did a lousy job anyway, and that was a primary consideration. Certainly the California PRO spent more time getting its government contract renewed than worrying about the review work, and it was filled with people in authority who should have been retired or selling real estate years ago. These people hired people less competent than themselves so they'd look better and keep control, so the review organization was afflicted with injellititis. The corporate Medical Director spent half his time in Washington with his old navy buddies. From Laxton's perspective working for them would be doing

274

an ineffective, low paid, job but with security. Montpellier might be a nice chap, but he was ineffective. He told himself he was counting on pie in the sky, the Governor wasn't even elected, and who was Papadopoulus anyway?

"I hope you had a good rest," Megan said. "I have some news I don't like and I don't think you're going to like. Herb wants me to go to Switzerland with him."

"What precipitated this?" Laxton said.

"Two things really. Herb was furious about the sale of the hospital but none of them could do anything about it because they weren't voting partners. The feature that really made him angry was all the physicians got almost nothing for their shares. Do you know anything about it?"

So, Laxton thought, Gotcher and the board had screwed the medical staff out of their rightful retirement pensions. He tried to keep a bland expression but what came out was a sneer.

"They screwed Terry Card and he had to threaten to expose Aysgarth's AID's before they gave him a decent settlement. They gave me a decent settlement when I left, but I was off the board and out of board decisions before anything like that was done."

"The medical staff were thinking of a class action suit against Gotcher and the rest, and Herb was right in on that, but it turns out Smiley was into some kind of bribery and to do a suit might open up a lot of stuff with the Justice Department, which would freeze distribution of funds for sure and might reveal stuff that could mean we didn't get any money for a long time, if at all," Megan said.

"So they dropped the idea of a suit?" Laxton said.

"Yes. They dropped it."

"What's the second thing?"

"Just as you predicted the Board of Licensure reprimanded Herb for his surgery at Valley and fined him. They told him he could retain his license to practice as long as he did not participate in surgery."

"How specific was that determination?" Laxton asked.

"It actually said in the State of California."

"He can actually do surgery in Arizona then. If they'd known about that they might have been a little less specific. And you're telling me he wants to take you to Switzerland to celebrate all this? What are you going to do?"

"So much depends," Megan said.

"Depends on what?"

"It depends on what we decide should be done."

"You mean you and Herb?"

"Don't be offensive; you know that's not what I mean."

"What exactly does Herb think the two of you are going to do in Switzerland anyway?"

"I don't have to go over the fact again this relationship with Herb is business and not anything else," Megan said.

"The only kind of business I can think of that you can do in Switzerland is funny business."

"Jealousy doesn't become you."

"Things are getting to a point where you're going to have to make a choice, Megan. This best of both worlds has been very difficult for me and I believe very good for you. I know now is a bad time for you, but there is less to stop us getting together than was ever present before today. I've made money, you have money, so that's not a worry."

"One thing I need is stability in a relationship, and you're still unsettled. You don't seem to realize how the world works and that it doesn't matter where you are, people are the same. It's been very difficult for me too, because I'm in love with you. I have a steady job at the nursing home, of which I'm a part owner in addition to everything else. You're not happy with what you're doing and you're restless, angry sometimes, frustrated and haven't figured out medicine isn't a profession where there are many doctors around who aren't on the make and there aren't any hospitals who aren't on the make either."

Laxton thought of Aysgarth who was mixed up with cocaine, with organized crime, but wanted medicine to be practiced in a clean way, and wanted to run a class hospital. He had a mixed record Laxton thought. Smiley was worse because he knew what the stuff was doing to kids and didn't care. Either he wanted to be a criminal or was too stupid to know the difference. In any case standards of care didn't bother him. Megan didn't even know about these people and had come to a conclusion about the whole medical profession which he couldn't buy. Laxton believed it was the system which coerced the majority of physicians who went off the approved path, not their individual greed.

"I don't know what to say to you Megan, because one thing you've got right is I'm not satisfied at the moment and another thing is I do have a mission."

"Are you going to tell me not to go to Switzerland?"

"I don't have that right at the moment."

"If I go, it won't be for love, sex, or anything personal. It will be to support a business partner."

"It's a decision you're going to have to make for yourself. I won't make it for you."

Back at Bay Hospital Laxton had been called before the Board. It was a friendly meeting but there was an agenda.

"Now we have a problem," said Duncan Gedes, chairman of the board. "We have three suits against the hospital all because of this so-called gynecologist Ching. Our insurance company is screaming and wants to know how he got on our staff. We have to get rid of him."

"How did he get on your staff?" Laxton said. "There must have been at least two hospitals where he was thrown out. He was thrown out of Valley Hospital. How come no one called the Chief of Staff there?"

"They did and he was recommended."

"No, they did not," Laxton said, "and I know because I was Chief of Staff there."

"Wait a minute," Gedes said, looking in a file, "they called a Doctor Smiley who recommended him to us."

"The one that's going to jail," said another board member, "or so's the word."

"What is really needed," Laxton said, "is a National Data Bank which has the qualifications, habits, and malpractice suits of all doctors in the country and it should be available to all hospital medical staffs."

"That's well beyond our jurisdiction," Gedes said. "I know you're skilled in dealing with this kind of thing and I know you've gotten rid of menaces before, and we need you to move on this one."

"Have you talked to an attorney yet? I'm sure you have your own," Laxton said. "I should warn you that such meetings with an attorney should be secret and you should not use the meeting to strategize removal of the doctor."

"Why not?"

"Because if he is removed you, as the board, are his last court of appeal. You cannot connive to remove him and then sit as a court of final appeal because you run the risk a civil court will not uphold the decision if it ever came to light you planned this."

"I'm meeting with our attorney tomorrow. In the past we've not had problems with people we wanted to leave the staff, but in this case our Chief of Staff and the Medical Executive Committee talked to Ching and he refused. In fact he threatened to sue everybody on that committee and they all backed down."

Laxton knew from the tone he used that the Chairman wasn't

going to back down. He was sure tremendous turmoil would result from the whole thing, and from the sound of it Ching might create publicity even though it wasn't in his interest to do that.

"We just thought we'd get you in the picture early on," Gedes said.

As Laxton drove home he thought: "Here we go again." It seemed to him little nibbles at major problems weren't getting him very far. His endeavors, although successful, had not made major improvements. They were small local stuff based on the Rugger concept that you could only protect the hospital you were in.

Megan was on the telephone.

"Can you have lunch with me?"

"You want to come over to the apartment for lunch?" Laxton said, incredulously.

"Oh, no, he's out of town and I want us to go out for lunch. I need to talk to you."

Laxton chose a restaurant called the Fireside, off Beach Boulevard, mostly because it was dark inside, because there were booths, and there were unlikely to be prying eyes. He wouldn't have to drive that far either.

Megan was dressed for business and he assumed she had come from the nursing home. How smart and attractive she was he felt, and he sighed.

"Sighing so soon," Megan said.

CHAPTER 40

WHERE TO GO

Laxton had called the University and it was clear they were very interested in him and they wanted him for teaching purposes. Teaching students was one way of trying to get the message across, but it seemed to Laxton to be a cop out for him. How much of the country could he affect by grinding concepts into medical students in one state and what would be the percentage of those who retained ethics?

He had been very busy at Bay Hospital and it looked as though there was going to be a major battle to get rid of Ching. Laxton remembered how easy it had been to get Ching out of Valley, because he had made it easy, but Ching had entrenched himself at Bay Hospital and put fear into medical staff members with his threat of suits. It was deja-vous for Laxton and he didn't like it.

Alone in the condo he watched the Presidential election results to try to get his other problems off his mind. Elections had never excited him, and didn't now. He was surprised to see the Republicans taking a beating and it was clear there was going to be a Democrat in the White House. But what kind of Democrat he wondered? From what he had heard and read it had looked to him as though the Governor had no chance, and in fact when his sexual indiscretion had come out Laxton remembered how the last Democrat who might have become the candidate had lost all credibility because of sexual indiscretions. But this time there had been a glib explanation which had worked. Who had engineered it? He was surprised when the country was swept by a man no one knew much about, and amused to think Giocomani and his cohorts could have had anything to do with the election. He hadn't discussed or mentioned his trip to the south with anyone. When he got back from the Arkansas he dismissed the whole idea as some sort of ploy by Giocomani, from whom he had no wish to ever hear again, a ploy to make him believe he was getting a special return for his efforts and that organized crime had real power. He had heard nothing anyway as he watched the President sworn in.

The HMO had taken over Valley Hospital and they had cursorily asked Laxton if he was interested in going back to work for them. Gotcher was comfortably retired and Smiley bound for court and possibly jail. Nevertheless, Smiley had pulled a lot of money out of the sale of the hospital; the only question was how much the attorneys would take from him.

"I really believe," Laxton said to himself out loud, "maybe I should take the cut in pay and become a Professor at UCLA medical school, with tenure within a year, and set myself up for life with a decent pension to look forward to at the end of it all."

Laxton realized he was being morbid. He'd made the mistake of putting in too much time with Megan. He'd invested all his off time with her at the cost of having no real friends. She had been everything and they had hidden their relationship from others, never getting out together, and never meeting others together. Laxton knew the way he operated socially had to change and he had to become a member of society, and cut out the isolation he'd let happen. He'd allowed himself to become obsessed with Megan with the inward knowledge that her apparent stability was probably just a convenience for her, but he'd never let that thought come into his head for proper analysis. Where the hell was she anyway? He reminded himself grimly that Megan had made a choice, and he wasn't the chosen one. By now she was in Switzerland.

Almost a month had passed when Laxton received an unexpected phone call from Papadopoulus. He knew who Papadopoulus was by now. He'd seen him on the television news often enough.

"Here's the call I promised. This isn't a secure line so I won't say too much. Your income will become public anyway, and you'll get around eighty thousand plus all expenses and federal pension benefits. We'll pay off anything to the people you work for so there won't be any problems there. You'll find that because you're moving to work for the President people will be flattered they knew you. You'll have an office in the White House and I'm getting accommodation arranged for you which will be suitably close. All the FBI clearances are complete and we don't see any problems there. I phoned to warn you that the announcement will be made tomorrow so you might have to deal with your local press. Just don't say too much."

"When do I have to be there?"

"You have an appointment a week on Thursday to see the President, so you'll have your airline tickets worst case scenario Monday and you can leave Tuesday."

"I suppose I should tell the hospital board chairman about this?" Laxton said.

"Do as you want, but if you wait until the day after tomorrow they'll have been told we called for you at short notice. You'll be met at the airport by agents and brought directly here for processing, so you'll have your pass and clearance documented. You're going to be very happy here because this is going to be a great administration which gets things done. You'll participate in the greatest overhaul of medical services this country has ever seen. See you next week."

Laxton hadn't even demurred. He needed to get out of town. He ran all the things he'd been told in the past through his mind, from Rugger's advice that, "You can only look after your own hospital, you can't control what goes on in others," to Megan's view that the medical world was filled with physicians and hospitals, and even people, who were all after a buck and nothing else. Smiley believed that too. Megan had said that Laxton was an idealist and the medical profession was no place for an idealist. He decided to believe in Papadopoulus, "You'll be surprised what you can do from the top."

There was no one to celebrate with. He couldn't very well take off anywhere when he wasn't entitled to time off, and there was the matter of getting someone to replace him permanently under very difficult circumstances. Ching was not killing Medicare patients. The deaths were with newborns which was even worse, but no government agency was overlooking obstetrics, other than the State Board of Licensure. The malpractice suits against Ching might get their attention, but it would be years before they did something. Laxton had devised a scheme whereby he fed the evidence against Ching to the Board of Licensure, asked them to investigate, which they could hardly refuse, and set things up by leaving out some of the hospital material they needed for their investigation. This had the effect of putting pressure on the hospital because the Board would be requesting information and evidence from staff members, and no physician was going to be showing reluctance to testify to the Board of Licensure. It would offer them great protection as well. It would still be a battle to remove Ching from Bay Hospital in a timely manner.

Laxton spent some time looking for a replacement. He wished Rekuf was interested, but he had his contract with the HMO as well as his outside X-Ray offices, and he hadn't really liked the whole Trevellian matter. He was very qualified for the job and maybe, if they paid him enough, he would handle this one matter for them. Laxton knew he would be effective and thorough. When the Bay Hospital chairman went to see Rekuf he got an adamant refusal at first, but later Rekuf relented and a deal was negotiated.

The news of Laxton's appointment was in the newspapers as he expected. He had been careful to be unavailable when the news hounds were looking for him but couldn't avoid them forever. The

Board members at Valley were overawed by the appointment and the board chairman had talked to the press. Laxton was amused by the glowing account of his abilities that had been given to the press and felt they would not have said all those nice things if he hadn't been going to Washington.

It was silly, he thought, but he was reluctant to give up his condo in California. He had plenty of money since leaving Valley. That wasn't the problem. It wasn't rational to keep the place because he had no reason to return to California. He expected to be busy, and he needed to move into a new life, make new friends, and get into the Washington social scene. He sold his car anyway. It was a first step. The following day he sublet his condominium furnished, and moved to a hotel near the airport. That's where the press caught up with him. He didn't care because he was already back page news, except when the paper came out they had a picture, so the news was given more prominence than he had expected, and to his annoyance they told readers he was staying at the Marriott on Century Boulevard and when he would be leaving for Washington, but he didn't expect any crowds. At his request The White House had sent his tickets to him at the hotel and he was pleased to find he was traveling first class. To him, it meant he didn't need to arrive until the last minute, but he didn't think there would be reporters and photographers there anyway. He just wanted to be sure everything ran smoothly so that he had every opportunity to guarantee his new life would be successful. He had never felt more determined.

Laxton got his baggage checked in early and retired to the Club Lounge until the flight was boarding. It was a beautiful day in Los Angeles and very clear due to the light rain which had fallen the previous night, but the climate wasn't worth thinking about, it was the opportunity ahead.

Laxton left the lounge and walked to the gate, relieved to find no reporters. As he was about to hand his ticket to the agent a voice called, "Hello."

He turned slowly to see Megan standing about ten feet away. "I thought you were in Switzerland," he said.

"I didn't go. I made sure Herb went alone."

Laxton didn't say anything. He just stood there looking at Megan dressed smartly and as beautiful as he had always remembered her.

"I'll come, whenever you send for me," Megan said.

.